Books by B. V[illegible]

STAR FORCE S[illegible]ES

*Swarm*
*Extinction*
*Rebellion*
*Conquest*
*Battle Station*
*Empire*
*Annihilation*
*Storm Assault*
*The Dead Sun*
*Outcast*
*Exile*
*Gauntlet*
*Demon Star*

REBEL FLEET SERIES

*Rebel Fleet*
*Orion Fleet*
*Alpha Fleet*

Visit BVLarson.com for more information.

# Storm World

(Undying Mercenaries Series #10)

by

B. V. Larson

**Undying Mercenaries Series:**

*Steel World*
*Dust World*
*Tech World*
*Machine World*
*Death World*
*Home World*
*Rogue World*
*Blood World*
*Dark World*
*Storm World*

ISBN-13: 978-1728918907
BISAC: Fiction / Science Fiction / Military

*"No one can say with confidence they will still be living tomorrow."*
Euripides – 401 BC

## -1-

During my many long years of living with my folks down in Georgia Sector, I'd brought home any number of ladies to visit. I think my parents had long since given up on the idea of me settling down and raising a proper family. But they continued to mention it, from time to time, so I knew my habits still bugged them.

The day they discovered Galina Turov staying with me in my shack, however, was a shocker even for them. My long-suffering mother in particular couldn't believe it.

We were standing on my porch, with my dark doorway yawning open behind me. The interior of my little house was always full of shadows—I liked it that way.

"James..." Mamma began in a falsely sweet tone. "Isn't your guest... an officer?"

"Yes, Mamma. Just like I'm an officer. She's in my legion, too."

She exchanged glances with my dad, who shrugged his shoulders. Then she reached out and pinched him just behind the elbow.

Frowning, he rubbed at the spot and sighed. "Son, would you and your guest like to come out to breakfast with us?

We're thinking of driving into Waycross and getting some waffles before church. There's a fine platter being served every Sunday at—"

"This is Sunday?" I asked.

"Why yes, son. It sure is."

Just then, we all stopped talking. Someone small had stepped out of the dark interior of my shack. She blinked like a sleepy cat in the morning light.

"Hello," Galina said, "you must be the McGills."

"Uh..." my dad said, blinking.

He was thunderstruck, and I knew what the problem was right off. Galina Turov was many things, but she wasn't a shy woman. This morning, she was wearing one of my tee-shirts—and nothing else.

Barefoot—and almost bare-assed—she looked like a runaway cheerleader. In reality she was at least ten years older than I was, but she looked like a kid because she kept her body stored at around nineteen years of age. Whenever she managed to get herself killed—not a difficult thing to do in the legions—she came out alarmingly young again.

"Mom, Dad... this is Galina Turov. I've known her for years."

"Really?" Mamma said. "She looks like she just joined up."

"She has the same problem I do," I said. "I'm twice as old as I look—at least."

"You'd never know, James," Mamma said.

Galina laughed at us. She reached out to grab one of the posts that held up my sagging porch, and she began to stretch.

"We'll do it," Galina said.

"Do what?" I asked.

"Go to eat with your parents, of course. You never listen, James."

"Oh..."

Now it was my turn to look shocked. Were we *really* going to do the meet-the-parents thing? Really?

Galina's stretches started off politely enough, but they quickly became dramatic and even startling. I realized she was doing a sequence of yoga-type moves, saluting the morning sun that glared onto my porch in a reddish slant. By the time she slipped from the mountain, to the cat… or the monkey—or whatever the hell people called these poses—both me and my dad were grinning. Broadly.

Everyone seemed to be enjoying the show, in fact, except for my mother.

"Hey!" Dad complained, rubbing at his arm again. He gave my mom a reproachful look. "Um… well kids, what do you say? Should we get going?"

"James…?" Mamma said, still using that sweetness-and-light tone.

"Huh?"

"Maybe you should take your friend back inside and get freshened up. If she doesn't have anything proper to wear, I could—"

"That's very kind," Galina said, interrupting. "But I always travel with a full kit. Here James, get my bag out of the back of the air car."

She tossed me a capsule-shaped key, and I caught it out of the air.

"Galina?" Mamma said. "Would your mind if my Frank here took a look at your air car?"

"Hmm? Why no, not at all. In fact, I'll take us all to Waycross in it for breakfast."

"Ooooo!" my dad said enthusiastically.

My mamma soon shoved him, and he tottered after me, crunching over the leaves and sticks that always seem to cover my sorry excuse for a yard.

"This one is quite a looker, James," he said when we were at a safe distance.

I glanced at him. He looked pretty happy. From his point of view, this Sunday morning was shaping up nicely. He had an air car ride, waffles, and an extroverted young lady to look forward to.

"She is that, Dad. But I'm a little surprised she's interested in the family."

My dad's face fell. "What? Are we lame hicks from the sticks?"

"Yeah…" I said. "But that's not really the problem. You see, she's my tribune."

He blinked at me, and he stopped walking. “What are you telling me, boy?”

“Just that. She’s the CO in charge of Legion Varus.”

“Not just any tribune then… she’s *your* tribune?”

“That’s right.”

He shook his head. “Hard to believe. She looks like a kid.”

“Yeah… She’s ambitious, see, but she’s also kind of vain.”

My Dad frowned. He shook his head. “Why can’t you ever get involved with an honest, normal woman, boy?”

I shrugged. I’d asked myself that same question many times.

“Well sir,” I said, “it probably has something to do with my chosen profession. Normal people can’t deal with it. Legionnaires who marry outside the service always end up quitting or getting divorced. Imagine if I came back from deployment, and my wife was three years older, while I was a couple years younger than the day I left?”

He thought that over, shaking his head. “They do have longevity drugs now,” he said. “They slow down the aging process. I’m over seventy, but I feel like I’m fifty.”

“That’s great, Dad,” I said, and I turned away toward Galina’s car again.

It was hard for people to understand the life I led. In a way, I’d given up a normal existence for the legions. My old friends from school—they were growing big guts and bald heads. They had grandchildren, some of them.

And me? I was almost as bad as Galina. I’d frozen my body scans at about twenty-six. I figured I was in my prime then, and I was sticking with it. Hell, I still got my tapper scanned whenever I bought beer.

While I dug Galina’s bag out of the trunk, my dad crooned over the sleek air car. He ran his leathery hands over the fenders like he was touching an idol of carven gold.

“This is one sweet ride,” he said, his eyes glowing.

Half an hour later we parked at Banjo’s, a waffle place near the puff-crete highway on the north edge of town. It was a dive, but the food tasted good and the interior was well air-conditioned.

Unfortunately, we didn't get all the way through the meal before one of my many lies got everyone at the table tangled-up.

It had been bound to happen, of course. I'd even vaguely worried about the possibilities.

You see, I tended to tell different groups of people different things, according to my personal mixture of whim and circumstance. In this case, the topic was Etta, my daughter—and no one at the table except for me knew what had actually happened to her.

"...and I wanted to say," Galina told my parents in a hushed tone, "I understand why James sent Etta away to Dust World. It was a good move—a safe move. I plan to check up on her personally through government channels when I get back to Central."

My parents took about three seconds to digest her statement. During the interim, they blinked and stared, like two robots that had just been reset.

The problem was a layered one. In cases like this, I hadn't actually *lied* to anyone—not exactly. I simply hadn't bothered to correct them on their false assumptions concerning Etta.

It was a flaw in my character, I suppose. I'm a man who lets things slide if sliding is at all possible. Dishes had to stink before they got done, for instance—and maybe not even then.

As a result of my general sliding through life, I tended to allow people to believe whatever the hell they felt like believing about any given situation—especially if their mistaken impressions were better than the actual truth.

In Galina's case, she'd assumed earlier that I'd sent Etta away to Dust World to keep her safe. When she'd initially made this assumption, I'd liked the sound of it, and I'd decided on the spot to let her run with it. As far as she was concerned, it was the God's-honest truth.

Unfortunately, my parents were following an entirely different—but no less false—logical track. They thought Etta had gone to visit her grandfather on Dust World because he was feeling poorly.

That too, of course, was total horseshit.

The real truth was this: Etta was a brat. She was mad at me for interfering with her plans to join Legion Varus, and so she'd sold a valuable book to Claver and taken off with the money.

But that version of reality wasn't going to make anyone feel good, so I hadn't bothered to explain things to anyone.

"Uh…" I said, unable to come up with a distraction or a smooth cover. "Are we going to church after this?"

"Wait just a damned minute!" my mamma said. "What's this about Etta being in danger? James? You didn't say anything about that. Are you hiding something from us?"

My father narrowed his eyes. He'd never been easy to fool—possibly, that was due to having a solid fifty years of experience with my particular brand of shenanigans.

"James," he said sternly. "I recall now… When Etta first vanished, you called me over and over that night, and you raced back home from Central. Etta's in trouble, isn't she?"

"Oh, shit…" Galina said quietly.

I glanced at her. She looked embarrassed.

"I'm sorry, James," she said. "I should have kept my mouth shut."

"Well James?" my dad demanded. "Tell us what the hell is going on!"

"Uh…"

I might sound like a dullard much of the time, but in actuality my mind is often racing. It was a rare and unpleasant circumstance to be caught in a lie by several people at once, each of whom was even now calling into doubt the version of events they'd believed up until this very moment.

Glancing toward Galina helped me make my choice. She looked upset and willing to help. Therefore, in this instance, she was likely to back anything I said.

"I was worried," I said firmly. "That night when Etta left… there were… threats."

"Threats?" my mamma gasped. "Against your family? By who?"

"It wasn't just us," I said. "There were threats made against Varus officers in general. Still, I thought it might be best for Etta to leave town."

"To leave the planet, you mean," my dad added.

"Who would do such a thing?" Mamma squawked. "To threaten a young, innocent child? It's barbaric."

"There are people out there," Galina said, surprising me by joining in. "People who oppose us for political reasons, petty jealousies and even personal gain."

"But *who*?" Mamma insisted. "Who did this? I demand to know!"

Galina caught my eye. She had a questioning look on her face. "Do you want me to tell them, James?"

"Um… sure," I said, wondering what she'd say next.

Galina turned back to my parents, and she spoke a name in a hushed voice.

"His name is… *Claver*."

She said this as if she were speaking the name of a fork-tongued devil.

Perhaps, in a way, she was.

# -2-

My parents, for their part, seemed resigned to another weird, short-lived relationship between Galina and me. They'd seen plenty of girlfriends over the years, and I guess they'd given up hope that their only son would have a normal home life.

None of this bothered me much. I was just happy that no one had freaked out completely. When the subject of Etta had come up, I'd expected someone to lose it and blame me for lying. But they hadn't. They'd made up their own explanations, and I'd nodded and grunted in agreement.

I think it had to do with Etta being a young girl. I had a certain degree of automatic sympathy from all interested parties, as they knew I was raising a teen alone. Accordingly, Galina figured I'd done all I could to protect an innocent from that evil-doer Claver. She also realized my parents were in the dark about the Mogwa connection, the genocidal poisons and all the rest of it, and she was smart enough not to bring any of that stuff up.

My folks, on the other hand, figured I'd been protecting them by not mentioning the stranger known as "Claver". They were used to me keeping legion business under my hat, and assumed I'd been skipping details because it was all classified and hush-hush.

When they suggested such an explanation, Galina had blinked twice then nodded.

"Yes," she said. "Yes, that's exactly right. I shouldn't have brought it up at all. James was only following orders."

My parents ate that up, but they were still worried that Etta was somehow in danger.

Galina stepped up again, helping me out. She explained that she'd only *assumed* I'd sent Etta away due to a security risk. The fact that Etta had left for unrelated reasons was clear to her now.

After that, we ate our food awkwardly and tried to smile. Everyone seemed disturbed—except for me. I'd dodged two bullets, and I couldn't help but grin about that.

We headed back home, and my parents went to church. Galina stayed with me instead, apologizing for messing up my morning.

Pretending like I was feeling upset about things, I suggested we should indulge ourselves with a nooner.

She played coy for about five seconds before I grabbed her.

The day got old after that and slid away from us. It finally died in the west and became dusk. To my surprise, Galina didn't climb into her air car and fly back to her home in Central City. She said she had a lot to do, but she was enjoying her quiet vacation with me.

She began making various suggestions about our evening entertainment. Dancing, watching a feely, talking to my parents about boring stuff—but none of her ideas struck home with me.

Then, I got an idea. I dragged out Etta's autoscope and set it up on the porch.

It was an expensive, alien-made piece of scientific equipment. Galina watched me, intrigued.

"I've heard about these things," she said, "but I've never seen one outside of a lab."

"If you've got the credit," I told her, "you can buy damned-well anything these days. Check this out. Just tell the unit what you want to see."

She looked at the autoscope, then back at me, then the autoscope again. Finally, she seemed to come to a decision.

"Scope," she said, "show me Zeta Herculis."

I glanced at her in surprise as the scope immediately began to whir and slew around toward the southern horizon. It seemed to be aiming at the tops of the trees—but it soon displayed a glowing image anyway.

There it was, on the primary screen. An orange-colored K-class star, Zeta Herculis was a little smaller than our home sun.

"Are you upset?" Galina asked me. "It was just the first star I thought of."

"No," I lied. "I'm not upset. You want to zoom in and see the planet itself?"

She blinked at me. "What? There's no way this tiny device could have the resolution to…"

"You're right," I laughed. "It's not real—not exactly. I mean, the scope cheats. It picks up data from the Galactic net and fills in details of the imagery it can't actually pick up with its limited optics."

"Ah…" she said. "Very clever." She addressed the auto-scope again. "Scope, show me Dust World."

The scope whirred a tiny fraction, but seemed not to move at all visibly. Only the focusing knobs spun.

On the screen, however, the image changed. Dust World, a dirtball resembling an overgrown version of Mars filled the visual field. There were no polar ice caps and only a few wispy clouds. Dust World was, as the name suggested, a desert planet.

We stared together, fascinated as the scope played over the planet, zooming in to give details. Virtually all life on Dust World existed in deep fissures in the star-baked surface. These cracks were called valleys, and they were green and dank at the bottom.

Guiding the scope with her voice, Galina focused in on the most interesting oasis of life of them all. It was purplish and shaped like a bat's wing, standing out on what was otherwise a craggy, sun-blasted landscape.

"That's it," I said. "The valley where Etta was born…"

"The only human colony in existence…" Galina said thoughtfully. "Such a tough group of people. To think we sent them out from our world a century ago. They were exiles from Earth originally, you know."

"They're still pariahs, in a way."

She looked at me. "The scope can't zoom in any closer?"

"Nope. That's probably a good thing. I would freak out if I saw Etta waving up at us—even though I know it's all an illusion."

"Are you thinking about going out there?" Galina asked me. "To get your daughter back?"

I glanced at her in surprise. She was a sharp one. She was catching on, somehow, to the idea that everything wasn't perfect in my family tree.

"Uh..." I said. "There's no need. She'll come back when the time is right."

Galina nodded quietly, as if confirming a dark suspicion. Heaving a sigh, she put her arms around my neck.

This was only possible when she stood on her tiptoes. Even then, it wouldn't have worked if I hadn't been bending over to look into the scope. She was a petite woman, after all, and I was a solid two meters tall.

Putting my hands on her hips, I slowly straightened up. Her feet lifted off the ground, and she wrapped her shapely legs around my waist.

We kissed, and I began to get ideas—but she put a finger to my lips.

"I have to go," she said. "I'm sorry. I must report to work in the morning. Even with my air car, the drive will take hours. I might even be late to the office."

"Damn," I said. "How about you stay, I drive you, and you sleep on the way?"

"You'd do all that? Just for one more round of passion?"

I shrugged. To me, the answer seemed obvious.

She craned her neck, looking back at the auto-scope. Dust World still glimmered there.

She turned back to scrutinize my face. She was still in my arms, with my big hands holding her butt up in the air. As a consequence, we were pretty much nose-to-nose.

"Tell me the truth first," she said. "What is Etta doing out there on that irradiated rock?"

"Visiting relatives," I lied flatly.

She made a little pffing sound, as women often tended to do when talking to me.

"James, the Dust Worlders don't dote on one another. They're more like a swarm of sharks than a tight-knit family. The more I've thought about it today, the more I've begun to wonder..."

I almost dropped her. She was killing the mood, that was for sure.

"Do we have to talk about Etta? What difference does it make why my daughter does anything? Is this all some kind of elaborate ploy on your part?"

She looked shocked. "Elaborate ploy? What are you talking about?"

She slid out of my arms and down to the creaking porch floorboards. Her hands formed tiny fists, and they planted themselves on her hips.

"I'm talking about you coming down here, seducing me, and then asking a lot of questions."

She slapped me. I let her do it, but I watched her hands and her feet to see if she'd go for more. I wasn't going to play punching-bag for long.

She seemed to sense this, and she just glared at me.

"You're ruining everything," she said, turning away. "We had such a nice time—and now you're suggesting I'm some kind of manipulative witch who—"

I touched her shoulders lightly and whispered in her ear. "I'm sorry," I said. "I'm just a little sensitive about some topics. You can understand, can't you?"

She took a few deep breaths and relaxed a few notches.

"Yes," she said at last. "I shouldn't have pried. I'm too suspicious sometimes. Let's go back to where we were."

We tried, but the magic seemed to be gone. The evening was a cool one, and Galina began to pack her stuff.

An hour later, she was gone. I watched her air car vanish into the black sky. After a minute or so, it was only one more star among millions—one that glided away to the north until it vanished behind the treetops.

Along about then, I heard a twig crack out in the bog.

Now, I've been living alongside a swamp for many, many years. When you live in a place like that, a place of nature, you get to know the sounds of it.

Maybe it was because of Galina, but I'd failed to notice how quiet things had become out on the bog. The natural peeping and chirruping of insects and animals had died away to almost nothing.

My hand reached for my sidearm, but it came up empty. All I had in my hands was a half-empty beer bottle. I must have left my gun inside.

Women could be very distracting.

A voice spoke then, surprisingly close. My eyes strained, but I couldn't make out the source. There was nothing there, not even a shadow cast by the bright blue-white light of the Moon.

"I thought she'd never leave," the voice said. "How do you get women to stay so long of their own free will, McGill? You must release some kind of an ape-musk that drives them wild."

The voice was well-known to me. It was Claver.

# -3-

Looking around wildly, I still couldn't spot him. But judging by the nearness of his voice, he had to be close.

Then, I caught on.

"Wearing one of those Vulbite stealth suits, aren't you?" I asked, looking in the direction I thought he was.

"More like a Vulbite stealth trash-bag, if you ask me," Claver said. "Have you ever been inside one of these things?"

"Yes, as a matter of fact. What do you want, Claver? And what are you doing sneaking around on my property without permission? The last time you pulled that, it didn't go well for you."

I had, in fact, murdered him upon our last meeting. Maybe that's why he was wearing a stealth suit.

"I'm sensing a general lack of trust, here," Claver said. "Let's put our cards on the table, McGill. I'm an injured party, seeking restitution. I'm hoping you will provide satisfaction, rather than further abuse."

He'd said all this in the tone of a Texas lawyer. But his words left me blinking and confused.

"What are you talking about?"

"So that's how you're going to play it? Falling back on the tried and true dummy routine? You were born to play dumb, McGill, but I'm not buying it this time around."

"Huh?"

He sighed, and at that moment I thought I saw something move. I quickly realized I *had* seen something unusual. There were two shoe-shaped depressions in the grass. They wouldn't have been easy to spot, other than for the fact that the grass came half-way up to the man's knees.

Spotting him like that made me feel vindicated. This was precisely the kind of moment I was always explaining to various women who saw my lack of gardening skills as a sign of pure laziness on my part. You never could tell when a more natural environment might come in handy.

Turning away from him, I gave no hint I'd pinpointed his location. Instead, I crossed my arms and stared at a tree that was about ten meters off to one side, as if I thought that was Claver. I gave that imaginary Claver my best blank-faced, moronic stare.

Inside, I was feeling happy.

You see, I don't like when people I view as enemies make unscheduled visits. Such events always seem to put me in a terrible, territorial mood.

"You're actually going to play this to hilt, aren't you boy?" Claver asked angrily. "Well, that's just fine. You obviously know what your daughter did! I'm owed a debt, and I'm here to collect!"

The mention of Etta put me into a new zone of heightened tension.

"Aw now," I warned, "you don't want to be threatening my daughter."

"What? Try listening for a change, dummy. I'm demanding you make good on the deal I made with her."

I shrugged. "You'll probably have to head out to the stars for that. She's gone, and she's not coming back."

"To Dust World, I know," he said, making another error.

Like I've said before, I'm not quick to anger, but I don't take threats toward my family lightly. Etta might have stolen my property, sold it, and run off with the money—but she was still my little girl.

Slowly, I turned toward Claver—toward where he was really standing. I locked my eyes onto the spot about six feet above those two shoe-size divots in my overgrown lawn and stared.

"Can you see me?" he asked quietly.

I continued to stare.

"Shit," he said, and the grass at his feet rustled.

I had to move fast, before I lost him. Accordingly, I cocked back the beer bottle in my hand—it was all I had—and threw it. I threw it *hard*.

The bottle flipped end-over-end once, then thumped into something in the night air. There was a curse and a crash. A man-shaped area of folded-down grass appeared.

Springing after him, I launched myself as he scrambled up. I landed on nothing, but I sensed he was close.

I could hear him, but couldn't see him. Snatching wildly, I caught an ankle—and I pulled it up into the air.

He did a facer on the ground, and a needler sang. A hot beam lit up my hair just above my right ear, but I didn't let go.

Instead, I stood and yanked his ankle high. He went down as his foot went up, tangled inside the stealth suit. His foot was visible now, having slipped out of the suit entirely.

"Let me go! You've got no damned sense of hospitality, you frigging gorilla!"

I didn't speak. Instead I kicked out, landing hard blows with my size-thirteen work boots. I kept kicking, and he fired a few more times, but missed. At some point he lost his grip on the needler, and it went rattling onto the ground.

"All right, all right!" Claver called out, panting. "You caught me. Now, let me get out of this damned poncho so we can talk."

After one more mean, sweeping kick, I let go of him. He peeled off the suit and dropped it in disgust.

"Worthless tech," he complained. "I had big plans, but it doesn't work worth a shit if the other guy knows you're wearing it. Besides, it's almost as hard to see out of it as it is to see in."

Putting my hands on my knees, I leaned over him. "Any last words, Claver?" I asked.

"So that's it, huh? Murder again? I thought you got your jollies the last time we met."

"I did, and I'm fixing to enjoy myself all over again."

"Vicious, amoral killers. That's what all your Varus legionnaires become eventually."

"That's it, huh? Just insults? Kind of a waste for your final moments."

My big hands plunged toward his neck.

"Wait!" he called out, and I hesitated, easing my grip. His windpipe convulsed under my fingertips.

"You owe me," he rasped. "Etta took my money, and she ran off with it. The book was a fake."

I froze, considering his words.

Right about then, it occurred to me that I'd never dug into my hiding spot, the place where I'd stashed the book out in the older of our two barns. Could it be that Etta had given Claver the wrong book?

I laughed suddenly—long and loud.

Straightening up, I released him.

Claver had a coughing fit and glowered up at me in the moonlight.

"You McGills are all cheats," he complained.

"You want to know why I killed you the last time we met?" I asked him. "And why you almost died again just now?"

"I think that's abundantly clear. You're a rabid dog. A beast that should be put down."

"That's part of it, I suppose," I admitted. "But I got mad when I learned you'd approached my teen daughter. My family is off-limits, Claver. You've got your private little planet full of clones stashed away among the stars, and I've got sixty acres of swamp here on Earth. Can we agree to stay out of those two zones in the future?"

Claver climbed slowly, warily, to his feet. He brushed himself off and slouched, appearing relaxed.

Claver was a weasel, but he was no coward. As long as he thought I wasn't going to kill him right off, he was at ease in my presence. That was a dramatic difference between him and other weasels, such as Winslade. Lesser men behaved like pathetic piss-and-shiver dogs when I was in one of my intense moods.

"We can agree on that," he said after a moment. "But I still need my property. Imagine my embarrassment when I delivered the product and was informed it was bogus."

"Maybe we never had the real deal," I said. "Maybe I was mistaken as to the book's—"

"Uh-uh," he said. "That's not going to fly. The book had the right cover and the title page matched—but the pages inside were all wrong. It was some kind of crappy, self-help book. Old, sure. Made of paper and about the right dimensions—but it was a fake."

I grinned again. I couldn't help myself. Etta really was like her old man. "She pulled one over on you? For reals? That's a hoot."

For some reason, knowing Etta had screwed Claver in a deal brought me great pride. She was a true McGill, after all.

Laughing, I slapped him one on the back that made him stagger. He glared at me and my offending hand, which now rested heavily on his shoulder.

"Take your paw off me," he complained, but I took no heed.

"Look," I said, "you and I are going to have a little talk about that Mogwa-killing formula you're so anxious to sell, and then we're going to figure out how to handle this situation. But we're going to talk, first."

"What about?"

"Who's your buyer?"

Claver shook his head. "I can't say. In fact, you don't *want* to know. It would only sink you and your family deeper into this mess."

I gripped the back of his neck and gave him a little shake. He growled at me and cursed, but I could tell he was willing to die over it.

Sighing, I let go of him again. "All right. You don't want to say—I can understand that. Next question: What's in it for me if I help you get the real book?"

He blinked. "I already paid! This is a shake-down—literally!"

"It's *my* book, and I haven't gotten one thin credit-piece from you."

His eyes narrowed to slits. "I get it now. You're in cahoots, trying to get paid twice. You made a crude fake, but you knew

I'd be cautious about accepting the book from you personally, so you had your little girl do the hand-off. Diabolical."

These words were ironic coming from Claver who, to the best of my knowledge, was the king of double-dealing in Province 921.

"Do you want the damned book, or not?" I demanded.

He presented me with a list of further complaints.

"All right, damn you," he said at last, when he realized I wasn't even listening.

"Good... That'll be one million credits."

To my surprise, he brightened. "A million? Done."

I frowned, wondering how much he'd paid Etta. *Dammit*, I'd ripped myself off.

Shrugging, I waved for him to follow me. "This way."

He trailed me across the bog. "How can you even see out here in this stinking mud?"

"Don't have to. I know the way."

He slipped and slapped along another hundred paces, but then halted. "You're taking me to a secondary location, aren't you? A staging spot for a killing? What, wasn't your own overgrown yard optimal for murder? The grass was so high I doubt they would have even found the body."

"Are you coming or not?"

Grumbling, he followed. In the light of the Moon, we made our way to the second barn, the old one way back on our property. No one had used it for decades.

The door creaked, and the single bar of lights flickered, casting bluish light over the dusty interior.

In my own head, I hadn't decided yet what I was going to do with Claver or the book. I was keeping my options open.

Prying back a floorboard, I dug in the spidery dark and pulled up a metal case. Claver reached for it, but I slapped him away.

"It's booby-trapped," I told him.

"Of course it is..." he chuckled, and he stepped aside.

I opened it carefully after disarming the bomb inside, and the case opened with a snick.

Inside... it was empty.

# -4-

"Another trick?" Claver demanded. "Does it have a false bottom or something?"

I sighed. "I wish it did—but no. She took it."

Claver stared at me, and the empty case. "Seriously? You're not bullshitting me? The girl took it with her?"

"I think so.'"

"What kind of a lame scheme are you running here, McGill? I followed the bump-up for the extra pay—but this doesn't make any sense."

"I guess I should explain a few things, then."

I told Claver the truth then—with some mild editing, of course. I told him Etta and I had had a falling out. That she'd wanted to join the legions, and I'd forbidden it.

"So…" he said. "She took my offer because she wanted money to start a new life. I get that. A teen dream. But then she gave me a fake book and ran off? Didn't she know I'd come looking for my property?"

"She probably doesn't realize who she's dealing with."

"Right… I get that a lot. Okay, I think we both know where this is heading next."

I slewed my eyes toward him and locked there. "What are you talking about? It's over. We don't have the book."

He snorted. "I'm not giving up so easily. A million credits is nothing. I'm going out there to collect my property."

I laid a heavy hand on his shoulder again. "You know, one thing about this old barn, there's no wireless reception out here. We're off the grid."

"That's riveting information," Claver said. "But I'm—"

"Uh-uh," I said. "If you die now, your mind won't have been backed up. You won't remember what happened out here in the bog. You won't know about the hiding place, that Etta has the book—nothing."

He smirked at me. "I was wondering when you'd get around to murder again. But it's pointless, McGill. I've got another clone here on Earth, working another angle. He won't give up. He'll keep coming. A deal is a deal."

Thinking that over, I knew he was right. Claver was a trader and a persistent one. He wouldn't give up. He'd send more Clavers at me until he was satisfied with the outcome.

"All right, what's your plan then?"

"Didn't I just say it? Or was I talking too fast for that micro-brain of yours? No matter, I'm headed out to Dust World."

"You have a ship?"

"No, dummy. I'm porting out. I still have a fair number of jump-suits. That's how I got here, in fact."

"Hmm…" I said, mulling that over. "Let's go take a look."

"At what? The suit? There's no point, it's one of those old-fashioned units the squids made."

I smiled. "Big enough for a nine-foot Cephalopod? Or two men?"

He stared at me in surprise. "Now hold on, I'm not giving you a ride to Dust World on top of it all."

"Have you ever been out there, Claver?"

"As a matter of fact, I have."

"Did you find the locals to be friendly and easily swayed with pretty words?"

He paused. "No. They're outright bastards. Dishonest, cruel, and tricky."

I nodded. He really had been out to Dust World.

"So, do you think you'll have an easier time of convincing them to give up the book with me along, or without?"

“Them? What do you mean, ‘them’? It’s your daughter who has the book.”

I shook my head. “Her grandfather is the Investigator. He’s probably got it by now.”

“Oh…” Claver said, turning that over in his mind. “He’s not an easy-going man.”

“Nope. Now, are we jumping out there together, or are you interested in drinking some of that bog-water outside?”

He watched me warily, realizing I didn’t make deadly threats in vain. Claver and I had killed one another many times in the past.

While we’d been working in the barn, a gentle rain began to fall. By the time we exited, leaving the creaky door groaning in our wake, the rain had become strong. Silver sheets were falling, and we were quickly soaked.

“McGill,” Claver said. “Your place sucks. Seriously, I hate it.”

I shrugged. “Southern Georgia isn’t for everyone,” I admitted.

Together, we looked for his arrival point. The rain died down and he had some trouble in the wispy fog that welled up to replace it, but at last he found the spot.

We stood directly under a big mangrove tree on a small hump of land. It was higher and drier than most of the surrounding region.

There, he squatted and pulled a teleport suit out from under the big tree’s roots and slapped the mud and worms off it. He worked with a control box, targeting our destination. Zeta Herculis wasn’t far by interstellar standards, only about thirty lightyears, but it would be quite a jump from the point of view of teleportation travelers.

“This will be a tight, unpleasant squeeze,” he began. “I don’t even—”

He got no further. His words cut off, and he turned slowly to gape at me, his mouth hanging wide.

“Sorry,” I said with a shrug. “There’s been a change of plan.”

“Why?” he croaked out.

“You really shouldn’t make deals with a man’s teen daughter. It’s unacceptable—even if she cheated you.”

Claver tried to say something else, but he lost control of his body at that moment. He collapsed and shivered on the mud at my feet.

A trowel—just some rusty tool I’d picked up while we were in the barn—was sticking out of his sternum. I’d driven it into his heart.

“Too bad you won’t remember this lesson, Claver,” I said, standing over him as the light went out of his dying eyes. “You shouldn’t mess with a legionnaire’s family. Maybe you’ll figure that out on your own… Eventually.”

I dumped his body into a deep puddle of mud. It was a spot I knew well, one I’d warned Etta about. It was the bubbling top of a sinkhole, and I knew his body might never be found—if anyone ever cared to look for it, which I doubted.

Sliding into the teleport suit and checking the gauges, I was pleased with the results. The suit booted cleanly when I powered it up, and it still had a charge.

As an afterthought, I took the bag-like stealth fabric with me as well. Rolled up tightly, it fit in the roomy teleport suit.

Looking around at the noisy swamp surrounding me, I sucked in one last breath of the dank air of my homeland, and I slammed the faceplate closed.

My hand moved to the actuator, and I engaged it.

The world melted into a glowing blue, and it began to throb. Faster and faster the light pulsed until it blinded me.

My last thought before I ported out was really more of a hope. I wished with all my heart that Claver had targeted the suit accurately—without any final tricks thrown in for laughs.

# -5-

Dust Word came as a shock after leaving Earth behind. Both were warm places, but rather than the cloying dampness of my home marshes, Dust World exuded the heat of an open oven.

The sun blazed overhead, painfully bright and oversized, due to our nearness to the central star. Zeta Herculis was actually smaller than old Sol, but it was closer to this world, making it seem hotter. It was a glaring eye that ruled the sky, and I had to shade my dazzled eyes with a hand.

It was then, as I squinted and peered at my surroundings, that I got the worst shock of all: I was out in the open.

Now, you have to understand that Dust World is a giant orb of blowing sand and rocks. There's very little that survives on the exposed, sunbaked surface. All the life we knew about existed in the dozen or so deep crevices that dotted the planet, mostly near the two poles.

"I'll be damned…" I said to myself.

Immediately, I tried my tapper. The seeking-connection icon spun and spun—there were no repeaters within range. That wasn't a big surprise, but it was disappointing.

I was in serious trouble.

Examining my surroundings for hints of my location, I saw a sandstorm off to my left, and a mountain range of parched spikes off to my right—but neither of these landmarks meant shit to me.

Dust World was, for the most part, a trackless wasteland. There were no roads, no hotels, no gas stations—nothing but a few scattered oases of life, hunkering down deep in the crust, seeking shelter from that burning eye of a sun overhead.

My next move was to check the teleport suit again. If it still had a charge—but no, it was bone dry. I should have expected that.

Already, I was wishing I hadn't lost my cool and killed Claver on impulse. But it was too late to cry about that now. What was done was done.

"Think, James," I said aloud. "Claver was planning to come out here. He planned to land at this exact garden-spot. He wouldn't have gone to all this trouble just to perm one bad-tempered dumb-ass named McGill."

My own words hurt, because deep down, I knew that's what I was. A dumb-ass who'd lost his temper and killed the single man who knew the lay of the land out here.

Maybe he had a spaceship hidden just over the horizon, or a buried base, or a few clones waiting in orbit for a signal to swoop down and rescue him when he arrived.

But whatever his scheme had been, it had died with him. I kept peering around at the rocks and grit, hoping a thought would impinge—but it didn't.

I considered committing suicide in hopes of a catching a revive later on, but I soon passed on that idea. No one back on Earth knew I'd come to Dust World. No one except Claver would even *suspect* that's where I'd disappeared to. Given the circumstances, I doubted he would launch a rescue effort on my behalf, even if he did figure out what had happened.

In short, I'd probably just permed myself.

Sucking in a dry, gritty breath of air—at least Dust World had a breathable atmosphere—I chose a direction at random and started walking. From the angle of the glaring star in the sky, I figured a path straight ahead would fit best, as it didn't go toward the sandstorm or the mountains. As best I could judge by the slant of the star's angle, that direction should be south, toward the pole. All the best valleys on Dust World were huddled around the poles, where it was slightly cooler.

Since any valley would do for shelter, I felt heartened when I approached a rougher region of ground. Was that…? Yes, I thought that it was. A darkened zone ahead looked like a rocky outcropping, but grew to become a widening hole and then a chasm opened up at my feet. I guess it was my lucky day after all.

It was a valley. I grinned and released an echoing war-whoop. I'd done it! I'd found my way to life and hope again.

Staring down into the dark, purpley bottom of the pit, I felt a pang of worry. How was I going to get down there? Sure, there was a lake in the center of the valley—most of these valleys were really bubbling craters with deep pools of water at the bottom. But I couldn't survive a jump. A fall of a kilometer or two was certain to be fatal.

Just then, I thought I heard something behind me. Turning, I saw two strange beings.

They were men wearing helmets with face shields—only their lower face showing. Large men, nearly my size, they had uniformly broad shoulders and moved almost as if in synchronization.

Behind them was an aircraft they'd landed, a flitter. It was an antigravity vehicle, capable of silent flight.

"I'm glad to see you two!" I shouted at them, approaching and offering a grin and a handshake.

They closed to a range of three meters, and then stopped.

"Where is the Prime?" asked the man on my right.

"The what?" I asked, confused for a second.

The man on the left pointed toward my chest. "You're wearing the Prime's teleport suit. Where is the Prime?"

Suddenly, my dim brain lit up. I'd seen these guys before—or a pair very much like them. They were low-ranked Claver-clones. He'd called them class-threes. They were workers, brutes. Not too bright, but born with the inbred loyalty of dogs.

Claver had created a small army of himself, somewhere out in the cosmos. I'd been there, but I didn't know where it was, exactly. A planet full of clones of varied abilities and designs—all based on his own original set of genes, biologically.

"You're both Clavers," I said. "Class threes, right?"

They didn't even blink. "Where is the Prime?" they asked again.

A big smile curled up on my face. I sucked in a breath and stepped toward them. "Well boys… that's a long story. You see, he sent me on ahead as he was injured in an accident back on Earth. I'm supposed to reclaim his property, which is down there in that valley yonder."

The Clavers didn't smile or even blink. They peered at me, slowly rotating and cocking their heads as they listened to my words. The effect was kind of eerie, like watching a couple of beagles try to figure out what you were telling them.

When I was about a meter distant, my smile was as big and round as a Georgia peach. I halted and pointed to their flitter.

"Now," I said, "if you two boys want to follow Claver-Prime's orders, all you have to do is take me for a little ride on that flitter. We'll sail down into the valley, retrieve the goods, and I'll teleport the package to Earth."

"The package isn't going back to Earth," said the one on my right.

They seemed a little confused. They weren't the brightest of clones, after all.

"That's okay," I said. "If you want, I'll hand the package over to you two and you can get it back to Claver-land any way you want."

"You are the McGill," the one to my left said suddenly.

I turned toward him. "The light just went on in your fridge, didn't it, son? You're absolutely right, I *am* James McGill, the man who knows where the pack—"

That was as far as I got. Two sets of arms shot out, with a grand total of four knobby sets of fingers reaching for me.

Now, you have to understand that I wasn't just your typical soldier. Sure, these walking genetic freaks had been designed for strength and speed—but they didn't have my decades of combat experience to back them up.

A combat knife appeared in my hand. It wasn't my own, as I'd stupidly forgotten that back on Earth. It was from the man on my right flank. He'd stupidly left it there on his belt, unguarded.

One upstroke, and the two men were down to three hands between them. I felt that would even-up the odds some.

But the injured Claver didn't back off. He didn't fall, keening and grasping his wrist in shock. Instead, he coldly proceeded to struggle with me. Hot blood sprayed out of his stump, splashing all the way up to my face.

It was disgusting, but I didn't have time to worry about the salty flavor in my teeth. Focusing my efforts on the right hand Claver, I tried to knife him in the gut—but the two of them managed to wrest my weapon away and drop it into the dust.

The three of us exchanged hammer-blows whenever we got a hand free. I kept punching the one-handed guy—but soon that wasn't needed.

In shock, losing blood fast, he sank to his knees. He kept struggling to stand up, but he couldn't. Now and then, he asked me where Claver-Prime was with a weakening voice, but I was too busy to give him a smartass answer.

That left me with one vicious Claver to deal with. He wasn't going down easy, either. He kept up the fight, and I was honestly impressed by his design. If I ever got the opportunity, I'd have to bring that up to the original model and compliment him on his craftsmanship.

But still, the final conclusion was preordained. I was too big, too strong, and too damned mean to be beat by any version of Claver in hand-to-hand combat. It just wasn't going to end that way.

He hung on determinedly, and he never gave up. I'll give him that. He just wouldn't stay down.

Finally, I grew tired of the game, and I walked him to the edge of the cliff and threw him over the side.

"McGill!" called a voice behind me.

I turned. The one-handed Class Three had made his way to the flitter and retrieved a gun. He had the muzzle trained on me.

"It's about time you thought of that," I told him.

"Where…?" he said, seeming to have trouble breathing. "Where is the Prime?"

"He's back on Earth. Dead—at the bottom of a sinkhole. Are you happy now?"

He didn't answer me. Instead, he fired his weapon. I caught the blast and spun around. A hazy moment later, I realized I was falling.

I'd followed the first Class Three and tumbled right off the cliff.

I fell through space for what seemed like a very long time. The wind whistled, and my sinuses stung because the air was so dry.

It took about twenty seconds to hit the bottom, if my perceptions were right.

During that long fall, I had time to regret some of my recent choices. For instance, I thought maybe I shouldn't have tried to kill three Clavers in a single day.

After all, a man has to pace himself.

# -6-

Waking up an unknowable time later, I felt an overwhelming sense of curiosity.

Who had bothered to revive old McGill this time? And why?

One thing I could tell right off: it hadn't been a standard-issue revival. I wasn't lying on a gurney with some bio-worker shining a light into my eyes.

Instead I was in a quiet, dark place. It was cool and windowless—almost like a tomb.

That single thought made me suck in a breath and struggle to sit up. One of the greatest nightmares every legionnaire entertains now and then is that of being buried alive.

It *has* happened. From time to time, a grow is discarded while still breathing rather than recycled for raw materials. Awakening from whatever stupor they were in, they might find themselves buried alive.

"Ah," a voice said. "Our guest stirs."

*The Investigator.* I recognized his distinctive tones immediately. The fact I hadn't been left for dead someplace did put me at ease—but only to a degree.

The Investigator was an older man. He was Della's father and Etta's grandfather. He was also the leader of the Dust World colony. For all of that, he wasn't a friend of mine. He was a strange man, driven by obsessions and a cold, clinical nature.

"Hello, sir," I croaked. "Thanks for reviving me."

"You might want to save your gratitude," he said.

"Why's that?"

"It's best that you rest now—we'll discuss it later."

Alarm bells went off in my head. My eyes snapped all the way open, even though the scene they revealed and transmitted to my foggy brain was both dim-lit and blurry.

Was that the pallid shape of an approaching arm?

The glint of a needle?

For a Legion Varus man, to think was to act. Anything else led to death more often than not.

If it had been anyone else, I probably would have punched him. But the Investigator was a relative, of sorts. Reaching out I grabbed the needle, feeling a tiny sting, then snapped it off. It fell to the stone floor with a tinkling sound.

"What have you…? You are a most difficult man."

"No time to sleep now," I said casually. I held onto his wrist, so he couldn't rearm himself. "I've got things to do."

The Investigator tried to slip out of my grasp. He was surprisingly strong for an older, lanky man. Dust Worlders had always been tough in both mind and body. They lived in a deadly environment such as few humans on Earth ever experienced. The civvies back home were like fattened rabbits by comparison.

But he couldn't break free. I was hazy-minded, and my hands felt a bit rubbery—but still, my grip was like an iron band around his wrist.

Finally, he relaxed.

"All right," he said. "We'll talk now, if you'd like."

"I'd like that very much, sir," I said in as friendly a tone as I could muster. "The last I remember, I was falling about two kilometers down into a valley."

"Yes, exactly... We have sensors up on the rim. The illegal vehicle that transported you here tripped our defensive network. After careful inspection of the site, we realized several individuals must have been involved in some kind of altercation. It was a simple matter to retrieve the bodies from the lake below."

"Right…" I said, letting go of his wrist.

He withdrew his hand and examined the tip of his syringe. "Surprising dexterity and effectiveness so soon after revival. I shall have to make a note."

"You do that."

I was able to see him pretty clearly now, and I was looking around the chamber I'd found myself in. The place looked like a medical lab—Dust World style. The tables were slabs of polished stone.

The Investigator reached out a long arm and snapped on a light. This created a yellowy glow rather than the white glare Earth doctors preferred.

"Uh…" I said, gazing this way and that. "Where's the revival machine?"

The Investigator shrugged. "Already, my decisions bear thc fruit of misfortune."

"Um… what?"

The Investigator was a pretentious man. He absorbed everything you told him in a deep way, thinking constantly about some third ramification that no one else in the room had yet considered. I figured he was having just such a spell of daydreaming right now.

"They warned me not to do it—not to revive you," he said. "But I did it anyway."

"Who warned you?"

"The Council," he said with a shrug. "Those who seek to advise me in my leadership."

"Hmm…" I said. "My mind is still a little fuzzy, but I'm catching on now. You can revive people without a machine?"

He made a vague gesture toward a series of stinking vats full of thick liquids.

"The process is somewhat similar to the wet-printing the alien machines perform. We have modified the procedure somewhat, as we only bother to recreate human flesh—the system doesn't have to work for any biotic morphology. That simplifies the design."

"Huh…" I said, looking around at his tanks and dripping, oily vats. "If you don't print people… how do you…?"

"It's more of a seeding process of our own design. We start with a clean strip of DNA, incubating it until it's the size of a grain of wheat. Then we allow it to spin up into a larger mass. Cell differentiation is encouraged, of course, if not exactly guided. The process is therefore slower, but no less effective."

When he said the word "slower" I snapped my neck around to look at him.

"How long? How long was I gone?"

"Precisely forty-two days—within the margin of error of an hour or two."

That was a gut-punch—no one likes to learn they've been dead and gone for a long time. It makes a man's mind wonder about existence. But then again, I'd been dead for as long as two years in the past. Six weeks shouldn't be a mind-blower for me.

"What about my mind?" I asked. "My memories? They seem whole, up to the point of my death. How did you manage that?"

He pointed at my tapper. "Earthmen all bear these integrated devices. They store memory up to the point of death. We retrieved the data from the arm of your corpse."

"Yeah..." I said, looking down at my tapper. "Makes sense."

Standing carefully and stretching, I began rolling my neck and flexing my fingers. The Investigator watched and made a few careful notes.

"I'm surprised at your effectiveness," he said, "and even more so by your calm demeanor. Past test subjects didn't become fully functional so quickly."

"They probably haven't died as many times as I have," I said. "You get your head wrapped around it eventually, and it doesn't bother you."

He stepped close again, peering into my eyes. He was only about five centimeters shorter than I was—a rare thing at my height—which allowed him to study me face to face like few could.

"Death and life don't intrigue you? How is this possible? Most humans are obsessed with these things."

"Yup—but not me. Dying is old news for the likes of James McGill. To me, the process is akin to going to sleep and waking up again."

"An interesting adaptation…" he said, walking around me and squeezing my bare arms now and then, poking at my flesh as if to test its quality.

It was weird, but I let him do it. After all, I did owe him my life. He was fascinated by me—he always had been.

"Do you ever wonder where you mind goes every night?" I asked him. "Are you *really* yourself then, or are you partially dead—or at least in suspended animation?"

"You're equating our natural comatose state with non-existence," he continued as he crept around me. "In a way, the analogy holds up. When we sleep, we're out of control, unaware, and generally motionless."

"Right…" I said, but my eyes began to wander. I was becoming bored with the Investigator and his odd ways.

Looking at his various tanks and vats of goop, I frowned. "You know… this entire operation is a Galactic violation. You can't just build your own revival machine."

"I've explained to you the critical differences in my process. My efforts in no way represent an attempt to duplicate currently patented technology."

"Um… right. But that's not how the Galactics will see it. They'll consider this a clear criminal case."

He stopped pacing around me and checking me over like some kind of prized pig. Instead, his eyes came up to meet mine again.

"Are you thinking of reporting this incident?"

I jutted out my chin and thought it over. "No," I said at last. "No, I would never do that. Not for several reasons."

"One being the fact that you're now an illegal grow? A deviation which the Empire would deal with harshly?"

"Yeah… that would be reason number one," I admitted. "But there's also the fact that I don't want Dust World to be erased. My own daughter is staying here now. On a larger scale, and perhaps most important, humanity as a whole may be held liable and condemned for your shenanigans."

I'd meant to slip in the bit about my wayward child casually, but the Investigator took immediate notice. Like I said, he wasn't born yesterday.

He drew back a step. "Etta? You *are* here to run her down, then? She told me she suspected as much the moment she learned of your arrival. I'd thought that might be a delusion of hers."

"Nope… she's right," I said, deciding to come clean. "I came here to see Etta."

The Investigator studied me closely, and at last, he seemed satisfied. He was a walking, breathing lie-detector. That's why I'd gone with the truth in all my dealings with him so far.

Nodding, he went back to poking at me.

"Say, Doc?" I said. "You got any clothes I can put on?"

"Is it too cold in here?"

"Nope. But on Earth, most of us don't wander around naked all the time. I'm not used to it."

He waved toward a dusty row of lockers, and I helped myself. After pulling on some stained coveralls, I felt better.

"Does Etta know I'm alive again?" I asked.

"She's known for weeks. She's come here, now and then, to study your form as it floated and slowly expanded in the tanks."

For some reason, that made my lip curl. I didn't like the idea of my little girl seeing me in such a sorry state. But, what was done was done.

"Can I go see her, then?"

He looked at me in surprise and spread his long-fingered hands wide.

"It's nothing to me. You've got the right to walk among us."

"And this place—this process you've developed—that will all stay secret. I won't tell anyone about it."

He nodded, and I turned to go. I felt his strange eyes on my back. They crawled there while his mind filled with unfathomable thoughts.

"One more thing, McGill," he called after me.

Reluctantly, I turned back to face him from the doorway.

His glowing blue eyes captured my gaze. He aimed a long arm at the vats, and he extended a single index finger.

"What about the next man in the vats? Have you no curiosity about him?"

Alarmed, I turned back. Six fast strides took me to the tanks again, where I gazed down into the murky liquid.

There he was, sleeping in a tank of oily amber gels.

That face—I'd know it anywhere.

The Investigator was reviving Claver.

# -7-

The new Claver looked fully-formed. He couldn't be far behind me in the process.

"He looks like he's fully cooked," I said. "How long until he wakes up?"

The Investigator made a vague gesture. "This isn't yet a precise science for us. We planted a seed, and we fed it. The fruition should come soon—he was planted the same day you were. In fact, most of my staff thought he would quicken before you as his total biomass is considerably less.

I stared down at Claver, frowning.

"This isn't the man I fought up on the rim," I said. "He's not a Class Three."

"A what?"

"Claver creates many clones of himself. Some of them operate with reduced mental capacities—most of them, in fact. The men you found flying that flitter up there on the rim were Class Threes. This man… I think he's a Prime."

The Investigator came near and stood with me, gazing down at the thing in his tanks. Now and then, a puff of bubbles rolled out of the nostrils. They were feeding him oxygen somehow.

"I don't understand your accusations. We took a DNA sample from the man who fell. There were no others."

"No Second-man? No one up there, wounded?"

"No."

My eyes searched the chamber, but I didn't notice anything that clarified the situation.

"I don't understand..." I said. "Claver clones himself illegally all the time. He has a base on a planet full of variations of himself. But how could one of those dumb, muscle-bound Class Threes be carrying the DNA of the original?"

"Ah... it's very possible," the Investigator said. His strangely lit eyes were wide, excited. My words seemed to have filled him with curiosity. "He must be manipulating the DNA during processing—as opposed to before setting the original seed. I want to meet this man and study his science."

I shook my head. "No, I don't think you do. If he has any cool tech gadgetry, rest assured he didn't develop it himself. He either bought it or stole it. He's no scientist. He's more like an interstellar pirate."

"Hmm..." the Investigator said, looking a bit disappointed, "I suppose I only have to wait for a time and ask this clone more about it."

"I don't think that's a good idea."

"So you said... Didn't you have a visitation to perform?"

"You mean with Etta? Where's she living now?"

"In the Grand Cave, most likely. Earth has softened her somewhat. She doesn't like the heat and dust as she once did. She haunts the shores of our lake and the coolest depths of our caverns, avoiding the blazing eye of our sun."

"Yeah..." I said, thinking about it. "I guess I'll be going. I'm looking forward to catching up with her."

Before leaving, I considered asking the Investigator to stay quiet about my presence on Dust World, but I passed on the idea. He would do whatever he wanted anyway, and he wasn't a man who was prone to lying. It probably didn't even occur to him to speak anything other than what he saw as the truth. He was brutally honest, but he wasn't always right about his take on things.

I left him there, poking at the Claver he was growing in his vats. If Claver was about to wake up, I didn't want to be around when he did.

Moving through the tunnels, I found the denizens of Dust World inclined to stare at an Earthman in their midst. I would have thought it was rude if I hadn't been familiar with their habits. They didn't know it was rude to stare.

After checking out the Grand Cave and making a few inquiries, I found Etta wasn't there. Moving up through the passages and galleries, I made my way to the surface.

There, along the lakeshore, I saw swampy ground. Bulbous growths, most of them bearing large fleshy-flowers, flourished everywhere. These plants stood over three meters tall.

Avoiding the relatively quiet beaches, I made my way to the overgrown spots. I sought land that was overgrown, mushy.

It wasn't long before I found Etta. She wasn't trying to hide, fortunately. If she had been squatting out here in these alien reeds, I'd never have found her.

Instead, I found her crouching over a pile of bones—very large bones.

I approached her quietly from behind, but she heard me before I reached her. It's hard to sneak up on someone when you've got huge feet and squelching mud to contend with.

Her head jerked to the side, and a blade appeared in her hand. But then she saw me, and she relaxed and put the knife down again. She went back to arranging her bones.

"Come see what I found, Father," she said.

Wading in up to my knees in the mud, I sloshed closer and stood over her, dripping.

Her form reminded me of Della's, but Etta was at least ten centimeters taller. Together, we examined the bulky skeleton she was assembling. The bones didn't look human. They were too big. They were as thick as a horse's bones.

But the skull gave it all away. It was clearly humanoid, but twice the size of any man's. It looked like the skull of some long-extinct great ape.

"Is that…?" I began. "Is that a heavy trooper? A Blood-Worlder?"

"Yes. That's right."

"Where'd you find him?"

She stood up and faced me for the first time. She swept the valley with her arm. "Don't you recognize this place?

Something like thirty years back, you fought right here. Maybe you killed this littermate yourself. There's no sign of the usual nanite-etching Dust Worlder weapons leave behind on a victim's bones. Just a few broken ribs over the heart. I think he was shot to death."

"That does sound like the work of the legions," I agreed.

For a few moments, we didn't speak. We just stood side by side and gazed at the bizarre specimen that was splayed on the big flat rock at our feet. Back on Earth, Etta had exhibited a strange fascination with digging up bones out in the marsh. I'd always hoped she'd get over it—but I guess she hadn't.

I didn't say anything because part of me was enjoying the moment. I'd felt for months like I'd lost my daughter. This activity, as morbid as it was, felt homey to me. I didn't want the feeling to end.

"I wondered if you would come out here after me—and you did," she said in a quiet voice.

"There was never any doubt of it," I lied firmly. When you lie to family, you have to go whole-hog. You can't have any reservations, no hemming or hawing. They know you too well for that.

"How'd you get out here?" she asked. "Did you die knowing my grandfather could be convinced to revive you?"

I blinked. In a way, that was exactly what I'd done. That hadn't been my intention of course, but things had turned out that way.

Shrugging, I nodded. "That's right. I arranged for the Investigator to get my DNA, knowing he could revive me. Then I offed myself and zap, after a regrow I'm on Dust World."

Etta leaned close, suddenly, and she wrapped her arms around me. My privates were doing a dance of fear, I don't mind telling you. The girl was mean with a blade.

But I let her hug me, and I patted her awkwardly.

Was she crying? I thought she was, just a little.

"I'm sorry Daddy," she said. "I shouldn't have run out on you. I guess I was in a bad mood."

"I'll say."

"But Claver told me about the book. About the poison—and about Earth's plans to use it."

My mouth opened up to say something, but then it clamped shut.

The book in question was called *The Eaters of Lotus,* and it hid inside its pages the chemical code for a deadly genetic poison. Floramel had figured all that out while I was off running around on Dark World last year.

I'd known all about that—but I hadn't known about any plans by Earth to use this bio-weapon.

"Uh..." I said. "What did Claver tell you, exactly? About Earth's plans?"

"Just that Central wanted to weaponize some kind of spore. That the weapon would be released and allowed to hollow out the populations of the Core Worlds."

I peered down at Etta, wondering if it could be true. Claver knew things, secret things—but he was also frequently full of shit.

"Is all that stuff true, Dad?" she asked me.

"I think it *might* be," I said. "The book and the poison definitely exist."

She nodded, and she knelt again over her bones. She had dug out a plastic-wrapped package.

"This is it," she said, handing it up to me. "The real book. There's no cover—but the contents are still there. I took it because... because I didn't want to let anyone have such terrible power."

"But didn't you sell it to Claver? And give him a fake one?"

She looked a little shy. "I needed the money."

"Right... to come out here. Are you happy on Dust World? There's some pretty good swamp-land."

She looked around the scene. It was alien, but lovely in a way. Natural beauty abounded. The total population of Dust World was about the same as a small town back on Earth. Spread out over an entire planet, humans weren't exactly elbow-to-elbow like they were back on Earth.

"I'm not sure..." she said. "Maybe when I'm a little older, I'd like it better. It's so empty here, and I miss my grandparents."

I felt kind of bad for her. She was a girl without a planet, in a way. Sometimes, for a young person, having two homes was like having no home at all.

Before I finished contemplating the situation and figuring out what to say next, I heard a splash behind us.

Etta and I turned as one.

"The McGills..." said an odd voice.

It was Claver's voice, but it wasn't *quite* right. It sounded a little deeper, a little raspy.

"Claver?" I called. "Come out and show yourself."

"Gladly," the man said.

Reeds snapped and bent. Claver appeared.

He was nude. Slathered in mud and dripping blood from a dozen spots, I thought I might know what had happened. Inside the Investigator's makeshift gestation tanks, there had been many attached tubes to the bodies he was growing.

My own tubes had been removed by the time I'd awakened. I still had a dozen itchy round holes in my skin, but I'd never had to endure the pain of their removal.

Perhaps it had gone differently for this clone of Claver. Or maybe, the Investigator had seen fit to speed up the process since I was awake, and he'd stimulated this man's fresh body into quickening.

After noticing the nudity, the dripping blood, and the yellow glint in his eyes, which seemed crazed—I saw the weapon. He had a pistol in his hand.

The bulky gun was shaped like a power drill. Dust Worlders made these guns themselves. It was an oversized but effective weapon.

Automatically, I shifted myself between Claver and my daughter. Etta took her cue, diving backward off the flat rock where she'd been painstakingly assembling an alien skeleton. She vanished into the soupy bog.

Claver charged forward, aiming his gun after her. He sent one hot bolt after her retreating form, melting a dozen fleshy plants. A misty explosion of heated gasses puffed up around us.

I stepped toward him to distract him, and his gun swung to cover me again.

I held the book up between us. Maybe that would give him pause.

"What do you want, Claver?"

"Where...?" he said, his lungs rasping. "Where is the Prime?"

I laughed. "Don't you know? *You* are the Prime now. Think about it: aren't you having new thoughts? Isn't your head clearer today than it's ever been?"

The Claver looked tormented, haunted. I could see my words had struck through.

Wondering what it might be like to be an idiot awakened in the brain and body of a genius, I could almost feel pity for him. Almost.

"I can't be the Prime..." he said, sounding lost.

His weapon hand sagged a little, and that's when I charged at him.

I was too far away from him to start with—I knew that. But I hoped that his slow wits might impede his reaction time.

But they didn't. His weapon flicked upward, and as I raised my hands to shield myself the gun sang again. I felt a gush of heat.

First, a fireball blossomed in my hands. In a singular fraction of a second, I realized he'd unwittingly obliterated the book.

I also realized this Claver didn't care about that. He wanted his leadership, his society, his planet of Clavers to order him around. Without that, he was completely lost. He'd asked me over and over where the Prime was because he needed a boss Claver to lead him through life.

None of that mattered now. The beam didn't take long to burn through the book. It lanced onward, stabbing into my skin a moment later.

The beam burned away the flesh covering my chest, then it popped the marrow inside those gray-white ribs, turning them black and making them smolder.

Toppling backward, mortally wounded, I saw a cloud of steam rising from my ruined chest. I'd been burned—burned badly.

There was a growl from the reeds then. It was an almost inhuman sound. If it hadn't been high-pitched, I wouldn't have been able to credit the source.

The idiot Claver who stood over me shivered repeatedly. His eyes widened in shock. I heard the repeated thrusts of a knife sinking in.

Before I died, Etta crouched over me in the mud. She was crying—something she hadn't done for years.

She was saying something. Holding my dying hand and telling me something important—but I couldn't understand her.

Then… I died.

Lying on my back in an alien swamp, my body quit functioning on me. The whole thing was a nightmare, and it was probably the worst death I'd gone through in decades.

# -8-

When I woke up, I fully expected to find myself floating in the Investigator's turd-tank again—but I didn't.

"What have we got?" asked a male voice.

"This is a backorder revive," a woman said. "Questionable docs."

"Meaning what?"

"No body was found. At least nothing that's been confirmed on Earth."

"Well… why the hell are we doing this, then?"

The other voice, the female voice, down-shifted to a low tone. A whisper. I couldn't make out what she said.

"Is that so?" the male asked. "Well… I don't like it. Let's reroll."

"He's not a bad grow."

"I don't care. I'm not losing rank over some kind of cluster-fuck upstairs. It doesn't matter who ordered it, we're going to recycle. Get his legs."

Two strong hands gripped my ankles. I was pulled off the gurney. Wet and slimy, I flopped onto the cold floor. My limbs groped, but they lacked strength. My fingers felt like half-inflated rubber balloons.

My eyes tried to open, but they were fluttering, rolling in my head. I only saw vague shapes, bright lights, shadows.

Lashing out with my hands, I caught an ankle, heard a curse and my fingers exploded with pain. They'd stomped my groping hand.

"Turn it on, dammit!" the male bio said. "Turn it on! He's waking up!"

"Adjunct," the woman said. "Don't you think we should check—"

"Shut up and turn it on! That's an order."

Then I heard the most terrible sound a fresh revive can hear: the whirring of angled blades. Sounding like a cross between a wood-chipper and a vacuum cleaner, the recycling machine was on, and soon my foot would be going into it. Once part of your body went in there—well, there wasn't any escape from death.

*My feet.* That was the thought that struck through to me then. For the past thirty seconds of awareness, I'd been trying to operate my arms, my hands, my fingers.

But I'd never tried to use my feet.

Now, I'm big man by any measure. A solid two meters tall and well over a hundred kilograms in weight. My foot was built to match and unreasonably large.

Using my left leg, I drew it back and kicked out blindly. The person dragging that foot turned out to be the woman on the team, and she was taken for a ride. Dragged almost to her knees, she stupidly tried to hold on. When my foot jacked back out, catching her in the belly, she didn't sound too happy.

She made a whuffing sound and went ass-over-tea kettle into a rack of equipment. Instruments, tools and the like clattered and rained down on the tile around me.

The male adjunct came toward me then, growling. He had something in his hand. I could see well-enough to catch onto that fact by now.

My hand caught his. Surprised, he put his second hand onto his first, and he tried to drive the spike into my chest. It was probably a syringe loaded with a kill-solution, or at least a sedative. I was pretty sure of that.

My other hand worked well enough to join the fray. Grunting, we struggled. He was on top of me, and his body was operating fully. Fortunately, he didn't possess more than half my strength.

Every second that passed, my mind became clearer, my vision grew sharper, and my muscles functioned more precisely.

The woman got to her feet, but she didn't jump in and help the adjunct.

"Go get help!" the adjunct told her.

"Yeah," I said in a husky voice. "You'd better get help."

She scrambled off the floor and rushed out the door.

The bio bared his teeth at me. In return, I grinned.

"This isn't going to be your day, hog," I told him.

With a sudden burst of power, I reversed the syringe and jabbed it into his neck. The bulb pulsed and throbbed, automatically pumping its load into his bloodstream.

He screamed and his eyes flew wide.

While the adjunct writhed and curled up into a ball on the floor, I got to my feet with a groan. I almost slipped and fell again, but I caught myself.

"That was a close one, hog," I told the dying man on the floor. "You should have checked the roster. I'm a Varus man. You don't go around recycling real, star-going legionnaires without cause. You just don't."

Stepping over him, I gave him a solid kick in the ribs. He seemed to wheeze in response, but it could have been his death rattle. Sometimes, it's hard to tell.

By the time a pair of blue-tunic wearing MPs rushed into the revival chamber, I was dressed in a smart-cloth jumper. I'd found a beret, which I put on at an appropriate angle. In the insignia box, I found my centurion's red crest and slapped it on.

The floor slished with sliding boots. Breathing hard, the two MPs came into the room. They had their shock-batons out, and they regarded me warily.

"Gentlemen," I said loudly in a commanding tone. "You're late. The incident has passed."

Their eyes flicked over me and my rank insignia then down to the bio, who was curled up like a stone-dead beetle on the floor.

"Don't worry," I said. "It was just a misunderstanding. I'm not going to press charges."

“Who the hell are you?” one of them demanded.

“I’m Centurion James McGill. Legion Varus. I’m here to report to the brass upstairs.”

My eyes were functioning well enough now to recognize this was a revival chamber inside Central. Only the Lord above knew how many times I’d awakened in a room just like this one in the past.

The hogs relaxed a little, and they switched off their batons.

The smaller female bio behind them peered past their elbows. When she saw them standing down, she was immediately outraged.

“What’s this bullshit? He assaulted me and Adjunct Harrison while we were performing our assigned duties! I demand you arrest this man! He’s slated for recycling!”

“He sure doesn’t look like a bad grow to me,” one MP said.

“That’s not for you to determine,” she said officiously. “Are you going to help me or not?”

The MP shrugged and threw up his hands. “Not my job, lady. If you want to recycle him, be my guest.”

The two hogs walked out, and I made a mental note to buy them both a beer if I happened to meet up with them later on.

When they were out of the place, the bio watched me warily. I walked over to the lockers and fished around for any personal effects—there were none.

The bio girl trotted quickly to Harrison’s side. She bent over him and gasped.

“You *killed* him! That’s murder!”

I laughed, and I kicked on the recycler. It whirred and buzzed and made greedy slurping sounds. They all had the ability to vacuum up debris.

“You want me to help you stuff Harrison in there?” I asked.

She opened her mouth to say something nasty—but then she thought the better of it and clamped her lips shut again.

“Just get out.”

That was good enough for me. I left the place.

As I headed to the elevators, I thought I heard the buzzing slow down and choke for a moment.

I smiled grimly, knowing it was the sound the recyclers made when they hit a hard lump of bone.

# -9-

As it turned out, it was night time. Inside Central, the hallways weren't completely empty, but they were pretty quiet. Most of the staffers had gone home to bed.

Of course, being the headquarters of a military establishment that spanned a dozen star systems, Central never truly went to sleep. Probably a third of the usual daytime shift was on duty, along with plenty of janitors and other support personnel.

I got into an elevator, and I let it scan my tapper for a few long seconds. For a grim moment, I thought maybe I'd had my clearance pulled—but it wasn't so.

The doors shut, and the elevator car began to hum. I chose to go up, not down, and I was lifted a few hundred floors higher. Walking out along a long corridor, I passed various tribunes' offices.

Victrix was first in line. They usually were. Their famous crossed swords emblem was a half-meter wide, covering most of the door. Next was Germanica, with a stylized bull's head on their entrance. That was Taurus—a cow-god, or something.

I passed them all, one by one. Solstice, Teutoburg, the Iron Eagles. The parade of offices continued until at the very end of the road I came up to a door with mean-looking wolf's head on it.

Smiling, I tried the door. It hesitated, then opened.

That was good. I was still a valid officer in Legion Varus.

There was no one home inside. That wasn't all that unusual. Varus wasn't on deployment, nor were they gearing up for a mission. We were on shore leave until we got called up again. As we'd finished a mission on Dark World only a few months earlier, I didn't expect to get such a summons for quite a while.

Sighing, I made myself at home on the couch in the tribune's waiting room. Before I knew it, I was sound asleep.

What seemed like moments later, I felt a sharp blow to my over-large feet.

"Get your boots on, Centurion!" a familiar voice said.

"Yes sir," I said, sliding around into a sitting position and stretching. An uncontrollable yawn howled out of me.

Galina Turov, tribune of Varus and my CO, stood over me with her arms crossed.

"What is it this time?" she demanded. "I've gotten several odd reports about you vanishing and reappearing on Earth. Is it possible you've gotten yourself into some kind of trouble *again*?"

"Uh…" I said, glancing over at her secretary and the two staff-primus types she had with her.

I got the feeling they'd had a breakfast meeting, walked into the office, and discovered me snoring on the couch.

The two primus-ranked pukes were hogs. They smirked at one another behind Galina's back.

Now, Galina and I had had an inappropriate relationship going, that was true. But me showing up in her office like this broke our rules. Sure, she'd spent a weekend at my parents' place a few months back—*damn, had it really been that long already?* Time sure flew by when you were dead.

But despite our special moments together, I wasn't supposed to embarrass her whenever I felt like it.

"Sorry sir," I told her. "But I've got some important, classified information for you."

She stared at me with the narrowed eyes of a pissed housecat. Women often suspected me and my motives. Usually, they were right to do so—but not this time.

"McGill?" she asked. "Can this information wait?"

"Sure," I said. "It's no more important than, say, your average lost library book might be."

Galina stared at me, and then she blinked—once.

Finally, she got it. She sucked in a breath, and her spine straightened.

Turning back toward the bemused group that stood in her wake, she clapped her hands together loudly.

"Gentlemen," she said. "I'm going to have to postpone our meeting. Gary, please reschedule them."

So saying, she spun around on her heel and marched into her office. Her door hung open behind her. I presumed that was for my benefit.

Calmly, I stood up and followed her at a leisurely pace. I spoke to Gary, her latest secretary, before I entered her office.

"Better clear the schedule until after lunch, my man," I told him.

He gave me a spiteful glance.

"McGill?" Galina called out. "Get in here!"

I touched a couple of fingers to my beret in the direction of the two primus hogs and marched inside. They lingered in my wake, confused and annoyed.

When I got into her office, safe and sound, I closed the door behind me. Then I looked around for some breakfast.

There wasn't much. She had some chocolate candies on her desk, so I munched on those.

"What the *hell* have you been doing?" she demanded, her arms crossed tightly over her breasts. "You are officially AWOL, did you know that? We finally got word from Dust World that you'd died out there, and I green-lit a quiet revival. How did you manage to turn that into a bloodbath—right here in frigging Central?"

"Some bio downstairs got cold feet during my off-book revival."

"You mean he tried to recycle you?"

"He tried, and he failed."

She sighed, rubbing the bridge of her nose. "You've been off-planet for two months. Then you come back and immediately make a violent splash. That's unacceptable."

I shrugged, not caring one whit. "When a man tries to kill me… well sir, he'd better not miss."

"All right. Forget about that. Tell me about the book."

"Uh…" I said, looking around.

Not seeing any cameras or other recording instruments, I turned back to her. "Are you going to let me slide on these details?"

"You've got it, then?" she asked with sudden intensity. "You've stolen it back from Claver?"

I munched on her chocolate candies, staring at her.

She snatched the bowl away from me and put it back on her desk.

"All right," she said, heaving a sigh. "I know how you operate. I'll exonerate you from all legion-based charges. That won't exempt you from Hegemony, if they decide to prosecute."

"That's good enough," I said, and I told her my story.

I told her most of it, anyway. I left Etta out as much as possible. Her name didn't need to be associated with these types of goings-on. I wanted her to make it to adulthood without being prominent in someone's database as a troublemaker. When she grew up fully, I was pretty sure she'd make her own waves, but it wouldn't be due to anything I'd reported while she was a kid.

Galina listened with a sour face. Her expression softened somewhat when I told her about Claver coming to my place.

"So… Claver came out to harass you after I left? I can understand how violence ensued. But then you blind-ported out to Dust World? That seems insanely risky."

"Remember who you're talking to?"

"Right… Where's the book now?"

This was the part I hadn't told her about yet. I filled her in on my final moments, about how a confused Claver had blasted it to ashes.

"It's *gone*?"

"Yes. But don't worry, it has to have been scanned by Central when Floramel had it."

Her teeth exposed themselves in a wild snarl. Her thin arms came away from her chest, and she grabbed me by the shirt. I would have been alarmed, but she'd never been very strong, or much of a fighter.

"James, there are *no* copies! *Nothing*. I checked. I went through everything down there a year back."

"Is that so? When you say 'down there' are you talking about our secret underground lab levels?"

"Yes," she said, letting go of me. "I can't believe it. It's gone. The book is gone."

I chewed that over. Looking past her tousled hair and angry face, I spied that bowl of candies. I was really hungry.

"You got plans for breakfast?" I asked.

She hissed in disgust. "Why do you always shrug off disasters? Is it because you take them in stride, or because you really don't care?"

"A little of both, I suspect. But in this case, you don't have to worry. I can get you a copy. I swear it."

Her eyes probed my face. I looked back at her blankly.

"Really?" she asked, her tone almost pleading all of a sudden. "That would be a miracle. Perhaps I didn't make an error reviving you."

"An error? I thought you and I had a good thing going just eight weeks ago."

She made a flapping, dismissive gesture with her hand. Then she began to pace around her office.

Galina did that often, and I'd always enjoyed the show. She wore skin-tight smart clothes that molded themselves to her shapely form. It was almost like she was wearing body paint.

"James?!" she shouted at me.

"Um… yeah?"

"Are you listening at all?"

"No… I'm hungry."

She made an exasperated sound. "If I get you some food, will you give me another copy of that book?"

"What's the rush?" I asked, suspecting there was more to her interest than she was letting on.

She was instantly on her guard again. She cocked her head as if listening to a voice I couldn't hear then nodded as if coming to a decision.

“This visit is no accident, is it? You found out about Hegemony’s deal, and you moved to secure the merchandise before we could.”

At this point, I was entirely in the dark as to what she was going on about. But I knew that if I kept quiet long enough, she might just tell me. Galina loved to talk.

“I see…” she said, taking my silence in the worst possible light. She sighed. “I’d hoped our relationship had moved forward. That we could trust each other more now that we’ve been getting along so well.”

That made me frown. She had a point. I was treating her like the old Galina, the conniving witch who’d done everything but perm me in years past.

“You’re right,” I said, nodding. “We should trust each other more. Let’s go get some breakfast, and we’ll talk about it further.”

“I’ve already had breakfast. I hereby *order* you to tell me where the other copy of the book is right now!”

“Okay then,” I said, deciding to call her bluff. I stood up. “I’ll go eat by myself. I’ll be back in about an hour.”

She made a growling sound of frustration. I walked out and left her in her office.

Not three seconds later, I heard her quick, light steps behind me.

“Wait, James. I’m coming with you. You’re not going to get away with dying on me—not again.”

She followed me out of the office, and I again tipped my hat to the two hog officers. They were still sitting quietly in Galina’s waiting room. They frowned back at me and muttered among themselves.

# -10-

One would think that Tribune Turov could simply order me to spill my guts about any given subject, and that would be that. Ordinarily, I'd agree with that thread of logic. The problem was things were more complex than that.

Galina and I had been involved in countless adventures, some public and legit—others secret and downright criminal. Because of that history, when we dealt with a matter that was outside the formal boundaries of a military operation, we reverted to a secondary set of rules that existed only between us.

"James," she growled as she walked beside me, "if this is all bullshit, you're going to pay. I want you to know that."

Picking up the pace a little, I left her following in my wake. She almost had to trot to keep up with my long strides. The situation had a smile playing on my lips. Often, I got to play the part of the puppy on the leash, but today I was enjoying the reverse.

"Don't worry, Tribune sir. You won't be disappointed."

At least, I *hoped* she wouldn't be. I hadn't bothered to check up on my hunches, but I felt pretty good about them, so I'd gone with it. When bluffing, it's best to go whole-hog, I always say.

Galina followed me down to the officer's commissary, where I ate heartily. She picked at a bowl of fruit I'd insisted on ordering for her.

After several plates of scrambled eggs, country fries and heaps of crispy bacon, I sat back and pushed the table away.

"Oooo," I grunted. "I'm full now."

"I should frigging hope so. Are you willing to talk to me now?"

"Actually…" I said. "I could go for a—"

Galina snapped. She leaned over the table, put her hand on top of mine, and dug in her nails.

"Are you shitting me?" she hissed. "I'm going to bust you back down to veteran if you don't—"

"Okay, okay!" I said, throwing my arms wide in surrender. "Let's go find your book."

"What?"

"Come on, it's not far."

I got up, stretched, and let her pay the check. She did this with poor grace, but I didn't care. After all, I was doing her a favor.

We were back in the elevators and heading downward. I needed Galina for the next leg of the journey. I didn't have the clearance to hit the underground lab zone without a special invite.

As former Hegemony brass, she still had the proper clearances. She touched her tapper to the elevator panel, and a whole mess of optional destinations swam into view on the panel. I selected one about a hundred and fifty floors below the surface, and we were whisked into the depths of the Earth.

Once arriving, a security team greeted us. They ran us through fluoroscopes, metal detectors and Lord-knows what other kinds of sensors. Our weapons were removed, even my knives, before we were finally allowed to enter the lab complex.

Even so, I knew we wouldn't get far down here without an escort who had room-to-room clearance. Accordingly, I thought hard before I crafted a text and sent it.

Lowering my arm, I waited for my tapper to buzz me back. Nothing happened for a solid two minutes.

"James," Galina said in a whisper. "What are we doing down here? This is a need-to-know level. Even with a clearance, that's not good enough to be loitering around down here. We can't just—"

"Floramel?" I called out, ignoring Galina. I stretched out a greeting hand, put on my best smile, and waved.

A door had cracked open down the hall. The room beyond was dim-lit, and I couldn't see the figure who stood there clearly, but I would know that long-limbed shape anywhere.

"Floramel, let me explain," I said, walking slowly toward her.

My hands were out and up, and I approached her the way a man might approach a wary squirrel in the park. I only hoped she was interested in peanuts today.

"James…" she said, still standing behind the cracked door. "You brought Turov with you… why?"

"I can't come down here on my own. I don't have the clearance."

"Then you shouldn't be here. Those are the rules."

The door had never been open very far, and now it narrowed to a slit.

"Hold on!" I called out. "Galina here revived you. Remember that."

She hesitated.

Behind me, I sensed Galina was following with wary steps. At least she had the good sense to keep quiet and let me do the talking. Often, brass felt they should take over when tricky negotiations were underway. The results were usually disastrous.

Finally, the door was kicked wide.

"Come in here," Floramel said. "I'm on break—you have three minutes."

I slipped into the doorway, and behind me Galina managed to catch the closing door with her fingernails. The door was heavy, made of steel, and once it closed it would take a grenade to blow it open again.

Cursing quietly, she slipped inside behind me.

"There are cameras everywhere, McGill," Galina said. "I bet security bots have already opened a file on all three of us."

"Probably," I said in a bored tone.

My eyes and my complete attention were all focused on Floramel. She was as tall and long as Galina was small and petite. Her face was very pretty, but in a sort of stretched out, almost unnatural way.

Floramel was a near-human. She'd been bred primarily for her intellect, and on Earth she served with our military scientists.

Over the years, I'd figured out that the squids who'd engineered her genes had also purposefully designed her to be attractive to brutish males. That was because, back on her home planet Blood World, the females often served as brood mothers to create soldiers of various types.

"Why are you plaguing me today, James McGill?" Floramel asked. "I'm going to be on report for this. I would not be surprised if I'm soon arrested and interrogated."

"Yeah, I get that," I said. "I'm real sorry, too. But listen, do you remember a few years back when I had you read a book for me?"

Floramel's eyes widened a fraction. They flicked toward Galina, who stayed quiet, then back to me again.

"What about it?"

"As I understand it," I said. "You have a good memory. Could you reproduce the text of that book, exactly as you saw it?"

Again, she flicked her eyes over the two of us. She looked concerned.

"Of course. My memory is eidetic."

Galina seemed to be catching on at last. She looked at Floramel the way stray dogs look at pork chops.

"You can reproduce the book?" Galina demanded, stepping closer. "Exactly as it was? No error in punctuation, spacing—"

"That's what I said."

"Do it, then," Galina said. "I *order* you to write the book and submit it to me personally. Do not transmit it with your tapper. You must give me a physical copy."

Floramel studied us for a second. "Why?" she asked at last.

"Why are we interested in the book? That's none of your—" Galina began hotly.

"Hold *on*, ladies!" I said, stepping between the two women. "Now Tribune, we don't want to be rude, do we?"

I gave Galina a sharp look. She bared her teeth and crossed her arms.

Turning back to Floramel, I was all smiles. "What about it, Floramel? We're all friends here. Friends do each other favors."

"Why?"

"Well," I said, taking the question at face value, "when people have a certain level of affection for one another—"

"No, James. I mean why should I help you two? You're independent military. I'm part of Hegemony, Government Services. You don't have any authority over me."

"Yes, right," I said. "That's why I've been talking about friendship."

It was Floramel's turn to cross her arms. A stubborn cast came over her features. I'd seen that look countless times before, but not on her face.

"You've changed," I said.

"Yes, I've become much wiser during my years on Earth."

"What do you want, hog?" Galina asked rudely.

That statement made me turn to Galina and give her a small shake of my head. She didn't seem interested. Floramel and Galina were squaring off, and they were already in a full-fledged stare-down.

"I want Raash revived," Floramel said.

"What?" Galina squawked in surprise. "That murdering lizard? He was an enemy agent."

"He was my friend."

"He killed you and McGill both."

Floramel shrugged. "So what? You legionaries kill one another now and then. I want to give him a chance to explain himself."

Stepping close to Floramel, I made a big mistake. I smiled widely and nodded to her—then I rested one of my big hands on her shoulder.

"Sounds like a reasonable request…" I said. "Too bad we don't have his DNA, or his memory engrams. If only…"

I stopped, because Floramel had produced a dime-sized disk of plain metal.

"Raash's data is imprinted on this memory device," she said. "Use it to revive him, and you'll have your book."

Galina's eyes flashed from me, to Floramel, then to the disk. She looked pissed all of a sudden. Her shoulders were hunched, defensive. Her eyes were slits.

Catching on, I pulled my hand off Floramel's shoulder. Galina was clearly jealous.

"This is all bullshit," she told us. "It's a setup. McGill, you cheating bastard. You're trying to manipulate me, the same way you always do. I was a fool."

She turned away and straight-armed the door. It popped open, and an alarm sounded. She ignored that and marched toward the elevators.

"Uh…" I said, realizing the entire operation had just gone to shit right before my eyes.

Reaching out, I snatched the disk from Floramel. "I'll see what I can do," I told her, and I hurried after Galina.

She wasn't in a good mood. She almost didn't let me into the elevator. Only the fact the hog MPs were watching and snickering at us changed her mind. I got into the elevator car, and we were whisked away again toward safer ground.

"James," she said, her arms crossed. "I've made several key decisions."

"Um… like what?"

"Do you know who those gentlemen were who you brushed aside this morning in my office, embarrassing me horribly?"

"They were fat-assed hogs, right?"

"They were Hegemony controllers. Mission planners, working with Drusus and others. Legion Varus is going on deployment again soon."

I blinked in surprise. Usually, a starfaring legion got a year or so of shore leave between deployments. Seeing as we were often killed on alien worlds, and that our tours might take years to complete, it only seemed right to give us a break in-between.

"That seems premature, Tribune."

"It is. I was going to fight it—but not now. I have plans. New plans. They involve you, me—and your old girlfriend with her bad attitude."

To my way of thinking, it was Galina who held the bad attitude award today—but I didn't mention that. I couldn't see how it would do me any good to do so.

# -11-

True to her word, Tribune Galina Turov managed to get us all shot up into space within two weeks' time. Damn if that girl wouldn't cut off her own nose to spite her face!

During the interim, I couldn't get ahold of her. She seemed angry and distant. It was more than a cold-shoulder, she was actively avoiding me. There was some talk of her being sick, or something—but I didn't buy that for a minute. She was pissed off.

About two weeks after she'd marched off in a huff, I found myself sitting on a lifter. My unit was with me, and they were downright mutinous. There wasn't a set of lips onboard that wasn't cursing the name of our hotheaded CO.

"This is unacceptable," Harris kept saying. "Do you know I'd just started cutting and pouring a new pool at my place? I couldn't finish, and I had to ditch the whole project."

"A new pool, huh?" I asked him. "You digging it yourself?"

"Of course. I don't have the cash for a team of bots. But the rest of it—I had to schedule everything and pay up front. Do you know what a puff-crete machine costs to rent these days?"

"No clue," I admitted.

"Too damned much! Six months' pay, down the shitter! Turov knows the rules. If Earth's not under threat, we should be rotated off active duty for at *least* six months. That's a minimum!"

I made sympathetic noises, but my attention was already wandering. I let my eyes travel over the faces in the harnesses all around me. The lifter was full of people—most of them familiar to me.

Carlos was sitting next to Kivi, and both of them were bitching up a storm. Leeson was farther down, looking glum but determined. He was a hard-bitten soldier, the oldest man I knew next to Graves himself.

Primus Graves wasn't in sight. He was upstairs, riding in the command module. As a centurion, I could have chosen to join him, but I'd decided to sit among the troops instead. Sometimes, it was good to get the lay of the land, and you could only do that properly from ground-level.

About the only happy person I spotted was Veteran Moller. Built like a fireplug with arms, she seemed to like active duty. I suspected she didn't have much of a personal life to go back to when the legion was marooned at home on friendly dirt.

Leeson spotted my wandering eye, and he climbed out of his harness. He came close, shoved a recruit out of the seat next to me and buckled in again.

"What do you know about this particular Charley-Foxtrot, Centurion?" he asked me.

I shook my head. I'd long ago decided to play dumb on this trip.

"Nothing," I lied. "I was taken completely by surprise, just like the rest of you."

He eyed me for a moment, and I eyed him right back. At last, he sighed.

"Okay. I can buy that. No one knows where we're going, or why we were mustered up with only three days' notice before an undetermined deployment. This is just the kind of bullshit that makes me envy hogs."

"Aw now, don't say that Adjunct. There's no need to stoop to that level."

"Yeah… you're right. But it seems unfair. We were fighting and dying back on Dark World not six months ago. Now, we're on the way out into space again, and they haven't even bothered to dust us with any shitty lies as to why we're doing it. I mean, I don't mind getting fucked. Hell, I'm used it.

But I like to get kissed first. Call me old-fashioned if you want to."

"Uh-huh…" I said, checking my tapper.

A red message blinked there. My tapper was shivering. I slapped Leeson's shoulder with the back of my hand.

"I've got a summons. Keep them all from wetting the bed, Leeson."

"You got it, Centurion."

Harris turned a baleful eye after the two of us as I left. I'd just left Leeson in charge of the unit in my absence, and for some reason, that always pissed off Harris. He wanted to be my second in command, despite the fact he didn't have the seniority with officer's standing.

All of that was just six kinds of too-damned-bad. With rapid tugs on a series of rings on the walls and ceiling, I negotiated the null-G environment and got myself flying in the right direction.

Catching the hatchway with one out-flung hand, I swung myself inside and shot up a tube to the upper chambers.

Here, the officers and crew enjoyed the kind of space and comfort that was unknown below on the troop level. Up here, there weren't any armored knees and elbows hitting you in the side, or vacuum-powered drains crusty with puke. It was fresh-smelling, roomy and even brightly lit.

Graves' office was at the end of the main passage, but I skipped that and headed for the conference chamber adjacent to the bridge. There, I found a group of centurions encircling our primus and a central viewing tank.

A few more centurions arrived before the tank flickered into life. Primus Graves shushed us all with a glare, and we listened up without being told to do so.

First, the Legion Varus symbol blazed in the midst of the tank. It was a Wolf's head, stylized and standing out in metallic relief. It spun around and then seemed to fall away from us, shrinking to a point and vanishing.

Tribune Galina Turov loomed next. She was standing too close to the pick-up, to my way of thinking. Her head was about a meter across—but maybe she liked it that way.

"Officers," she said. "I know you're all wondering why we're going on deployment again so soon. Let me assure everyone, it's for a good reason."

We squirmed a little, and several of the centurions threw a glance my way. Everyone knew Turov and I had a thing going. It was hard to keep a secret of that nature under wraps.

I played the situation the way I usually did: I ignored everybody. With a deadly serious look on my face, I stared at Galina. The truth was, I didn't know where we were headed or why. She'd cut me off from insider information the same day she'd gotten all jealous about Floramel.

"Legion Varus has been honored by a direct call to service from Hegemony," Galina said. "As your leader, I felt compelled to take advantage of this unique opportunity."

"Turov sounds like she's selling a condo," Centurion Manfred commented.

We all chuckled—except for Graves. The primus tossed Manfred a quick glare, and he quieted.

The scene in the tank changed. I realized now, for the first time, that Galina was already aboard the transport ship. She had to be, as she was in a very large chamber on Gold Deck. The lifters were coming in, closing on the transport and docking. Even as I watched her speak, I heard our lifter's braking jets light up.

The hull shuddered as we made course adjustments. In a few minutes, we'd begin unloading and walking onto the decks of our new transport vessel.

"Welcome to *Legate*," she said, indicating an external view of the ship.

Galina's own shapely form was superimposed on a star field, and it looked like she was a goddess pointing out details of our new ship from the outside. A few of the centurions whistled appreciatively, but it wasn't entirely clear if they intended to praise the lines of the new ship, or Galina's form.

The ship was large—very large. If I had to guess, I'd say it was twice the size of our last transport, *Nostrum*.

"*Legate* is the first ship with a radical new design," she told us, running her hand along the spine of the ship. "We've maintained prior functionality and added new elements. Here, for example, is a pod containing a full broadside of sixteen cannons firing fusion shells. That is still our primary armament."

We quieted, as this was getting interesting.

"The nature of our missions in space has been changing, however. It is perceived that we may face naval combat as well as be involved in planetary invasions."

"Well, no shit!" Manfred said.

Another glare from Graves was followed by silence.

"Accordingly," Galina said, running her fine fingers to the bow of the ship, "we've added a smaller battery here, here and one more in the stern."

At her touch, the modules seemed to blossom. A spiny set of missiles sprouted up.

I whistled at that.

"These missile pods are new," Galina continued, "in more ways than one. They contain a new kind of missile. One that kills enemy crews with x-rays. Therefore, it doesn't need to strike a ship directly in order to deliver death."

"Hey!" I shouted suddenly. "I know where they got that idea! The Rogue Worlders gave it to them. They fired missiles just like—"

"McGill," Graves said. "Shut the hell up."

"Yes sir. Sorry, sir."

We were really listening now. We weren't fleet-lovers, far from it. But as men who got to ride to their deaths among the stars, we'd often commented on the superior nature of rival navies. Since the Empire's battle fleet seemed to be stuck off somewhere among the Core Worlds, we needed all our ships to be armed.

Galina went on detailing more of our ship's capabilities, both offensive and defensive. It seemed to be a dramatic set of advances. This new ship, *Legate*, was sleek and deadly.

When the briefing was over, I realized we still didn't know where we were headed, but I almost didn't care.

"Did you see those new missile pods?" I demanded of Manfred. "Do you see that? It's like the brass listened to us for once!"

"Nah," he said. "They'd never do that. They looked at the numbers, and they decided it was too expensive to keep losing ships. It's all about the budget."

"There's another factor," Graves said, stepping up to join us.

"What's that, sir?"

"It takes time to advance your technology. We first witnessed weapons like those Zeon missiles back at Rogue World several years back. But you don't just witness a new tech, steal the scientists who built it, and then roll your own version out the next day. You have to research, develop, design and build. And yes, allocate the budget for each of those vital steps."

"Well…" I said, "whatever the case is, I'm glad they finally did it. Maybe this ship—*Legate*, right? Maybe *Legate* won't blow up the first time out like the last one did."

Graves gave me a hard look. "That might be up to you, McGill."

"How's that, sir?"

"Is it my imagination, or did you do severe damage to several of these transport ships in the past?"

"That, sir, is not just a lie. It's a damned lie!" I boomed.

He sighed. "Right…"

Then he spun around, raising his arms for attention. They all shut up.

"Listen up everyone. The lifter is docking right now. There will be another briefing, including target planet information, at 0700 tomorrow. Get your men into their modules and bedded down. We're going into warp tonight. Any questions?"

My hand shot up. Graves looked around in vain for another hand, but he didn't see any. He called on me in defeat.

"What is it, McGill?"

"Sir? What happened to the Blood Worlders on our rosters? I noticed there are no squids, heavy troopers, or—"

"The last trip out was an experiment involving integrated units. It didn't work out well for a variety of reasons. Henceforth, Central has decided Varus is all-human, with a few auxiliaries—"

His voice was drowned out by my cheering. Manfred and a few others joined in and soon we were chanting: "No more squids! No more squids!" at the top of our lungs.

Graves waved for order. "Shut up until you hear the rest, you apes. We've still got Blood Worlders aboard—did any of you notice that there are more than ten lifters out there heading toward *Legate*? The number is closer to thirty."

"Come to think of it..." I said. "I did. And that transport is big, anyway. The whole ship looks pregnant."

"She's fat all right. Fat with troops, not just new weaponry. She's designed to carry a human legion *and* a Blood Worlder legion at the same time."

A chorus of groans rose up from the group.

"Don't worry, they won't be in our faces—not much, at least. They've got their own modules and training zones. Except for a few exercises, we probably won't see them at all until we hit our target planet."

There was scattered grumbling, but overall, we weren't too upset. Graves dismissed us all, and we went below.

Reaching my former seat, I buckled in and passed along choice pieces of information to my supporting officers and noncoms.

Soon thereafter, we were jostled as we docked. Huge metallic groans and clangs filled the lifter. It was like robots were drumming on the hull.

It was Carlos, however, who asked the most critical question.

"That's all cool, sir," he said. "But where the hell are we going, exactly?"

"That's classified," I said confidently. "You'll find out soon enough,"

They groaned at this, but no one argued outright.

Of course, no one had told me our destination either, but I didn't see any advantage to admitting that to the rank and file.

*No wonder officers always kept their troops in the dark*, I thought to myself. It was just easier that way.

# -12-

As it turned out, our new pot-bellied ship carried two full legions. One was a regular professional Human legion, while the second... Well, it was made up of near-humans.

Most of them were heavy troopers. Overgrown hulking men we called littermates, they came in batches of nine from Blood World. Each unit of heavies had Cephalopod officers and an auxiliary squad of slavers for scouting.

What impressed me most, however, were their giants. These monsters hadn't gone into combat with us back on Dark World. That was about to change.

I was summoned to Gold Deck early the next morning. All the Varus officers were ordered to attend a briefing—at least, everyone with the rank of centurion or higher.

When we first got there, the tribune and her pack of primus-ranked staffers were having a pre-meeting. Probably, they were making all their decisions before they met with us, so they could dump them on us as a done deal during the briefing.

I didn't care much about that, but I was bored. There were a few female centurions in the group, so I moved to the closest and began to pester her. I knew from her first sneer I wasn't getting anywhere, but a man has to try.

There had to be over a hundred of us in the main meeting chamber. Being Varus regulars, we weren't quiet and orderly. Things got pretty loud as we talked, laughed and speculated concerning what kind of a shithole we were likely to be invading this time out.

Twenty long minutes passed, during which things got louder and more unruly with every passing second. Line combatant Varus officers were, after all, just senior troops with rank. We were still a rough lot, older and meaner in the mind, but not in the body. Physically, most of us were in our late twenties.

"Hey, McGill!" Manfred called out. "Get off that poor lady and come talk to me!"

Manfred was another centurion like myself. He ran the sixth unit in Graves' cohort, while my unit was Graves' old one, the third. I counted him as a friend, so I did as he asked.

We clasped hands and slapped each other on the back.

"What's up, Stumpy?" I asked him.

He curled his lip at the name, and others laughed nearby.

Manfred was built like a barrel. He had short, thick arms and a chest that was almost as deep as it was wide. To me, he looked like a bulldog somebody had taught to walk on his hind legs.

"Let's wrestle," he said, throwing out one of those lumpy arms of his.

A whoop went up from the gathered centurions. I knew right off I was committed. To back down from a direct challenge like that…? Well, it just wasn't done.

I grinned and threw my arm up into his face. "And here I thought you were chicken all this time!"

We squatted around a table, and a small crowd formed. Bets began to flow.

We were both grinning, sizing each other up. He had the leverage on me, there was no doubt about that. But I'd kept in good shape. A lot of that was related to dying a couple of times over the last month. My body-scans had taken in my prime, at about twenty-five years of age. In that period of my life I'd been a weaponeer who worked out constantly.

Sometimes, I fell into bad habits between deployments and even managed to grow a few extra pounds of blubber on my waist—but as soon as I got killed, I popped back out lean-and-mean all over again. As that had happened only a few days earlier, I had an edge on fitness.

Manfred hadn't died for months. I could tell that just by looking at him. It could have been my imagination, but he was definitely packing more than one six pack around his middle.

Of course, that didn't mean I could beat him—but I thought I had a chance.

We clasped our hands, and another centurion name Doyle wrapped his fists over ours. He rocked our knotted fingers back and forth, forcing us to move.

"Loosen up, boys. Let's start this even-like, now!"

Our self-appointed referee was a pro, and I recognized him, but I didn't know Doyle well. He came from another cohort, I was sure of that much.

Now, I don't know much about this world, but I know how to arm-wrestle. I crunched up tight, but so did Manfred.

"You guys gonna kiss?" Doyle asked.

Manfred backed off a little, and for that tiny favor, I mentally thanked the ref for his interference.

"Okay… GO!"

Doyle took his sweaty hands off ours, and we went for it.

At first, Manfred's hand felt like a block of steel in mine. I threw my weight and power into it—but he didn't budge.

Then, an evil smile came over his face.

"Is that all you've got, McGill?" he asked me.

I felt a tickle of worry, and I braced myself, wrapping my legs around the table struts for leverage. Someone was pointing and saying I was cheating—but I didn't recall anyone specifying a rule about that.

It was a good thing I'd braced myself, too, because Manfred began to pour it on. His arm was an unnatural thing, proportioned all wrong. It was just too damned thick and short.

He moved, and I began to give.

This pissed me off. One thing about my colorful personality that has been a constant since I was a kid annoying everyone in grade school, was my strong desire to win contests of this sort.

Usually, I could do so with ease—but not this time.

Snaking my legs out farther for leverage, I bent my neck, lowered my head, and heaved for all I was worth.

The contest locked up then. We weren't moving, but I was probably an eighth of the way gone. Any arm wrestler can tell you that when you're about a quarter gone, you're screwed—but I wasn't there yet.

I think my efforts surprised Manfred at least. He wasn't smiling that evil little smile anymore. He was deadly serious, face red and running with sweat.

A matching trickle of sweat ran down out of my hair to make my left eye burn about then. I didn't care at all. I was barely aware of it.

The crowd was cheering, and I was howling now, roaring and carrying on. So far, Manfred had endured this contest in confident quiet, but when my arm started to gain on him—maybe it was a matter of flagging endurance, I wasn't sure—but he began to shout, too.

The fight went longer than such things usually do. My world had focused down to just the two of us, and I was barely aware of the rest of the noisy meeting hall.

Suddenly, however, something impinged. A different group now surrounded the two of us. Was that Primus Graves? And that lithe, strutting form—could Galina Turov herself have stepped up to watch?

The officers were saying something. Talking to us. I couldn't have given a single shit what they were saying, however. All I cared about was Manfred's unnatural frigging arm, an arm made of steel that I just couldn't bend.

"McGill!" Graves shouted into my ear.

His head was bent down now, even with my face and Manfred's. He looked kind of annoyed.

"Can we start the meeting now, gentlemen?" he demanded.

That was the critical moment. Manfred shifted, and he looked up. I think he pulled back his legs, too, which had been braced on the steel table just like mine had.

It was a crucial error. I half stood up, and I lifted him high, then I threw him over. As he was a smaller, lighter man, he rolled right out of his chair and did a facer on the deck.

Panting and standing tall, I shouted and shook my fists over my head.

"McGill cheats, and he wins!" Centurion Doyle shouted.

Cheers and boos filled the room.

Shaking out my aching fingers and arm, I offered a hand to Manfred, who was glaring at me from the deck.

At first, I thought he'd spit on me or something, but then, his face softened.

"Well done, Centurion," he said, and he took my offered hand.

A second round of cheering went off, then everyone shuffled toward their seats. Those who had placed bets handed off cash or touched tappers to exchange credits.

All this was watched by several frowning cohort leaders. Every primus in the place seemed annoyed—but not old Turov herself. She smirked at me.

I wasn't surprised. I knew Galina pretty well by now. She liked to watch men struggle like apes. I'd often thought that moments like this formed the very basis of our mutual attraction.

Still shaking the kinks out of my hand, I sprawled in a chair. Manfred came to sit next to me, and I was gratified to see he was clenching and unclenching his fist as well.

We traded tired smiles, and we might have spoken, but the briefing began.

Primus Graves kicked things off. He was Turov's senior primus as indicated by his rank insignia consisting of a basic star emblem with a red ruby in the center. They called that a blood drop, and it meant he was the second in command of the entire legion.

"Officers of Legion Varus," he said. "I welcome you back into Earth's service. This time, we have a challenging mission ahead."

A few officers muttered at that, mostly saying "no shit" and similar remarks. No one was surprised or impressed.

Despite being officers, most of us slouched in our chairs. Varus people weren't known for pomp and shiny kits. We were known for killing stuff. Aliens, mostly.

"In the past, we've met up with countless alien species. One of the most challenging of those was an unusual population called the Wur."

"God help us," Manfred muttered.

I groaned softly, seconding the motion.

The Wur consisted of a very strange set of intelligent plants. They infected planets, rather than colonizing them, by planting growths that eventually took over the entire surface area of the host world. So far, I'd tangled with them on two occasions—and I wasn't looking forward to a third encounter.

For about a minute, I experienced a flashback. I recalled walking trees, ferns that released poisonous gases, spider-like things that came out of cocoons—and giant brain-plants that ruled all the rest of it.

"Megaflora," Graves was saying when I managed to pay attention again.

He was flashing through a series of short vids. He showed us giant trees the size of a skyscraper. These trees didn't move themselves, but they grew pods to defend their territory.

"The mobile forms look like this," he said, and we watched as a charging wave of the monsters overran our lines.

"That day sucked," I said, remembering the battle.

"It sure did," Manfred chuckled. "Because I was dead that whole week."

I glanced at him. "You missed Death World?"

"Most of it," he admitted.

"Gentlemen," Graves called out to us. "Could I have your attention, please? Or do you two love-birds have an engagement to announce?"

A chuckle swept the room.

My hand shot up, and Graves called on me reluctantly.

"Primus Graves, sir? Why are we fighting the Wur again? Is the target world inside Province 921?"

"A good question, for once. I'll hand that off to our tribune to answer."

"Thank you, Primus Graves," Turov said.

She stepped up onto the center of the stage. There was always a stage when Turov gave one of her little speeches. I'd figured out this was due to two simple facts: one, she liked being up high and in charge. Two, she also enjoyed the ogling looks all the men in the audience tended to give her as she stood at the front of the room.

"Graves has given us the basics," she said. "The who, but not the where or the why."

She swept her arm over the wall behind her, and the starscape shifted to display the frontier region.

"As you know, we have a province to protect for the Empire. But we also have a difficult frontier border to worry about. In this region—"

Here, she caused a large zone to light up that was past the edge of the Empire proper.

"—certain independent worlds exist. We control a few of them, such as Blood World, in the very heart of the region. Keep in mind, we have legal claim to all of them—but that's not good enough. You also have to be strong enough to enforce that claim."

Suddenly, the point of this new two-legion warship was striking home. Maybe it wasn't an extravagance, but a necessity to Earth's long term strategic goals.

"Rather than gathering a fleet and visiting all these worlds, demanding obedience, Hegemony has decided to answer calls for support. There are always, after all, downtrodden planets in need of our aid."

She turned to the map then, and she began to zoom and pan. This action caused her to stand on her tiptoes, and that was a lovely sight. Somehow, a girl in high-heeled boots looked best when she lifted herself up on her toes.

Even Manfred was affected. Out of the corner of my eye, I saw him squirm in his chair and cant his head slightly to the left, probably to get a better angle.

"Here it is," she continued, making dragging motions to pull a star down closer. The visual panned and focused on its own. "M244-H. An unimportant star, a red dwarf. It's a little bigger and brighter than most red dwarfs, but… so what. They are common and usually without value."

As she spoke, she kept facing the wall. Was she doing that on purpose?

Along about then, I began to frown a little. Was her butt shaped differently today? Was I seeing things?

"I'll be damned…" I said.

Manfred tossed me a glance, but I ignored him and continued peering at Galina.

Now, it has to be said that I'm something of an authority on the topic of a woman's hindquarters. I liked to think I knew every variety of hip-structure and shape available. Turov had always possessed a very nice, carefully manicured posterior. It was a natural shape, the kind that was girlish rather than broad-hipped and fully mature. This was probably due to the fact she kept her body-scan from her earliest years in the legion.

But… today she looked a bit different. Those hips were wider, somehow. And that butt… yes, I'd stake a months' pay on it!

"She's had a butt-job!" I said aloud.

Fortunately, my words were spoken quietly. Only Manfred heard me. He could hardly help it, as he was sitting right next to me.

Manfred bust out laughing.

Everyone turned to look at him, including Turov. Graves wore a particularly grim expression.

"What is it, Manfred?" Graves asked.

"Uh… Sorry Primus. McGill is cracking jokes back here."

Graves swiveled a pair of unfriendly eyes in my direction.

"Dick," I hissed at Manfred.

"What's the joke, McGill?" Graves demanded. "Please share it with all of us. I'm sure we could use a good laugh."

"Um…" I said. "It was nothing, sir. Manfred likes knock-knock jokes, see. He can't get enough of them."

Graves eyed me coldly, not believing me for a second. "Can both of you shut-the-fuck-up now?"

"Yes sir," we mumbled in unison.

"Such infantile behavior," Turov said.

She turned back to her wall again. Continuing to reach high and then low, she generally fussed over that big display of hers. She showed us the target planet, the continents, the prospective LZs—everything. She even talked about the alien race that lived there, and how they were being overrun by the Wur and were asking for our help.

Daydreaming, I missed most of the details. The woman was hypnotizing me.

I knew full well what she was up to, of course. She was showing off her new purchase. Some lucky surgeon had taken her best feature and improved it a bit, and she damned-well wanted to get her money's worth.

Sure, she could have turned around and faced us. She could have had an underling manipulate the board, or she could have at least spent more time looking out at her audience—but she didn't. She'd had some special work done, which was why she'd been out of sight for a few weeks. What's more, I was pretty sure I knew why she'd done it: misguided jealousy.

Deciding I might as well enjoy the fruits of her labor, I stayed riveted to the rest of the briefing. Galina had always commanded the attention of any audience she got in front of—and that was never by accident. She *wanted* to make sure every man in the place got an eyeful.

And brother, looking around the room to check out the crowd, I can attest that she'd gotten her wish today.

# -13-

Manfred and I had always gotten along, and I think now we were tight. We marched back to our modules, laughing and high-fiving each other.

"You know, McGill, I've always watched your particular flavor of bullshit from afar. I never really participated before—but now, I'm hooked. That was hilarious!"

We grinned and parted ways, agreeing to do our damnedest to destroy one another on the training grounds. That was the peak of compliments among rival officers in Varus.

Sinking into my office chair, I felt pretty good inside. I'd been an officer in the legion for several years, but I'd always felt somewhat out of place. The older types hadn't appreciated my swift rise through the ranks, or my genuine talent for pissing off the brass.

After today, I felt like all that had changed. For whatever reason, my fellows were accepting me as a welcome peer.

Harris thrust his head into my office first that day, and I could tell by the stink-face he was making that he was bound and determined to rain on my good mood.

"McGill?" he asked. "Did you know all this crap about the tides?"

"Um..." I said, casting my mind back to Turov's skin-tight uniform and lengthy briefing. It did seem, to my hazy memory, that something had been mentioned about the harsh weather. "I heard about it at the briefing, sure."

"Wet-suits? Grav-boots just so we can hold onto the ground during the tidal shifts? Hot geysers, deadly terrain—this planet sucks!"

I blinked at him, and I slowly began to frown. It occurred to me, as it so often did after a mission briefing, that I should have daydreamed a little less.

But instead of mentioning these things, I lifted a finger and wagged it at him.

"Now, don't go spreading your deepest fears among the troops, Harris. You hear me? Just because your panties are all wadded up with tears, that's no reason to lower morale."

"Say *what*?" he demanded, becoming angry. "Since when have I complained in front of the troops?

I rolled my eyes. "Since before I was born, probably," I told him. "Just make sure that if you feel the uncontrollable urge to cry, you do it in private. Got that, Adjunct?"

He slammed my door and left. That was disrespectful, of course. I could have put him on report or worse—but I let it slide. After all, his actions had brought a smile to my face as I'd been goading him for fun anyway.

But after he left, I began rerunning the recording of the briefing on my tapper. Adjusting the video so it only caught the big screen—rather than Turov's distracting display—I was better able to absorb what was being said.

The planet in question did look kind of shitty. It was a weird, wet world. The land to sea ratio was worse than on Earth, with over eighty percent of the surface underwater. The continents that did exist were smaller and… nastier.

"Hmm…" I said aloud. "Continuous atmospheric disturbances. High winds, heavy cloud-cover, constant tidal shifts from the six moons… Crap!"

*Six moons.* That was the detail I'd somehow missed before.

Back home on Earth, our single moon did us a lot of good. It kept the oceans stirred up, driving waves, tides and many other natural phenomena. Without our moon, the Earth would be kind of dead and quiet most of the time.

But this world had taken that logic to an extreme. Being a relatively small planet encircled by no less than six satellites, the place was churned up all the time. The ground itself sometimes swelled up and popped a new volcano due to the intense yanking it got when several of the moons aligned.

And the storms… they were legendary. Planet-wide rain was the norm, not the exception. The result was a lashing stew of water and wind. Sometimes hot, sometimes freezing cold an hour later, the weather depended on vicious twists in the upper atmosphere that drove the climate like a raging cowboy beating his poor horse to death.

As I absorbed all this, Leeson showed up at my door next. He tapped instead of simply nosing his way inside, and I told him to come on in.

"Centurion? You ready to talk seriously about our new situation?"

"Uh…" I said, looking up at him. "You mean about this washing machine of a planet were supposed to invade? Or Harris?"

He waved these ideas away. "Nah, I already figured we would be fighting on some kind of bucket of puke planet. I also wanted to tell you you're right about Harris. He's a big baby."

"Okay then…" I said, leaning back and putting my boots on my desk. "What's bothering you?"

"It's the new adjunct, sir. I'm not sure she's going to fit in."

I blinked at him twice. Frowning, I lifted my tapper and glanced at it. I tried to make this look as if I'd just gotten a text message.

And I had, of course, gotten about a hundred of them this morning alone. Unlike most people, I didn't feel the driving need to read them the second they came in. I liked to let them stack up for a few hours before giving them the eye. Pacing myself that way made my life feel less disrupted.

"Just a second," I said, coming up with a covering lie. "Just got something in from Turov."

Leeson smirked. "Is there a pic? I hear she—"

I waved him to silence in irritation. It was unfortunately well known that Galina and I slept together from time to time. Leeson, in particular, seemed fascinated by that fact.

Scrolling, I soon came to the reassignment orders. My eyes read the notice—and I swallowed hard. I gave up on all pretense that I had already known who they'd assigned to my unit without consulting me.

"Damn..." I said. "I was hoping we'd get someone we knew."

"Fat chance. The brass hates promoting us. Why pay us more when they know we'll work for less? Besides, the fresh face on the other side of the fence is always cuter. Eh, McGill?"

Another dig about me and Turov. I ignored him and eyed the new adjunct's record.

"Adjunct Barton," I read. "From Victrix, no less. She's experienced, but she must have done something pretty bad to get herself reassigned to Varus."

"Maybe she's into screwing her commanders, eh?" Leeson suggested, leering at me.

I frowned at him. "That's enough of that talk, Adjunct."

"Sorry sir," he said in a disingenuous tone. "At least she's a better looker than Toro. Let's hope she's a better officer, too."

"Hmm..." I said, tapping on her profile and digging deeper with every tap into her history files. "Looks like she used to be a centurion... Maybe she *did* get herself into some trouble."

The woman's face came up on my screen with the crossed swords of Victrix emblazoned over her head. They hadn't even bothered to change her insignia yet. That meant she'd been fired out of Victrix on a rail.

Either that, or she was some kind of spy.

I studied the face. Sharp, large features. Eyes that were big and olive shaped. Her chin and nose seemed to come to a point. Her shoulders were broad, but not brutish. Overall, she was a fine specimen of womanhood, but with a meaner look than usual.

"You thinking about going for it, McGill?" Leeson asked. "Already?"

"Dismissed, Adjunct," I said. "When you meet her, be respectful."

Leeson gave me a dirty laugh. "Oh, I've already met her. You're gonna love this lady."

He walked out and I frowned after him. It seemed to me that my unit lacked discipline and respect for rank.

It was a serious problem in the legions that grew over time. You got to know each other too well after living and dying together for decades. There was rank, there was protocol—but then there was reality.

To me, it seemed like everyone had gone to seed over the summer. Sitting in my office and thinking hard, I pondered different means by which I could kick some subordinate tail and gain team spirit at the same time.

Thinking about that caused the first smile of the day to break out on my face. It was a grim smile, but I enjoyed it no less for all of that.

Drills were coming. Cruel exercises that would straighten out my people.

"Centurion McGill, sir? Am I disturbing you?"

"Huh?" I said, craning my neck back to the door again.

There she was. The woman on my tapper display. In person, Barton didn't seem quite as threatening as her headshot appeared on her profile.

She was as solidly built and fit-looking as anyone could hope to be, but there seemed to be a hint of trepidation in her expression. Maybe she wasn't comfortable with Varus yet.

If so… well… that was just too damned bad. There'd never been much in the way of hand-holding here in Varus. You lived, you died, and you lived again. That was pretty much all of it.

"Adjunct Barton," I said, standing and giving her a tight smile.

We gave each other a salute, and I followed up with a handshake. "Welcome to the third, the best outfit in Legion Varus."

"Thank you, sir," she said, standing at attention.

Sizing her up, I immediately decided Barton was a sharp troop. I liked that right off. Unlike my other overfamiliar, nosy, complaint-and-joke-filled supporting officers, she'd yet to give me a single ration of shit. I thought to myself I could get used to that.

"At ease, Adjunct. Take a seat."

She did so, and I sat across from her. We mouthed some small talk for a few minutes, but I soon got to the matter that was burning on my mind.

"So… you got kicked out of Victrix and exiled to Varus. Is that right, Barton?" I asked her point-blank.

She blinked. "That's rather direct, sir."

I shrugged. "We're a fighting outfit here, Adjunct. Not a color-guard. I like to know what I'm dealing with before I go to war depending on a new officer."

"I… I understand, sir. Yes, I'm from Victrix. You might have heard of them."

There was a hint of pride there. I could hear it clearly. But then she looked down.

"I was transferred out."

"Transferred…? No one leaves Victrix for greener pastures. There aren't any."

"I guess that's accurate, sir."

"Okay. So why'd you end up with Varus?"

She looked back up from the deck. "Because I didn't want a desk job. They tried to move me to Hegemony—but I'm not ready to be a hog. I hope I'm *never* ready for that. So, I asked if I could switch to Varus instead. They agreed."

We stared at each other for a second or two. My obvious next question would be to ask her *why* she'd been kicked out and transferred to Hegemony. It didn't say on her profile.

But I didn't want to ask that question.

"So you like to fight…" I said. "That's good enough for me. Varus is the land of misfits. Here, each soldier's history is largely their own. For that reason, I'm not going to ask you why you were booted… I don't really care."

Barton smiled. "Thank you, sir."

My return smile was grim.

"Don't thank me too fast. We're going to start training tomorrow, at 0500 hours sharp. You'll be taking over Harris' platoon of lights. Some of them are fresh recruits."

I stood up again, and she stood with me. She looked alarmed. Her big eyes studied me.

“Do I gather this will be a combat exercise, sir?” she asked. “With fresh recruits? They won’t know their asses from their hats, Centurion. I haven’t even met them yet.”

“Then introduce yourself! Tomorrow we’ll see to it that they learn *real* fast. Dismissed, Adjunct.”

Looking a little shell-shocked, Barton walked out of my office.

# -14-

Della visited me later that evening. This was an eyebrow-raiser for me, as she and I had been through a lot of life together.

We'd had a child—without my knowledge at the time, mind you—and we'd tried forming a real relationship when the mood struck us. The results had always been somewhere between humorous and tragic.

"James?" she asked, leaning into my office. "Have you got a moment?"

My heartbeat accelerated a notch. It almost always did when Della came around.

This wasn't just because she was pretty and moved with a dancer's grace—it was also because she'd killed me on several occasions, and I'd returned the favor now and then.

Like Etta, she was a Dust Worlder. The real deal, born and raised. That meant, essentially, that she wasn't entirely civilized. She was kind of like a feral cat—and if you've ever tried to adopt one of those furry bastards, you know exactly what I mean.

"Hello Della," I said in a falsely cheery voice. "Sure, come on in. What's up?"

She stepped inside my office and closed my door. That's when I saw the pistol in her hand.

I was out of my chair and standing with my combat knife in my hand in a flash. I might have tried to draw my pistol, but it was snapped down at my side. My knife, on the other hand, had been lying within easy reach on my desk.

Still, for all my alertness and speed, I couldn't beat her on the draw. She had the pistol trained on my face. A tiny red dot played over my eyelashes, making me blink.

"We need to talk," Della said in a calm voice.

"Uh…" I said, thinking of a half-dozen crimes and misdemeanors I'd committed lately. When a woman came at me in a war-like mood, there was always a good reason—or several of them.

"Put the knife down, please," she said. "I only want to talk."

"Um… okay. But if you're in a talking mood, maybe you could take that heat lamp off my eyeball too."

"I'm the injured party herc," she said. "Or at least, I'm representing her. So I'll keep my weapon for now."

"Della, dammit," I said, thunking my blade into the desktop. "This kind of insubordination is exactly why I didn't want to transfer you into my unit when you first asked."

She shrugged. "It's a bit late for that now, isn't it?"

Sighing, I flopped back down in my chair. "All right, fine," I said. "Shoot me for whatever petty, jealous hysteria you've got burning in your mind. But this time, I'm not going to drop the charges. You'll head to the stockade and serve your time like anyone else would."

Della slid into the chair across from me. She kept that annoying beam on my forehead, which was beginning to piss me off.

The trouble with living and dying together just about forever was the relationships that naturally formed over the years. We didn't have the discipline we should have in the legions—and we were especially lacking in that department in Legion Varus.

"All right," I said, "can you tell me what's on your mind?"

"You can't guess? Really? Are you still so thick-headed after decades?"

"Um…" I said, thinking hard. "Is it about Turov?"

"No, you big idiot. If you want to waste your lifetime entertaining her, it's none of my business."

That response didn't sound like she was a completely disinterested party, but I decided to let it go. If the woman said it didn't bother her, well, I sure as hell wasn't going to poke at the wound.

"Um…" I said.

Then, it struck me. Struck me hard.

"Etta," I said. "You heard about what happened with Etta, right?"

"Of course I did. She's *my* daughter. Did you think you could keep a violent exchange of gunfire all to yourself? I still have connections to Dust World natives, you know."

"Right… Okay, here's the deal."

I quickly sketched out the events, leaving out all details that might have shone a bad light on my actions. In my version, I was something between a saint and a bounty hunter chasing down the bad guys.

She took all this in with a frown and a stare. It didn't seem to me that my explanation was pleasing her too much, however, as she was still heating up my eyebrows with that damned laser sight.

"That's all you've got to say?" she asked when I'd finished. "A pack of brash lies? Really? What about our daughter, James? Did you go back and check on her? Did you make sure she was all right?"

"Um… I did send a text."

"That's right. I heard as much from Etta herself. A single text, after a traumatic experience. Did you think that was sufficient?"

"Interstellar texts cost some serious credit…" I pointed out, but I knew even as the words left my lips it was the wrong thing to say.

Her expression darkened. The laser stopped circling on my face and became an angry glare burrowing into my left pupil.

Della stood up suddenly. "Why did I ever seek to mate with such an uncaring man?"

I'd always wondered about that myself, but I didn't think it would be a good idea to delve into the topic now.

"Look," I said, trying to be soothing. "Etta is fine. She didn't die out there, and the men who came after me aren't interested in her. Now that I'm out in deep space on a mission, they'll just have to wait for their satisfaction."

"Men?" Della asked. "You said Claver was after you."

I kicked myself mentally. I'd simplified the story to make it all sound less dangerous. I'd failed to mention the army of Claver-clones that were involved.

"Uh… Claver may have supporters."

"Henchmen?"

"Yes, something like that."

I thought of the Claver-Threes and their relentless pursuit. Describing them to her now might induce a panic.

Della was the kind of mother who tended to wander off from her young, but when Etta was in danger, she turned all mama-bear on you.

"Well?" I demanded. "Are you going to shoot me or not? Get on with it, Specialist. I've got work to do."

That seemed to break the spell. She lowered her gun and put it on the table between us.

"I'm sorry," she said in a faint voice. "I just don't like the idea of our daughter going through her first death."

"I don't want that, either," I said truthfully. "But she's growing up. I think you need to talk to her directly if you want to guide her path. There's only so much a part-time dad can do."

Della studied the deck. "I *have* talked to her. A dozen times. She still wants to join the legions, even after almost dying. Even after watching her own father die before her eyes while defending her."

"We can't protect her forever."

"We've barely tried. You and I are both so selfish it's disgusting."

"Come on," I said. "The kid herself is impossible. She's largely responsible for her own fate now. You're still thinking of her as a child, and she is inexperienced, but she's very much her own woman."

Della looked miserable. It seemed like I couldn't say anything to cheer her up.

Taking a chance, I stood and walked slowly around the desk. She didn't move, so I put hands on her.

She let me hug her, then she waved at her gun on my desk.

"I'm sorry about that. I got emotional. I've been listening all day to the tone of your voice. I was expecting to hear some hint of the same kind of worry I've been feeling about Etta. When I finally realized you didn't care at all—I became angry."

"Well now, hold on a minute. I *do* care. It's different for me, but I still care. I went out there to Dust World, didn't I? I found her, and I made sure she lived. Isn't that good enough?"

I thought I heard a sniffle. That was a shocker. She was normally made of steel.

Della turned to me suddenly, and my gonads clenched up in an automatic bolt of fear—but then I relaxed again.

She'd pressed her face into my chest, and her arms were around my waist.

My hands slid up to touch her shoulders. Looking down, I had certain thoughts, but I steered clear. The rest of her stayed untouched.

After a long hug, she went up on her tiptoes to kiss my cheek, then she took her pistol and left.

When she was gone, I let out a long sigh of relief.

A few hours later, when we sounded lights-out, I was still thinking of her.

# -15-

The next morning came too soon. I felt like I'd barely gone to sleep—because I had.

Hammering and yelling, the noncoms were kicking groaning troops out of bed all up and down the module.

That was how we lived in the legions. Every transport trip was like a refresher course through boot camp. Effectively, this *was* boot camp for the newest recruits. They were expected to get their training and their general cultural reeducation on life during our journey to the target star.

As for those of us who were experienced, we always seemed to need a few lessons repeated for our benefit as well. A few had managed to get flabby, and that wasn't a good thing to do, not even if you were an officer. Superiors at every level liked nothing more than to send a man through a revival machine to thin him down to a lean, mean fighting weight.

Fortunately, my team hadn't gone completely to seed. We'd only had about four months between deployments, and that was entirely different than taking a year off. All we needed was a rough spring-training, and we'd be back in the saddle again.

Standing at attention in a ragged line, I took charge. Noncoms were still walking the ranks, kicking at ankles and slapping at hands that were out of place, but I began speaking anyway.

"Proud members of 3rd Unit," I began. "It's an honor to serve with all of you. Even the lamest recruit in this outfit is going to earn my respect over the next few months, let me assure you of that."

My eyes swept over them, and they stood at attention, not meeting my baleful stare.

"Today, I mean to give all of you an opportunity to prove you haven't gone soft."

A hand shot up in the back. It was Cooper, and I wasn't in the least surprised.

"What is it, Cooper?"

"Sir, do I take it we're going to be killed in some kind of pointless exercise?"

I felt like smacking him, but everyone felt like that when Cooper opened his mouth, so I shook it off.

"Absolutely not," I said. "If anyone dies in today's wargames, I'm going to be very disappointed. The purpose here is to make the other side die—we're here to win."

A small cheer rose up, and I smiled. They weren't all smartasses like Cooper.

"Here's the deal," I said, pacing in front of them. "We're going to face a large body of troops. An entire cohort of them, and we're going to put them down."

My soldiers looked stunned.

Cooper's hand was up again, but I ignored him. I pointed to Kivi instead.

"A *cohort*, sir?" she asked. "How's that possible? Are we fighting on the outer hull, or the tops of the modules? Nowhere else could possibly—"

I stopped her with an upraised hand. "You're wrong, Kivi. This isn't a regular transport. This ship is *big*. We're going to have a large, pitched battle. A wargame, like I said."

"But how—?"

Jabbing a finger upward as if I was pointing out the Almighty himself, I got her attention again.

"Green Deck is *big* on this ship. A lot bigger than the exercise rooms aboard our past transports. I'd say it's about ten times bigger than the Green Deck was on *Minotaur*."

Kivi nodded to me. She was catching on.

I forced a smile and paced in front of the troops.

"That's not the only scrap of good news," I said. "The kicker is this: the other side will be made up of Blood Worlders."

A groan rose up then, and I frowned.

"What?" I demanded. "Are you guys chicken? The Blood Worlders aren't—they're raring to go. They say all the time that human legionnaires are wimps, and I guess they might be right."

People became angry upon hearing my bald-faced lie. I made up specific Blood-Worlder names for the chief culprits, the biggest insult-slingers on the other side. One name I invented was Bluto, who I described as a full-fledged bastard. I was especially proud of that effort.

The Blood Worlders hadn't said anything about humans, of course. The males rarely spoke at all. But none of that mattered. Within ten minutes, I had them raging for revenge.

Marching down to Green Deck was a pleasure. Instead of leading a group of bored, somewhat apprehensive troops, I had a snarling pack behind me. Other units passed us in the tunnel-like passages, but they never seemed as fired up as my gang did.

Arriving before a big set of metal doors, I saw a large blue light at the top—and a full unit of pukes standing around underneath it.

Centurion Manfred pushed his way through his team and frowned at me.

"This isn't your entrance, McGill," he said. "Keep moving."

I frowned down at him. He'd always been less friendly when his troops were listening. I figured it was part of his tough-guy act.

"Ah!" I said. "I get it—they changed the plans, huh? Are we supposed to slaughter your gang now? It will be a real pleasure."

"What?" he barked, then his face softened. A moment later, he laughed. "You didn't read the brief, did you?"

"Uh… I might have missed something," I admitted.

Internally, I kicked myself. I'd never been a man who could stomach a long boring talk of any kind. You could confirm that with any teacher who'd had the misfortune to be given the task of instructing me. Any of them… ever…

"Big moron," he muttered, shaking his head. "Your gate is two doors down. We're a team. Our side is blue, and the other side is red."

"Two doors down? How many doors are there?"

"Twelve, I think—on this side. Red team gets its own twelve."

Harris, who'd come up to listen in, whistled. "Twenty-four entrances? You weren't shitting us when you said this place was big, McGill."

Turning, I ushered my unit toward the correct door. Harris lingered behind, and I heard him question Manfred.

"What flavor of bullshit are we in for today, sir?" he asked.

"Nothing ground-breaking. It's just them or us. This Green Deck is big, and fancy—but it's still just a city park inside a bubble. Now, get going."

Harris trotted after me and soon caught up. I was leading the unit at a jog, not wanting to be late to reach my station on top of everything else.

"Did you get yourself… ah… *distracted* last night, sir?" he asked me.

I glanced at him, and I didn't like the big shitty grin on his face.

"Yep," I said. "Turov kept me up all night again. Damn, that girl is a screamer. Didn't you hear her?"

He frowned in confusion and amazement for a second, then his face shifted into a disbelieving sneer. "Very funny, sir. What are my deployment orders?"

Harris was leading my heavy platoon now. Leeson, as always, had command of my auxiliaries. Mostly, that meant he led weaponeers, bio people and a few techs. Barton, of course, had Harris' old command, a platoon of lights with snap-rifles.

"You're team is taking the center, walking advance. Barton will flank left, scouting and moving faster. Leeson's knuckle-draggers will bring up the rear. See that you don't leave his people behind and unguarded."

Harris grinned. "You're going to angle back left, aren't you? To screw over Manfred?"

I shook my head, and I showed him the briefing on my tapper—tossing it to him with a flick of my finger. He read it on his own tapper as we marched.

"Two sides..." I explained. "This is no free-for-all. Manfred said it's blue against red. All the humans are on the blue side."

Harris frowned, reading further down. "We're facing... Blood Worlders? Hundreds of them? When did this turd drop onto your tapper?"

"This morning, I guess."

"You knew about it? And you didn't tell us?"

The truth was I hadn't bothered to read it at all. But that wouldn't be a good thing to tell anyone now. Harris needed to believe in me just as much as the rank and file did.

"It's no big deal," I said. "It's just a bigger op, because we have a bigger deck to play on."

"But... Blood Worlders? What kind of Blood Worlders are we talking about?"

The truth was I didn't know—I hadn't skimmed down to that section yet.

"All I know is that they're already in there, setting up camp in the center."

"They get a *fort*?" Harris demanded. "That's totally unfair, sir! We should protest."

"Complain to Primus Graves all you want. I hear he loves whining."

Harris grumbled. "So, we've got to dig them out? We're expected to overcome an entrenched force?"

"That's right. You all done crying now? What matters is that we win. Now, get to your platoon and keep them organized. They're the core of this formation."

Grumbling, Harris moved to his line of heavy troopers and began examining each kit in person. When he found something out of place, he cursed, cuffed and generally abused the soldier in question.

I shook my head. In his platoon, his noncoms didn't have much to do. He was still a veteran at heart. I guess decades of doing one job made it stick with a guy, promotion or no.

We were standing under the big blue dome light by now. The door stayed closed for about two minutes after we got there, which gave me just enough time to talk to all of my adjuncts and get them organized.

A buzzer sounded while we were still shuffling around. The light went green, and the big door slid away, vanishing silently into the walls.

"Unit, advance!" I shouted.

Immediately, Barton's team jogged off to the left. They were moving fast and stepping smartly. I could see Barton was already having an effect on them. What's more, she was at the head of her platoon, not hanging back in the rear ranks. Noob troops really appreciated a visible leader.

The thickest trees turned out to be there on our left, and I was glad for that bit of luck. It appeared like I'd planned for the lights to take immediate cover—but in truth, it was happenstance.

"Harris, advance at a walking pace. Barton, report a deer with the shits if you see one."

"Roger that," both said in my headset.

We were on tactical chat, which was normally pretty lively, but the troops were quiet today. They all knew some of us were about to die. Knowledge like that tended to maintain discipline without a lot of effort from the officers.

Harris' armored troops formed a double line, walking about three meters apart. They kept a ragged formation and moved slowly but deliberately. Each carried a morph-rifle, which had many different modes and capabilities.

After the armored troops had advanced perhaps fifty meters, I pinwheeled my arm, signaling for Leeson to follow.

He did so in good order. His weaponeers encircled the other specialists, walking with their oversized belchers in their hands.

Belchers were plasma weapons with a lot of variability. They were line-of-sight, but they could be used to fire a powerful narrow blast that could take out an armored vehicle or a broader beam that could incinerate a squad of infantry all at once. Created originally for larger beings, our weaponeers tended to be very muscular males.

In the middle of the weaponeers were our most vulnerable troops, a knot of bios and techs. This last team busied themselves by flying small drones called buzzers everywhere, searching for the enemy.

Normally, Leeson's group would have a few 88s with them—but not today. No artillery was allowed on Green Deck. I guess someone was afraid of a hull breach in flight, which could theoretically take out the transport and kill the entire legion.

As we marched forward, I had the chance to scan more details of the exercise on my tapper, including my assigned role.

Frowning, I read the final words.

*Remember officers, this exercise is designed to train and build morale. It is therefore weighted in favor of the Blood Worlder troops, as they have greater need for reassurance in our leadership. They're meant to win this conflict, so don't be surprised when the inevitable outcome materializes.*

Graves had signed the bottom.

"That cold-hearted prick..." I muttered to myself.

# -16-

I don't mind telling you, I was a mite pissed.

Graves often set up bullshit exercises like this. It seemed to be his specialty. But even so, this shit-cake took the prize.

He'd set up a whole cohort of human troops—*his* cohort, no less—to take a deadly fall. He actually *expected* us to fail, and that's why he'd given the Blood Worlders a head start to fortify the center.

My mind churned. I didn't like the situation or the circumstances. Most of all, I was wishing I'd read the mission details when they'd first come to my tapper mailbox—but I'd decided to let that wait until this morning. Then… I'd never quite gotten around to it.

Switching to officer's chat, I contacted Manfred.

"Hey, Centurion," I said. "Are you marching straight in?"

"No frigging way," was his immediate response. "Let me guess: You want to commit suicide real quick to protest this cluster, is that it, McGill?"

"Nah," I said. "I want to win."

Manfred laughed. "That ain't happening."

"What if we all charge—all at once? If we could talk the other centurions into an early rush—"

"McGill?" Graves broke in.

I wondered right off if he'd been listening. As our primus, he had the permissions to break into any conversation on this channel, private or not.

"Yessir!" I answered promptly.

"You're not to hit the central fort for three more minutes. You got that? Set a timer on your tapper."

"It's as good as done, Primus."

He grunted and left the channel.

"There's your answer," Manfred said. "Seems like you've got a guardian angel listening to your every thought."

"Yeah…" I agreed, and I closed the channel.

We trudged forward toward the center of the field, but before we made it very far scattered fire began peppering Harris' line.

"Snipers!" Harris roared. "Take cover!"

Everyone scattered and ducked. I couldn't even see the enemy yet—but I did see a structure ahead. Gray puff-crete walls encircled a building that looked like a pile of large blocks with dark, slit-like windows.

Enemy fire poured out of these windows with increasing frequency. They weren't just shooting at us, fortunately, but at all the advancing units as blue team emerged from the bush.

The quick-growth trees were taking a beating all around us. The leaves jumped and slapped at their trunks. The foliage itself was kind of tropical in nature. Mostly palms with big fronds and fat trunks.

As the incoming fire died down, we counted our casualties.

"Six wounded, two dead," Leeson reported.

His bio specialists crawled over the landscape, administering aid or quick death as was required. It was their job to make sure any soldier who couldn't fight anymore was sent to Blue Deck for a quick revival.

During this interlude, the sky darkened. I was surprised when it began to rain.

"That's new," I muttered, looking up.

The artificial sky was *gushing* raindrops. Soon, the hot landscape began tossing up curls of steam. Could this be what fighting on the target world was going to be like? I suspected it would be even worse.

"Adjunct Barton!" I shouted on tactical. "Advance under cover, find good firing positions, and keep the enemy honest. Make them duck with your rifles in sniper-mode."

The firing out of the thick copse of trees to my left began almost immediately. Barton must have been anticipating my order.

"No wonder Victrix recruited her," I muttered to myself. Not for the first time, I wondered why she'd been kicked out of that elite group.

Our two sides traded fire, and both scored a few hits. One heavy trooper slid off the battlements and did a facer in the mud.

That's when I noticed the mud. It was growing in depth as the rain soaked in. I got onto the officers' chat channel immediately.

"3rd unit is requesting permission to attack," I said.

"You want to die early, McGill?" Graves replied.

"No sir, but there's a growing mud puddle all around the central fort. If we don't go for it soon, we'll be mired in soup up to our assholes."

There was a few seconds of quiet, then Graves came back on the line. "I see that now… All right, most of the units are in position, and the fight is getting dull. Time to kick the show up a notch. I'll contact each of the units and get back to you."

I heard a chair creak over the com channel, and I frowned. Just where was the primus? I suspected he was watching from somewhere safe, perhaps with a foamy beer in his hand.

Leeson had crawled over to my position, and he was listening into the chat channel. Adjuncts could hear the traffic, but they weren't supposed to talk much unless offering up critical information. Otherwise, it would be chaos on the shared voice line.

"McGill," Leeson said, shaking my armored shoulders.

"What?" I demanded.

He pointed upward. I followed the gesture—and then I saw it.

A cupola, circular in shape, sat above us. It was an observation booth. Windows went all the way around, and I could see figures up there, watching us.

"Well, I'll be damned," I said. "Just like a private suite at a football game."

"Use your zoomers," he said. "You won't believe it."

I did as he suggested, and my faceplate lit up. It zoomed sickeningly, and I could see the figures in the observation booth.

Every primus in the legion seemed to be up there, along with other fellows I didn't recognize. After a moment, I realized they had to be commanders from the enemy legion, the Blood Worlder leaders.

"Is that a friggin' *squid*?" I demanded aloud.

Incensed, I stood up and shook a fist at them.

A few stray rounds popped nearby, and Leeson tugged at me. At last, I let him pull me back down.

Feeling a fresh surge of anger, I decided it was about time to take unauthorized action. After all, if you couldn't innovate on a fake battlefield, when could you?

To start with, I muted my microphone. Graves was obviously listening to my line directly. I would have to talk to my troops the old-fashioned way.

"Leeson," I told my top adjunct, "get all of your weaponeers to focus fire on the base of that turret over there."

I pointed to a nearby corner of the fortress walls. It was something like two hundred meters off—close enough for a point-blank gush of plasma to do some serious damage.

Leeson looked at me. "Graves hasn't ordered us to attack yet, Centurion."

"I know that. When he does, he'll probably tell us to charge the walls. But we're not going to die in the mud for nothing. Get every beam you've got, tightened down to the narrowest setting to hit that corner. Have Sargon coordinate the op. He's to fire the second he gets lined up."

Leeson trotted away, bent over double to avoid sniper fire. He didn't look happy, but I didn't care about that.

Sargon was a senior noncom who'd spent a lot of years as a weaponeer. I trusted his judgment. While he squirmed the men into position, I talked to Harris privately.

"Switch every morph-rifle you've got over to grenade fire," I said. "When they come out of that castle, let them have it."

"Why the hell would the enemy give up their advantage?" he asked me. "They'd be crazy to come at us."

"Just do it."

Grumbling, Harris shook his head, but he passed the orders along. The heavy troopers had morph-rifles, weapons that had several configurations. The trouble with them was it took at least thirty seconds to switch over. If we were caught in the middle of this operation, things would go badly.

Kivi was the last member of Leeson's platoon I gave orders to. I told her to send every drone buzzer the techs had into the castle, over the walls, to buzz-bomb the inhabitants.

"Nail the squids," I told her. "Any squid you see, take him down. Poke his eyes out if you have to."

She smiled at me. "It's about time we did something. This whole exercise is bullshit."

Kivi didn't hesitate or complain at all. She just talked to the other techs, passing the word to other units as well.

Soon, a flock of buzzers rose up from our lines. It looked like a bee swarm. In unison, the massed drones swept over the walls and vanished into the fort.

At about the same time, Sargon began burning a hole in the wall at the base of the nearest turret. It blackened, and the rain drops that were caught in the converging beams wisped into steam as they encountered raging heat.

It wasn't until a few more beams began cooking the walls from various angles that the officers above us took notice. Several units, perhaps assuming the general attack was underway, were hitting the other towers the same way I was. As my tapper began to blink urgently, Centurion Manfred's team joined in the fun, blasting the base of the nearest tower.

"McGill?" Graves' voice boomed into my headset. "What the hell are you doing? No one ordered the attack yet!"

"Well sir," I said, "you might want to step up the schedule a little. Apparently, some of the boys got antsy."

As I spoke, I watched the base of the nearest puff-crete tower blow apart. The heat had become so intense and concentrated, it had vaporized a hole.

Then the unexpected happened. The tower leaned and toppled. We'd taken out the support to the structure. Apparently, it wasn't completely made of stuff as tough as puff-crete. Either that, or we'd got a lucky hit on the central struts and melted them.

A few Blood Worlders were flung free of the structure to crash down into the mud. One slaver was among them, flailing with his tremendously long arms. Barton's light troopers shot him to death eagerly.

The battle was on, and Graves was beyond pissed. "3rd unit! You've engaged without orders!"

"It was Leeson's weaponeers, sir," I shouted. "They're bloodthirsty. You just can't hold back an angry mob forever."

"Goddammit, McGill!"

Leeson frowned at me. "That's bullshit, Centurion," he complained. "You can't blame this all on me. You're the one screwing this cat, I'm just holding the tail!"

I waved away his arguments. A moment later, Graves came onto the general chat channel, broadcasting to the entire cohort.

"Blue team, you seem to be very eager. I'm ordering a full charge on every flank. Storm that castle, and take it—now!"

A roar went up, and it rang in my ears. Light troopers stood and advanced—including mine.

The charge was suicidal, of course, but that's what Graves apparently wanted. I gritted my teeth. It was one thing to jump the gun and fire without orders, it was quite another to disobey a direct instruction from your CO. I had no choice but to go with it.

"Barton, you've got the ball," I said. "Advanced to contact, set every snap-rifle to full-auto. These Blood Worlders aren't going to die easy."

Even as we prepared to charge, however, the enemy beat us to it. The front gates fell open, and through the gap where the tower had been, hulking figures appeared.

Daring to smile, I realized the Blood Worlders were taking the bait. They hated sitting inside fortifications. They liked to close with their enemy and get personal.

My smile faltered when I saw the monstrous troops they'd sent against us. These attackers were too big to be heavy troopers—they were true giants.

Standing about seven meters tall, they looked like barrel-chested men. Their heads were slightly too small for their bodies, however, and their eyes had the shared light of madness and idiocy in them.

Each wore a harness and a backpack. Their backpacks contained a power generator that fueled a beam projector and a shimmering personal body-shield for each of them.

Our light troops were just moving into the mud when the giants appeared. They paused in horror, then began hammering away with their snap-rifles. They were firing wildly, close to panic just at the sight of these approaching monsters.

Each giant's shielding sparked and flashed around him, as if a thousand tiny gnats were hitting a bug-light.

"How'd you know, McGill?" Harris demanded. "How'd you know they'd charge us?"

"Because we used drones to nail their squids. Blood Worlders lose their minds when you take out their officers. Now, grenade these monsters!"

The battle became wild and violent after that. The snap-rifles were useless against shielding, but our light troops still served a valuable role. They caught the attention of the angry giants, who used their beam projectors to cut them down like wheat before a dozen buzzing scythes.

In the meantime, Harris and his heavies got organized and lobbed grenades at the feet of the giants. The grav-plasma charges pulsed blue and overwhelmed the enemy shielding. One by one, the giants fell.

When they'd been swept away, I was surprised to see some of my light troops still lived. Barton herself led the final seven toward the walls.

"Damn," Harris said in surprise, "that girl is really going for it!"

"Graves said to charge. He's ordered us all in now. Have your armored troops switch their rifles over to shock-mode, and follow Barton into the breach. Leeson, gather up Sargon's group. We're advancing behind Harris."

"Lord help us…" Leeson said, but they all obeyed.

That's what Legion Varus troops were really good for: a solid fight to the finish, no matter the odds. We were a strange bunch. We were disrespectful, but highly skilled and willing to die on command.

Barton made it to the smoldering wreck of the tower—but no farther. Enemy guns took her team out to the last man when she tried to press inward.

Slogging through the mud was slow-going. Every step was a challenge. Overhead, the enemy had climbed the damaged walls and manned the towers that still stood intact. They raked our advancing lines, killing dozens.

Harris made it to the breach first, and he managed to score some hits—but it was too little, too late. The enemy had formed up a half-circular firing squad in there. They executed my men as they rushed through the hole.

"Sargon!" I shouted, grabbing his arm.

He whirled to face me. "We're all going to die in there, sir," he said.

"That's right. But I've got an idea: I want you to overload your last belchers and throw them into the breach."

He blinked at me. After a second, he understood, and he grinned.

"You're a first-class asshole, sir."

"Better than being a third-class kiss-up. Can you do it?"

"With pleasure—but Graves isn't going to like the property damage."

Sargon's weaponeers were shocked by the orders—often, equipment was valued more than human flesh in Legion Varus, and that went double during exercises.

But in the end, they followed my orders happily. Everyone wanted to do these Blood Worlders some serious harm by now. We were hunkering outside the walls, pinned down by fire from above, facing certain death in the breach ahead—but at least we now had a plan.

As one, Sargon's team rushed up and heaved their belchers. Sargon himself was hit as he made the final, squelching run.

He spun around and went down.

Encircled in his arms was a hot belcher, glowing and pulsing brighter blue every second. The fallen weapon was right in the middle of the last knot of troops I had.

Scrambling, I got to the belcher on all fours. I picked it up and made for the breach to heave it inside.

But as I got there, the timers began to run out. The belchers the other weaponeers had tossed inside went critical. A sweeping, overlaid series of blasts shook the place. Troops were knocked off their feet and killed all over the place.

I fell as well, slammed down by a rolling blast wave. I spun around, slipped and fell, still hugging Sargon's belcher.

One of my eyes wasn't operating—I didn't want to know why—and my ears were ringing and singing—but I didn't care. I had to toss one last bomb into the stew.

Cradling Sargon's weapon, I felt it go hot in my arms. With a desperate motion, I tried to toss it far into the fortress.

Then it went critical too, and I was obliterated in an explosive gush of radiation.

# -17-

When I next became aware of my surroundings, I don't mind telling you I was concerned.

I'd gone off the rails big-time in the exercise room. I knew that, and I was willing to own up to it. My only hope was that I wouldn't be punished *too* harshly for my actions.

Graves presided personally over my birth. That was a bad sign right off the bat. He never came down to greet newly hatched subordinates without a very good reason. In my case, I didn't think he was down here on Blue Deck to wish me well.

"McGill?" Graves said.

I felt fingers digging into my arms, but I didn't move a muscle.

"Can he hear me? Is this a bad grow?"

"Shouldn't be, Primus," a nervous sounding bio-girl answered. "All his numbers look good."

A fist slammed into my belly a split-second after she said this, while the other fist nailed me in the ribs. A sick explosion of pain snapped my eyes open and set me to coughing and curling up on the gurney.

"Primus!" the girl complained.

"Playing opossum isn't going to get you out of this one, Centurion," Graves told me.

His face had to be close, 'cause I could hear him breathing. My eyes fluttered open. The room was too bright, and Graves' craggy face was almost in kissing range.

"Morning, sir," I croaked out. "I must have overslept."

"Get off that table and get into uniform," he ordered, letting go of me and stepping away. "Gold Deck in five minutes. Be there."

A much more attractive person came close then, and she peered at me in concern. She ran deft fingers and instruments over me, casting angry glances over her shoulder after the primus. Either Graves didn't see her do it, or he didn't care.

I took the occasion to call out after Graves. "Give red team a hardy congratulations from me on winning that exercise, sir," I said to his retreating form. "It was quite an honor to do battle with them."

Graves flipped me the bird without even the courtesy of turning around to do it. The door swished shut in his wake, and he was gone.

"One cracked rib," said the girl working on me. She massaged my aching chest tenderly. "No sign of a punctured lung or hemorrhaging… You should be okay."

Grunting, I sat up and groped for my uniform. The bio-girl came at me with a patch before I closed the top, and I let her put it over my bruised mid-section.

"This is a smart-patch," she said, as if I'd never been injured before. "Leave it on for three days, and it will fall off in the shower on its own."

"Say…" I said, catching her small hand as she pulled away. "You wouldn't be looking for a date later on, would you?"

She gave a small, surprised snort. "I don't know." Our eyes met for a moment.

My face split into a grin, despite my aching ribs. Anything less than a flat no was a good sign in my book.

"What's your name?"

She touched her patch.

"Adjunct Kelly Walsh," I read aloud. "That's a nice sounding name. I always come back to life hungry, Kelly. You want to share dinner with me tonight?"

Kelly flashed me another glance, then she looked around behind her as if suspecting someone might be listening in.

She shook her head. "You're trouble, McGill," she said, not meeting my eyes. "I don't think it would be a good idea."

"Well now, don't you worry about old James! When I'm in trouble, I always find a way to dig myself right back out again."

She flashed me a small smile. "I don't know... Talk to me in a week—if you haven't been permed yet."

"You've got it, girl!" I said, staggering out of the room. "I'm gonna hold you to that, Kelly!"

Leaving, I wandered down the passages of Blue Deck, whistling an old tune. I felt pretty good, all things considered.

Sure, Graves was pissed off, my ribs hurt, and the rest of the legion brass was probably hating on me right now as well.

But I'd shown those Blood Worlders what a human legion could do. If that battle had been remotely fair, we'd have cleaned their clocks. I was certain of it. As it was, a quick check on my tapper showed we'd killed over half of them. By my accounting, we'd done ourselves proud.

Hitting the elevators, I checked my tapper again.

That was a downer moment. I'd expected there would be an unpleasant message or two in my inbox, but *damn*! There had to be at least fifty red-liners. They just kept coming, too, cascading in from the local server after having waited around for me to get revived again.

Getting the gist of them in a second or two, I ignored most of the texts, swiping them away to oblivion without reading more than a few words.

There was even one from Floramel. That surprised me. I almost opened it when I caught sight of the length. It was frigging *long*. Way too long. There were no pictures, either. Just words.

Sighing, I figured she'd outdone herself, giving me some hundred page text-wall. Most likely, it was full of her feelings, thoughts, and lots of recriminations as well.

Shaking my head, I knew I just wasn't in the mood. In fact, I knew myself well: I would *never* be in the mood to read this.

Accordingly, I swiped once and deleted the monstrous message. Whatever manifesto she'd sent me, I made a mental note to pretend it was riveting and thought-provoking the next time we met. After all, the girl had obviously worked hard on it.

But then I saw one from Graves. Apparently, there was a party arranged up on Gold Deck, and I was the guest of honor.

Frowning for a moment then giving it a shrug—after all, what was done was done—I marched to Gold Deck and touched my hand to the plate. There was only one option for that part of the ship, so I took it and was whisked away toward the upper decks.

What had that little cutie Kelly Walsh said? Something about me not being permed in a week?

Could she know something I didn't? It wouldn't be the first time I'd walked into an ambush.

Frowning a little, I slapped the elevator plate. The car stopped, and I dinked around with the control panel.

There was no way to redirect it. That was the kind of crap they pulled on legionnaires these days. They didn't trust us to tie our own shoes. Frustrated, I tapped at the plate until the emergency screen came up.

"What's the nature of your emergency, Centurion McGill?" the AI asked me.

"I've just been revived, and I suffered an injury in the process. I need to go back to the infirmary."

To my surprise, a scanner flashed over me. "No serious injury has been detected. Skin is unbroken. Internal organs appear—"

I didn't listen to the rest. This damned machine wasn't going to make this easy on me. But where there's a will, my Daddy always said, there was a way.

Wincing, I ripped off the smart bandage Kelly had put there, I drove in a fingernail, digging for gold. It took a second, but I had a few drops of blood and a bruise underneath.

"Scan me again. You missed it," I told the AI, which had been droning on about protocol for nearly a minute now.

"Minor injury found."

"I'm bleeding, dammit. Take me back to Blue Deck."

The elevator sat there for a second, as if weighing its options. At last, it reversed course and bore me back down to where I'd started off.

When the doors swept open, my smile faded.

Two specialists stood there, dressed in white. They were Blue Deck goons, the kind of men who shoved people into recyclers when the mood struck them.

Neither man had his gun out, however, so they clearly didn't understand the kind of mood I was in.

My smile grew back. I walked forward, leaning and dripping blood. "A little help, boys?" I asked.

Surprised, they reached out their arms, and I leaned on them heavily.

Now, as I might have said before, I'm a large man, easily taller and heavier than ninety-nine percent of Earth's sons who were fit for duty.

The man on my left was relatively small, and his legs almost buckled when I put fifty kilos of force on his shoulder.

But what really surprised him was my left foot, which snaked out and hooked his ankle. He hadn't been expecting that at all.

He did a facer, and I went down on top of him. I planted a knee in his back, and I could have sworn I heard a crackling sound.

The Second-man was getting smart about now. He reached for his belt. I grabbed his wrist and kept that gun planted in its holster. Getting to my feet, I made short work of him. These Blue Deck pukes weren't seriously combat-trained, after all. They usually fought the helpless while mouthing hushed platitudes.

When the second guy was on his knees, I plucked out his gun and backed onto the elevator again.

Examining the gun briefly, I was surprised. It wasn't a needler, standard-issue side arm or even a laser pistol. It was a kill-gun—the kind of thing that shot a bolt into the skull of an animal in a slaughter house.

"By damn…" I said to no one.

Then I applied my hand to the plate, but the AI didn't want to cooperate.

"Injury detected. Blue Deck return and replace authorized."

Return and replace? Shit. Could that mean those guys really *had* intended to recycle me and send a fresh McGill upstairs to whatever special fate awaited him on Gold Deck?

“Override,” I said. “I’m feeling better. See?”

Clumsily, I put the bandage back into place and smiled for the scanner. After another ten second delay, during which I sweated a few greasy droplets, the damned machine finally began going back up again.

I tucked my half-assed weapon into my tunic and enjoyed the rest of the ride up to Gold Deck. After all, it was likely to be a one-way trip.

Thinking of Kelly Walsh and the missed opportunities she represented, I felt a pang of honest regret.

## -18-

On Gold Deck I was greeted with guards that impressed me. Two hulking brutes took me by the elbows and guided me down the passages.

They were Blood Worlders. The smell alone would have identified them at a hundred paces. Coming from a desert climate on a planet not well known for amenities of any kind, these near-humans weren't big on deodorant—or bathing in general, for that matter.

Half-dragging me like a kid between them, the two troops marched me to a conference room. Once inside, I was allowed to stand on my own.

My eyes swept the room. Graves sat on the right. Turov sat on the left.

But… there were only two?

My face almost split into a grin, but I managed to stop that. I looked worried instead.

Internally, I relaxed. You see, in order to properly perm a man, our Hegemony bylaws clearly stated you had to have a quorum of three officers in the defendant's chain of command at the trial.

And unless someone was visiting the head, I only saw two in the room, which meant perming was out.

Now, sure, it was true that these two didn't look especially happy to see me. But there were only two of them.

*Demotion*, I thought to myself. That's what I was facing, I was ninety-percent sure of it.

To be honest, the thought bothered me a little, but not too much. I'd been demoted before, after all. When you spent your life in the service of a notorious military outfit like Varus, there was bound to be misunderstandings and hiccups in any man's career.

"James McGill..." Turov began, sighing. "Destroyer of worlds... That's what they call you back at Hegemony, you know. Those who have managed to trace the wreckage you leave behind back to its original source, named you that years ago."

My mind seethed with retorts. After all, Turov's half-assed leadership had resulted in any number of serious military disasters over the years. Hell, she was largely responsible for the near-capitulation of Earth back when Home World had been invaded by the squids. And that was just to name a single occasion.

But I didn't bring any of that up. Sour grapes weren't called for today. This was an occasion requiring a dash of solemnity, along with only a hint of my usual defiant attitude. Just enough to make them feel certain I'd felt the stern lashing I was about to receive.

"I do believe that's an unfair characterization of my record, Tribune," I said.

Graves blinked. Were my words too tame? Maybe he'd expected fire and brimstone—but he wasn't going to get any of that out of me today.

"If anything, my rebuke is too mild," Turov said. "Let us review today's damages."

She started listing things then. Lost equipment, dead near-humans—it was an impressive laundry list of broken and expired stuff. Under different circumstances, I might have been prideful.

But I tamped those urges down. I did my best to look forlorn, like a dog left out in the rain.

At some point, Turov strutted around to the door behind me and opened it. She looked up at the two Blood Worlder guards and waved at them, her nose wrinkling.

"Out, you two," she said. "Stand guard outside."

They lumbered away, and I was glad for it. They stank, and I knew the scent had finally driven Turov to action.

As she retreated toward her desk, I took a long, lingering glance until the moment she was safely out of my view again.

"McGill!" Graves said loudly, and I tuned in to hear what he was saying, just in case he was saying something I cared about. "Do you realize what you've done? Those Blood Worlders aren't coming back. Only the squids are being revived."

"What?" I asked.

"What Graves is telling you is correct," Turov said. "You have permed nearly a cohort of our new Blood Worlder legion."

"Why permed?" I asked, feeling a churn in my guts. I had a feeling I knew what she was going to say.

"Because we don't have the facilities to revive them all. Hell, even if we had a stack of revival machines big enough to get their stinking carcasses all processed by the time we reach M244-H, it would cost too much. We can't afford it."

My mouth hung open. "I know you weren't reviving them on the last campaign…" I said, feeling a little lost. "But I figured you must have sorted that out by now."

"No, McGill, we haven't," Graves told me.

"Well then why the hell did you have them fight us on the exercise deck?" I demanded. "That's kill-or-be-killed, sir. What did you expect a Varus army to do?"

"I expected you to follow orders. I don't know why, but I did. Maybe I'm the one that should be permed."

"But if you're not going to revive them all, how are they going to deploy on the target planet?"

Even as I asked this question, the answer occurred to me. "Wait… you're going to use gateway posts, right? Shipping fresh troops from Blood World directly to our landing zone. Is that it?"

"That's the plan," Graves said. "Didn't it occur to you, McGill, that we were making the battle easy on the Blood Worlders precisely because they couldn't be revived? Humans come back, Blood Worlders don't. If there's to be any use to a training, it has to be nonlethal for their side."

"That's why you held us back..." I said, feeling the puzzle pieces fit together inside my thick-skulled brain. "You wanted them to slaughter us on the walls, learning to fight our way, figuring you could revive us. You had us play the part of target practice dummies."

"Exactly," Turov said. "It was also training for the human troops to be familiarized with the fighting conditions of the target planet. But you couldn't even do that right! So... now that you understand your gross errors, do you want to know what's happening next?"

I didn't answer her. The truth was, I was feeling a little bit sick. The Blood Worlders were gross and vicious, but they didn't deserve to be permed in a lousy exercise. How many had I killed? Five hundred at least, by my estimate.

*Damn.*

I turned to Graves angrily. "You should have told me what was going on, sir," I said. "I had no idea I was perming those men. If I'd known... well, things would have gone differently."

"A confession?" Turov purred. "You're slipping, James."

I didn't care about that, so I didn't even look at her. My glare was entirely aimed at Graves. This was a big mess, and I didn't think it was fair to blame me for all of it.

"Maybe..." he said. "Maybe in retrospect, you're right. I should have let the centurions in on the nature of the game. But tell me, would you have been happy to know that any percentage of the Blood Worlders you fought were going to be permed?"

"No."

"Right. So, I was balancing two problems. Both of them were rooted in the typical lack of discipline that's rampant in this legion."

"You can retire, sir. Any day of the week. But this will still be Legion Varus, even after you're gone."

Graves looked at me thoughtfully. "I wonder..."

"Gentlemen," Turov said, clearing her throat. "If you two are done swinging your dicks around, it's time to send James on his way."

"Yes... it's overdue."

As Graves said this, he began checking his sidearm. He stood up and walked around the desk, approaching me.

"Hey," I said. "I thought you guys were going to demote me, or something."

"There's been a change of plans, James," Turov said. Her voice seemed to have softened a little. Could she be regretting what was about to happen? "You see, we've got to execute you. The Blood Worlder legion officers are demanding it. We'll revive you later and slip you back into active duty, if all goes well—once we arrive at the target world."

"Huh?" I said, confused. "You mean you're putting me on ice for a few months? I'm going to stay dead until you need me again?"

"Sort of," she explained. "Now, if you'll—"

But I never heard whatever she planned to tell me next. Maybe she wanted me to kneel or something—I could have told her that wasn't going to happen.

Graves approached me confidently and put the muzzle of his pistol up against my temple.

I didn't flinch, I didn't even look at him. But I'd been hiding that bolt gun, and so I put it up against his chest and fired it.

This was a pretty big breach of protocol for me. Normally, I took my beatings and executions stoically, like a good soldier should. But this time, I'd reacted emotionally. After all, I simply didn't think any of this was fair. They'd put me in a pit and told me to fight—well, I'd fought to the best of my ability. It's not right to tell a man whose life is on the line to pull punches.

The kill-gun's blast wasn't a loud one. The charge was just enough to fire a length of steel through his sternum and into his heart.

He fired his weapon too, but I'd already batted it away from my head.

As he sagged down, his eyes registering shock, I considered that he shouldn't have gotten so close. You would have thought he knew me better than that by now.

"Overconfidence," I said to him as he slid down onto his back.

“Dammit, McGill!” Turov snarled. “You’re blowing everything! This is being recorded, you fool. The Blood Worlder officers must not see shit like this! They already think we’re insane!”

“Sorry about the mess on your carpet, Galina,” I told her. “I guess you’ll have to revive Graves and bring him back up here to have another go at it.”

That’s when she shot me. Sneaky woman. She’d kept her distance. With nothing but the tiny range of my bolt-gun and my fists, I didn’t stand an even chance.

“Now,” she said, standing over me.

I lay on my back, gasping. There were holes in my chest—plenty of them. Way more damage had been done than I could ever hope to repair with smart bandages.

Galina sure was pretty, I reflected. But she was also a serious bitch when she was angry.

“I’m going to tell you what’s going to happen next,” she began in a deceptively calm voice, “just so you don’t screw anything else up. You’ve got the full text of the Mogwa book on you right now. We’re using you as a courier. You’ll be revived at a secret destination, far from here. They will take the text, and you will let them. Do you understand?”

“I…I don’t have it…” I wheezed.

“Yes you do, James,” she said confidently. “It’s on your tapper. Floramel wrote it all out, and sent it to you. The message is encrypted, of course, but—”

My hand shot out, forming a bloody claw that grabbed her by the calf. She squeaked and tried to dance away, but she couldn’t escape. Her gun came up, but she hesitated when she realized I wasn’t trying to kill her.

“No…” I said, understanding something now with grim certainty. “I deleted that message.”

“You did *what*? You deleted the message from Floramel?”

“Yes…”

“But *why*?” she demanded, lowering her face into mine.

My vision was dimming, and I thought to myself that if this was my final moment, it wouldn’t be a bad way to go. At least Galina looked a lot better than Graves did.

"It…" I said, struggling with the words, "…it was too damned long."

"Are you fucking kidding me?" she screeched. "Xlur will freak out!"

She straddled me, and she grabbed my bloody tunic with her two small fists. She shook me.

She might have slapped me too, or even have pistol-whipped me, but my nerves weren't reporting much up to my distant brain any more.

"McGill? Don't die yet, damn you!" she shouted, and she might have said more, but I never heard it.

A final thought did impinge on my dying mind, however. *Had she said something about Chief Inspector Xlur?* I thought perhaps that she had…

But it didn't matter a moment later because by then I'd died on the floor between her sweet, blood-soaked thighs.

# -19-

Coming to life again was like waking up from a strange night of bad dreams. I was hazy, confused…

It felt like it had been a long time. Could they have given up on sending me to the Mogwa and simply revived me back on *Legate* instead? I dared to hope that was the case.

But strange sounds and scents soon dissuaded me of any such comforting thoughts. The environment I was in—it was all wrong.

First off, the air was *sticky*… As a man from southern Georgia Sector, I was no stranger to humidity, but revival chambers on human transport ships were always cool and dry. Always. This room was humid to the extreme—I could feel it on every exposed stretch of my skin.

It was brightly lit and hot, too. My eyes weren't open yet, as fresh-grown eyes are always overly-sensitive—but this level of light was unprecedented. I felt like someone was aiming a hot headlight into my face.

Squinching up my eyes, I did the opposite of opening them. I closed them even tighter.

The sounds were wrong, too. Normally, I awoke hearing medical jargon between human bio people as they scanned me and discussed my vitals. Instead, I heard some odd clicking noises. They were rhythmic and varied, coming out in organized bursts.

Could those be alien words? I thought they probably were. I'd heard enough samples to know the way they usually sounded.

Something poked me in the ribs about then, and I groaned, slapping it away. The touch was nasty. Kind of like a wet, bony hand. I almost opened my eyes at that, but remembered to squinch them shut. The bright light here was going to hurt if I opened them now.

A warbling sound began a moment later, and I heard a series of tones that sounded human. As if tuning-in a radio signal, the tones focused and became clear at last, dividing into intelligible words.

"It will stand and exit the chamber," an automated voice said.

That was a Galactic translator. I talked to Nairbs with these things on many occasions.

"It's too damned bright in here," I complained. "Turn off some lights so I can see."

"Ah, of course. You are a pathetic dark-worlder. I'd forgotten your disabilities."

There was a rustling, and the room dimmed. I opened my eyes at last in relief.

The Mogwa stood at the window. He'd adjusted the light that glared in from outside—apparently these windows could be shaded at will, like those in every hotel room on Earth.

But even when dimmed down to a tolerable intensity, what a view it was!

The exterior of the building—whatever the hell building I was in—looked out upon a sprawling city. We were apparently high up in a spire. The strangely shaped structures, mostly built with dull metals, stretched to the horizon and perhaps beyond.

My brain was still a little hazy, but I had the presence of mind to reach over and touch the record button on my tapper. The sights, the sounds and a dozen other things began to be tracked. If I ever made it back home, the nerds under Central would go nuts for this stuff.

"That's quite a view," I said. "What's this city called?"

"It has no name. It is 'the City'. The planet itself is known as Trantor. You are very fortunate to have a surface view. Too bad its glory is wasted on your dull eyes."

Getting down from a cold metal table, I walked to that window and looked around. After a moment of studying the endless city, I glanced up.

That was a shock. I'm used to starscapes, don't get me wrong—but this!

An explosion of suns hung overhead. They were like stars, but much bigger and brighter than any that have ever graced Earth's skies. Each star was like a moon, brilliant, intense, varied in hue and size. There were dozens of them, and dozens more smaller orbs hung in between the brightest.

I gasped. "This is a star cluster. A tight cluster, by the look of it."

Glancing back over my shoulder I saw the Mogwa who had attended me. He was working a device, something like one of our tappers. Doubtlessly, he was reporting my status to his masters—perhaps to Xlur himself.

"What's your name, Mr. Mogwa?" I asked.

"It is improper for a lesser being to so directly address a superior. However, I will let it go today, as you are a frontier barbarian."

"Thanks," I said.

A silence followed. He never did tell me his name.

"Uh…" I said. "What are we waiting for, your supreme overlordship, sir?"

"The arrival of your master. Here, put this on. It bears his mark."

He handed me a big bracelet. It was ridiculously oversized, but I tried it on my wrist anyway.

The Mogwa made some of those nasty farting sounds their kind did when they laughed.

"No, imbecilic being," he said. "It goes around the neck."

Finally, I caught on. It was a collar. A slave collar.

Spinning it around carefully in my hand, I found an engraving. It looked like a spider holding a flag or something. Could that be the "mark" this other bastard had been talking about?

Just then, a door appeared. It occurred to me then that I hadn't seen any doors in this chamber, only a single window. The door was indistinguishable from the rest of the wall until it was activated, then it seemed to melt away to nothing.

Another Mogwa appeared at the entrance.

He took one look at me, then admonished the technician who'd revived me. "The beast isn't collared? Why have you failed me?"

"He only just arose," the first Mogwa complained. "He's slow. Are you sure his mental capacities haven't been impaired?"

The newcomer sniffed and stepped closer. He inspected me briefly.

"This is the McGill-creature."

"How can you tell them apart?"

"This specimen is of unusual size for the species."

That's when I caught on. I thought this second guy looked familiar.

"Chief Inspector Xlur!" I shouted, giving him a smile. "Good to see you, Your Holiness, sir."

Xlur eyed me disdainfully. "Your grunting syllables do not entirely translate. No matter. We require very little input from you. Follow me—and put that collar on before someone sees you."

For a second, I balked. I didn't like the thought of collaring myself, not for any reason.

"Um… could I have some clothes, sirs?"

Both of them made their blatting noises. "The temperature here will be survivable without adornment. Besides, slaves require no clothing, and we have nothing programmed to fit your odd form anyway."

Shrugging, I decided I'd just have to go commando today. Lifting the collar, I got an idea. I put it around my neck, but I didn't click it closed.

Walking out of the room in Xlur's wake, I took a last glance over my shoulder at the window.

"That's an amazing view, sir," I said. "We've got nothing like it back in Province 921. What province is this, if you don't mind my asking?"

He cast me another dismissive look. “Ignorance is your forte, human. This is Trantor—Mogwa Prime.”

Then, it all hit me. I should have known right off, but I hadn’t caught on for some reason.

*I was on one of the Core Worlds!* That realization was a shock, let me tell you.

What’s more, this was the fabled Mogwa Capital. The city-world that was at the very heart of our portion of the galaxy.

A chill ran through me. It was a true honor to be here. I had to wonder if any other human had ever slapped his bare feet on this floor before—I thought it was unlikely.

“Good old McGill,” I whispered to myself, “you crazy bastard, you made it all the way out to the Core Worlds! Hot damn…”

# -20-

It may come as a surprise to learn that I'm a man who's relatively at ease while naked. Some people might feel an urge to cover themselves with a hand, or walk funny, or something. But not old James McGill. Hell, back when I was a kid, my momma had a devil of a time keeping me dressed at all until I was seven or eight years old. There were many family tales of me streaking into rooms full of ladies playing bridge and whatnot.

So today I found myself marching among the Mogwa with my wang fully exposed, and that wasn't really a problem for me. It didn't seem to bother them much, either.

We walked for what felt like kilometers. Mogwa's have six limbs, each of which is terminated by an odd-looking appendage that could operate either as a foot or a hand. Their six hands could all be used to manipulate objects or aid in locomotion. Either way, the Mogwa looked funny, like funky spiders with a wobbling step.

During that long walk, I let my tapper continue recording. I took vid shots of every random thing we passed. I figured intel was intel, and the people back home could sort the good clips from the bad later on.

The Core World was kind of tight-knit. Despite the massive size of their city, I got the feeling they were cramped for space.

"Hey, Chief Inspector? Just how many Mogwa are there on Mogwa Prime?"

He glanced back at me. “A telling question for a saboteur. But I will entertain it nonetheless. We are nearly three trillion strong on this world.”

“Holy shit…” I said, looking around in wonderment. “Then this city… it can’t be skin deep. It has to go down and down, deep into the crust.”

“The mantle is our limit,” he agreed. “We’ve been forced to immigrate to hospitable worlds recently, due to lack of space here at home.”

“Um…” I said, thinking that over. “You mean you haven’t colonized a thousand planets already?”

“Heavens no! Leaving Mogwa Prime is a form of banishment for any of us. *This* is our home. We only truly enjoy ourselves here.”

That got me to thinking… if the Mogwa were contained so tightly on this single planet, well… killing them all would be a whole lot easier.

Suddenly, I began to understand the power of the bio-terminator I’d been chasing after. The book Floramel had transcribed verbatim from memory was a recipe for genocide against these people.

Before seeing Mogwa Prime, the feverish hunt for a poisonous formula had never seemed too rational to me. Sure, it would be a good way to kill a population, but I’d always assumed any ancient race would be spread far and wide across the stars.

But… what if that wasn’t true for the Mogwa? What if they were such stick-in-the-mud types they didn’t like living anywhere else? Like salmon that were only really happy in the river of their birth, these guys had always complained when they traveled.

They looked down their noses at everyone, calling us all kinds of names. And I recalled as well that the officials I had met were generally considered outcasts. Grand Admiral Sateekas, for instance, had said he was out of favor back home in the Mogwa courts. Maybe that was why he’d been sent so far from home to run a fleet in our far-flung province.

Chief Inspector Xlur was of the same sort. He hated Province 921, the very place he’d been assigned to rule.

"So…" I said aloud, "when they assigned you to be governor of 921, that made you into a sort of exile, didn't it?"

Xlur halted. Slowly, he turned to face me.

*Crap.*

"Uh…" I said. "I hadn't meant to say that out loud, Chief Inspector. Please disregard my rudeness."

He studied me, looking me up and down. "I remember you now. You were a disruption back on Earth. A plague they didn't know what to do with. That other being—the female Turov—she described you as such to me."

"Um… that's right, sir. I'm a barbarian. Rude and uninformed."

"Normally, I'd have you flailed and boiled for your remarks. But unfortunately, I have need of you. Besides, you are essentially correct. Every moment I spend out on the rim is a moment forever lost to me. A tragic waste of my life-essence."

"Hmm…" I said. "Can't you get any nice lady-Mogwas to share your palace with you—or whatever you have in Province 921?"

"Palace? Your province has nothing that would qualify. But in any case, no female of my species would ever ponder joining an official like me in banishment. The size of my domicile would not matter. Only a male's proximity to the city-world can impress a female."

I thought about the various women that I'd dealt with in my lifetime. "You know, I think I've had the same experience for decades. Now, don't get me wrong, I've managed to entice more than my share of females out to my shack in the swamp, to be sure. But those brief visits always turned out to be a temporary fling. They've always started yearning to return to some city or another..."

He eyed me coldly for a moment. "Are you mocking me?"

"Um… I don't think so."

He turned away. His sides puffed up then slowly deflated, making a long, drawn out farting sound.

Could I be witnessing a Mogwa releasing a long sigh?

"You've deepened my self-disgust," he said. "The mere idea I could have shared life-experiences with one of you brutes—it's too depressing to contemplate."

We pressed onward. Soon, we passed factories, spaceyards, food dispensaries and slave pens. None of them looked all that appealing to me.

Mogwa design, I slowly began to realize, wasn't artistic or expressive in any way. It was almost purely functional. They wouldn't have known how to build an attractive structure if their cold little hearts depended on it.

As a result, this Core World was impressive due to their advanced tech, the sprawling nature of the city, and their glorious sky. But it was also cramped and drab for the most part. Maybe that was due to the fact it had to be home to trillions. When you had those kinds of numbers, you didn't have a lot of room left over for bric-a-brac.

"Here, this is the download station," Xlur said, stopping and guiding me into another small chamber.

I entered cautiously. Inside, I found a lump of brown flesh in the shape of a mushroom. It was about the size of a footstool, and it sprouted all kinds of living tubes and insulated wires.

"Ah," I said, finding a port I recognized. "Here's a Galactic standard connector. Is this for power, or data?"

"Either, depending on the need. Kindly plug in and download your data. When you're finished, I'll send it to the labs to be analyzed."

"What happens to me after that?"

"Depending on the results, you'll be returned to Earth quickly… or slowly."

"Um…" I said, thinking that over.

I was pretty sure I got the idea. If they liked the quality of my work, I'd be killed quickly and a revival order would be sent to Earth. Death was the only way I was going to get home, I'd already figured that out.

But if they weren't happy with the data I was carrying, they'd take it slow. Torment? Perhaps a permanent death afterward? The possibilities didn't warrant thinking about.

Now, I'm not a man who sweats easily. But this was a tough spot, even by my standards. The key to my troubles was simple enough: I didn't have the data they wanted. Not a word of it.

Feeling a tickle of perspiration under my arms, I sniffed and lifted my tapper. Giving it a shot, I checked the virtual trash can to see if I could undelete my deleted message.

Of course, that didn't work. Encrypted messages stayed deleted on modern tappers—especially after you died.

"Hmm…" I said, taking up the Galactic standard cable again.

Xlur shuffled a pace closer, watching me.

He was no dummy, but he clearly had no idea what I was thinking. My immediate instinct was to rip the cord out of his fleshy bio-computer, wrap it around his slimy neck and strangle him.

I almost did it, too. But then I had a better idea.

# -21-

For many years I'd gotten by on my brawn at least as often as I had my brain. Seeing no other option, I considered killing the Mogwa—that would be, what…? the third time around for old Xlur? The thought made me smirk.

But I quickly passed on the idea. It would be satisfying, sure. I might even indulge myself in a few extra minutes of existence afterward, having a good laugh before about a trillion of his relations got smart and came to check on his flat-lined vitals.

Nope… for once, violence didn't seem to offer any kind of satisfactory solutions. I was going to have to use my brain instead.

"What is the source of this delay?" Xlur demanded. "Can you be so ignorant? Plug into the device, human. I'm anxious to see the merchandise you've brought me."

Sighing, I plugged in the cable. There was a port under a flap of skin on my lower forearm. I rarely used it, as practically all communication was wireless these days.

The bulbous living computer I'd plugged into throbbed and pulsated when I connected myself to it. That was freaky. I was used to indicator lights, beeps and tones—but not to a slow throbbing.

The bio-computer searched my tapper thoroughly. It downloaded everything it could, and then it released a small, unpleasant smell.

"What the…?" I asked, wrinkling my nose.

"The process has finished. I will now send the contents of your tapper to the labs for analysis."

The Mogwa turned to go, but I spoke up.

"Um… Mr. Mogwa, sir? I mean, Chief Inspector?"

"What is it, creature?"

"I'm not sure you can read the file I brought… It's encrypted."

He blinked at me. "Avoidance? Extortion? You dare?"

"Um…"

"Know this, McGill-creature: I'll not be abused. I've been as patient and cordial as possible. You've been honored with this opportunity to visit the greatest of the Core Worlds, a fantastic boon. But that will in no way stop justice from exacting revenge upon your person. You—"

"Hold on, hold on!" I said. "I'm not trying to make any demands. My concerns are all practical. I'm not sure you can read all the files I just gave you: especially the one that really matters."

He organized his clusters of optical organs to study me.

"Why would your superiors send you all this way to the center of the galaxy with useless data files?"

"They're not useless," I said. "I can translate them if needed."

The Mogwa squinted at me. It was one of the few gestures that seemed familiar. Almost every species protected its eyes in some manner when they examined something unpleasant.

"Very well," he said. "We will await the response from our labs."

A few long minutes passed. I tried to make conversation, but he wasn't interested. He just thumped around me in circles, clicking and farting to himself. I could tell he was stressed.

"Chief Inspector?" I asked. "Can you tell me what this means to you, personally, if I can get you the data you've been promised?"

Xlur finally took notice of me and stopped muttering to himself in his strange language.

"How do you seek to twist my responses to your advantage?" he asked.

"Um… I don't, sir. Just making idle conversation while we wait."

Xlur ruffled his lobes. It reminded me of the way a pissed-off bird might fluff up then slowly shrink again when it's annoyed.

"The facts can't hurt, I suppose, and they should be obvious to any thinking creature. You must be mentally challenged if you haven't figured it out by now."

"I'm a card-carrying retard, sir. That's what they call me back home."

"Unsurprising… To answer your question, I hope to reveal a valuable threat to the crown. By doing so, I'll elevate my status. With luck, I'll be brought home, leading the cruel life of an exile no longer."

"Ah-ha!" I said, grinning. "I kind of thought that was what you'd say. You want to come back home and start a family of little Mogwas, don't you?"

"These words, coming from a crude frontier creature such as you, are painful to my spirit."

"I'm sorry about that, sir. I truly am. I hope you get home again—permanently."

"Your well-wishes aren't necessary. All that is required is that you perform your function as a messenger— Ah! The lab has just returned the results."

"And?" I asked brightly. "Let me guess: they managed to convert it all, didn't they? I shouldn't have even doubted your Galactic geniuses, sir. I knew in my heart your techs are so much better than ours that we'd never be able to encrypt anything that they couldn't—"

"Silence, creature! The labs have discovered many files, but they are all useless garbage. Reports, images, advertisements for questionable products—all completely useless."

"Oh…" I said, lifting an index finger into his face. "You see, that's the genius of our encryption. The files aren't altered using some methodical mathematical formula. No, no, it's all based on idioms, see. Details of my life history, woven together to tell a story that only I could—"

"Yes, yes, yes. Whatever. Can you translate it? Quickly?"

“Like greased-lightning, Chief Inspector! You won’t even believe how fast I can work once I’m all warmed up and in the zone.”

His eyes followed me for a time, and I sensed a malevolent light in them. Had I, perhaps, pushed things too far? Was he beginning to suspect I had absolutely nothing and was just stalling for time?

“Why would Earth send this data in an encrypted format? Especially using a method so elaborate and arcane?”

“Why, I’d think that was obvious, sir. We wouldn’t want something so dangerous to fall into enemy hands, would we?”

Xlur shuffled uneasily. “Enemy hands? What do you know of our enemies?”

“I know you’re in a struggle here in the Core Systems. A long, drawn-out civil war.”

“That description is overly dramatic,” he stated. “We’re merely experiencing differences of perspective among the leadership of the galaxy. The Galactic Council has made appreciable headway recently, and all is sure to be resolved promptly.”

“Thousands of worlds scorched bare?” I interrupted. “Suns exploded, turned inside out and driven to nova? That’s some difference in perspective.”

“That information shouldn’t be available out on the frontier!”

“I’m sorry, sir,” I said. “But I don’t see how hiding facts is going to benefit our side in this righteous conflict. What are you going to use this formula for, if you don’t mind my asking?”

He looked at me guardedly for a moment before answering. “I suppose I can confide safely in the courier-beast that possesses the formula itself. My plan is to enlighten and elevate the Mogwa elite. I’m sure to gain notoriety and importance with this frightening discovery. As a hero who has removed a deadly threat, they’re sure to listen to my clever contributions. So armed, our envoys will be able to present an unassailable argument for the throne.”

“You don’t say… Well then, how about I get to work? This book isn’t deciphering itself.”

For about five long seconds, the Mogwa studied me again. At last, however, the spell was broken.

"All right," he said. "You will live for now, human. My plan was to dispatch you, of course, the instant the message was cleanly transferred to my data system. Clearly, my plans must be time-shifted forward."

"Sorry for the inconvenience, sir."

"Your sorrow is pointless. Begin the translation immediately."

"Sure thing, sir. I'll just need a few things to work with…"

"What's this? Demands?!"

"No, no, no, sir. Far from it. But I came to your world buck-naked, with no tools or food. I'll need something to write with, and something to drink—and eat, of course."

Xlur made some nasty sounds. "This process sounds lengthy. You will do no writing. You'll dictate your words into this organ."

He indicated a conical ear that had sprouted up on this mushroom-shaped computer.

"Okay… and what about the food and drink, sir?"

"Bah… very well. I will procure suitable items."

"Excellent!" I said. "Steaks would be best to start with. I've never been much of a salad-man. Three thick cuts will do the trick, along with some beer if you've got it. You've tasted these flavors before, I believe, back on Earth?"

Xlur made a lot of bad smells and evil noises as he left to find me some grub. I'd honestly expected to see him summon up a servant to bring the stuff to me—but he went to get it himself.

I couldn't help but grin as I saw him hump his way out into the permanently crowded walkways.

By this time, I'd figured out I was sitting in his apartment. He had no staff, and he was doing all this on the cheap. Among his kind, Xlur really was a low-caste individual.

Chuckling to myself, I stretched out on his bunk for a nap. It was short and damp, but I didn't mind. After all, how many earthmen could truthfully say they'd been waited on by an honest-to-God Mogwa governor?

# -22-

Needless to say, the translation of the secret document I'd erased on my tapper didn't go well—mostly because the document was imaginary.

On top of that, I'd read the original book years ago, but I'd pretty much forgotten everything. I'd found the book to be kind of boring, if the truth were to be told.

Naturally, I couldn't afford the truth to come out. On a philosophical note, I'd often found the truth was a luxury beyond my reach under the best of circumstances.

As a result, the mess I dredged up from memory didn't sound much like the original. Worse, my version of *The Eaters of Lotus* seemed to deviate further with every page I wrote.

What seemed to bug Xlur the most, however, was the speed of my progress—or lack thereof. I'd be the first to admit I'm not a terribly fast writer. Anyone who's had the misfortune to try and teach me a course in English could attest to that.

Finally, after about three grueling days, Xlur lost his cool.

"All you do is eat!" he boomed at me. "You are a useless creature!"

"That's not true," I said. "I sleep a lot, too. Translations like this take time, Chief Inspector. Isn't patience a virtue among the Mogwa?"

He was enraged. I've pissed off a lot of humans and aliens in my day, so I knew the telltale signs all too well.

"This venture is pointless," he said. "I will demand restitution from Turov. She will be punished the next time I go back to Earth—perhaps your entire species will be erased with her."

"Uh..." I said, thinking that over.

To my mind Xlur had just made a critical error. He'd informed me in no uncertain terms that the game was up. Compounded with several of his additional errors, the primary one being the fact he'd given me a few days to plan things out, he was skating on thin ice.

He had no idea what I was thinking, of course. The Mogwa are so accustomed to abject obedience they've become over-confident and arrogant, in my opinion.

As I watched, he calmly took out some kind of gadget. It looked like a brass nozzle a man might screw onto the end of a hose to water the garden with.

But I knew better. It was a weapon, a regional disintegrator.

Disintegrators were pretty cool devices, actually. Like magic wands, they detected a mass in nearby space, figured out where its boundaries were, and then broke the molecular bonds between the atoms that made up that mass. The target—in this case my outsized body—was then transformed into an ashy mound of powdery gray dust. The entire process took less than a second.

Fortunately, Xlur's actions didn't take me by surprise. Over the last few days, I'd done a bit of creative writing for him, but I'd also researched my environment. I'd found the disintegrator and modified it.

That might sound like an intensive technical chore, something that only a genius like Natasha was capable of. But in this case, the device was so simply constructed that all I had to do was take out the central parabolic crystal, turn it around, and insert it back into the weapon.

Xlur's eventual use of this odd weapon was all part of my grand plan—but I'd miscalculated. I'd figured he'd threaten me with it first to get more work out of me.

But he didn't even bother. Xlur was a decisive alien. He clearly intended to erase me from his apartment without making so much as a single doom-laden ultimatum.

"Uh..." I said, watching him pick up his toy. "That's not a good idea, Xlur."

"It's the best idea I've had since falling for this fraudulent scheme," he said. "I should have done it the moment I identified your shivering body. The mere stink of your person is unbearable. Living here with an ape for days—"

That was about as far as I could let him get. He'd been lifting his weapon, now fully activated, and aiming it toward my chest. There wasn't much time left, and I could tell already I was never going to talk him down before he pulled the trigger.

I moved. There was a flash of metal and a thunking sound. Then, to finish things off, we both heard a wet slap as something fell away from Xlur's body.

Xlur shivered in pain and slithered away.

"You slashed off my hand!" he complained.

But then, he began to laugh. "You're an abject a failure, human! You can't even rebel properly. You missed and cut off the wrong appendage."

I shrugged and waved around the monofilament knife I'd used to cut him. It was the only weapon I'd found in his apartment that I knew how to use.

"You'd better get on with my execution, then," I said. "I'm liable to hit the right spot next time."

He lifted his gun—but then hesitated. Could he possibly smell a rat?

He was right to be worried. There was a two meter long rodent staring back at him, waiting for him to fire—but he didn't do it.

"Your demeanor is all wrong," he said. "No begging, no gnashing of teeth. Why are you facing nonexistence with such total calm, McGill?"

I shrugged, which made him flinch. "I've died many times before."

"Not like this, you haven't. A creature destroyed by this weapon is simultaneously removed from every data core in the galaxy. You can never be revived. Even if someone were foolhardy enough to try—there will be nothing left. Even searching the Galactic Grid will turn up nothing."

"Sounds pretty dangerous... Please don't shoot, Mr. Mogwa!"

"That's better. At least you're begging. But it will do you no good. You're about to become an unperson, McGill. Say goodbye."

"Goodbye."

Ruffling and making those farting sounds that were laughter for him, Xlur pulled the trigger.

The gun had been reversed, naturally. I almost felt bad for him as he melted away into an ashy heap. After all, I'd been his houseguest for days, and we had a history together that went back more than two decades.

"One piece left..." I said, picking up the foot-hand appendage that I'd sliced off.

The lopped-off flesh contained Xlur's tapper, naturally enough. That's why I'd chosen that limb to sever. If he'd disintegrated his entire body, I'd have been left with nothing to work with.

As it was, I had to move fast. Xlur might not be an important Mogwa on his home planet, but I was pretty sure I'd tripped up more than my share of emergency alarms.

Using his tapper, I transmitted a message. Fortunately, his tapper wasn't password protected. The Mogwa didn't feel the need since their tappers were always with them, and they were the masters of their universe most of the time.

The message went off to Turov, of course.

"Package received," it said. "Courier performed superbly. I recommend you promote him after revival."

That was it. I sent it, and as the Galactic net could get a packet to Earth without much in the way of charges, it zipped away across thousands of lightyears.

All that was left now was to kill myself. Originally, I'd planned to use Xlur's disintegrator. But that idea was out now—removal from the data core? No thank you!

While I thought about it, I fixed Xlur's disintegrator. I didn't want them figuring out it had been tampered with.

In the end, I decided to use the knife. It was messy, but I didn't have anything else, and I didn't want to risk exiting the apartment to throw myself off a cliff or something.

With my wrists opened up, I began to feel a little lightheaded almost immediately. I doodled with the growing pool of blood then got a bright idea. I wrote a suicide note on the floor in my own blood.

*Xlur took his life. As his faithful servant, I feel I must leave the cosmos with him.*

It wasn't as cool as one of those samurai death-poems, but I was proud of it.

My vision had dimmed by the time Mogwa emergency bots broke into the apartment. They ignored me, fussing over the stump of Xlur's foot-hand and the loose pile of ash on the floor. They clearly didn't know what to do.

Lying there among what seemed like a pool of gathering shadows, I listened to them whir around in confusion.

Whenever I die with a smile on my face, I chalk it up as a good death. This time, I went out grinning. Grinning hugely.

# -23-

Revival came as an interruption this time. At least, that's how it felt.

I'd been dreaming while I was dead, and I woke up wanting to finish the experience. The whole dream was an illusion, of course. Like déjà vu. People often came back to life under the impression they'd been sleeping, not lingering in nonexistence.

But this time the sensation was stronger than usual. I could remember… faces.

"What have we got?" an official-sounding woman asked while I dozed on the table.

"This is a weird one," an orderly responded. "The revival order is… well, there isn't one. This is unofficial. Off-grid."

The woman was quiet for a second. When she did speak, her voice tones had changed dramatically. She now spoke in a hissy-sounding whisper. "Are you telling me Turov green-lit another illicit revive? Without even asking us if we'd do it or not?"

"Looks that way. There's no record of death. No official military GPS coordinates on the subject prior to death, either—I'm guessing he died off-world."

"Then this is bullshit," the bio said. "We've *got* to get approval from Central. Otherwise I'm recycling."

The other guy sighed. "I'll check, but there won't be anything. You know that."

"This is bullshit!" she repeated.

My eyes fluttered open about then. My dream… it was still lingering. I'd dreamt about being revived earlier, I was pretty sure of that. Or maybe that was an illusion. It was hard to tell.

A cold thought struck through my hazy state of mind. Could I have been revived somewhere else recently… and died? Was my dream really a flickering memory of a very short lifespan?

That could be the situation. Maybe what I'd assumed was a half-remembered dream—was a reality. In support of that theory, these two didn't seem keen on bringing me back. Maybe they weren't the first to balk at the idea.

In my dream, two bio people had hovered over me, just like they were doing now. In the end, they'd finally decided what to do—and the dream ended abruptly. They'd moved like ghosts, and they'd whispered like these two—but I'd felt a sting in the final moments.

"Is he awake?" the woman whispered.

"He should be… but he looks like he's still out."

My left eyelid was rudely pried open. A brilliant light stabbed into my fresh-grown eyeball.

In order not to give things away, I rolled my eyes way up into my head. I didn't want them to get a clear pupil response.

"He's still recovering," the orderly whispered.

"Okay then… we have time to think. What if we just grind him and say it didn't work out?"

"Turov has given us cash for illegal stuff before—she'll know we pulled the plug. She might dox us."

"Screw her. She didn't even give us a courtesy call," the bio complained. "She's got huge clanking balls to pull this shit. Just sending us a random revive, obviously illegal, no talk of payment, nothing? You've got to be shitting me."

"If she wants to, she can report us—for what we did last time."

The bio woman made a small growling sound of frustration.

While these two argued about my fate, I was feeling stronger every second. Like always, I'd come back with rubbery fingers and hazy vision. But as a veteran who was all too familiar with the cycle of life and death, I had a distinct advantage. Legionnaires who die a lot grow emotional armor about these things. We're not freaked out by death, so we don't awaken in some strange metaphysical mindset.

In short, I was ready to make a move.

"I'm not going for this," the woman said suddenly, coming to a fateful decision. "Put him into the recycler."

"Are you serious? He's a good grow. Turov might tear us a new one."

"Look," the bio said in a low tone, "we have to call her bluff right away. If she thinks she can order us to do whatever she wants, she'll do it forever. We have to let her know we're not going to stand for this treatment, or we'll be her slaves."

"All right… All right…"

I heard feet shuffling, and I felt big hands clamp onto my biceps. I was hauled off the table and onto a cart. It rolled, and I let my feet drag.

"Jesus, he's a heavy bastard."

"Just do it."

I waited until I heard the blades whirring, revving up. Then the orderly grabbed me by the neck—at least he was a nice guy. He was going to put me into the grinder head-first. Bad grows suffered less that way.

But I didn't care about his chivalry. By this time, I was in a bad mood.

My own arms came up, but I didn't grapple with him. Instead, I sought out his eyes.

I poked one out—I was pretty sure about that. The other finger missed, but I'd done what I'd wanted to.

The orderly staggered away in shock, screeching. I got up and slid off the gurney. My limbs weren't too strong yet, but my legs held me up. I reached out a foot, hooked it behind the orderly's ankle—and down he went.

He slid into the chute on his back, headfirst, the same as he'd planned for me. The blades struck his skull, bit in, and spun. For a few seconds it sounded like a chunk of wood had been caught between two gears. Then the recycler sucked him in, and it was all over within seconds.

I almost didn't hear the bio. She hadn't screamed and run out—she was a tough one. She came toward my bare-assed backside with a syringe ready.

Fortunately, I turned to face her in time.

Giving her a tight smile, I spread my hands wide. "If you want to go for a ride like your friend, here, I'm ready."

Snarling and breathing in little puffs, she stood indecisively. "You murdered Jake!" she said. "I'll kill you for that, I swear…"

"Now, now," I said. "No one has murdered anyone. He's just been recycled. Maybe he was feeling poorly."

"What the fuck are you talking about, you—?"

"Listen," I said in a reasonable tone. "I know all about what you've done for Turov. I know *everything*. But I'm not talking. Not in this lifetime, or my next. Can't you do me the same favor?"

She blinked. Her brain was starting to process again. She was slipping out of her fight-or-flight mode and back into rational higher functioning. It was a good thing to see. I'd already had enough of killing today.

"We'll stay quiet," she said at last. "We'll all stay quiet."

"What about him?" I said, nodding toward the recycler.

Her lip curled. "He tripped and fell into the blades. Could have happened to anyone."

"Accidents are terrible things," I agreed. "Now, if you'll excuse me, miss."

She stepped back, giving me a wide berth as I sauntered by and pulled on some clothing.

"Who are you, anyway?" she asked when I reached the door.

"I'm a legionnaire, miss."

"I know that, fool. What legion?"

I gave her a little smile. "Varus."

She nodded as if confirming a dark suspicion. "Of course... I should have known."

My exit from Blue Deck went smoothly after that. She didn't ask any more questions or make any more threats. Sometimes, it helped to come from a legion with a bad rep. People tended not to mess with you as much.

To my surprise, I found I wasn't on Blue Deck aboard *Legate.* Likewise, I wasn't on my legion's target planet, or even inside the echoing, endless halls of Central.

At least I *was* on Earth. I'd been revived at a military outpost in Central America sector.

I was sure Turov had her reasons for bringing me to life down in Old Mexico City, but I barely cared what the story was. I was just happy to be alive again.

My escape from the Core Worlds had been a dangerous one. My excuse had been thin, my murder of Xlur blatant, and even my return to life had been eventful.

When I walked safely out of the local Hegemony Center, an institution which served this region as a local headquarters and recruitment station, I attempted to contact Turov. Maybe the legion had finished the mission out at M244-H, or they'd returned early for some reason.

Now, I can't say that I expected to get to see her beaming face appear on my tapper screen with inviting eyes and scant clothing—but I'd at least expected her to answer the call.

She didn't. She bumped me straight to voicemail, like I was some kind of sales AI.

Could that mean she was still off-planet? Then why had she revived me back on Earth?

"Uh…" I said, talking to her social bot. I left a dumb-sounding recording. "I'm back. Thanks for the revive. I'll head back to Central—I guess…"

Heading to the nearest sky-train station, I bought a ticket at the gates with a flick of my tapper and found a seat. Crying babies, people with their belongings in sacks—it wasn't the best way to travel long distance, but it was the cheapest.

Falling asleep on the flight, I found the bright light of morning digging into my eyes as we dropped out of low orbit and made landfall over Central City.

For some reason, my proximity to the city triggered several events. I'd often suspected people kept tabs on me with grid-alerts, and this just about proved it. As soon as I came close to the city, they used my tapper against me—to alert them as to my whereabouts.

In this case, I got a personal call from Winslade.

Now, good old Winslade had been out of Legion Varus for months. He'd taken a cush job with Hegemony, and he hadn't looked back. Probably that was for the best, as he hadn't been a crack officer during his tenure with Varus, anyway.

"McGill…" he said, looking out of my tapper at me. He said my name like it meant "stench" or something else unpleasant.

"That's right, sir," I said. "How're tricks dirt-side? What's it like being a hog at last?"

His face twisted a notch. He normally looked kind of pinched and rodent-like anyway, but when I called him a hog, he became extra sour.

"Enough with the insults, McGill. You're AWOL."

"Um… I didn't know that. I've been off-world, but I was serving my legion faithfully up to the last moment."

"It's been that long since you've been breathing, hmm…?" he mused. He looked aside, as if checking some data. "My goodness... you've been abroad for… four *months*? Why is it the data core lists you as being aboard the transport *Legate* when it took off?"

"Uh…" I said, thinking hard.

The trouble was, not even *I* knew why I wasn't aboard *Legate* right now. For some strange reason, that made it harder to lie. How was a man supposed to fabricate a new reality if he didn't even know what had actually happened?

"You see, sir," I began, "the story goes like this—"

He never even let me get on with my cock-and-bull tale of woe and heroics.

"Stuff it, McGill," he said. "I don't care to hear it, whether it's lies or truth. Just get to Central. We'll sort it out."

Warily, I landed at the spaceport and made my way to the big building that formed the axis of the city. When I got to the elevator, I tried to punch up Winslade's floor, but it wouldn't let me.

Instead, every floor I was authorized to visit seemed to be far underground. Those floor-level numbers… there was only one thing down that far. The secret labs?

Touching the first one on the list, I began to plunge into the Earth.

I soon felt a tickle of sweat inside my tunic. Historically, I hadn't had the best of experiences down here on the most secretive levels of Central.

When I arrived, I was greeted by Winslade with a team of hogs at his back. The hogs were armed, and they had their guns trained on me the moment the elevator doors yawned open.

"So good of you to join us, Centurion," Winslade said. "This way, please."

Marching with a color-guard of hogs surrounding me, I began to whistle a tune.

"What is that annoying racket, McGill?"

"I think it's called: *The Battle Hymn of the Republic*, sir."

He gave me a strange glance. "Isn't that an illegal tune?"

I shrugged.

Sighing explosively and shaking his head, he led the way to a caged set of gateway posts.

"Uh…" I said, looking them over. "Do those go somewhere, sir?"

"You'd better hope they do, because you're walking through them. I'm kicking you out of my hair, and out of my life, McGill. Hopefully forever."

I eyed the gateway posts. They were lit, and they seemed to be actively resonating with some distant matching target.

Modern travel took many forms. We had starships, of course, most of which were driven by the Alcubierre warp drive. In addition to that, we had teleporting suits and one other device: gateway posts. When you walked between them, they instantly transmitted your existence somewhere else.

That was all fine and dandy, but what concerned me was the unknown nature of gateways such as this one. When you first set one up, there was no way to know for certain what was on the other side—other than to step through and take your chances.

Winslade and his hogs watched me expectantly. So, I stood up straight and tall. I wasn't going to have them telling everyone how I'd chickened at the sight of some possibly ungrounded gateways.

"These go to *Legate* then, right?"

"Actually," Winslade said, "your transport made planetfall over Storm World a month back. You'll probably arrive at some pathetic bubble-tent being lashed by the endless rain and wind."

"Any more news or advice you can give me, sir?"

"Certainly. Watch out for the amphibians. By all accounts, they're more likely to give you a rotting disease than the Wur themselves."

"That doesn't sound too encouraging…"

He laughed. "What's the matter, McGill? Are you chicken?"

I glanced at him, and for a few seconds, I entertained grabbing him by the neck and dragging him through the posts with me. Dark places always seemed brighter when you brought along a friend.

But in the end I didn't do it. Instead, I waved and marched between the glimmering, vibrating posts alone.

After all, I really didn't want an angry Winslade coming along on this trip. In fact, I didn't want any kind of Winslade. None at all.

# -24-

Tumbling through space-time was as unpleasant an experience as it always was. But moments later I stepped out into a chamber.

I knew several things right off, the minute I got there. For one, I hadn't been expected.

The guards, who consisted of two heavy troopers slumped against one wall, snapped to attention. They crunched forward, their guns lowered to my chest-level and their lumpy faces deadly serious.

For another, I was on an alien planet. The gravity was light—probably two thirds that of Earth. What's more, the air was dank, kind of like my swamp back home.

"Hello troops," I said. "I'm Centurion McGill, Legion Varus. Where's your commanding officer?"

The two hulking near-humans froze. They'd looked like they'd been intent on killing me at first—but I'd slowed them down with that wall of words. Blood-Worlder troops weren't generally geniuses. They were slow, deliberate, loyal—all of that, yes—but morons, mostly.

"The McGill?" the one on the left rumbled.

I rewarded him with a smile. "That's right. The man who once stood as the proud hero of all Blood World."

They looked at each other again, then they both began to side-step, stomping slowly from one foot to the other. They swayed back and forth in a solemn fashion. I knew from experience that meant they were doing some hard thinking.

"The sub-centurion," the one on the left spoke again. "That way."

He pointed his long, tree trunk-thick arm toward the only door.

I touched my cap and marched smartly toward the door.

A gunshot rang out. A chip the size of a cue ball appeared in the door jamb. That was impressive, as the entire wall was made of rough puff-crete. We were clearly inside a bunker of some kind.

Pausing, I turned around, nice and slow. "Is there a problem, boys?"

The one on the right spoke this time, impressing me. "No one supposed to use the gateway."

I glanced back at the humming posts. "No, no," I said. "You're supposed to stop people from *leaving* here—using the gateway to desert. I'm returning to the field. I've just come from Earth with important news for Tribune Turov."

More frowns and stumping from side-to-side. They weren't all that good at English, despite years of training. It took them a long time to puzzle out sentences that were more than three words long.

That was my fault, really. I should have dumbed it all down about six notches, but I'd been surprised by just about everything lately, and I wasn't yet at the top of my game.

Grinning like an idiot, I stared and waited for them to make a decision.

"The McGill should go, then," said the one on the right at last.

Turning slowly and taking cautious steps, I moved to the door and pushed it open. All the while my neck was craned back over my shoulder to watch them. If either one got the bright idea to take another potshot at me, I didn't want to be surprised.

Neither man moved. They just watched me go.

Once out in the hallway, I breathed a sigh of relief. Unfortunately, my mood crashed down again when I saw where I was.

The hall was wide. *Way* too wide. And the ceiling—that was twice as high as it needed to be.

Then I saw the marching troops, and I knew: I was in the camp of the Blood Worlder legion. This was their territory, and this entire bunker had been hollowed out in dimensions meant to fit their outsized bodies.

Slavers, heavy troopers, groups of hopping gremlins—they were all here. The place was a regular hive of near-humans.

Not having a clue where I was going, I marched off to the left at a smart pace. When caught in enemy territory, always appear decisive. Never hesitate or give any other sign that you don't belong.

It worked at first. I made it about a hundred steps down the central hallway before anyone did more than give me a puzzled glance.

Finally, however, a voice burbled words at me.

I could hear the alien words, which sounded like the garbled voice of a drowned man, then the translation box kicked in.

"Centurion? Why are you in our bivouac?"

Spinning around on one heel, I confronted the creature who had addressed me. It turned out to be a squid.

Checking his rank, I saw he was a sub-centurion. That was good, because it meant I cleanly out ranked him. Blood Worlders were subservient to Earth troops in our army.

"Sub-Centurion," I said. "Your name wouldn't happen to be Bubbles, would it?"

He *looked* like Bubbles to me, a squid I knew pretty well—but then, almost all squids looked alike to human eyes.

"No sir. I'm Sub-Centurion Churn."

"Ah, okay. Nice to meet you. Now, if you'd show me the way to Legion Varus headquarters, I'll be on my way."

He gave me an odd look. "There is no path to such a place."

"Why not?"

"The sea is between this rock, and that rock, for at least another ten hours."

"I understand," I said, and I meant it.

Storm World, as people were apparently referring to this turbulent rock, experienced almost continuous atmospheric disruptions. With several extra moons, the climate was continuously stirred up to a violent degree. Tides weren't just low and high, when moons combined their gravitational tug, they became near tsunamis.

The winds, too… Listening for a second, I thought I could hear a howling sound outside. Could that be the wind? I felt, with a sinking sensation, that the odds were high that it was.

"Then why did you ask such a foolish question?" Churn demanded.

That was just the kind of asshole thing any squid would say. They liked catching you in any tiny twist of the facts. They had no concept of saving face, or politeness. It just wasn't in them.

Instead, they seemed to get a charge out of proving others to be wrong—wrong about damned-well anything at all. Nothing gave a squid a hard-on quicker than calling you out on something stupid you'd done.

But I wasn't in the mood for that game.

"Sub-Centurion Churn!" I barked out. "Come to attention!"

Surprised, he did so.

I walked around him in a circle twice, taking every step slowly.

"Eyes front!" I ordered.

He'd been following me with all eight of his orbs.

He looked a little puzzled, but he did it.

Squids had to be dominated. They were like mean dogs. Either you were the alpha, or they were. Nobody was on an even playing field. Everyone was somebody's master, and somebody else's slave in their society.

"That's better," I said. "I'd heard discipline was very lax here in this legion."

"That's untrue," the squid complained. "We are very—"

"Quiet! You haven't been given permission to speak."

He shut up. I proceeded to tell him what a piece of livid shit he and his entire unit were thought to be by Legion Varus brass. He looked alarmed, but he held his drippy blue tongue still.

As my lie took over my thinking, the story quickly expanded. I was here to inspect the Blood World legion. It was, of course, a surprise inspection, and Churn himself was under a dark cloud of suspicion for slovenly behavior.

At last, I let him talk. He complained a bit, then I cut him off and chewed on him some more.

By the end of it, the squid was cowed. That's how you had to treat them, or they'd walk all over you every time.

"Permission to speak freely, sir?" he asked when I'd finished ranting at his expense.

"Granted."

"Are you the human who killed so many of our troops during our exercise aboard *Legate*?"

"Uh..." I said. "Yes. Yes, that was me. I'm a harsh man."

"You are a murderous tyrant. Therefore, I respect you."

I glanced at him, and I figured he was deadly serious. Killing great numbers of his troops in a mock battle—that was cool, according to squid thinking.

"I'm surprised you survived," I said. "If I'd seen you, Churn, I would have killed you myself."

"I have no doubt of it. I now understand better why these simpletons still revere the name of McGill."

"They do?"

"Absolutely. They speak of their planet's hero with awe, fear and respect. They do not understand why you left them, but they still believe you are their conqueror."

I felt a twinge of guilt to hear his words. After all, I'd beaten their world in a series of trials by combat, winning their loyalty. But then... I'd gotten bored with their nasty desert planet real quick and gone home.

"That's good," I said. "Adulation pleases me."

"As it would please any thinking being."

"Listen, Churn, when the weather breaks, or the path to walk home opens, I want you to guide me back to Legion Varus."

"That would be most irregular."

"Do you have a sub-primus that needs convincing?"

He did. I had him lead me to his commander, who turned out to be a human. That surprised me a little, but I guess it shouldn't. The whole legion couldn't be made up of a giant stack of aliens. How would they stay loyal to Earth if it did?

What I found even more surprising was the man who was running things. He was known to me.

It was Primus Fike of the Iron Eagles.

I'd first met Primus Fike back on Dark World. He'd been serving under Deech back then, and he'd been one arrogant SOB.

Today, he looked a lot younger. He'd died back on Dark World while I was watching. I guess he hadn't died for a long time before that, because he was at least a decade younger today.

"By damn!" I said. "Primus Fike? As I live and breathe, sir! I haven't seen you since we fought the good fight back on the orbital factory together."

"Speak for yourself, McGill," he said sourly. "I found nothing about that battle to be satisfying."

"Just so, sir. Just so. But look at you! You've lost a lot of years, sir. A *lot* of years. You can't be unhappy about that."

Apparently, he was unhappy. He gave me a sour stare. "Is there something this sub-legion can do for Varus?"

"Uh… sure. I need to get back to my unit, sir. I want to do so at the first opportunity. As I understand it, the tides and the storms should break in another eight hours or so. I'd like to quickly rejoin my comrades then."

"Impossible. You're not even supposed to be here on my turf. I don't get why you're here—and knowing Turov, I probably want to keep it that way."

"Um… why would it be impossible, sir?"

"Because we never get a break on this shit planet, McGill!" he snapped. "If it's not a storm, then it's a tide. And if it's neither of those, the enemy attacks our walls. We're in a state of continual siege. You wouldn't know it by the way we're all hunkered down in this hole, but we are. The moment the conditions are right, the enemy will attack again."

"Hmm…" I said. "Well then, how am I supposed to get back to my unit, sir?"

While we'd been talking, Primus Fike took out a pistol and screwed on the barrel slowly. He aimed it at me.

He gave me a little grin. "I'll take care of that personally."

Then, the bastard shot me.

# -25-

I was revived in a crappy bunker about fifty kilometers away in another compound. Needless to say, I found Fike's "decommissioning" and "sudden transfer" process extremely rude. Accordingly, I came out of Blue Bunker in a sour mood.

Locating 3rd unit's module, I was greeted by an enthusiastic throng. Leeson seemed happiest of them all.

"Glad to see you're back, Centurion," he said, pummeling me on the shoulder.

Despite my frown, I almost smiled to see how excited Leeson was. As my senior adjunct, he'd taken over as unit commander in my absence—but he'd never been all that comfortable in the role. He didn't mind the mid-manager job of being an adjunct, but a centurion? At that level, you really had to think for yourself.

Taking in a deep breath, I tried to let go of all my pent-up, pissed-off feelings toward Fike.

"It's good to be back with 3rd unit," I managed to say in an even tone.

"Where have you been all this time, Centurion?" Harris asked. "If you don't mind my asking in public…?"

Harris had that suspicious-dog look on his face. He probably figured I'd wangled a vacation of some kind.

Pondering the nature of my response for a few moments, I came up with an angle and ran with it.

"I've just come from the Blood Worlder camp. Primus Fike decided I was needed here… so here I am."

"What?" Leeson demanded. "You mean he offed you just to get a Varus man out of his hair? That's rude. Uncalled for."

"That depends," Harris said.

"On what?"

"On what said Varus man did to deserve it."

A chuckle ran through the group. That put me right back into my sour mood. I could see what was happening. My long absence, unavoidable though it may have been, had eroded respect in my unit for their rightful centurion.

What's more, Harris seemed to be leading the charge on undercutting me. Adjunct Barton, at least, had the good graces to keep her mouth shut. Every time a critical moment came up, she'd been playing it straight. I was beginning to like the woman, and I was also beginning to appreciate what it must feel like to command a group of pros from Victrix who didn't mouth-off all the time.

"At storm-break," I announced. "We're going on patrol."

"What? You mean outside the walls?" Harris asked me.

"That's what I said."

"Dammit. Uh… sir, did you anger Turov as well as Fike…?"

"Put a sock in it, Adjunct."

He shut up at last. His giggle-partners shut up as well. Being experienced Varus troops, they knew exactly the *wrong* time to piss off your commander was before a dangerous patrol. Unpopular soldiers tended to get dangerous assignments on hostile planets like this one—and they often didn't make it back to their bunks at the end of the day.

As the group broke up, I pulled my favorite noncom aside. "Veteran Moller," I said, "I'm reassigning you to Barton's light platoon."

Moller looked surprised. She was the most barrel-chested woman I'd ever served with. She was competent, quiet, and dedicated. Even so, I could tell she wasn't happy to be joining the platoon with the lowest probability of survival in the unit.

"Did my dog shit on your lawn, sir?" she asked.

"No, no. To the contrary. I want Barton to have the best support I can give her."

Moller nodded resignedly. "Understood."

She stumped off to talk to Barton. While she did so, I worked my tapper.

I'd decided it was time to confess to Turov that I was breathing again. I'd been avoiding reporting in, if only because my last experience with her hadn't been completely positive. More importantly, I couldn't know for sure if my little venture to the core of the galaxy had sent shockwaves all the way back to the frontier. Hopefully, no one would ever investigate Xlur's death and follow the trail back to Earth.

Turov picked up right away.

"McGill? You're here on this godforsaken rock?"

"Yes, sir. And for the record, I'm not a man who minds a little rain now and then."

"No..." she said, "considering where you live on Earth, I guess that's clear. Well, come to my office. Immediately."

I glanced around uncomfortably. My officers were glancing my way too. Clearly, they expected to talk to me in private. I was sure that there was plenty of politics and dirt to catch up on with all of them.

"Uh... all right, sir. I'll be right there."

There were a lot of eyes on my back as I walked out. At the module doors, I turned back to face them.

"Remember," I said with a stern expression. "We're out of here at the first ray of sunshine. Pack-up, gear-up and be ready."

They got moving then, and I felt glad I'd left them with something to do.

Naturally, there hadn't been any orders to go on patrol when the storm broke. I'd invented that detail. But the fabrication had worked wonders. They all had a task to perform, something to fear and worry about that was coming at us within hours. They were moving quickly and with purpose.

Leaving the module, I had to smile. A unit *needed* a centurion. They just never felt good without that single individual on hand to keep them all on target—even if the target was imaginary.

After checking my tapper a few times, I hunted down Turov's office. It was in a separate bunker across the compound. At the stairway that led up to the bunker doors, I was stopped by an armored specialist who laid a hand on me.

"Sir?" he asked me. "Where are you going?"

Now, as an officer, I wasn't accustomed to being grabbed by specialists. I yanked out of his grip. "I've been ordered to report to Gold Bunker—if that's any business of yours."

"Well sir, it's not, but you might not want to walk out there on the surface right now. It's not safe."

My eyes slid off the noncom and up toward the puff-crete stairs. At the top, I saw the heavy doors. They were shut and sealed, but as I watched, they shivered with a powerful gust of wind.

I frowned. I couldn't recall *ever* having seen bunker doors affected by winds. Just how bad were the storms on this particular shit-bucket of a world?

"Uh…" I said. "What's the wind speed out there?"

"A steady hundred kilometers an hour right now," he answered brightly. "Technically, that's not even a hurricane-force wind. But it can gust up on you. We've tracked wind speeds of over two hundred earlier today."

"Huh…" I said. "Is there another way to get from here to Gold Bunker?"

"Nope. Most of the bunkers are connected with tunnels—but not that one. The brass voted to keep themselves off the tunnel grid. That's because of the scuppers, of course."

"Um… how's that? Scuppers?"

The noncom was frowning at me now. "Are you feeling all right, sir?" he asked. "It's like you have amnesia or something."

I drew back my shoulders and straightened my spine. "I'm fine, Specialist. Thanks for asking. Now, open those doors. I've got orders from the tribune herself to report immediately."

"Right sir," he said, shaking his head. "But take it easy. Even in armor, it's dangerous."

The moment they released the outer locks both the doors began to lift and flap. Between the two bouncing steel doors, I could see a gray light. Splattered rain flew through the crack in silvery strings.

The doors flapped and drooled like the jaws of a rabid dog. I hesitated for about two seconds, but then I steeled myself. After all, the two guards were watching me.

Moving with purpose, I marched up the steps and pushed my way out into a howling maelstrom.

# -26-

Marching through the storm was a daunting experience. The winds were fierce, driving against me like I was a leaf in a gale. Leaning into it, I headed toward Gold Bunker. Mud whipped up into my face and got all down into my suit—despite my having sealed most of it.

I could have gone back and put on an exoskeletal unit, of course, and powered right through it. But I didn't feel like limping back to my module and commandeering a power suit. Doing that would have made people laugh. After all, they all knew how rough the storms were.

Why was I taking this difficult path? Sheer stubbornness, plus a desire to avoid embarrassment. I'd been left out of the first half of this shitty campaign, and I didn't want to look green in front of my troops.

So, I toughed it out. Fighting the blasting storm, I focused on putting one foot ahead of the other. My universe was reduced to my immediate surroundings. I kept telling myself to keep my head down, lean into the wind, and keep marching…

Then a reversal came. It was a shock. The wind that had been blowing directly into my face shifted. Instead of propping me up as I leaned into it, the wind now angled from the right, and it knocked me off my feet.

A big, wet, silvery hand of water and wind slashed in and I slipped down to one knee. I threw out my hands, feeling them sink deep into mud. With a grunt and several loud curses, I pulled my arm out of a sinkhole. I tasted blood in my mouth—

maybe I'd bit something. Cursing some more, I got back to my feet and began marching again at a new angle.

This time I moved more warily, as I realized the wind was tricky. It could switch on you without warning.

Twice more the fickle winds switched angles and velocities—but I never fell again. I was getting the hang of it.

Hammering on the steel doors of Gold Bunker, I got no immediate response. Growling, I unlocked them manually and threw both leaves wide.

The doors clanged onto the puff-crete walls, ringing like two church bells. The stairway had two surprised-looking noncoms at the bottom. Without asking permission, I stumped down toward them. A small wave of water came with me, along with at least a hundred liters of mud.

The two veterans rushed up the steps, reaching out their hands. They grabbed either arm.

I think they meant well, in retrospect. I really do. They were probably just trying to help me out, a man staggering out of a bad storm.

But I was in a rather bad mood by this time, so I shoved them both away. They stumbled into the walls of the bunker.

"I'm fine," I said. "I'm Centurion McGill, here to see the tribune."

"Um… that way, sir. Hang a left at the second intersection."

Marching onward, I ignored the mud, grime, dripping silt and large limp leaves that had accumulated on my kit during the crossing. They fell off and stained the floor behind me.

After being ushered into the tribune's office, I pulled off my mask and hood. Another gush of water and mud splashed the carpet.

Carpet? I was amazed. Turov liked the good life, even when she took to the field with the rest of the legion, but it seemed to me that a carpet didn't belong on Storm World. Not even in the driest room on the planet.

"Centurion McGill reporting, sir," I said loudly.

Turov glanced at me, and to my pleasant surprise, she gave me a neutral smile.

Around a conference table sat a number of officers. They all held the rank of primus, which was one level above mine. Each of them commanded ten units like mine.

My immediate supervisor, Primus Graves, was in the room. He sat at Turov's side. He was her senior officer, second in command of the entire legion.

Unlike Turov, however, he wasn't smiling at me.

"McGill," he said. "You should have worn powered armor. The storms are dangerous on this planet."

"Nah," I said. "Just a little rain."

Turov's face brightened further. "You see?" she demanded of the others, looking from one to the next. "This man rushed right to my side without hesitation. He isn't interested in creature comforts, or fearful of stepping in a mud puddle."

The rest of the officers looked sour. They fidgeted. I got the feeling I'd helped win an argument for Turov.

Graves didn't change his expression, however. Not one iota.

"We're not talking about toughness and willingness to obey, Tribune. We're talking about safety and—"

"Silence!" Turov said. "I've heard enough defeatist talk. We can't fight only when the skies clear. If we continue to do that, we'll be here for years."

Graves glanced at her sourly. I knew he didn't like being accused of being defeatist—but he didn't like to argue with his commander either. That wasn't his way.

"We must attack the moment the winds drop below gale force," Turov continued. "We're not delaying a minute longer. There will *never* be a clear day on this miserable planet. Waiting around for it will only allow the enemy to gather more strength."

"I feel it necessary," Graves said, "to warn you as I've done before: the enemy are far better adapted to these conditions than we are. After all, they're plant-based."

"Too bad. Each of you must give me at least one able unit. These units will march at first light tomorrow. The weather will be sufferable by then, according to AI predictions."

At this point, I slowly raised my gauntlet. As I did so, a shower of muddy droplets fell onto the carpet, but Turov didn't seem upset about that.

"Sirs?" I asked. "I'd like to volunteer for this patrol duty. My troops are bored sitting around in their bunker. Besides, it's not all that bad out there."

"A volunteer!" Turov said, beaming. "Do I hear another?"

A few of the officers offered up units of their own. She made notes, then quickly "volunteered" one unit from each of the cohorts that hadn't spoken up.

"At first light, you will all choose a patrol path. McGill gets first pick. You'll march out into the jungle and loop around, returning with news of any contact you make. Don't go more than ten kilometers from the walls. That's it then. You're all dismissed—except for you, McGill."

There were a lot of muttered words and a few grunts—but they didn't argue. They all knew it wouldn't do them any good to grumble and moan aloud. Instead, they stood and marched off into the passageways, already working their tappers to pass along the unwelcome news.

After that, I knew they'd go off to the officers' mess and bitch about Turov over a drink. They'd do their complaining privately, to each other.

As they filed out past me, one of them flipped me off. I touched my soaked cap in return.

When they'd gone, I felt small hands touch my back.

"You know," she said. "Any other day, any other time, I'd cut off your parts for this stunt. You do realize that, don't you?"

"Of course," I lied. I had no idea what she was talking about.

Her finger pointed downward, and I followed the gesture.

"My carpet is ruined, but… I think it was worth it. Your example humiliated all my other officers, as I'd hoped."

"You knew I would march here despite the storm?"

"Of course. You were hoping for a sexual greeting, right?"

"Uh…"

"Besides, I know you anyway, James. You're just the kind to ignore a tiny hardship like a storm on Storm World. What

I'm uncertain about was this business of tracking mud in here. Was that for dramatic effect? Did you realize I wanted you to make a grand entrance?"

The truth was I'd been annoyed with her summons in the rain, and so I'd decided to stomp off some of that fresh mud I'd accumulated inside her office. But it wouldn't do to admit that now, so I went with another approach.

"Primus Fike mentioned it," I said.

"He did...? When did you speak to…? Oh yes, the gateway goes to his bunker. It's set up there to allow reinforcements to arrive directly from Blood World."

"That's right. He's a friendly fellow, that Fike. He told me all about your troubles here with Varus."

She flashed her eyes dangerously. Her hands left my drippy form and slid to her own hips, where they formed fists.

"Oh really? What else did he say?"

"It was just a short briefing, really. Something about limited command skills, lack of authority… Oh, and a general problem with unpopularity—that coupled with running the worst troops in the cosmos. Something like that."

Galina's expression had shifted dramatically as I spoke.

"That slippery bastard," she said. "He's so polite when he speaks to me. He must still be pining away for Deech, his past commander. She ditched him, you know, after that disastrous attack he led back on Dark World. You remember that, don't you? He marched four units to utter destruction right past your encampment."

"How could I forget? He told us he'd show us how things were done… but he sure did make a mess of it."

I laughed, and Galina softened.

"In any case, I'm glad you're back. You did well. I got a message from Xlur over a month ago. I was very worried when you left that you'd deleted the book."

"I managed to get that back for him," I lied with a cheery smile.

"Yes, I assumed that. Afterward, I couldn't revive you here directly—the entire affair was illegal, from top to bottom. To cover the trail, I brought you back on Earth, then had you transferred here in steps."

I grimaced. On several of those steps, I'd died—but there was no point in complaining about that now.

"It's good to see you again, too, sir."

Saying these words, I began to take liberties. After all, I felt I'd earned them. How many men have died a half-dozen times to return to the woman who'd murdered him in the first place?

My hands shucked off my gauntlets, which slapped down onto her wet carpet. Then, they snaked forward, reaching for her waist.

She danced back a step, giving me a tiny frown. "Not so fast. Tell me about the Core Worlds. What was it like?"

Reaching for my tapper, I brought up an edited file. It had only a few highlights such as my view from the high windows of the revival room, and my march across the passages inside the city. With a flick of a finger, I passed the recording from my tapper to hers.

She began to watch, fascinated.

"It's so… normal. I see advancement, but I don't see fantastic wealth and displays of glory. Don't they have monuments? Statues?"

"I didn't see the whole planet," I admitted. "But what I did see gave me the impression that the Mogwa are a practical people. What's more, Xlur told me there were around three trillion of them on Mogwa Prime. I guess that doesn't leave them much room for monuments and such-like."

Her eyes came up to stare at me, and they were huge. "Three *trillion*?" she gasped.

"That's what he said."

"And thousands upon thousands of planets they must inhabit. We're a microscopic species by comparison."

"No… not exactly. He also said most of the Mogwa species lives on Prime. They don't like to live anywhere else. They consider governorships like the one he's been serving out here in Province 921 to be a form of exile."

"Really…? That's fascinating… There's so much information here to take in, McGill! I'll have to use backchannels to get these files to key people at Central. I'll tell them I've slipped a spy into the capital. That will put fear in their bellies. I'll demand favors…"

She was walking away from me now, and I caught sight of her tight outfit. She hadn't lost any of her charms. In fact, she'd improved things somewhat. She'd reshaped her hips a little and probably stored a new body scan to make the fix permanent.

"You've still got it, Galina," I said aloud.

Almost without conscious thought, I followed her and put my hands on her waist again. From behind, this time.

She allowed my touch. I could tell she was in a fog of grandiose thoughts. I could almost see the gears spinning inside her little head.

Shedding my jacket, I kissed her neck. She barely noticed, but she did tilt her face to one side enough to kiss me back.

Over her shoulder, I watched the vid I'd passed to her. She'd already transferred it onto her desktop. She played it again from the beginning, and the blue flickering light filled her face.

"This is amazing…" she said.

My hands moved over her, and although she never said another word, she never gave me a complaint, either. Not even when I slipped her out of her uniform.

All the while we made love, she gazed down at the sights and sounds of a true Core World. Most likely, she was only the second human in existence to have ever seen such amazing sights.

The images were forbidden fruit, and they worked their seductive magic. Entranced, she never stopped playing that vid. She paused it, expanded it, playing certain scenes over and over.

I didn't mind her distraction. I enjoyed myself thoroughly, and I thought that she did, too, in her own way.

## -27-

The next morning, dawn broke over a different world. The sky was still gray, the ground was still swampy—but the rain and wind had paused for now.

The doors creaked and clanged open, and I marched out of the bunker at the head of my unit. Behind me, the armored troops had the hardest time, squelching and sinking into the mud. I gave them permission to power up their exoskeletal support systems, which burned their batteries, but allowed them to move freely.

We left the puff-crete walls and marched out into the countryside. Two rocky outcroppings thrust up on either side of my unit. In between them, an overgrown bog stretched for a good three kilometers, according to my HUD. The region amounted to a gully, a spillway for floodwaters. Storm World was built for storms, it seemed. Every feature of the landscape had been eroded by eons of rough weather.

Harris came up to me. He spoke in low, earnest tones. "You don't want to march us into that bog, sir. A man might take fifty paces, then sink into oblivion one step farther out."

"Let's follow the higher ground then, to the left," I said, and I set off.

Behind me, a single field group marched. They strung out pretty quickly, as often happened in rugged terrain.

The dark rock and the green-crusted bog reminded me of the rough-hewn fjords of Norway. This planet was lovely and strange all at the same time.

Leeson was the next man to come puffing up to get my attention.

"Uh… Centurion McGill? Sir?"

"What is it, Leeson?"

"There's a forest ahead, sir."

"I'm well aware. It's on the map-app."

"Um…" he said, sounding stressed.

I stopped to look at him. Leeson wasn't a man who would bother his commander for no reason.

"Unit, halt!" Moller shouted back down the line without being told. She was good that way. She seemed to know what I was going to do next almost before I knew it myself.

"What's the problem, Adjunct?" I asked Leeson.

"Well, you see… the forest is where we'll find the Wur, Centurion. They've got some of those giant trees down there—plenty of pod-walkers and those weird spider-things, too."

He looked at me earnestly, and I considered his words. Nodding, I made a choice.

"Cooper!" I shouted. "Cooper, get up here!"

A light trooper with a slight build and a sour attitude came trotting up the line to join us.

"Centurion?"

I looked him over. "You still want some rank, Cooper?"

"Uh… I sure do, sir," he said warily. He looked interested, but not quite eager. Rank didn't come easily to junior troops in Legion Varus. The price tended to be high.

"Good," I said. "You're my man. Have you heard of the new specialist rank for recon?"

"Recon, sir?"

"That's right. They call them Ghosts."

"I didn't think Legion Varus…"

"They're quite new," I said. "We've got some new equipment we can issue to help out our scouts."

For once, I wasn't bullshitting. Legion Varus had undergone some changes. In the old days, we'd been designed to function as a complete outfit. These days, we were more likely to operate as a single legion in a much larger force. Instead of hiring out to alien princes, we were being used as elites to spearhead invasions.

We were still technically independent, however, and we had a rental price which was negotiated for each mission with Hegemony. I'd never paid that much attention to the economic side of Varus, but costs mattered. They always mattered.

"You see," I told Cooper. "The Blood Worlder legion we've been teamed up with has three times our weight in troops. They're the regulars now, and we're the spearhead of the army. Accordingly, there's more need for on-the-ground intel."

"Uh, sure… but can't we just use buzzers for that?"

"Buzzers don't have sniper rifles, Cooper. Buzzers don't plant mines, demo bridges or anything like that. What's more, if we give you a few buzzers, you'll reach farther into the field than any tiny drone can on its own."

"I get all that, sir, but I—"

I clamped a large gauntlet onto his shoulder and grinned. "This is where you come in, Cooper. I want you to be my first Ghost."

"That's sounds real nice, sir, but—"

"Look," I said, lowering my voice. "Let's be realistic about it. Do you think you're big enough to be a weaponeer?"

He looked startled. "Um, no. Not really sir."

"Right. How about a tech wizard? You got circuitry in your brain? You love gadgets?"

"Well… no. I get bored by computers very fast."

Already, he was looking down, staring at the mud and frowning. I had him on the hook, I could tell. All I had to do was reel him in.

"What about the medical fields? You think you want to run revival machines, clean bed-robots, learn to perform surgical—?"

"No way, Centurion! I'm a killer, not a meat-repairman."

"Exactly. So, let's be realistic. If you're ever going to advance in the ranks, you've got to become some kind of specialist."

He sighed. "Yeah… and I know you're trying to help me out, sir, but I've been ground up and shit back out of revival machines so many times already… I don't know if scouting—"

"Fine," I said gruffly, stepping away from him. I turned and scanned the group. "Sarah!" I boomed. "Sarah, come up here."

"Wait!" Cooper said.

I turned back to face him. "What?"

"I'll do it," he said. "I'll play bunny-rabbit."

"*Ghost*, Cooper. Get it right. You're a ghost in training now. Here's a sack of buzzers and a special rifle."

"Got it, sir."

He examined the equipment with interest. The one thing that caught his eye was the fold-out poncho that slid from a bag. It shimmered like a cloak of woven silver.

"Is this…?" he asked. "Oh, cool!"

Happily, he put on the stealth suit. It had been copied from captured Vulbite designs but tailored and redesigned to fit a human. With the suit on, he vanished from sight.

Sarah came trotting up with her blue eyes peering up at me under a fringe of blonde hair. Bright and eager, she reminded me of the indulgent thoughts I'd once had regarding her during a meeting in my office.

Managing to keep it professional, I made the same pitch to her about becoming a spook. Cooper watched closely while stealthed. Sarah ignored him—I don't think she even knew he was standing there with us.

But Sarah had different ideas. "I'm not cut out for that kind of work, sir. I passed my finals and I'm about to be promoted out of here as a bio specialist."

"Congratz," I said, and I meant it. "But… um… what if you don't like recycling folks?"

Sarah made a disgusted face.

"I'm not looking forward to that part," she admitted. "But this is the end of the line for me. If I hate my life as a bio… well, I'm going to ditch this legion entirely."

I nodded. "Good enough. I'm already looking forward to your tender mercies. But for now, go on back to your platoon… and Cooper? You're my bunny. Start hopping."

Making a vague gesture forward, I aimed a finger toward the massive trees.

A region of air moved and there was a slight flapping sound. Sarah looked startled. "Cooper has a stealth suit?"

"That's right," I said. "You want in as a Ghost after all?"

Sarah shook her head. "I'll stick to what I know."

I watched as she returned to the light platoon. Everyone else in the unit was staring at the rugged mountains and the looming forest of alien trees. Now that we'd gotten close, the mist had broken, and they could see the towering mega-flora.

"Holy shit…" Harris breathed.

"What?"

"We were out here, sir, not more than a week back. That forest—it's grown. It's grown a lot."

I nodded, unimpressed. "The enemy is comprised mainly of trees, Harris," I said. "Storm World just watered the hell out of them. What'd you expect?"

Hushed by the looming presence of the trees, my unit struggled forward. We soon left the hills of crumbling black stone and walked among the trees. The ground was much more firm here.

Could it be that these monstrous growths had sucked the water and nutrients from the land with such greed they'd changed a swamp into solid ground? Its effect seemed odd, but undeniable.

We found our first walker less than a kilometer deep into the forest. Cooper found it, actually. He reported in to say he'd spotted the monster, and he wanted to know what he should do about it.

"You think he sees you?" I asked.

"Probably not, sir," Cooper admitted in a whisper. "He looks fresh-born. He's just standing there, swaying as if confused."

Pod-walkers were akin to mobile trees. They had long limbs of brownish green and skin like wet bark. There were no eyes or a face, but there were fronds that hung from the body. These sickly-orange fronds ended in polyps that flopped and pulsated. They were sensory organs—bulbs of nerves that could sense light, heat and even sniff the air.

The walkers were born out of the gigantic mega-flora, which also resembled trees. These trees were hundreds of meters tall and grew very quickly. When threatened, they grew pods which contained the walkers to defend them.

"The Wur are true freaks," I said, paging through the stills and video Cooper was taking as he scouted the scene.

Suddenly, the pod-walker we'd been observing stirred. Instead of standing there with dangling orange fronds puffing and contracting, it turned its body.

A chill ran through me, despite the fact I was far from the scene. The walker had turned to face Cooper.

Could it have seen through his stealth gear? Of course it could have, I realized. The stealth suit was intended to disguise a man from human eyes, operating in the visual spectrum our species could see.

Walkers were an unknown. We weren't even sure whether they could see in the infrared or the ultraviolet—or really "see" at all. In a worst-case scenario, it might be able to detect a moving body in both those frequencies of light.

Wisely, Cooper had hit the dirt and stopped talking. I stayed quiet too, but he'd probably squelched my voice anyway. I was still getting an optical feed, however, from the sensors on his helmet.

Working my tapper, I transmitted the feed to Natasha. She'd recently rejoined my unit, and I was glad to have her back. She was the best tech I knew.

"This is amazing," her voice spoke in my ear. "I'm coming forward, sir."

I didn't object. I needed her input.

The Wur were possibly our worst potential enemies. They had, long ago, been the power behind the throne of the Cephalopods. They were everywhere, tucked away on small forgotten planets.

They operated like a disease that slept in the body until triggered. We suspected they were in several provinces of the Empire as well as the frontier regions. Often dormant, unseen and unchallenged, they waited until the time was ripe for an infestation.

But, for all their skill and frequency of appearance, they'd only attacked Earth once. We'd gone straight out to Death World afterward to return the favor. Perhaps because of our vehement counterstrike, they'd decided to leave us alone for decades.

They were masterful terraformers, seeding worlds previously thought uninhabitable. Most planets weren't even tracked inside the Empire itself—there were billions of them, after all. On those forgotten worlds, they dug in and made a habitat until that world was swollen and popped, spreading more of their spores into the cosmos.

Natasha arrived, and we knelt together, staring into the hanging mists between the gigantic trees. The forest was so dense, the trees so massive in size, it looked like a cave ahead of us. It didn't help that the skies above were crawling with clouds, blocking the sunlight.

"It's the Wur," she said. "It's been so long since I've seen them."

She shivered, and I put a hand on her arm. Natasha didn't have fond memories of the Wur. One version of her had been permed, in fact, by these creatures. Fortunately, another copy of her had lived in hiding on Dust World. I'd brought her home, and helped her keep Hegemony in the dark concerning the switch.

"One unit can't fight an army of these things, James," she said.

"There's only one pod-walker right now, and it's just staring at Cooper."

"There will be more."

As if she were the voice of a doom-laden prophesy, Cooper swung his head and the vid pickup caught another cracking motion. Another pod-walker, closer than the first, stepped out of its husk and stood there, swaying.

"Cooper," I said quietly. "Withdraw."

"It's too late," he whispered.

He shifted his point of view gently again, scanning the horizon around him. There were seven pods now. He was surrounded.

# -28-

It kind of pissed me off that I'd just gone out of my way to recruit Cooper, despite his concerns, and the damned pod-walkers had come for him less than an hour later.

"We'll distract them," I said. "Then you'll withdraw. Creep south, come around…"

"Thanks, Centurion," Cooper whispered back, and I knew he meant it.

Natasha's eyes caught mine, and she stared at me in alarm. "James, we shouldn't—"

"We should go back inside our walls and hide, yes, I know. Let the Wur eat Cooper—so what? Then tonight, maybe we'll get lucky enough to hide behind another storm. Then we can ignore what's going on out here in this forest for another day, or another week. Natasha, they're getting stronger every day. We've got to push back, or we're doomed."

She looked down and nodded. I wasn't sure if she agreed with me or not, but she wasn't going to argue. That was good enough for me.

I ordered my light troops to fan out and advance. If they could start sniping at the walkers, we could draw them off Cooper's tail and let him escape.

It was a risky move, of course. If there were only seven freshly-hatched pod-walkers, well, we could take down that many, no problem.

It was the unknowns in the forest that worried my troops. There might be ten more—or a thousand. It was hard to tell.

"I need intel. Kivi, Natasha, fly your buzzers everywhere. I don't care if they're spotted. Give me a count on the enemy."

They did as I'd ordered, and Barton's platoon of lights formed a widely-separated line that marched deep into the trees and the low-lying mists swallowed them up.

"Harris," I said, "take your heavies and advance in the second rank. Set your morph-rifles for maximum punch."

He looked at me for a long second. His eyes were wide, and I knew he thought I was crazy. But he just shook his head and signaled his armored troops to advance.

"Let me guess," Leeson said, coming up to crouch beside me. "My weaponeers are supposed to kill these things while everyone else does a dance to distract them, right?"

"That's about the size of it."

He sighed. "Where do you want me on this field?"

"You know your job. You stay in place—but don't sit back too far. The forward troops won't last long in close quarters."

Grunting, Leeson rallied his troops and they broke out special equipment. Belchers and two 88s were on hand. Leeson had insisted on dragging the light artillery on the backs of two pigs—walking drones—all the way out from the base. I realized now that might have been a critical move. It was hard to take out walkers with small arms.

If Cooper was good at one thing, it was sneaking around. Glancing at his feed on my tapper now and then, I saw the pod-walkers still hadn't nailed him.

They were moving, however. Roaming now and milling around the area, I could tell they were still a bit confused by their birth and not fully cognizant. They moved like zombies sniffing for a scent.

Cooper stayed low in a spot encircled by thick tree roots. I could see the intelligence of that. The pod-walkers weren't likely to find him, and even if they did, they wouldn't want to damage the root system of their parent trees in order to dig him out of his bolt-hole.

As I watched, I heard snap-rifle fire from the forest. Glancing up, then back at the tapper video, I saw one of the pod-walkers shiver.

More firing, followed by more reactions from the walkers.

“They’re taking the bait!” Leeson shouted. “McGill, pull the lights back! They’ve done their job.”

I checked out the data from a swarm of buzzers. He was right. The walkers had begun moving with purpose toward the stinging snap-rifle fire.

“Adjunct Barton,” I said, “time to skirmish. Keep pecking at them, but withdraw at a trot back to our lines.”

Like clockwork, I saw the light troops reverse themselves. Barton had excellent control. She’d been drilling her men night and day ever since we’d left Earth, and it was obviously paying off.

The walkers, however, were speeding up. They were moving with purpose now. Their massive legs, easily five meters tall, swung through the ferns and undergrowth, picking up speed.

I’d seen this sort of behavior before. The Wur underlings—moronic creatures like these pod-walkers—would often work themselves into a frenzy. They’d mass-up, forming a charging wave, and surge right over us.

“Harris, tuck your people into that root structure out there. Keep them separated, and wait to fire until the walkers are on top of you.”

“Permission to edit the plan, sir!” Harris barked back at me.

I winced. I’d made a point of letting the commander on the spot alter my orders. Since I was only a few hundred meters away from his position, it seemed like Harris was abusing my policy. Still, I decided to stick to my philosophy.

“Permission granted.”

He broke off and began shouting detailed orders to his platoon. In the meantime, I moved to where Leeson was setting up his two 88s.

The weaponeers had them off the pigs, and the tripods were quickly extended.

“Right here?” I asked him. “On open ground?”

“Yep,” Leeson said. “I want to get a clear field of fire. If Harris can ding them up, I can finish them with a kill zone right here. 88s don’t shoot through tree trunks as big as these, sir.”

“All right,” I said, shaking my head.

I could hear the Wur now. They were hooting, raising an odd, warbling cry from their upper bodies. To me, they looked like gigantic headless men.

Finding an extra belcher, I knelt and added my weight to our line. Our thin line was manned by white-faced troops. No one was joking around, not even Carlos.

About half our number had fought back on Death World. The rest had heard stories and watched training vids on the topic. The Wur were dangerous, if only because plants always seemed to be harder to kill than creatures of flesh and bone.

Soon, we could hear their footsteps. The sound swelled up and each step turned into a booming report.

Out on the front line, Harris had indeed edited my instructions. Instead of firing point-blank, he waited until the line of walkers had passed overhead. Then, in unison, his armored troops lit up the walkers, hitting them hard in the ass.

A series of whoops went up from my own side. Two of the creatures went down, thrashing. One got up, but the other was missing a leg entirely. It turned and crawled toward the attackers, dragging its injured body behind it.

Excited, Harris' troops advanced and pounded heavy shots into the ass end of any Wur they encountered.

The move was dramatic and powerful—but I felt it was premature.

"Harris, get your men to pull back. Keep your line hot and ready."

"They're mostly coming to you, sir," Harris objected. "There are just two here, and one of them is down already."

As I watched, the armored troops advanced on the Wur that crawled toward them. They fired their morph-rifles again and again. White patches appeared in the dark smooth bark that served it for skin. Bleeding sap and other less identifiable fluids, the walker shivered and thrashed about—but it kept crawling.

"Shit..." I said, watching events unfold rapidly. I didn't have time to argue with Harris. The main line of pod-walkers was about to sweep up and hit my light platoon at a dead run.

There's something about big creatures—truly, monstrously large creatures—when they charge at you, you can't help but feel a wave of fear.

I'm sure that somewhere in the back of my monkey-brain, some distant McGill ancestor had faced a charge like this. Maybe it had happened back when the world was young, when mastodons, saber-tooths, and a thousand other giants roamed the Earth.

They came so *fast*. Once a walker was committed to a charge, each step came more swiftly than the last. Already, they had to be running faster than a dog could run. Huge legs, each as deadly as a swinging tree trunk, brought them closer with shocking speed.

I almost gave the order to fire—but Leeson beat me to it.

"Begin sweeps! Merge center!"

Two beams leapt out to the far sides of the charging enemy line. There were only five of them, as two had been held up by Harris, but that felt like plenty.

The outer two monsters took the brunt of the 88s shocking power. Flash-fried, they were turned into running torches. The orange fronds melted away. Like nests of frenzied snakes, these sensitive organs tried to withdraw into their host bodies, but it was hopeless. They were vaporized in a split-second.

The torsos were tougher. They burned, yes, but they didn't disintegrate the way a smaller mass would. Men, when touched by these awful weapons, were struck dead immediately.

Still, the outer two went down hard. They pitched forward, thrashing and flailing. Berserk with agony and blinded, they tumbled and shook the ground. More weaponeers working belchers lanced their bodies repeatedly, trying to finish them.

The 88s were on a sweep, and they converged toward the center from each side. The second two were caught next, and they were taken out as well. If anything, they died faster. Maybe that was because we were at shorter range and the hot beams from the 88s hit that much harder.

The last pod-walker, however, was just moving too fast. Leeson and I had both miscalculated. The walkers had been accelerating, and the two converging beams didn't make it to the center walker before he got to us.

The monster didn't even bother to halt. It crashed right into our lines, wildly smashing the 88s that had so tortured his brothers. In one hand, a stocky figure was snatched up and hurled to the ground again with fantastic force.

I could sense the anger in that throw, the rage. The killed gunner bounced a few meters into the air, flopping and thumping down near me.

It was Sargon, and he was deader than yesterday.

# -29-

One might wonder what in the nine hells I'd been up to until this point. Well, I wasn't asleep at the switch. I'd been holding my fire for the right moment.

When facing the Wur, I'd learned a well-timed, well-placed bolt of energy was far better than a thousand pin-pricks. When you fought one of these abominations, you were either going to kill it, or you were going to get busted up and die. So, it was best to choose your moment wisely.

Around me, my troops scattered, naturally giving ground. The towering figure in our midst, easily twelve meters in height, was hard at work. He stooped, bending at the waist, and grabbed up a fleeing man with either hand. Bringing the two together, he smashed their heads to pulp. Bits of helmet, brains and gore flew down in a rain that made the leafy undergrowth patter.

With the aperture open about a quarter-turn, I nailed the sensory fronds on its right side first. They burned like dry grass hit by a blowtorch.

The Wur shivered, and the fronds on the left side were sucked up into its body. I tried to nail them as well, burning a streak across the trunk—but I didn't get there in time to blind it completely.

"Shit," I said.

Several other weaponeers were joining me now, firing from multiple directions. What's more, Harris was leading his armored troops back toward my position. Even Barton was getting in the game, showering the surviving beast with snap-rifle fire.

Small-arms couldn't do much against a walking tree, but they could distract and madden it, giving those with heavier gear a chance to finish the job.

In the end, the Wur was left crawling. One arm was blown off, and it couldn't walk, but it was still dragging itself around the field of battle, making grasping motions. Snap rifles had shredded what was left of those weird sensory organs when they had reappeared.

Blinded and dying, it managed to crush one more light trooper who'd gotten too close and overconfident before it too, died like the rest.

After it was over, my unit began hollering. I let them, as it had been a good fight, and we'd won in the end.

Reporting in to Graves, who was running all the patrols, I relayed my after-action-report and uploaded all my data back to camp. A few minutes later, he called me personally.

"Grandstanding again, McGill?" he asked.

"Whooping tail, sir!" I said.

Carlos slapped me on the back as he went by. "That was cool. Hardly any wounded to worry about, either."

I grinned at him. Carlos was a bio, and he loved battles where people either died or survived unhurt. That kept him from having to do a damned thing.

"McGill?" Graves was saying. "Centurion, can I have your attention, please?"

"Yes sir. Sorry, sir."

"I'm seeing two damaged 88s… who requisitioned those expensive units?"

"Uh…" I said, thinking it over.

It was Leeson, after all, who'd really wanted to bring them along. I could have tried to blame it all on him—but that was a chicken-shit game, the kind I didn't play. After all, Leeson had been right to bring them.

"I did, sir," I said. "Without them, the Wur would have knocked out my entire unit."

"Is that your opinion, McGill?"

"That's right, sir."

He grumbled a little more. Graves always had valued equipment over manpower. After all, it was easier to grow a fresh soldier than it was to requisition a new artillery piece.

"All right," he said at last. "You're cleared to withdraw to the walls."

"Really?" I asked. "The day is young, sir. I'd like to finish my tour."

"Say what?" Harris demanded.

He had to be a good thirty paces away, but he'd still overheard me. Or maybe he'd been listening in on command chat. Either way, I tossed him a sour glance which he promptly returned.

He stumped toward me, putting his hand over his mic and glowering.

"We did our tour. We're still breathing—most of us. Let's go back in!"

I turned away and walked a few paces over the mud and slimy muck that served the Wur for blood.

"My men are eager to finish our tour, sir. We've got ninety-percent effectives."

"Yeah," Graves said, "but what are you going to do if you run into another angry tree dropping pods? Your 88s are out of commission."

He had a point, but I had a counter.

"I've got an excellent scout now, sir. Cooper is trying out for the new specialist rank of 'ghost'. I'll use him to make sure we don't walk into any more ambushes."

"Really? He didn't do shit to keep you out of the last one."

"Uh..." I was in a spot now. I really didn't want to tell him Cooper had been useless—that would hardly help the kid get rank.

On the other hand, I could tell him what really happened. After a long second of indecision, I decided to go with the God's-honest truth. That hurt, but I knew it was the right thing to do. So I swallowed hard, and I did it.

"The truth is, sir... I drew the charge. Cooper would have probably died if I hadn't."

"That's a genius move, Centurion. You saved one man, but you half-crippled your unit and got another dozen killed."

"Excuse me, Primus," I said. "Maybe I've made a mistake, but I thought we were here to do more than sit inside our walls and play with our dicks."

It was harsh language, but Graves was beginning to piss me off. He didn't seem to be gung-ho to win this war—no one did, not since I'd gotten here.

"Good point," he sighed. "All right, here are my orders: complete your patrol. Do not lose more than another ten percent of your force or gear. Report to me personally when you get back. Oh, and don't take too long, another damned storm is likely to blow in tomorrow."

"That's good news, sir," I said. "I was thinking I would die of thirst out here."

He laughed and closed the channel.

When I turned back to my unit, I faced my three adjuncts. They'd all gathered around, and they'd apparently been listening in. Leeson looked glum. Harris looked pissed, and Barton looked determined.

Of the three, I liked Barton's reaction the most.

"Good news!" I announced to all three of them. "We're going to continue the hunt. First off, strip the bark on this tree, full circle. Make sure you kill it. Then let's do a few minutes of clean-up. Gather up any lost gear you can find, and be ready to march in ten minutes."

I heard some grumbling, but I ignored it. Dumping water in my face, I sighed and drank my fill. Battle always seemed to make a man thirsty, even on Storm World.

Cooper came up to me a few minutes later. I noticed him on my HUD inside my faceplate first, as he was wearing his stealth gear.

My officers' HUD had features most of the troops didn't have access to. The inside could light up with all kinds of arrows, symbols and text. That could be quite distracting, particularly in battle, so they didn't outfit regular soldiers with the full info-systems.

But in this case, I saw a green dot very close. The word Cooper was written on it in a tiny, slanted font.

Stopping suddenly, I pretended to yawn—sweeping my arms out to my sides.

My left hand grazed Cooper, who was standing there invisible.

Letting out a war-whoop, I whirled, grabbing the smaller man. He almost got away, no doubt dancing madly to escape my outstretched hand, but I managed to hook a finger into his collar. I yanked him back hard and dashed him to the ground.

Ripping out my combat knife, I grinned when he screeched and flailed to get his stealth suit off.

"By damn!" I said. "Is that Cooper? I thought one of those trees would have shat you out by now!"

Cooper's eyes went from fear to disgust. He'd read my shitty grin correctly.

"That was a funny one, sir."

"Would have been funnier if I'd gutted you."

"That's just what I was thinking."

I offered him a gloved hand, and he took it warily. I yanked him off the ground and stood him on his feet. Then, I began walking again.

"Hey, Centurion? I just wanted to say… well."

"I love you too, man," I said.

"Right. It was cool what you did back there. I feel kind of bad for Sargon, though."

Turning around, I looked him in the eye.

"Don't," I said. "Sargon did his job. Leeson's the only one who screwed up slightly. He took too long to order those 88s to fire. Not that I would have done any better, but it was his job to time the sweep."

"Yeah… but you advanced to contact instead of writing me off. That's what I'm talking about."

I shrugged. "Another mistake, I'm sure. Won't happen again. But we're not out here in this godforsaken rainforest to live forever. We've got a job to do. These casualties—they're necessary."

He narrowed his naturally narrow eyes and looked at me. "Are you saying the brass is holding us back?"

"Damned straight they are. Look at this forest. All it does is sit out here and grow, while we've been shivering and pissing ourselves inside our walls for a month waiting for the rain to stop. Well, let me tell you two things: the rain is never stopping, and this forest is going to keep growing."

Cooper followed me while I checked on a dozen things. Soon, we were all marching again. I could tell he was thinking hard, so I didn't order him out on point immediately.

"Why are they just sitting in their bunkers, sir? It does seem odd, now that I think about it. We can't win this way."

"That's right. Now you know where my mind is wandering."

"Hmm… what are you going to do about it?"

I stopped, scanning the horizon. We were deep in the forest now. We'd traveled deeply enough into the quiet interior to lose sight of the rocky hills we'd left behind.

"I haven't decided yet," I admitted. "Now, start scouting."

Cooper trotted off without a word, vanishing completely before he'd taken ten quick steps.

I nodded to myself, thinking he was truly going to make a good ghost. He was a natural.

# -30-

As we moved through the forest on our sweep, we came to some surprising sights.

"Centurion?" my ghost Cooper whispered into my ear. "Can you check out my visual?"

I switched over to his channel, which I'd built up as a permanently available thread to my helmet. A moment later, my faceplate displayed what he was seeing.

"Hmm…" I said, "is that stripped bark?"

"That's right sir. Someone's ahead of us, doing exactly what we've been doing."

A tap came on my shoulder at that very moment. Glancing, I saw Leeson looking up at me worriedly. I turned away, refocusing my eyes on the images playing inside my faceplate. Leeson was always wetting his pants about something.

"If there's no blood or fire, I don't care, Leeson," I said.

He stumped away, shaking his head.

"Cooper," I said. "Give me a tree count, and if you spot who's doing it, I want a visual."

"Got it, sir."

Cooper moved off, and a vid began playing that showed giant fern fronds waving as he pressed through them.

"McGill to Graves, come in, sir."

"Channel opened. Talk, McGill. I'm busy. Haven't you gotten yourself slaughtered out there yet?"

“Negative, sir. Still working on that. But we have spotted a number of trees slashed through—is there another patrol in our vicinity?”

“No. One unit per zone. Unless you’ve gone outside your designated region—but no, I see you haven’t. I’ll check with the other commanders in the field. Maybe someone else has gone AWOL.”

“Roger, sir, thanks.”

I disconnected, worrying. Our patrol had two tasks, to spot enemy concentrations and do some harm along the way—but not too much harm.

The trouble was that the trees didn’t like getting slashed. They’d react. This was assumed, of course. They couldn’t grow pods quickly enough to defend themselves within a few hours, but there was always a tree now and then that did it in every region.

If we slashed too many, they’d all grow pods, sensing the pheromone release in the air. That could be dangerous, as thousands of pod-walkers could breach our walls.

Therefore, our patrol had been given orders to slash a tree every kilometer or so. Enough to do some damage and spark a half-hearted response later on—but not enough to ignite a widespread fury. It was a war of attrition tactic. We were just trimming them a little, keeping them in check.

But the Wur might react unpredictably if provoked too much.

Graves came back online a few minutes later. “No one is confessing. I’ve reviewed what you uploaded to me—this is a clear violation. No one is supposed to nail every tree they pass. That’s a clear violation of your rules of engagement, McGill.”

“That’s what I thought, sir.”

“So stop doing it, dammit! That’s an order!”

“Uh… wait a second! I’m not doing it! I’m reporting the activity—”

“Bullshit, McGill. Bullshit. This is just like you. I should have expected it, in fact. I was a fool to send out a hotheaded alien-hater like you into the field. No wonder you were so eager to go on patrol.”

I recalled the meeting. I had played the part of a man filled with excitement at getting himself killed—but Graves had taken it the wrong way.

"Primus," I said, "I was bored, and I wanted to get out past our rain-soaked walls, but I'm not crazy. We've been cutting trees, about every third one so far. I'll pass you the evidence. Check our GPS trail, if you don't believe me."

Grumbling, he went silent for a minute. I let him ponder the data. Graves was a "trust-but-verify" kind of officer. Fortunately, in this rare case, the facts were on my side.

"I apologize, Centurion," he said. "My assumptions were off-base. Even you, working with Natasha, couldn't falsify this much official data while in the field. I'm going to have to assume you've run into a Scupper patrol."

"Uh… a *what* patrol, sir?"

"Didn't you manage to stay awake through the entire briefing this time?"

"I resent that question, sir."

"Right… you didn't listen. The Scuppers are what we call the locals—weird-looking wet-skinned humanoids. They're really ugly, but they're on our side. This is their planet. The Wur are the invaders."

"Oh…" I said recalling something about there being some salamander-type aliens crawling around on Storm World. "Right sir. The salamanders."

"It must be them. They hate the trees more than we do, and they might be taking action. The problem is they're hitting the same area we are, and they're doing it too hard. McGill, I need you to do two things: One, stop slashing trees."

"Got it, sir."

"Two, find the Scupper war-party and tell them to return to the ocean."

"Uh…" I said. "Can they talk?"

"Of course they can talk. They've been mapped by the Galactics for nearly a century. Give them a translator, tell them to knock it off, and don't kill any of them. Graves out."

Seeing my conversation had ended, I felt another tapping on my shoulder. I turned around irritably.

"What is it, Leeson?" I demanded, but I caught myself.

It wasn't Leeson this time, it was Barton. She was standing close, looking worried. Her eyebrows were dark lines over a pair of crystal-blue eyes.

"Sorry. What is it, Barton?"

"Sir, we've got a problem. I'm missing two of my light troopers. They're not reporting in."

"Huh? How's that possible? Are there dead names on your list, or what?"

Every officer had a sophisticated HUD system. Dead troops showed as red names if they were in known positions and knocked out. Other colors showed various states."

"They're grayed out, sir. Beyond contact range."

"But they were green a moment before?"

"That's right."

Frowning, I called the column to a halt. I huddled with my officers.

"I tried to tell you," Leeson complained. "I had one tech go gray on me about twenty minutes back. I figured it might have been a malfunction, but nope. I checked—she's disappeared."

My eyes swept over the mushy ground we were crossing. Whatever was hitting my people, it had to be coming in hard and fast. There had been no warning. No one had witnessed anything.

"I don't trust this bog," I said. "Get everyone up on that big root system. We'll climb it and get some height for spotting."

"We'll be easy targets up there," Harris complained, eyeing the dark, humping roots.

The roots of these trees were just as over-sized as their trunks. They were often ten meters thick and gnarled with rampant growth. In order to support the massive mega-flora, the roots had to be commensurately huge themselves.

"If you want," I told Harris. "You can squat right down here in the ferns alone. It would be a good test-case, actually. Are you volunteering for that special duty, Adjunct?"

"Hell no!" Harris said, huffing.

He marched off and gathered his armored troops. They were the first ones up into the tree roots, slashing away fronds that got in the way. They looked like a column of ants crawling up a wet tree.

“Don’t do too much damage,” I called after him. “It will start defensive responses. We’re out here to trim the lawn, not to scorch the earth.”

He waved at me without turning back to make any formal acknowledgement.

*There it was again,* I thought to myself as I climbed the hulking roots after the rest. Disrespect. That’s what it was. Ever since I’d come back from a long absence without any clear explanation, my troops—especially my closest officers—were giving me a daily ration of shit.

It wasn’t anything overt, in most cases. It was quiet-like, stealthy, or maybe even subconscious. But I’d gotten the message, loud and clear.

And I didn’t like it.

# -31-

When we were all huddled up on top of the black roots, perched like rows of starlings on a wire, we gazed back down at the mud and ferns.

It was getting dark by now. The daily rotation period on Storm World was about half as long as it was back home on Earth. Days took just under thirteen hours to make a full turn, six and a half hours of light, followed by an equal period of moonlit night.

As it was hard to perform a serious mission in only six hours, command had seen fit, in their infinite wisdom, to have us serve out a full day and night as a single shift.

Using night-vision, however, the forest floor lit up as bright as day.

Scanning along with a dozen others, I saw nothing unusual. The forest was quiet. The ferns ruffled, but only with the breezes. For Storm World, it was a rare and beautiful night.

About then, I thought about Cooper again. I'd neglected to check in with him at the top of the hour, and he hadn't made his report, either. The disappearances and dramatic new orders from Graves had driven all thoughts of my scout out of my mind for a while.

"Cooper?" I called, using a direct channel helmet-to-helmet.

There was nothing but silence in return.

"Cooper?" I repeated. "Come back, this is Centurion McGill."

Three more long seconds of quiet followed, and I ran a diagnostic. The connection was solid. My helmet was linked to his—but he was too far off to get a body-reading. He didn't show up as a casualty—he didn't show up at all on my regional scanners.

I made my way down the slippery root in the dark to Natasha. She was near the forest floor, poking around and taking measurements.

"Hey girl," I said, and she squeaked.

Nearly losing her balance, I caught her arm and steadied her.

"Sorry," I said.

"It's okay. I'm a little spooked."

"Why?"

"This forest… there's something wrong out here. I've gone back over the unit logs. These people who vanished, they were all on their own at the moment of disappearance. About ten meters or more from any other member of the outfit."

"Okay…" I said. "So they were out of sight. Out of mind. Taking a piss, or something."

"Right. And according to the logs from the network sensors I've been paging through, they vanish very quickly. It's almost as if something reaches up out of the ground and snatches them away. They're there one moment and gone the next."

"Super. Let's move higher up on the roots."

"James…" she said as we made our way up to what we assumed was relative safety. "What if something is grabbing people?"

"Like what? The boogeyman?"

I laughed, and she laughed weakly in response. But we both knew we were on an unknown planet with all sorts of possible predators we hadn't identified yet.

"Look, James," she said. "This is a big deal. I can't call these disappearances in as deaths. We've got no bodies—we've got nothing."

That sobered me up. I hadn't thought about that angle before.

"You're saying that if we don't find them—or at least find their bodies—they're permed?"

"Pretty much, yes."

I stewed, thinking that over for a while. Then I stood up.

"We can't sit on this tree forever," I said. "Graves won't stand for it. Besides, a new storm might blow in at any time."

"It will be dawn in a few hours."

"Not good enough," I told her. "We're going on patrol again. Anyone who doesn't like it can grow a set of gender-appropriate gonads to deal with it."

"That's what I figured you'd say—but I'm still scared." She examined the ground around us.

Then I showed her the Cooper situation, and that didn't make her any happier.

"That's four gone now," she said, eyeing the data.

"We don't know that. He might be dead in a normal fashion, or there might be some other explanation."

"Do you really believe that?"

"I surely do!"

Natasha rolled her eyes at me. That was the trouble with knowing a woman for decades. You just couldn't fool her any more after she caught onto your tricks.

"Okay, okay," I said. "Something's up. But like you said, we can't sit on this tree any longer. We've got to finish the patrol whether we're losing troops or not."

She licked her lips. "Who are you going to put on point?"

I looked around at the prospects. They were sitting like monkeys in a big tree, many crouching. Most held their weapons nervously, scanning the open ground below.

"I'll do it," I said. "I'll lead by example. They can't all piss themselves at once if they see their commander is fearless."

"But you'll be risking yourself."

"That's the whole point!"

With that, I stood up and addressed the full unit on tactical chat.

"All right people, listen up. We're moving out. We can get to the point where Cooper found evidence of a tree-slashing war party in half an hour if we move fast."

I paused for dramatic effect, scanning faces. People winced and shrank. A few were surprisingly hard to see, as they were crouching behind big leaves and fern fronds.

"Follow me," I said at last.

Turning around, I marched down the root and onto open ground as if I hadn't a care in the world.

Startled, my troops got up slowly and walked in my wake. They'd been certain I was scanning for a volunteer. The relief of tension had them smiling and shaking their heads as they marched behind me.

That's what I'd wanted. Not a single man of them complained about walking into danger, not even Carlos. That was because I was leading the way in person. How could they whine if I wasn't even forcing anyone to play the part of the sacrificial lamb?

After about a hundred meters, I began to whistle. Now, anyone will tell you that I'm not the best at whistling, although I'm better at it than I am at singing.

Fortunately, I didn't care how many ears were offended today. I felt good, and my people were even starting to smile and talk again. They'd been pretty glum while they'd been perched on those giant roots, waiting to vanish into limbo.

My mood and the general upbeat surge among my soldiers all changed, however, when I took a final step.

I was, if I had to be precise, about two hundred meters from the big tree where we'd taken refuge. Since I was whistling and walking fast, I'd gotten ahead of the column. At least fifty paces ahead.

That might have been a mistake. Like the others who'd vanished, I was isolated from the pack.

I took a final confident step, and it seemed as if I'd walked off a cliff. I pitched forward, and the forest vanished. Falling, tumbling as a man might when he's stepped into a pit he had no idea was there.

Automatically, my hands reached out and I flailed, trying to grab for roots, leaves—anything at all.

But there was nothing there. Nothing but darkness. If I'd stepped into a hole, it seemed to be the biggest damned hole this side of the Grand Canyon.

Tumbling, falling, I finally understood what had happened to all my missing troops.

# -32-

I didn't go down screaming—not exactly. It was more of a series of thrashing roars and grunts.

Needless to say, I was surprised and seriously freaked out as I fell down into nothingness. The worst part was how deep this hole was—if it was a hole. The fall wasn't just a few meters, it went on and on. It felt like being in space, falling in orbit.

Absolute blackness swallowed me for several seconds. These moments were among the longest of my considerable lifespan. It felt like I was falling into Hell itself.

But there was no fiery pit below. I couldn't see anything. One moment, I'd been walking in the forest. The next moment I was falling. That's all I knew.

My sleeves ruffled with a fast, continuous passage of air. After a time, I realized it had to be a trick of some kind. Some kind of interdimensional hanky-panky was at work.

I happen to be something of an expert on getting lost in time and space. I've fallen between cracks in our trusted physical laws many times. Some aliens had a way of producing better tech than we did back home on Earth—mostly because they had a hundred thousand years or so of a head-start.

This felt like one of those times. It reminded me of the first time I teleported in a teleport suit, or when I'd stepped through gateway posts heading to Dark World, but ended in some kind of queued-up purgatory of non-existence.

After the first five or so seconds of skidding in what felt like a perfectly lightless, void of a universe, I began to get seriously worried.

What if there *wasn't* an end to this fall? What if I was trapped, bound to fall forever until I was a desiccated corpse—or worse, a mad-thing that was unable to die?

That was right about when I hit the bottom. In some ways, it was a relief to strike something solid. After all, I'd fallen a long ways, and it did bring an end to my previous questioning. Even if I died down here, that would be better than an eternal fall.

Standing up and brushing myself off, I noticed a number of things. First off, I hadn't died on impact—I hadn't even broken my legs.

Storm World had a lower gravitational pull than Earth did, but falling was falling. I should have built up enough inertia to be seriously hurt—but I wasn't.

"Hello?" I called out, peering around in bewilderment.

Wherever I was, it was small, cramped and pitch-black. I felt the walls, and found myself enclosed in a horizontal tube of sorts, about two meters in diameter. I was almost able to stand upright—almost.

Turning on my suit lights, I saw I was indeed in a chute of sorts. The ceiling opened up and had another pipe just like the one I was in, but it fed this one from above at a slant.

"Looks like a sewer…" I grumbled.

"Smells like one, too," said a familiar voice. "Or maybe that's the mud on your suit...?"

"Cooper?" I demanded turning around and looking for him.

Of course, I couldn't see him. He wasn't there—he'd kept his stealth gear active, even though it hadn't done him much good so far.

"Show yourself," I demanded.

"Feeling paranoid, McGill?" he laughed. Then he quickly changed his tune as I got out my pistol and aimed it where his gut had to be. "Whoa! Lower that gun, sir. I'm pulling this thing off!"

He appeared then, in chunks coming out of the air in a manner that was strange to watch. It seemed, for just a second, like I could see through his guts when he was partly visible and partly covered. Did the Vulbite stealth gear just bend light, or did it do more than that?

As neither of us was a tech, I figured we weren't going to get any of those answers today, so I dropped such thoughts from my mind.

"Come on," I said, heading off down the tunnel.

"Why do you think that's the right way?" he demanded.

I glanced back at him, over my shoulder. "You got something to say, ghost? Where does this one go?"

He shook his head. "I haven't done much exploring yet…"

"Bullshit," I said, laughing and splashing away—there was a little water in the pipes, but it was less than ankle deep. "You got scared and shivered down here, playing rabbit. Come on."

Cooper grumbled, but he followed me gamely enough. In a way, I couldn't blame him for squatting down here where he'd landed. There was no guarantee we'd find a way out by heading off at random, and his strategy of sitting around had gained him an officer for company.

We walked about a hundred paces, and the floor disappeared. I might have walked right out into space and fallen, but the sound of the rushing water gave it away.

"A pit," I said. "Another one."

"You're like a lucky rabbit's foot, sir. Just like Carlos said."

I gave him an annoyed glance. "Scout—start scouting."

"Shit."

He crept past me, let his stealth suit drop over him, and moved off around the rim of the big open space. There was a lip of sorts, a thin ring that spiraled along the wall. I could see where he was due to the water he was displacing with his boots.

Grunting and hissing, he slid around in the dark. In order to help him, I turned my suit's full spotlights on and aimed them downward. His feet made tiny splashes as he edged around the pipe, following the ledge.

"I've found something," Cooper said. "There's a door on the far side—or something like that."

"Well, open it."

He grunted and strained. “It won’t budge,” he said at last.

Sighing unhappily, I began edging my way around the big circular pit to his side.

“There isn’t much room over here on this side, McGill,” Cooper whispered.

Just then, a creak sounded. The door he’d found opened outward.

Unfortunately, Cooper wasn’t in a good position. He was directly in front of the door, trying to turn the wheel that sealed it. When the door suddenly opened—well, he was knocked off that thin ledge and went tumbling farther down into darkness.

I could hear him howling and carrying on for several seconds. It must have been a long way down to the bottom of that next run.

The door that had opened, knocking Cooper into oblivion, opened farther. I drew my pistol again and leveled it, waiting.

Another familiar face peered out of the circular doorway, making me blink in surprise.

It was Kivi.

# -33-

"What the hell are you doing down here, Specialist?" I demanded.

Kivi looked startled. "It's good to see you too, sir. I thought I heard voices out here, on the other side of this door, so I opened it."

I stared down into the darkness. There was no sign or sound of Cooper. I shrugged and began scooting along the walls to Kivi's side. I slipped inside the doorway and took a look around.

"Hmm…" I said. "I was kind of hoping for something better."

She watched me closely. "This is all there is: tunnels, pipes, it's like a subway system, I think."

I turned and stared at her. "How do you figure?"

"Well, someone uses the system for transportation. I doubt it's the Wur. I think it's the other guys—the local inhabitants of this miserable planet. The Scuppers."

"Not much of a subway," I said. "All you do is fall into a flat region, and then you have to walk."

She shrugged. "By the way, who were you talking to back there in the tubes? Before I opened the door?"

I eyed her for a second. She looked honestly curious. That meant she had no idea she'd knocked Cooper off into another freefall.

"Uh…" I said. "I guess I talk to myself now and then."

"I've never heard you do that."

"Maybe I'm getting old."

She snorted at that. Our bodies hadn't aged five years since we'd joined up decades ago. But she stopped arguing.

I'd skipped on the truth for purely selfish reasons. You see, Kivi and I had had an on-and-off thing going for many years—since I'd first joined Legion Varus, actually.

I wasn't a man who understood women well, or who even dared to make that claim—but I was good at making a connection when I felt like it. One thing you never did with a girl was tell her she was a fool who'd screwed up and killed someone by accident. Not if you wanted to get lucky later on, that was. A thing like that—she'd inevitably associate the horror she felt with you, the man who'd been dumb enough to tell her.

Instant buzz-kill.

So, I kept the details to myself. Who knew? We were trapped down here alone, and we might just get bored eventually…

The room we were in was about the same general size and dimensions as the last one I'd just stepped out of, but it had a floor. That was pretty cool. We walked around, finding several doors like the one Kivi had popped open and nailed Cooper with.

Experimentally, I opened each one. Tubes led off into the darkness in every direction.

Sighing, I sat down on the curved floor and tried to figure out what to do.

"We're cut off from every form of communication," she told me. "I had a few buzzers, but when I sent them off they zipped away and lost the signal. They never came back."

Kivi looked at me, and I saw a hint of fear in her face.

"Could this be some kind of storm drain system?" she asked. "If it is, water could come through at any time and sweep us away. We'll be permed."

It was a distinct possibility. We were cut off, disconnected from the grid. If we died down here now, Varus might never find us. We couldn't be revived without a documented death, so… game over.

"Nah," I said dismissively. "We're not going to get permed, girl. Don't even worry about that. What I'm wondering is who made this? And why?"

"It has to be the Scuppers," she said. "The Wur wouldn't do this. They deal in organic tech. It's not Galactic, either, so it has to be the native people."

"Hmm..." I said. "I thought they were fish-people or something."

"They're amphibious, yes," she said. "All that was in the briefing. You saw the pictures and read the reports, right?"

"Yep."

She frowned at me. "No you didn't."

"Well... I've been kind of busy since I got revived, you know. I had a unit to command, a patrol to set up..."

Kivi shook her head. "Same old McGill."

That bugged me, and I almost told her what she'd done to Cooper—but I held off.

"Okay," I said. "Let's think this through. There's no reason to panic, and this place has to make sense to an alien mind, at least."

"All right... Let's go over it," she said. "The tubes don't carry power. They don't distribute food. They might drain the forests to the ocean—but we haven't seen much evidence of that yet."

"They could just be a tunnel network—a way to get around without having to walk on the surface."

"A subway system? You already mentioned that idea. Where are the trains?"

"They might come along..." I admitted. "Any minute."

Kivi looked alarmed at the thought. "We'll be run over. There's nowhere to go. We'll be crushed against these walls and permed!"

She was winding up again, so I snaked one of my long thick arms around her shoulders.

"Hey, it's going to be fine. Old McGill is on the case."

"That doesn't fill me with confidence, I'm afraid."

Letting go of her, I paced the circular chamber and tested all the walls again. "Maybe there's a way to trigger this thing. I mean, if it's a transportation system, there has to be some way of calling a train, or something."

Circling around, I tried many things. I crouched low, I felt the walls for tiny buttons, I pounded and stomped.

Heading out into one of the side chutes, I repeated all my moves. Kivi sat down and watched me with one fist pressed up against her cheek. She clearly didn't have a lot faith in my efforts.

After tapping every wall, I finally tried hopping up and down. Maybe there was a floor plate I couldn't see. After all, alien tech didn't always work like human tech did. Especially when the aliens in question were some kind of tree-frog.

It was the second hop that was magical. For a fraction of a second, all four of my limbs left contact with the tunnel walls.

That did the trick. I was suddenly falling—sideways. As I fell, I whooped and howled. Naturally, I reached out a hand and touched the sides of the tunnel, trying to grab a handhold.

There were no handholds. The walls of the tunnel were quite smooth and rounded—but the sensation changed abruptly anyhow.

Slam! I was down and tumbling. Like a man thrown out of a moving tram, I rolled and flopped. It was a wonder I didn't break my neck.

Sharp clangs approached. Kivi was rushing to my side.

"Careful!" I hollered, but I was too late.

She took flight, the same as I had. I reached out as she flew by and batted her out of the air. She did a flipping, flopping fall.

I crawled up to her, and I grimaced.

Her helmet had been off, and she'd landed badly. Her neck was broken, and she was as dead as a doornail.

"Shit," I said.

I was alone again.

# -34-

It had cost Kivi her life, but at least I now understood where I was and how this tunnel system operated.

It was a transportation system, but there were no trains or cars. All you had to do was hop into the air. Gravity was diverted if no part of your body was touching the walls. That meant you "fell" in whatever direction the tube was built to send you.

What a beautiful system it was, when you thought about it. We'd been as dumb as a couple of dogs wandering around on a highway with the same predictable result: violent death. That didn't mean the system wasn't workable, however. I just had to figure out the details.

So far, I knew that if I hopped into the air, getting all my limbs airborne at the same moment while inside any given tube, I'd begin to fall toward the end of that tube. That part I understood.

But how did you stop the effect? Even falling sideways was pretty dangerous. Kivi gave mute testimony to this fact with her lifeless, staring eyes.

I read her tapper with mine, in case I managed to get a chance to revive her. Then, I stood up and took a deep breath.

It was going to take both balls and luck to survive this. I couldn't think of a better way than to just start hopping into the air for short falls. I couldn't just walk—the tunnels went on for countless kilometers. Worse, they went every which-way. I was already hopelessly lost. The only way to find my way out, before I ran out of supplies, was to fly.

Grimacing, I hopped into the air. Immediately, I was swept away down the tunnel. I only let that go on for about a second before reaching a hand out to touch the walls.

As before, I fell to the floor. Tucking my head down and curling up into a ball, I bounced and thumped, grunting until I came to a stop.

I lay there, feeling my bones. Bruises, maybe a sprain on my left wrist—I was okay.

Sitting up, I stared back the way I'd come. Kivi's body was a crumpled figure on the floor, no more than ten meters away.

"How the hell do I stop?" I asked no one.

Sighing, I looked up and down the tunnel. I was screwed. If I let myself fall for a long time, I'd keep speeding up. Pretty soon, I'd reach terminal velocity—about two hundred kilometers an hour. With that kind of speed, there was no way I could land without being seriously hurt or, more likely, killed.

How the hell did the aliens do it? Obviously, there must be a way. I thought about possibilities, such as wearing a parachute, or having a control mechanism on your person. There had to be something that slowed them down at each junction. Every hatch at the end of each tunnel was closed, and that meant the falling effect had to cut out in time to let you open the next door to go on another leg of your journey.

After a few more hops, none of which ended any better than the first one did, I finally got annoyed and hopped up into the air again.

This time, I let it go.

"Whoa! Whoa!" I found myself shouting.

My hands flailed, and I tumbled a little, but I did my best to avoid that. I was speeding up, and the walls became a blur. My heart raced.

*I've permed myself.*

That was the only thought that could clearly be heard in my chaotic brain.

*James McGill*, I thought, *you are some kind of a special breed of moron.*

My own grandma had often told me I was one part genius and three parts retard. This was one of the moments that proved it, to my mind.

Once I was really falling fast, I dared do nothing. Sure I knew at the end of this tunnel there had to be a hatch. It was almost certainly closed, and when I got there, I'd smash into it, crushing the life out of me.

But by now there was no jumping off this train, either. The tube was flashing by at an incredible rate. Just one touch, one brush with those walls, and *splat*—I'd be a goner.

With no better plan, I kept it going as long as I could. Sure, I wasn't likely to survive—but that didn't mean I wanted to check out early. In fact, it became kind of a game to keep the effect going as long as I humanly could.

Rolling a bit, I realized I was falling headfirst. In order not to touch the walls, I had to ball up, looking like a kid doing a cannonball. The wind whistled past me. It was scary.

A spin. I was in a spin.

I'd jumped out of a few aircraft before, and I'd learned a few things. There were postures you could take as a skydiver that would level you off. I used one of them now, putting "my dick into the wind" as they say. Curling back my arms and legs, I formed a potato chip shape, arching my back.

That did the trick. The spin stopped, but I almost grazed the walls of tube. I curled again immediately, imitating a cannonball again.

Why go to all this effort? I don't know. When you're dancing with death, I guess it's natural to try to keep the music going for as long as you could. I mean, why not? One touch against any of the walls of the tube, and it was all over…

The door.

It had to be coming up soon. I just felt it.

Sneaking a peak ahead, I almost panicked and began to flail about. I could see it now, right "below" me, coming up fast.

The end of the line. Old James McGill was going to be the biggest damned splat anyone had ever seen. For some reason, this struck me as funny.

The final second or so passed, and I wondered if I'd ever get another revive. In my honest opinion, the odds were slim.

That wheel that sealed the door—it was going to drive right through my chest and out the backside. I'd be flatter than a stray dog on a sky-train launch pad.

But something unexpected happened during the last second of my plunge to certain death: I slowed down.

It was shocking and kind of painful, to tell the truth. My guts were wrenched, twisted up. It felt like the fastest express elevator in the world was pulling at me, all over—but a little unevenly.

The effect would have made me sick if it had gone on for long, but thankfully, it didn't. I found myself landing on my butt and skidding a few feet to a stop.

Getting up with a groan, I looked around. The door was very close—less than a dozen steps away.

I began to laugh. "I almost shit my pants," I muttered aloud to myself.

It wasn't chance that had eased me down in front of the door. I knew that now. The transportation system was dead-simple and very fast. All you had to do was hop into the air, fall to the end of any given tunnel, then wait until it deposited you in front of the next door.

Experimentally, I gave a little hop.

As I expected, I began falling away from the door. I was headed back the way I'd come, toward the end of the tunnel where Kivi lay dead in the darkness.

My hand snapped out and touched the wall, and I tumbled again.

Climbing back to my feet and cursing, I thought I'd pretty much figured out this little bit of alien tech. Now, it was time to do some exploring.

Unfortunately, I heard something about then. It was a flapping sound, like a sail on a sailboat in a stiff wind.

Looking back down the tunnel, I didn't see anything, but a moment later I was struck by something all the same. I rolled and tumbled again.

I came up with my knife in my hand, and so did other guy. Then, recognition set in as the object that had slammed into me stripped off its stealth suit.

"Damn you, boy," I said. "That wasn't funny. I almost gutted you."

Cooper laughed hard.

"I just had to do it," he said. "Haven't you figured out how these tunnels work yet, McGill? Don't tell me you walked all the way down here from the last station."

"Nah, I flew. Kivi and I figured it out the hard way."

"Yeah…" he said, looking back the way we'd both come. "I saw her stretched out back there. Did she break her neck, or was she talking too much?"

I glared at Cooper, and he grinned back.

"Come on," I said. "Let's explore."

"After you, sir."

"No way. You're going first. Get out of the way fast when we reach the end of the next tunnel, or my size-thirteen boots will go right up your ass."

Cooper grumbled a little, but he led the way. He didn't bother with his stealth suit this time. The odds of an accident were higher if I couldn't see him.

Working together, we covered the local region of jumps. While we were falling through the tunnels with increasing confidence, we had time to talk.

"So," Cooper began, "I get this place. I can see why the salamanders built it and all. They have a permanently wet planet, and so aircraft or trains are never going to work here. This system is simple and pretty sweet if you don't kill yourself accidently."

"Yep, makes good sense. What I don't understand is how we got down here from the surface, though."

"Yeah, that was weird. I think there are access tunnels. Holes to the surface that we stumbled into."

"No markings, though?" I asked. "No signs, no way to know they're there?"

"Well, these are aliens we're talking about. Maybe the access points are obvious to them."

"You mean they might be using pheromones to mark them, or something like that?"

He laughed again. “Yeah, sure. Why not? Maybe they piss all over them and sniff them out like dogs. Who knows? Aliens are weird.”

The kid had me there.

We kept falling, taking each tunnel we could that fell “upward” hoping to reach the surface eventually. When we finally reached the end of the line, though, we were in for a big surprise.

# -35-

The last exit wasn't a hatch. It was different.

Looking like a spongy dark mass, I thought we were falling into a mud pit of some kind—but how could a mud pit be sitting on the ceiling?

Cooper gave a war-whoop as he fell into it first and vanished.

We were slowing down—but not enough. I hit at speed—maybe thirty kilometers an hour.

I clenched my teeth and hunkered down, bracing for what looked like a bone-breaking impact.

To my surprise, it wasn't that bad. It felt like I'd hit *something*—fabric, maybe. Something big and gauzy that covered me, then gave way and let me fall through.

A moment later, I found myself vomited out of the ground. I was back on the surface in gloomy daylight.

The next thing I noticed was that the forest was gone. We were on the beach. I staggered around in a circle, trying to take it all in.

"Careful, Centurion!" Cooper said. "You'll fall back in!"

I froze, looking around at the sandy beach. There were rocks, sand… but I didn't see a hole.

"Where is it?"

"Right near that rock, I think. Just walk toward me, sir. You should be able to get to my position without falling. I managed it."

I looked around, but of course, Cooper wasn't visible. I studied the ground next. I spotted footprints, and I followed them.

He trudged away then, and I continued to follow his trail. We headed inland, leaving the beach behind, as it was too open for my taste.

Using my tapper on high-gain, I managed to beam a short message to headquarters. We had com satellites strung around the planet by now, and it wasn't a hard thing to do.

"Did you report our dead?"

"Yep," I said. "Kivi will now get a revive."

"That lucky bitch," he said. "God only knows where we are."

"We're on a slate-gray beach," I said. "Why so glum? This has to be about the best summer day anyone has seen on this planet for a while."

"Yeah, but a storm is coming, sir. It's on your tapper."

I checked, and he was right. I cursed.

The storms on Storm World didn't seem natural to an Earthman. They were hurricanes—pretty much always.

In fact, the beach we were on wasn't all that normal-looking. On Earth, even a wide stretch of sand between the sea and the first grassy tufts wasn't usually more than a hundred meters or so.

This beach was different. It had to be a half-kilometer wide, made up of open sand and rocks. That was because the tides here were serious. They shifted the water level by up to fifty meters—every day.

As a consequence, the ocean itself was a stewing cauldron. Looking out to sea, I witnessed a terrifying series of whitecaps. Instead of nice, man-high waves, I was watching ten meter crashers out there. They came in hard too, and they meant business.

In the other direction, away from the beach, the mainland began with a black cliff. The rest of the land had been eroded away by harsh weather combined with relentless waves and tides.

We headed toward the higher ground, seeking a way to escape the churning ocean before the tide swept in to cover the beach.

"We're in for a climb," Cooper said

Looking up at the dark, rocky walls ahead, I grunted. "You got that right. I guess we should be happy we didn't find an exit that was entirely underwater."

"Why would lizards build something that terminated underwater?

"They're amphibious, remember? They can walk on the sea bottom or the land—it's all the same to them."

"That's weird," Cooper said. "Aliens are always so damned weird. Kind of makes you want to kill them all, doesn't it?"

"Uh… sometimes meeting a life form you don't understand can bring out the worst in a fellow," I admitted.

Cooper was a man with rough edges. I'd made a special effort to recruit him years back. Since then, he'd become a first-class regular who might become my unit's first ghost specialist.

That was all well and good, but I couldn't help wondering if moving a mean man like him up in the ranks would reflect badly on me someday…

That moment of doubt passed quickly. I didn't really care what people thought of my choices. Cooper was a good killer, and he was loyal enough to his own side. That was good enough for a man who was expected to fight and die over and over on shithole planets like Storm World.

A hundred steps later, Cooper spoke up again. "Uh-oh… the sky is darkening."

I glanced back and looked out to sea. Most of the really big storms started in these turbulent oceans, and what I saw out there didn't look good. There were black clouds now, pregnant with rain. As I watched they roiled and swelled, coming closer to the coastline. In the center of the blackest cloud, lightning flickered. A rumble of thunder rolled over us.

"Hmm…" I said. "We should probably get moving."

Picking up the pace, we began to hike up the crumbling cliffs. Fortunately, there was a path of sorts. It had probably started as a run-off for water spilling down the side of the rocky cliff, but I doubted it was completely natural now. There were marks from tools and even a few flat slabs of stone wedged into place here and there. I thought it likely our salamander friends had cut into the wall of the cliff, creating a slanted series of rough steps.

"This rock is so weathered and stained that the path looks like a random jog in the granite," Cooper said, "but it isn't. I think these lizard guys cut this into the cliff face. Good thing they did it, too."

"Salamanders," I said.

"What?"

"You keep calling them lizards. The Scuppers are more like Salamanders. Lizards have dry skin. These guys have wet-looking skin, and it comes in a variety of colors."

"Freaks either way."

I didn't bother arguing with him, and I kept hiking up the side of the cliff. We really needed to get to the top before the storm rolled in.

"Hey," Cooper said after another hundred steps. "Don't look now, but we've got company."

Glancing back, I saw a knot of figures. They looked kind of like men—but they weren't men. They were Scuppers. About a dozen of them.

It had begun to rain lightly, and the mist from the sea was whipping around the cliffs. The wind was picking up.

Still, I halted and stared. Zooming in with my faceplate optics, I got a good look at them.

They were weird-looking, just like Cooper had said. Walking upright with tails, they reminded me somewhat of saurians. But these guys were taller and thinner of build. They also seemed more primitive because they didn't wear much for clothing, just a harness for weapons. Their exposed skin was smooth and colored in various patterns. Most of them were a dark blue, or a sea green, but some had yellow and red splotches.

Most importantly, I noted that each one carried a long stick with a pointed metal knob on top.

"They have some kind of spear," I said. "With a metal tip."

"Yeah, that's what passes for a gun for these losers," Cooper said. "Those sticks can shock you so hard your balls will light up."

"That's all they've got?"

"Pretty much… why do you think they called Earth for help?"

Turning away, we marched up the cliff, moving faster than before. We were supposed to be on the same side as these amphibians, but misunderstandings were common on new planets.

When we got near the top, I was huffing a little. I'd turned off the exoskeletal power in my suit, as I wanted to save what power I had left.

"Cooper, you think these guys are dangerous?"

"They've killed men at times, now and then. But all that happened before you got here. We've been hiding inside Fort Alpha for weeks now, waiting out the storms."

"That's a waste of time. The storms are never going to quit."

"All you've got to do is convince Turov of that."

I stopped talking. Cooper had brought up Turov, and I knew what he meant. People generally whispered about my relationship with the tribune. It was considered unseemly, if not entirely against regs. At least we were both officers now, only two steps apart in rank.

When we got to the top of the cliff, the storm got worse. I think it was because we were exposed now without a single rocky wall to protect us on one side. At least the immediate threat of a fall to our deaths had passed.

But then I caught sight of a throng of oddly shaped figures. They approached from several angles at once. There had to be hundreds of them.

"Scuppers…" Cooper whispered.

He was invisible again.

"Slip away," I told him. "Evade and report. I'll talk to them."

"Luck, McGill."

From every direction, the ominous crowd of amphibians began to close in.

Cooper was gone, just like a ghost—that lucky bastard.

# -36-

The leader was an acid-green monster with one yellow splotch over his left eye. He was taller than me, and he had arms almost as thick as a normal man's—which still looked pretty skinny for his height.

He approached, and I turned on the translation app on my tapper.

"…inferior…" he said. "Poor quality. Abasement…"

Hmm… already, this guy wasn't filling me with confidence. I thought about reversing course and heading back down the cliff to take my chances with the storm on the beach, but the other party was moving up the path toward me, boxing me in.

As I watched, now and then they got down on all fours and scuttled along like dogs—or maybe more like swamp gators back home. They could move pretty fast when they wanted to.

"Hello there Mr. Scupper, sir!" I said in a cheery tone.

"Disgust… resentment…" he said.

"Uh… you don't like me?"

The odd head canted to one side. It was a universal pose of puzzlement. Maybe most beings did it in order to hear better.

"You speak the language," he said. "But you are still inferior. You are an insult."

"How's that?"

"Earth promised an army. Earth demanded fealty. Earth sends a paltry few troops—frightened worms that sit inside their strange walls, terrified of a few raindrops."

Speaking of raindrops, the wind was beginning to do that gusting and screaming thing. The rain was coming down, harder and harder. Soon, it would be lashing us.

The Scuppers took no notice of this. They weren't cold or uncomfortable. I got the feeling they liked it wet. The salamanders out in the bog behind my shack were like that. They were sort of like lizards with the skin of a frog.

If there was one thing I'd learned in my many travels among the stars, it was to remain calm if your hosts were calm. I was determined, therefore, to ignore the growing darkness and the lashing winds and rain. After all, to these guys, this weather wasn't a big deal.

"I'm not afraid of rain," I told him. "I'm not afraid of the Wur, either. I've killed thousands of their defensive growths. Lastly, I'm not afraid of you."

The big eyes blinked. The left one, the one with the yellow ring around it, leaned closer. It looked like a giant frog-eye.

There was no emotion there that I could read. No pity. No anger—but then again, it was hard to read a cold-blooded animal.

"You challenge Scuppers?" he asked me.

"Uh… no, I didn't say that."

"You are inferior. You are like an egg in its mother's sac, waiting to be seeded by a male. You are—"

"Hold on," I said. "I thought we were allies. I didn't come all this way to listen to insults. Do you clowns want help or not?

The translator on my arm burbled, and they reacted by shuffling around and hissing. I didn't care. I was getting tired of these slimy-skinned assholes. Cooper's words echoed in my mind, how he'd talked about wanting to kill all aliens, and I tried to calm down. Maybe it was natural for two species that were so different to become hostile upon meeting one another.

The Scupper leader, however, wasn't trying too hard to make friends. "We don't accept cowards as allies," he said. "Show us you are no coward."

"Okay… I came all the way out here, didn't I? I didn't run from you when you came from both directions."

"Foolishness doesn't translate to bravery. I see before me one who has run from every threat. A dry-thing that has fallen into simple traps and nearly died trying to figure out the tubes, a system every infant Scupper has mastered."

"You mean the underground transport system? Yeah, we figured it out. Works pretty well once you get used to it."

"Naturally. Scuppers do not build useless things."

I was beginning to grind my teeth again.

"Listen up," I told him. "You can welcome me, or you can get out of my way. Your choice."

A series of popping sounds went up from the crowd. Were they blowing spit-bubbles and popping them? That was my impression. As to what it meant, I had no idea. They could have been laughing or raging or farting—or all three. I really didn't care.

"To gain our respect, you must slay the leader."

"Um… kill you? But that's not why—"

He made a move then, one I wasn't expecting. He swung his big spear-thing at me. The knob crackled with electricity.

I was wearing a breastplate and some other titanium armor pieces. That made it hard to dodge, and he'd taken a poke at me by surprise.

Startled, I raised an arm—but there was a crackle and a surge of electrical current. It ran through my armor, and to a lesser degree, my body.

That knob had touched me. It had shorted out most of my subsystems.

That was bad, as I was now trapped inside a heavy suit of dead armor. My faceplate computer had died. At least my body hadn't given up the ghost yet.

Legionnaire armor was insulated on the inside with a sheath of flexible polymers. It was kind of like wearing a wet suit underneath the metal plates. As a result, I didn't have a cardiac arrest, but I did get a nasty sting on the collarbone, where he'd landed his stick on me.

Reacting without much thought, I levered up my arms to a defensive posture. It was hard to do, as my armor was no longer power-assisting my movements.

Still, I managed to club away his staff with one fist.

He croaked at me, staggering back a step. Then he caught his balance again and squared off with me. His stick was held high.

When he came at me again, I was ready. I managed to get out my combat knife. I slashed and took off his right hand at the wrist.

The skinny green arm leaked dark blood, but his severed hand still gripped that staff. Reaching out with my other hand, I shoved him, planting a gauntlet on his chest.

He fell back and landed on the rocks. Stepping forward, I put a heavy boot on his staff. He struggled weakly with his one thin arm to free it, but I could have told him it was hopeless.

"Yield, sir," I said. "You've been beaten."

"My life is at an end."

"Nope. Doesn't have to be. Become my ally and friend, and I'll spare you."

Saying this, I lifted my knife from his throat and stepped back.

Slowly, he got up and found his severed hand. He slipped it into a pouch.

"Why do you shame me like this?" he asked. "Did I slay your mother in her sleep?"

"Uh… I don't think so. Just be happy. I'm giving you your life."

The crowd around us made popping sounds.

"You hear that?" he demanded. "You've shamed me deeply. They laugh, and I'll never be able to live in peace again."

"Aw now, come on. Can't we work something out?"

He scuttled away on all fours, limping badly due to his lost hand.

As he moved through the crowd, several of them thumped him with the butt of their staves and kicked him in the sides. He left as fast as he could.

The rest of the army encircled me. Another Scupper stepped forward. This one was a lovely blue.

"I am Second-man," he said. "You are now First-man. What is your command, First-man?"

Gawking, I looked around at the horde of amphibians. They were all intent, waiting for orders.

"Um…" I said. "Let's march back to the human fortress."

They all stood there.

"Why aren't you walking?" I asked.

"You are our leader. You must lead."

"Okay… Right. You there, yellow-belly. You'll walk ahead as my scout. Start walking."

The yellow-bellied Scupper I'd indicated turned and headed west. I'd kind of figured that was the direction home, but I hadn't been sure. This way, the throng didn't know that I had no idea which way to go.

Following my scout closely, I marched off into the stormy night.

Surrounding me, a small army followed. There were hundreds of them, about seven hundred, if I had to guess.

I smiled as I had a new thought: Galina was going to *love* these guys.

# -37-

The storm came and really worked on my army. They had suckers on their padded feet, but when a gust came up, it could sometimes pry a Scupper loose.

That happened now and then, but usually the guy in question managed to survive. He'd curl up into a ball and let the wind take him, rolling away thumping over rocks. When he caught himself, he'd limp back to rejoin the pack.

Twice, however, soldiers were flipped in the air and smashed into the rocky ground again with deadly force. Those men we lost.

There was no ceremony for the dead. The Scuppers simply tested the victim's reflexes, and if he didn't respond, they left him where he lay.

Soon we reached the edge of the great forest of the Wur. That was a relief, as the trees sheltered us from the storm and men stopped dying.

As we passed big Wur trees, the Scuppers cut them. They didn't skip any trees, either. They cut them all.

"Second-man," I said when I noticed what they were doing. "Why are these men cutting every tree we pass?"

"How else will we rid our land of these monstrous growths?" he asked.

"We humans cut the bark, too," I said. "But just once in a while. If we cut *every* tree we pass, they will all grow pod-walkers. If enough trees react and produce defensive growths, we'll be overwhelmed."

He stared at me curiously with his bulbous eyes.

"Can it be true, then?" he asked. "Was First-man right? Do you humans fear to fight?"

"No, not at all. We just—"

"How can you remove all the trees from our world if you don't cut every one you meet?" he demanded. "They have killed millions of our people. We intend to free both the land and the sea of this disease. We will not sit underground, or under the deepest waves, hoping the enemy will retreat out of kindness!"

I thought about it, and I figured old blue-belly was right. I was new to Storm World, but our rules of engagement made no sense. You can't win a war by sitting around inside a fort.

Then again, I knew Galina might have other plans. Maybe she didn't really care if she won or not. Maybe she just wanted to stabilize things here and wait for backup legions.

Our last foray to the frontier stars had taken us to Dark World. That forbidding place had been guarded by Vulbites, and we'd ultimately lost the fight to their masters, the Rigellians.

That failure could be the reason Turov wasn't taking any big chances on this planet. Maybe she'd decided to play it safer, the way Deech liked to do.

"Dammit," I muttered to myself. "Second-man, halt and stand here. I can see the walls. I've got to go forward and tell them who I am."

"You do not have to tell them anything," he said firmly. "You are First-man. You lead this army. We live and we die at your sufferance. Surely, these fearful humans will bow to your greatness."

"Um… that's all well and good, but I don't even know if these humans will accept your kind inside our walls. Trust me—you're going to have to wait here."

I'd said this last firmly, so he waited. He stepped from one big webbed foot to the other as if he had to pee or something. He was clearly agitated, but that was too damned bad.

At the gates, I used my tapper to hail the guards. The gate commander was none other than Centurion Manfred. He finally came out to meet me after delaying a few minutes.

"Centurion McGill?" he called down from the wall top. Fortunately, we had a radio link or we wouldn't have been able to hear each other in the rain. "Did you lose the rest of your unit?"

"I've brought along something even better," I said. "Nearly a thousand new men to man our walls."

Using his faceplate, he scanned the perimeter.

"Are you talking about those skinny primitives out there?"

"They're not all *that* primitive, actually. But yes, the natives want to join us at the fort. An attack is incoming."

Manfred shook his head. "I'm going to have to kick this up the line, McGill."

I felt like ordering my Scuppers to blow his gate down, but I knew better. The legionnaires were watching us. Hundreds of them manned the walls.

We waited for a few miserable minutes in the pouring rain. It was really getting soggy down here at the base of the wall. I could see why the Scuppers had evolved naturally shiny, wet skin.

"Check your tapper," Manfred called down to me.

I looked at the call that made my arm blink.

"Shit…" I said aloud.

It was Primus Graves. I injected a happy tone into my voice and answered.

"Primus!" I said. "Just the man I was hoping to talk to. I've got the most amazing story to tell, sir, and I—"

"Stuff a sock in it, McGill," he interrupted. "I've seen shots of your salamander army. I'm not impressed."

"Sir, these guys have pretty effective weaponry, they know the terrain, and they're willing to die to take down a tree."

"I told you to go talk to them, not to bring them back to the base!"

"Um… that's right sir. But they followed me. See, I'm like their mother-duck now.

"Why's that?" Graves demanded suspiciously. "Don't tell me you went and spawned with their queen or something."

"No, no, no," I said, suppressing a shiver. "I beat their First-man, and apparently, whoever does that becomes the new First-man."

"Whatever. Tell your new slippery friends to go home. By the way, where is your unit?"

"Uh…" I said. "I don't rightly know. Didn't they make it back?"

"No, McGill, they didn't. You're a centurion without a unit. That makes you useless. Go back out into the forest and find your people. Then, you can make your report."

"All right, sir."

"Oh, and McGill? Walk fast. There's a serious storm coming in."

To me, it seemed like I was standing in a full-blown gale already. How much worse was it going to get?

"Uh…" I said. "Sir, there's one more thing."

"What's that?"

"These Scuppers have been scarring up every tree they've met up with…"

"That's not policy, McGill."

"Right. I know, sir. But they *are* native troops, not regulars. It's occurred to me that they don't come under Varus rules of engagement."

Graves was silent for a second.

He was a by-the-book kind of guy, but he knew me well, and he also knew the advantage that could be gained by occasionally skirting standing orders from the brass.

"McGill," he said, "in the name of conducting relations with the native population, I'm going to let you keep your pets. They're officially marked down as local auxiliaries. Get me an official count and a write-up on their prospective needs and effectiveness."

Right then, I realized Graves was going to play ball. Maybe he'd been wondering why this war was stuck in low gear the same way I was.

"That's great, sir! Can I get them inside the walls, now? It's kind of—"

"I can't approve that. You'll have to get permission from Turov herself."

"Uh… okay. I can do that."

Graves was silent for another long moment. He knew I had a special relationship with Turov, and while he didn't approve of it, he knew it could be valuable.

Finally, he sighed. "I don't want to hear any more about any of this. You're on your own. Is that clear, McGill?"

"Absolutely, Primus."

"All right. Please control your native levies, and keep your own personal funny-business to a minimum."

"You have my word, Primus. There will be no deviltry, mischief or vandalism of any kind. I wouldn't stand for it."

"Great…" he said in a tone of defeat.

The channel closed, and I saw to the needs of my swarm of salamanders. Using Graves' name, I ordered up shelters, food and any other supplies I could think of.

Centurion Manfred doubted me. He contacted Graves personally to confirm. He was a friend, but I considered this to be a dick move on his part.

After listening for a few moments, he finally threw up his hands.

"I don't get it, McGill," he said, "but your lizards will get whatever they need."

"They're *salamanders*, man," I said. "Didn't they teach you anything in school?"

# -38-

It was late at night by the time I reached Gold Bunker. With each step I took in the raging storm, my foot was pushed halfway back by the screeching winds.

Brushing past the guards at the bunker entrance, I went in search of Galina's quarters under the unhappy eye of everyone who belonged down here. Despite the unfriendly welcome, her door swished open before I could even touch my tapper to the door to identify myself.

Galina was there, smiling.

"You lived," she said.

"Sure did! Mind if I come in?"

Not bothering to wait for her response, I stepped forward. Her small hand came up to my chest and pressed there firmly.

I halted, frowning down at her.

She was still smiling, but it was a tense smile.

"Uh…" I said. "Are you mad or something?"

"Why would you think that?"

I wracked my brain quickly, but I was still baffled. I'm not good at reading women's faces. If they try to fool me, or hide an emotion, it *always* works. I could only absorb the most obvious clues.

That tiny hand on my chest for instance, that was a clue. A bad one.

"Um… maybe I should come back later? You got that boy-toy of yours in here?"

She twisted up her face. "No, you idiot. I'm angry with you."

"Oh…. can I ask why?"

"You've been scheming with Graves, that's why."

Galina pushed me back outside, and the doors clapped shut in front of my nose. I frowned in utter confusion. Getting a little pissed off, my hand went up to the door again to demand entry—but I managed to stop myself.

When dealing with a woman, I don't read expressions very well, but I understand the rules that generally lead to success. One of the big ones was never to care too much. If you follow a girl around and beg for it, well, pretty soon she'll become contemptuous.

Shrugging, I turned and walked away. I did so slowly, working on my tapper as if making another call.

I stopped then, just a few meters from her door, and I put on a little show of talking to someone else. I knew she was watching me. She'd opened that door too fast when I'd first arrived—that had given her away.

The more I thought about it, the more obvious it was. She'd *known* I was coming, which indicated she was keeping tabs. Then she'd flashed that door open so fast… The only way she could have done that was if she'd been waiting right behind it, watching on her cameras.

That meant she really *did* care. She wanted to dramatically reject me, and she'd planned it all out beforehand.

Whatever else she had planned, however, wasn't going to happen. James McGill doesn't play that kind of game.

Pretending I'd gotten through to someone on my tapper, I brought it up close to my face so no camera could see who might be on it. Then I grinned. I grinned hugely, and I began to talk.

"I sure will, young lady!" I said. "You don't have to ask twice. I'm over in the gold-bricking bunker right now, so it will take a minute to get—"

Turov's door swished open behind me. I felt a heat on my back. I was pretty sure that was due to Galina's eyes, which were doubtlessly trying to burn a hole into my spine.

"McGill!" she shouted. "Report immediately!"

Turning around, I blew a kiss at my tapper and blanked the screen. Faking a slack-faced, dumb-ass expression, I spread my hands wide.

"What is it, sir? Is there a problem?"

She hunched her shoulders up angrily as I walked past her and into her quarters. Making myself right at home, I sank onto her couch. I don't mind telling you it felt great against my butt. I'd been marching around in the mud for damn near twenty hours straight.

"Mmm…" I said. "This is one comfy couch."

Galina parked herself as physically far from me as she could get. That wasn't very far in what amounted to a studio apartment, but she did her best.

Propping her butt up against the tiny kitchen counter—I was surprised to see she'd had one installed—she crossed her arms over her breasts and glared at me.

"Do you expect me to buy this charade?" she asked.

I blinked, and I almost blew it by laughing aloud and coming clean. After all, I *was* in the midst of performing a charade of sorts, pretending to make a midnight booty call to another girl and all. But something told me to keep going with my pretense. It had already gotten me into her apartment, and I'm a man who likes to stick with what works.

"Uh… could you give a clue, sir? Concerning what we're talking about, that is."

"You're trying to start a war, that's what. And Graves put you up to it. Don't try to deny it."

Now, she really had me confused. My mouth fell open a little bit, and it wasn't even an act this time.

"Uh…"

Angrily, she marched over to the wall near her bed. She swept her arm over it, and a bullshit image of sunny grasslands vanished. In its place, a map of Storm World sprang into existence. I saw our camp, the Blood Worlder camp, and several oily-looking areas that were labeled "Wur holdings."

She tapped the nearest one, which zoomed in. A trail of red spots drew two thick lines through the forest, crossing each other like an X.

"This is the path your patrol took. This other path—this is the one the Scupper war party took."

"Okay… but what's all the red stuff?"

"Those are wakening trees. They're releasing heavy defense pheromones. The wind is spreading them in this storm, far and wide."

"Oh…"

Galina turned on me angrily. "Is that all you have to say? You've awakened over a hundred trees, McGill!"

"We were killing them. Can they produce defensive pods if their bark is cut off?"

"For a time, yes. But more importantly, they release chemicals. That will light up all the nearby trees as well."

"That's what you wanted, isn't it? The walkers will charge the walls, get taken down, and that's that."

"No, you imbecile. That isn't how it will go. This storm will carry the winds to other Wur forests. The entire planet will be alerted. You can't kill this many trees without having them go into a frenzy."

I knit my fingers behind my head and leaned back on her cushions. Damn, they were good for a sore back.

"You got anything to drink?" I asked.

"Not for you. Now, what I want to know is what Graves offered you to pull this stunt for him."

"Um… nothing. There's no stunt. I think both of us were just wondering why we're sitting around doing nothing. You can't win a war sitting inside a fort."

Her finger came up, and it wagged in my face. I hated that.

"That's where you're wrong, McGill. I'm playing a different game."

Now, we were getting someplace. I was mildly interested. Since talking about defeat had gotten her to talk, I decided to push that strategy.

I laughed out loud. "A different game? You mean like, the-piss-and-shiver game? We look pathetic. Even the local guys with their shock-sticks have more balls than we do. Everyone knows it."

"They know nothing. We're waiting for a reason. We're waiting for the Rigellians."

Out of all the answers she could have given me, this one wasn't even on the list. The Rigellians were our arch-rivals out here in the frontier zone. They'd pretty much declared war on us back on Dark World.

"Uh…" I said. "We're waiting for Rigel? Won't they just send their fleet and wipe us out, like they did back on Dark World?"

A single thin finger sprang up again. Fortunately, it wasn't her middle one.

"No," she said. "The circumstances here are entirely different. The enemy risked it all back on Dark World, because the prize was so great. Here, things are different. Storm World doesn't have much obvious use."

"Right…" I said, not getting it at all. "So, why do you think Rigel would send forces out here at all?"

"Because they want this region. They want these worlds. Unfortunately for Earth and Rigel, the Wur are here. No one wants them to get a foothold on these planets. They must be eradicated."

"Okay… but how do you know they're coming?"

"Because these two-timing salamanders called for them."

"They called for help from Earth *and* Rigel?"

"Of course. How could you blame them? They're desperate."

Suddenly, the entire situation had taken on a different aspect. If another player was about to arrive, we didn't want to be found in a weakened state.

"Oh…" I said, staring at the map. "I think I get it."

"That's wonderful," she said sarcastically. "I'm so glad I can get the support of a single junior officer. It thrills me when I have to give private briefings in order for my directives to be followed."

"Well then…" I said. "I'm more than happy to stop that war party from cutting up a single additional tree. What's more, no patrol I'm in charge of will do it, either."

She looked at the map again. "Your change of heart might be too late."

"Probably not. Look at it this way: I brought the Scuppers here, and they're sworn to follow me. I thereby stopped them from cutting any more trees. I might have, in fact, averted disaster."

Galina frowned at me. "They follow you?"

"Yep. Like ducklings."

"Hmm… Why?"

"Uh…" I said, and I cleared my throat. "Their previous leader might have met up with an unfortunate accident."

She laughed then, a very good sign. "An accident? A *fatal* accident?"

"Let's just say he didn't look like he was in good shape when I last saw him."

She laughed again, and she stepped close to me. "I did miss you," she said. "You were dead for a long time."

"Sorry about that."

"Did you really call another girl for a meeting tonight?"

I looked startled, which was easy. But then I managed to appear guilty. I was proud of that bit of acting.

"Well… you did throw me out. This McGill, he's a virgin, see. Unfortunately, the girl said 'no.'"

"You lying bastard," she whispered. "I watched you. She said yes."

She was really close to me now. I felt a certain hot sensation inside my head as I looked down at her. But I still didn't reach out and touch her—not yet.

"There's one more thing, sir."

Her face flickered with annoyance. "What?"

"My new men… they need shelter. They need space inside our walls."

"Why? Have them dig a hole or whatever they do to survive on this shitty planet during storms."

Galina began to climb on me, to run her hands over me. But I stood firm, like one of the giant trees in the forest outside.

"Are you kidding me?" she demanded, jumping back and glaring. "You're trying to hold out on me? I don't believe this. You can go sleep with your frog friends!"

That was Galina Turov for you. She blew hot, then cold, then back again any day of the week.

Deciding to play hardball, I shrugged and turned away toward the door. To sink in the point, I glanced at my tapper as if I'd gotten a text.

Galina saw that. She was very perceptive, and she often jumped to extreme conclusions with alarming speed.

"You're still going to her?" she demanded.

I looked back. "I don't want to let my troops die in the storm. They want to help. They've got decent weapons, and they won't—"

"All right, dammit," she said between clenched teeth. "You can keep your skinny aliens."

Flopping back onto her couch, I was all smiles again. She glared at me, so I knew another act was required. I tapped at my tapper decisively.

"I erased everything," I said. "Take a look."

She grabbed my arm and ran a fine finger over my screen. She rolled through the recent history.

"You deleted it? But she could still contact you."

"Okay. When she does, I'll block her. I promise, you can watch me do it."

"I'm going to hold you to that, James."

"As God is my witness, we've got a deal."

Then she jumped on me, and we made furious love on the couch.

I'm a moth attracted to flame when it comes to evil women like Galina Turov, and I don't mind admitting it. I'd long since made peace with this and marked it down as one of my many flaws.

She was on top the whole time, straddling my wide form. She looked like she was riding an elephant or something, but I didn't mind the view.

While we were in the throes of passion, however, something happened that dampened my enjoyment.

Behind Galina, on the wall she'd turned into a tactical display of the region, the map began to change.

Contacts appeared. More and more of them showed up in the Wur forests. The red dots crept slowly toward our fortress walls. In reality, I knew that meant they were running at top speed, covering swampy ground at a startling pace.

My tapper began to light up seconds later, and so did hers. But her eyes were closed, so she missed it.

In the end, I decided to let us both finish our love-making. After all, this might be the last happy moment we shared for a long time to come.

# -39-

When we'd finished up, Galina immediately figured out there was an attack coming. She ordered me out to the walls to meet the charge head-on.

"You started this, James!" she complained, struggling with a smart-bra that seemed to have a mind of its own. "You're going to weather the storm on the front lines."

"Can I have a kiss for luck?"

"No! Out!"

Less than half an hour later, I was walking on the walls.

My friends, the croaking, web-footed Scuppers, had managed to get inside just before the big wave was due to hit. Fortunately, most of my unit had returned from their extended patrol as well. They were surprised to see me back home on the walls—but they were even more surprised to see a small army of Scuppers wandering around.

"McGill?" Graves called on officer chat. "My display says you're at the gates—that's the gung-ho attitude I like to see. Get your native levies ready for action. We'll see what they can do. I'm putting you in command of the frontline defense on the eastern side. Don't let one frigging tree get over that wall!"

"Your faith in me honors my soul, sir," I said.

Graves disconnected, and I noticed the gate-commander was eyeing me sourly.

"I'm taking command of this post, Centurion Manfred," I told him.

"I heard," he said bitterly. "So that's the deal, huh? I stand guard out here on this snot-slick rock-pile for a month, and the moment battle comes, you and your frogs take over."

"That's about the size of it," I agreed. My expression slowly transformed into a grin. I tried to stop that, sincerely, but it just wasn't in me.

"I'm asking to withdraw," he complained. "You've got enough troops in this sector."

"More than enough… But hey, you weren't a hog back on Earth when you started out, were you?"

Manfred's face reddened. As his cheeks were already kind of red, this was impressive.

"Fuck you, McGill," he said, and he stomped off.

I didn't care, as he was a friend. He'd get over it.

Manfred's unit of troops followed him, and I wished them all a good night's sleep in the rear of the defensive lines.

"You ladies don't have to worry tonight," I told them. "Don't piss the bed, or anything. We'll stop the big, bad trees right here. I promise."

They glowered at me as they filed by. At the same time, my own troops moved up to replace them.

Sargon hadn't survived the ordeal in the woods, but he'd managed to rejoin the unit after catching a revive at Blue Bunker. That made me happy, as I figured we were going to have a glut of people needing a revive real soon.

"Congrats," I told him. "You made it out of Blue Bunker before the rush hits."

"Yeah… I'm requesting permission to drive one of these 88s, sir. I'd like to disperse some payback on these trees."

"Permission granted. Get to your station."

Sargon moved off, and then I had to deal with the salamanders. They looked kind of lost standing on a wall with their funny electric sticks.

"Second-man," I said, tapping a blue one on the side.

"I'm not Second-man. He's down there, at the end of the line."

"Sorry. You all look alike to me."

I walked down to the man at the end, and I saw the splotch of green over his eye. Then I recognized him for certain.

"Second-man, we're going to issue some new weapons to your troops. They're called snap-rifles."

We didn't have time for a formal training, but snap-rifles aren't complicated. You slap in a box of needle-thin ammo, check the battery charge, then aim and spray fire at the enemy. The magazines held around a thousand rounds, but despite their small size, the projectiles did about the same amount of damage as an old-fashioned bullet.

The advantage of snap-rifles was mostly in the low weight-to-power ratio. You could hammer away at full auto, or with short bursts, all day long. The whole kit only weighed about five kilos, which allowed our light troops to move fast and hit hard.

As it turned out, this same kit was ideal for the Scuppers. Using only their spears, they had a real problem with range. Manning a wall effectively was almost impossible for them.

I was glad to see they took to the weapons readily and understood them without confusion. After all, they had a technological society. They'd built an amazing underground transport system.

Out in the forest, I heard an odd sound. A distant howl, maybe. Was that the wind? The skies were stormy, but the winds weren't up to hurricane force—not yet. They were releasing a serious outpouring of rain though.

Suddenly, my Scuppers began firing their weapons. Confused, I thought for a sick second that they'd turned their weapons on us. Could I have brought them into our walls, only to have them play a Trojan horse trick?

"Enemy sighted!" Adjunct Barton shouted.

I had posted her up high, on the watchtower. Our lights were supposed to play sniper from the best vantage point we had, and they didn't disappoint. They opened fire, joining the Scuppers.

Soon, a general storm of small arms rounds were heading downrange into the forest.

Wiping at my visor, I scanned for the enemy. I could see them now on my HUD. There were big red diamonds approaching in a ragged line. But I'd yet to see them with my own eyes.

A second later, one crashed into the open at the edge of the forest.

That's when I realized why I'd been missing them. This enemy wasn't a pod-walker. It was much smaller than that, only about two and a half meters high. Looking like a spider the size of a Clydesdale, the creature scuttled out and took a look around.

That didn't last long. We raked him with fire. Sargon even got excited and turned him to ash with his 88.

"Hold with the artillery on single targets!" I shouted.

"Sorry, Centurion! I've been dying to kill something for days."

"You'll get your chance, Veteran."

More spiders poked their way out of the ferns, but they were quickly driven back, leaving half their number behind thrashing in the mud.

"So far, so good," Harris said beside me.

I glanced at him. "Easy as pie. But I bet you soiled your armor when the first one showed up, didn't you?"

"Keep laughing," he said. "There are a hell of a lot of mamma trees out there making monsters."

He was right, so I didn't tease him any further.

After the first stragglers were quickly blown away, the big wave came. This time, it wasn't a bunch of puny spiders playing scout—it was the core of the enemy force.

What they did right this time was to come in all at once. Usually, we faced disorganized rushes broken up over time. Instead of that tried-and-true failure of a strategy, the Wur must have decided to gang up and hit us on every front at once with everything they had.

An avalanche of aliens charged out of the forest. There were a lot of pod-walkers on our scanners—hundreds of them. But even before the walkers arrived, thousands of smaller troops made their appearance.

Most of these were what we called acid-monsters. They were more sophisticated than the walkers, and we'd usually fought them in space. When I'd met my first Wur soldier, he'd been a space marine that burned his way into the hull of our transport with his sprays of concentrated acid.

The acid-monsters had brownish-gray claws with hard black nodules all over them. These arms were long and deadly in close. Unlike the pod-walkers, these troops seemed to have more brains, too.

To demonstrate their improved powers of thought, they'd come to this battle armed. They had launching devices that threw pods at us. These splashed on the puff-crete walls and began to smoke immediately. Anyone who was touched by the acid, or who breathed in the vapor, began coughing blood moments later.

Right behind what had to be two thousand acid-monsters were the walkers. Relative giants when compared to their smaller comrades, these guys halted when they came into view, and to our surprise, began scooping up and hurling the acid-monsters.

Our puff-crete wall was tough and about thirty meters tall. Nothing should have been able to penetrate it with traditional weaponry—but the Wur had never fought fairly. The acid-monsters balled-up and struck the walls with thudding reports.

Unfolding themselves like blooming flowers, they immediately crawled into our midst and began fighting in close quarters. Men, Scuppers and Wur were immediately locked into a wild melee.

"Sweep the 88s!" I roared, but Sargon and his boys were way ahead of me.

They beamed a steady gush of radiation into the forest, mowing down dozens of our attackers. Unfortunately, I hadn't been clear enough with my instructions. They were burning the pod-walkers rather than the acid-monsters, or the occasional spider officer who skulked among them.

"No, shoot downward!" I shouted. "Kill the little guys at their feet!"

The big guns dipped, but they still slashed the pod-walkers for the most part. Once an 88 begins a sweep, the beam is hard to redirect. You have to finish the pass or it's pretty much wasted. Then, after a cool-down cycle, you can sweep in a different pattern.

What these small artillery guns lacked in ease of use, they more than made up for in punch. As anti-personnel weapons, they were unparalleled in our arsenal. They simply destroyed anything smaller than an elephant instantly.

Unfortunately, these pod-walkers were bigger than elephants. When the radiation bath swept over them, their upper bodies exploded into flame, and their sensory organs were turned to ash at the first caress of the wide beams—but that didn't stop them.

Instead, the pod-walkers went mad. Injured, smoking and blinded, they still staggered forward. Their massive feet plunged down, smashing smaller Wur to pulp.

Some of the big guys tripped and fell, thrashing. Others grabbed comrades and tore limbs from one another such was their fury and agony.

But at least half reached our walls.

Blind, driven mad by pain, they clawed and scrabbled at the puff-crete. Their groping hands caught fleeing men on the battlements, crushing them in their man-sized fists.

When they caught one of the Scuppers, the naked aliens stood no chance. Croaking in dismay, the natives were squeezed until they popped like wet bags of gore.

Barton's light troops and my skinny-armed natives were shattered. Some were so desperate they jumped from the walls, falling to their deaths in the mud.

The 88s couldn't strike the Wur at this sharp angle. First of all, because they would have hit our own men, and secondly, because they hadn't been mounted to tilt down so sharply. It was an oversight, and my troops were paying for it with their blood.

Harris roared for his heavy troops to take to the walls then. I hadn't even given the order, he knew what to do. Except for Graves, he was the most experienced man in the cohort.

"Force-blades!" he shouted. "Stay low, and carve them up when you get an opening."

My single platoon of heavies rushed forward, and I joined them. Harris and I were up to our asses in aliens right off.

A huge arm like a telephone pole swept over my head. Harris and I ducked, but another man wasn't so lucky. He was knocked off the wall, and he roared all the way down until he broke his back on the ground thirty meters below.

Lifting up our force-blades, we extended them to about a meter's length and waited for the big arm to sweep blindly back. It did so a second later—and it was sliced clean off.

Harris and I hung on, but we were almost taken down with it. We spared a split second to grin at each other then moved to poke and stab at the Wur with our blades.

The alien was beyond pissed, howling and roaring, but it couldn't do anything about its torment. It needed one arm to cling to the wall, and with the other gone, it had nothing left to use to crush us.

Finally, it gave up the ghost and toppled, flopping flat on its back among the many dead at the base of our walls.

Two or three minutes passed in a blur after that. Leeson's weaponeers had switched to belchers, and they were blasting the Wur that still struggled on the battlements to fragments. Harris and I marshaled our surviving troops and marched as a knot, mopping up those that still struggled and clung stubbornly to life.

At last, the spiders called a retreat. The surviving Wur humped and scuttled back into the shelter of the trees that had spawned them.

Jubilant, Harris and I slammed our gauntlets together in a high-five.

Our celebration was short-lived, however. I was getting an urgent message on my tapper, my HUD… on every communication device I had on my person.

"McGill! Damn you!" Graves shouted. "Are you dead or just deaf?"

"Deaf, sir!" I shouted back, opening up the comm channel. "East gate is clear. Repeat, East gate held!"

"That's great. Now, please get with the program. I've been requesting reinforcements for the reserves at the bunkers. Take every other man you've got, and send them to the center. Immediately!"

Blinking, I examined my HUD. During a pitched battle, I usually turned it off or at least toned it down. It could be very distracting when you were fighting for your life in hand-to-hand combat.

Now that I took in the bigger picture, I felt a sinking feeling.

We'd held on our front—but two other zones of the fort walls had been breached. We were being overrun. Soon, the enemy would reach the bunkers in the center of our camp.

Flipping up my visor, I turned my face upward into the pouring rain. A gush of water, bitter winds, and fresh air immediately swept through my sweaty suit.

Then I slapped my helmet closed again, and I began giving unwelcome orders to my weary men.

# -40-

Legionnaires like myself are men of the stars. We'd long ago traded in a normal existence to fight and die over and over on hostile planets that are so far from Earth you can't even spot our home system in their night sky without a telescope.

It's only natural that, in such a state of isolation, we had developed elements of our own culture. One such item was an often quoted proverb.

*Don't trade a good death for a bad one.*

Only the oldest salts, the most experienced and hard-bitten soldiers would speak those morbid words. For a long time, my own comprehension of that nugget of wisdom had eluded me.

The idea that sometimes dying was for the best went against every natural instinct a young man has.

But today, I understood the proverb. Today, it was obvious even to me that those who had fallen fast and clean in the first hour of the battle had been the lucky ones. My envy for them grew as the day dragged on and transformed suddenly into night, which was normal on the fast-rotating planet we called Storm World.

By that time, banged-up and weary, I figured it would be a fine blessing to be all queued up, waiting in limbo. As it was, I could only dream of fresh lungs and clean air to breathe. Mine had long since been tainted by acid, blood and bile.

A peaceful rest was denied me, however. Instead, my unit had fought to the point of exhaustion. At our sides were the last two hundred-odd native warriors, and I'd come to appreciate their grit.

By the time night fell, we were huddled inside Gold Bunker, and we were nearly as crazy as the Wur themselves.

"They'll get in here," Harris said, his big eyes rolling around as he stared at the ceiling.

Outside, the walkers thudded around and scratched at our puff-crete bunker. They tried to pry open the steel doors now and then, making us all tense up, but so far they hadn't made the all-out effort that was required to tear their way inside.

"They'll get in here eventually," Harris continued. "It'll happen when the spiders come into the compound. They'll tell these morons they have to work together to pry our doors open. Then—that'll be it for us."

"Shut up, Harris," I rasped.

Even those few words caused me to go into a coughing spasm. I'd caught a lungful of acidic vapors a half-hour back, and it was still bothering me. Every now and then, I day-dreamed about making a run for Blue Bunker to get medical help, but that was just a fantasy. Even if I made it, I doubted our bio people would squirt any regrowth fluids into my lungs. They'd probably just decide to recycle me out of hand after a brief exam.

"First-man," my Scupper lieutenant said to me.

He'd been trying to get my attention for the last several minutes, but I hadn't felt like going through the ordeal it would take to communicate with him.

"First-man," he repeated.

Turning my burning head toward him at last, I regarded him with my one good eye. My right eye wasn't working anymore. After I'd taken a blast of acid in my faceplate, even ripping off my helmet hadn't completely solved the problem. Some of the caustic fluid had splashed onto my hair and skin. I probably looked like burnt hamburger.

My lieutenant didn't care about my looks, however. He didn't seem to have noticed my injuries at all.

"First-man," he repeated.

"What the hell is it? Talk!"

"Thank you. I don't wish to seem rude, sir, but it might be a good time to retreat."

I stared at him tiredly for a moment before I managed to bubble up a laugh. That turned into a cough, which subsided a few long seconds later.

"We can't retreat. The lifters that took about half the legion back up into space are all gone now—they can't land safely."

"That was the biggest cow-pie of all," Harris complained. "When I saw those ships coming down, I thought we were saved. But what Turov really wanted was to save our equipment. She took almost all the revival machines—did you know that, McGill?"

"Yeah," I rasped.

A loud noise interrupted our talk at that point.

*Bam-Bam-Bam-Bam!*

One of the pod-walkers was hammering on the doors again. The doors shivered, and mud squelched out of the cracks around the battered hinges—but it held. The abused doors weren't giving up, not yet.

Everyone grabbed up their weapons and aimed them at the entrance. We breathed with our mouths open, as if the monster might hear us otherwise. Who knew? Maybe it could.

My team had been charged by Turov herself to die on these steps if necessary to keep the Wur out.

After a long moment of quiet, we heard the thumping of massive feet. The walker had given up and moved off, looking for another way in—even though it should have been obvious by now there wasn't one.

"One more lifter would have done the trick…" Harris lamented. "I heard Turov tried to bring one more down to Gold Bunker. She was going to save her pretty ass and hopefully some of us with it. But the pilots refused to land after they saw the base was overrun."

"First-man we must retreat," my lieutenant began again.

I whirled around and grabbed his skinny arm. It felt rubbery, almost like there wasn't a bone inside at all. I reminded myself not to squeeze, and I let go of him.

"Second-man," I said. "There *is* no way out of here. We're trapped. Don't you get that?"

He stared at me with an unreadable alien expression. "Would it be bad manners to refute your statement, First-man?"

"Uh…" I said, turning over what he'd said in my mind. I shook my head and smiled with the good half of my mouth. "No," I said. "Go ahead and argue with me. I don't care anymore."

"Then, know this: The tubes are below us. There is an access point."

For the first time in an hour, a tingle of hope stirred in my mind. I turned to him slowly.

"There's a tube? A tunnel? A way to get down into your subway system?"

He took a second to understand the translation, then he spoke again. "Yes. That is what I said."

I whooped then. It was a startling Georgia battle-cry of the kind usually only heard in a bar, long after midnight.

A dozen dirty heads turned toward me. Two dozen eyes stared.

"What now, McGill?" Harris asked. "You got a crazy idea?"

"I do at that, Adjunct. Everyone, gather your kit. We're following this blue gentleman, here."

"Um… Didn't the tribune tell us to guard this spot with our lives, sir?"

"She did indeed, Harris. But I'm going to give her—and you—something she'll appreciate much more than pointless sacrifice."

Harris followed me, and I followed Second-man. A handful of confused troops crept after us.

The Scupper led us down deep into the bowels of the bunker. Like most, it had two levels, then a basement underneath that for storage.

There was an armory down here, but the cage doors stood busted open, the guards long since summoned away to man the walls.

Past that, generators thrummed releasing a steady trickle of fusion power. At least we still had lights and heat.

The last room was a storeroom, and Second-man led us there. At a bare spot on the puff-crete floor, he gestured with his odd, sucker-tipped finger.

"This is the spot, as closely as I can measure."

"Um… there's nothing here. Where's the entrance?"

"When the humans arrived, they covered it over with this hard substance. It was foolish of them, in retrospect."

I stared at the puff-crete floor, visualizing what must have happened. Legion Varus had arrived while I was dead, and they'd built this camp with their usual lack of concern for the environment or the locals who lived here. Apparently, they'd unwittingly paved over a Scupper tube station.

Snapping my fingers repeatedly, I rapped my knuckles on Harris' chest. He frowned down at this intrusion.

"Can I help you, Centurion?"

"Get Sargon."

"He's dead."

"Get any weaponeer we've got left. If we don't have any—find a belcher in that busted-up armory."

Grumbling, he marched off to obey. He was saying something about swamp-fever, but I didn't care.

There was the light of hope in my eyes again.

# -41-

After we'd managed to drill our way about two meters deep into the muck under the bunker, Turov showed up.

Her hands were on her hips, and her lips were twisted into a tight sneer. "McGill! You're flooding the entire bunker with the most awful fumes!"

"Right there, Moller," I said, directing my veteran to blast a new exploratory hole into the shifting wet dirt. "Burn me a new hole.

She nodded and went to work.

"McGill!" Galina exclaimed.

I stood up and looked at her.

That changed her expression. She put her fingers to her lips, gasped, and took a step back.

"Your face…" she said. "Half of it's missing."

"Nah," I said, giving her a painful grin. That effort sent a trickle of blood into my mouth. "It's just a scratch."

"Jesus… here…"

She got out a spray-can of nu-skin, and she started spraying.

That felt surprisingly good. Nu-skin is a liquid mix of artificial stem-cells, pain-relievers and disinfectant. We'd run out of medical supplies and bio specialists hours ago, so I hadn't had a chance to do much about my injuries up until now.

She clucked her tongue and gently worked the foamy stuff into the burns and crack of my cheek. The men behind her shook their heads and smirked.

I didn't mind. Everyone knew Turov and I had had our moments. It was about time she treated me with a touch of kindness in public.

"All right," she said. "Explain this to me. Why are you digging a hole in the bottom of my last bunker?"

"Last?" I asked.

The other men looked at one another.

"Well… there are survivors. But we are the last one that hasn't been broken into yet. Fortunately, I had the doors here overbuilt. They're way beyond required specs."

"I see," I said, and I did see. Turov never stinted herself when it came to government expense budgets. It made perfect sense that she'd built her own command bunker to withstand more punishment than the rest.

Now that my skin wasn't so sore and tight, I was able to talk to her and explain the nature of our plan. As I did so, she looked at the blue-skinned Scupper at my side in growing alarm.

"Are you insane?" she demanded when I'd finished.

"Some would say so," I admitted.

A small hand terminating in an even smaller index finger aimed itself at my Second-man. "We can't trust this… this being. What if it's all a trap? What if we go down there into a dungeon these lizards have dug, and we're all captured?"

"First off, sir, they're salamanders. Not lizards."

She crossed her arms and narrowed her eyes. Not a good sign. I decided to take a different approach.

"Okay," I said. "Moller, stand down. Let's wrap it up, boys. We're going back to the front entrance. We'll kill one or two of those pod-walkers when they break in. After that, well, they'll have the run of the place."

Turning to Harris, I thumped him with my knuckles again. He frowned at me.

"What is it now, sir?"

"How long have we got? Until they break in?"

"I'm no expert on Wur psychology," he said. "But the minute the spiders get here, they'll coordinate the efforts of the tree-things. Then… we're goners."

I grinned, even though it split some of the nu-skin and burned.

"There you have it! The kind of death every Varus man dreams of. We'll fight to the last, and we'll sell every life down here dearly."

I turned and began marching up the stairs.

Turov called me back. "Hold it!"

Feigning reluctance, I turned to face her with a quizzical look.

"Do you really think you can get us out of here, McGill? All I see is a steaming, scorched mud-hole."

I shrugged. "Maybe. Maybe not. Should we try? It's your call, sir."

She hissed and paced for a few seconds. Turov didn't like this kind of decision-making. She liked employing standardized plans that had been approved by Central back home. She liked designing fortifications and giving orders that had no chance to fail—but she didn't like going off-script into the weeds.

All that said, she didn't like dying, either.

"All right. Do it. But if they do break in, you'll rush up to the entrance and fight them off. Clear?"

"Clear as a mountain lake, sir."

She left, shaking her head. I watched her go, and so did the other guys. No one could help themselves. Whatever she'd paid to update her hindquarters, it was worth it.

"Hey, back to digging," I ordered.

They rushed to do so, and twenty long minutes passed without much in the way of results. We'd blasted the hole bigger by now. It was maybe five meters in diameter, with rough edges that were glowing hot.

We heard a crash and some screeching upstairs.

"That's it," Harris said. "They're breaking in!"

I waved to him. "Go up there and do what you can. Moller, hand over that belcher."

Reluctantly, she did so. Most of my men raced off, and I heard a firefight begin in earnest. The rasping and shrieking of the Wur acid-creatures answered our fire in the corridors. They were assaulting the entrance.

Second-man tried to hump his way after them, but I reached out a big hand and snagged him. He almost did a facer right there, but I helped him up.

"You are dishonoring me," he said. "You are dishonoring yourself as well. We must defend the bunker."

"That's a damned nice gesture, Lieutenant," I said. "But we all know those men are doomed to die. Now, I've gone and dug your hole for you. What I want is for you to find that entrance you promised would be here."

"I told you, it is difficult to be precise. The entrance *should* be here, but it has been obscured by human foolishness."

I still had a grip on his skinny arm, and I did a little march-around, taking him with me.

"Let's give it our best guess, shall we? Since this is about to be our final moment on this mud-pit you call home. Which spot is the most promising?"

He pointed to the far side, and I marched over there with him in tow. He struggled to get away and head upstairs to the battle, which was growing louder every second, but I hung onto his arm. My fingers were like a vice on his limbs, and he didn't even slow me down.

"Right here?" I asked, standing over the spot. "That's your best guess?"

"Yes, First-man."

"That's good enough for me," I said, and I kicked him in the ass.

He toppled forward into the hole, and, as I'd dearly hoped, he vanished as if the steaming earth had swallowed him up.

Clapping my hands and howling, I called for the rest of my men to fall back. They weren't listening, so I contacted Galina on my tapper.

"Hey!" I shouted. "We found it!"

"You found what? Get your ass up here and defend me!"

"I've got something better. You get your ass down here and survive with me. Bring everyone down. Withdraw everyone you've got to the basement."

She didn't listen at first, so I marched up the stairs. There she was, standing at the top and breathing hard. She was close to a panic. Galina Turov was a lot of things, but she wasn't much of a front-line combatant.

"Boo!" I said.

She jumped and squeaked, then she put a pistol in my face. "Jokes? Now? I should shoot you on principle."

"Come down here, sir," I said. "Just for one second. I found a way out, honest."

She narrowed her pretty eyes at me. Now, in her defense, I didn't have the best reputation when it came to truthfulness.

"You'd better not be bullshitting me, McGill. I'll rip off your centurion's crest and staple it to your balls."

"Well-deserved and purely expected, sir. Right this way."

I jogged back to the spot with Turov in tow. When we got there, she arched over the hole and peered in suspiciously, the way a cat might eye a pet cage.

"I don't see a damned thing," she said. "You're crazy. It must be the toxins in your blood or something. In fact, if you won't fight, I'm going to have to put you down—"

Her speech ended with a screech of dismay. I'd swept her feet out from under her and given her a shove. She fell into the hole, right where my Second-man had vanished.

To her credit, a beam flashed up and almost nailed me. As it was, I felt the heat of it on my scalp, and a number of hairs stank up the already foul air with that unique smell hair always produces when it's turned to vapor.

But Galina had vanished. The Scupper trick of interdimensional physics had saved the day again.

Patting at my hair to make sure it wasn't on fire, I contacted everyone on tactical chat.

"This is Centurion James McGill," I said. "Tribune Turov is down. Repeat: Turov is down. Everyone is ordered to fall back to the basement. Perform a fighting withdrawal. We've found an escape tunnel—get down here as fast as you can, boys."

That did the trick. Less than a minute later, I was tossing recruits into the hungry earth. Harris was one of the last ones to go.

He looked at me with vast suspicion. In fact, he seemed angry.

"If there's some kind of threshing machine down there, McGill, I swear I'll haunt you until the end of your days."

"Fortunately, my days are about done with. I hear something out in the hall."

A strange, hooked limb appeared in the doorway. It clung to the doorway and pulled itself closer.

It was one of the acid-monsters. Injured, it hadn't given up the ghost yet.

Harris and I blasted it, but it kept crawling closer. It was determined. Like all Wur creatures, it didn't die easily.

When it expired at last, there was no time for celebration. More were in the hall, rasping and whispering in alien speech.

Harris and I looked at each other.

"They're planning to rush us," Harris said. "Does this hole really go someplace?"

"Only one way to find out," I told him, and I jumped in.

Looking up, I saw Harris. His eyes were big, and I think he was realizing he was the last man in Gold Bunker.

As I fell, I saw him leap after me. His big boots were heading right toward my upturned face.

And then, everything changed.

# -42-

I fell backward into the tube. Someone under me grunted in pain. Just in time, I rolled to one side and dodged Harris' boots.

The figure below me turned out to be Moller. When Harris landed on her, she roared and kicked him off.

"I broke a rib already," she grunted.

"Get off the LZ, girl!" I shouted, helping her to her feet. "First lesson of any drop!"

"I'm sorry, sir. I'll be fine. I just got the wind knocked out of me for a moment."

"Right…" I said, doing a quick headcount. "Harris was the last man. What's our total strength?"

"Sixteen, sir—humans, that is."

I whistled long and low. That was pretty bad. I wondered how many of the thousands we'd left behind had made it out somehow. I suspected there weren't many survivors.

"What about Scuppers?" I asked Harris.

He pointed with an expression. I walked a few paces and stared down a side-passage. To my surprise, it was chock-full of Scuppers.

"What the hell…?" I asked. "How did all you guys survive? I didn't have this many with me in Gold Bunker, not even at the beginning."

Second-man approached. His blue skin had a few cuts in it, but he was easy to recognize and he could still move normally enough.

"First-man," he said. "This is your army. Do you not recognize them? They are your faithful followers."

"Yeah, but how did they all get down here?"

Second-man spread his odd, sucker-cup fingers. "It is easy to understand. Many were left behind at the wall when you left to defend Gold Bunker."

"Yeah, so?"

"Without you, sir, they lost heart. Scuppers do not fight well without their leader."

"But what does that…?" I trailed off, because I was catching on at last. "They ran out on the gate defenders, didn't they? They knew where the entry points were to these tunnels, so they found them and bugged out."

"We are nothing like insects," Second-man objected. "Insects are stupid, and they fight to the death like pod-walkers. These loyal troops waited for you here. Now, they have rejoined you, and they will serve you faithfully."

I wanted to give the crowd a good reaming, but I decided not to. After all, they were volunteer native levies, not regular soldiers. They were serving me and me alone. That meant I couldn't let them get out of my sight if I wanted them to fight hard.

Galina walked up to me about then. She stared around at the curving walls in wonderment—then she noticed the Scupper army in the side passage.

"Good Lord! Where did all these colorful frogs come from?"

"That's my personal army, sir," I said with a touch of pride. "They're here to help."

"I don't get how they knew to meet you down here… but I don't care. We need all the help we can get. I'm impressed by your army, and your tunnels. When I heard your report about an underground system of tubes, I figured the story was bullshit."

"Just goes to show you," Harris said. "You can't even trust McGill to lie properly."

He laughed at his joke, but I cast him a dark glance. He finally shut up and wandered off.

"McGill," Turov said. "Since you're familiar with this alien rat-hole, I'm putting you in operational command. Get us out of here."

"Roger that, sir."

I quickly explained how to use the tube system. As I did so, the human troops stared at me with growing alarm.

"We have to fall *sideways*?" Galina asked. "For kilometers?"

"Yep. But don't worry, it's kind of fun once you get the hang of it."

"Unless you touch the sides by accident and get smashed to a pulp," Harris said bitterly.

"Yeah, well… there is that."

"Lead," Galina urged.

After talking to Second-man for a minute, I got a handle on which way to go. We jumped into the air and shot in the correct direction.

Not long afterward, I landed and heard a distant, growing wail behind me.

Galina came tumbling out of the tube and slammed into me. Fortunately, she didn't weigh much more than an infantryman's ruck.

I caught her and set her on her feet, laughing. "It seems like lighter flyers go a little further down any given tube."

"Yes," my blue friend confirmed. "That's how it works, First-man."

"I must be the lightest person here…" Galina said, gasping for breath. "That means I should go *first* next time. Shit."

"Aw, come on. That was fun, wasn't it?"

"It was terrifying," she complained.

But, despite her misgivings, she jumped first at the next junction point. Trusting me and Second-man, she demonstrated she had guts. She was whisked away into the distance at about two hundred kilometers an hour.

Second-man followed, tucking himself into a perfect ball. His fellows followed him, as they were skinny people without much gear. The bulk of the human troops went next, one at a time. Lastly, Moller, Harris and I jumped, as we were the heaviest.

About three minutes later, we were deposited safely at the next station. No one had had a serious accident.

"This way," Second-man said, pointing up a long shaft. "This one goes to the surface."

"Where are we going to come out?" Galina asked.

I looked at her in surprise. "There's only one destination that makes sense," I told her. "This shaft leads up to the near-human legion camp."

"That's great," she said bitterly. "I'll be the laughing stock of the entire planet. When *doesn't* Turov wipe her entire legion?"

I didn't say anything, because she was probably right. The truth was people already said stuff like that about her without factoring in this fresh disaster. Galina had presided over several of the worst military defeats in modern history. Hell, we'd wiped on Dark World just last year under her leadership.

"Um…" I said. "You want me to go first?"

"No," she said firmly. "I'll do it."

Setting her lips in a tight line and looking straight up the shaft above us with determination, she squatted and then launched herself.

She jetted straight upward and soon vanished.

"Let's go," I said, and we all followed one at a time.

Our entire group soon came popping out of the ground like gophers exiting a flooded hole. We were noticed almost immediately.

There was a spat of gunfire, and several of the Scuppers were shot down. The rest had the good sense to hug the mud.

"We've activated automated turrets!" Harris hissed as I came out of the ground and did a little flip.

I landed on my ass near the exit point, and I started to get up.

"No! Don't!" Galina urged. "Stay motionless!"

All around me, our entire makeshift army of survivors was freaked out and kissing dirt. About the only good news was the storm was more of a drizzling rain here. We crouched on a layer of dead, wet leaves that frosted the thick mud.

Each man that popped out was tracked by the turrets. We shouted and even went so far as to pin them down. That kept casualties to a minimum.

Once we were all out of the tubes, Galina pointed toward the walls. I stared at the puff-crete defenses of Fort Beta, wondering what our next move should be.

Sure enough, I spotted an automated cannon up there, swiveling and chattering like a sprinkler. It kept swinging back and forth between targets with mechanical eagerness. The crappy AI didn't seem to know which of us it wanted to shoot first.

"McGill…" Galina said quietly. "Could you get rid of that thing, please?"

"Will do."

"I'll do it," Harris said, and I saw him reach out a long leg toward my Second-man.

Now, Harris was a master of putting the hurt on a man who seemed out of reach. His body seemed to stretch and stretch under these circumstances, almost like he was made of elastic.

My blue buddy had no idea what was coming his way, and I don't mind telling you I thought it was unfair. He was going to use the native as a distraction for the turret to shoot at.

When Harris had reached his greatest point of careful, slow extension, I intervened before he could kick Second-man. In the end it was me who gave Harris a push with my boot.

Harris lost his balance and rolled onto his face.

A sudden rattling sound told the tale of what was preordained to happen next. The auto turret, which had been guarding this lonely section of puff-crete wall, lost its cool. It put fifty rounds through Harris in a dramatic burst.

The rest of the group froze. They were surprised and alarmed—but not me. I took the turret's moment of distraction to toss a grav-plasma grenade at it.

The turret didn't like that. It was one of the newer models, and it could remember things. It put me on its kill-list and swiveled to shower me with bullets next.

*Whump!*

The grenade went off. The turret twisted up, smoked a little, and died.

"There you go," I told Turov. "All fixed."

"You got Harris killed," she complained.

I shrugged, uncaring. "He was the perfect distraction for the machine. Besides, he was kind of being a dick."

"Well, never mind. We must get inside these walls. The Wur have to be marching here next."

That idea made me blink in surprise. I mean, it stood to reason, but I'd never considered the thought until now.

"Who's running the Blood World legion, anyway?" I asked.

She glanced at me in surprise. "You don't know? I thought you were briefed—oh, but you missed all that. You were loafing around, dead."

"That's right. There's nothing as useless as a corpse."

She waved my words away irritably and made her way toward the nearest gate. I followed her, still wondering who the other tribune was, but figuring she wouldn't like it if I kept asking.

At the gates, we were challenged and identified. When the guards at last realized they'd met up with an honest-to-God human tribune, they changed their tunes and scrambled to open the door.

Gawking, two giants of the biggest breed watched us march inside their walls. They each stood a solid six meters high, with heads slightly too small for their gargantuan bodies.

The gate commander was a squid, naturally. I wasn't sure I recognized him—but then he identified himself and I whooped.

"Churn!" I shouted. "Is that good old Sub-Centurion Churn?"

He looked at me, blinking his overabundant eyes. Squids had more eyes than a tarantula, and they were at least as ugly to look at.

"Centurion McGill?" he asked. "I'm surprised to meet you again."

"You two can make out later," Turov said. "Churn, lead the way to your tribune's office, immediately."

"Ah… yes sir. But just for the record, I'd like to point out that your arrival is highly unusual. These natives with you, also—they're problematic. If you would please follow protocol—"

"Leeson, stay here and fill out whatever bullshit form he wants."

"Me sir?" Leeson complained.

"That's what I said. Now Sub-Centurion, lead the way. That's an order."

With poor grace, Churn led us toward their version of Gold Bunker.

# -43-

As we walked, I looked around and estimated the strength of the garrison here at Fort Beta. To my mind, the Blood Worlder fort looked stronger than the Varus fort had. They had a lot more troops, and each man was more physically imposing.

Looks, however, can be deceiving. Legion Varus troops had a lot more experience than any formation of Blood Worlders. Many of us had decades of combat experience behind us, and all of our skills are sharp.

That didn't mean the Blood Worlders couldn't fight—they were born and bred for that express purpose. They just didn't have our expertise.

Arriving at Gold Bunker, we were ushered inside. The bunker was similar in layout and design to the one we'd left behind at Fort Alpha, but it was bigger. Since Blood Worlders were often three times the height of a man, the ceilings were arched like cathedrals. The doors, too, were on a titanic scale.

Making our way to the end of the main passage, we arrived at the tribune's office. There were two more giants at the doors. They were imposing doormen, but they weren't heralds by any means. They reached out and pulled the doors open without saying a word.

Inside, an over-decorated chamber was revealed. That wasn't anything unusual to me—I'd become used to Galina's extravagant tastes.

What did surprise me was the nature of the décor. There were lots of trophy cases. The cases were made with real wood that darkened with age. Half-way up the very high walls was an arsenal of antique weapons.

Right about then, I caught on. I'd seen this kind of décor before…

"Don't tell me…" I said. "It can't be! Isn't he still commanding Legion Germanica?"

Galina smirked at me. "No longer," she said. "Drusus demoted him—sort of. He put it in complementary terms, of course. Lots of talk about needing an experienced man, one who could handle a new legion made up of non-humans. All nonsense, of course."

"Right…" I said. "They had to find experienced tribunes somewhere… but to be reduced to leading a Blood Worlder legion after having run Germanica for decades…"

Galina lowered her voice. "If I were you, I wouldn't bring that up. He's touchy about it. Xlur kept complaining about him, which is partly why he ended up here. Don't forget you had something to do with the tribune's fall as well. Don't forget that, McGill. I'm sure he won't."

I thought that over, and a new understanding dawned in my mind.

The last time I'd had direct dealings with Germanica was back on Blood World itself. The locals had arranged a series of arena battles between various groups. In order to ensure victory, Earth had sent not one, but two legions into the fray.

Germanica was the odds-on favorite to win the whole thing. Unfortunately, the locals had taken a shine to me and my troops. Because of this, Germanica had been forced to forfeit.

"Hmm…" I said, as more memories of those days flooded into my mind.

We stepped through the outer office, which was manned by a mix of real humans and a few squids. The next set of doors was smaller, only about three meters in height. I reached out and opened these by myself.

Inside, leaning back in his chair with his boots on his desk, was none other than Tribune Maurice Armel.

His eyes belied his relaxed appearance. He was gauging us both as sharply as a fox on the hunt. Those quick eyes slid over Galina to me, where they stayed.

Was it my imagination, or had his tight-lipped face just twitched a hair? Yes, I do think it did. He wasn't happy to see me, of that much I was sure.

This wasn't surprising. The last time we'd been in each other's presence, we'd killed one another. The only good thing about that fight had been the simple fact that he'd died first. That had left me the winner by default—until I'd bled out later on in private.

"Turov!" Armel said, sweeping his boots off his desk. He spoke with a French accent and wore an embarrassingly thin mustache over his sneering mouth. "I'm *so* glad to see an imperator has come to take proper command of this campaign at last!"

Galina's face had been brightening, but it fell immediately when the word "imperator" came out of Armel's twitchy mouth. She'd held that lofty rank, equivalent to a two star general—but that was in the past. She'd been busted back down to tribune before being deployed to Dark World.

Armel knew all this, naturally. He'd called her an imperator to slap her in the face.

"Oh!" he cried out, put his hand to his mouth. "Oh no, I'm a scoundrel! You lost that rank, didn't you? Please, accept my apology for that slip of the tongue. I'm so sorry for your loss."

"Thank you, Armel," she said stiffly. "My regrets echo your own. It's too bad we only have one *real* legion on this planet to fight with. If Germanica was here, instead of this stinking rabble of Blood Worlders, Drusus might have seen fit to assign us an imperator."

Upon hearing her insult, Armel's expression darkened a shade, but he recovered quickly enough.

The two clasped hands briefly. I watched, knowing that this universal demonstration of peaceful intent was a falsehood. These two already wanted to murder one another, and we'd only just arrived.

"Uh..." I said. "Maybe I should wait outside."

"No," Galina snapped. "Please sit with us, Centurion. After all, until the lifters bring down the rest of my legion, you're my highest ranked supporting officer."

Armel indicated chairs with a flourish. We sat in them—and we sank low.

Slightly alarmed, I looked around at Galina, she'd noticed it too. The chairs in front of Armel's vast wooden desk were low-slung. In contrast, Armel's seat was a bit high, allowing him to lord it over us.

Sighing and leaning back, I took full advantage of the seat. "This is nice and comfy," I said. "My limbs are sore after fighting all day long."

"Ah, where are my manners?" Armel asked.

He sprang up and opened one of the wooden cabinets he had standing here and there. Producing a large bottle of brandy, he poured three glasses and handed them around.

I didn't refuse the drink—in fact, I tossed it down.

"This brandy is the finest in the star system," Armel told us. "It's seven hundred credits a bottle, direct from the best cellars in Old France."

Galina sniffed hers, and she took a tiny taste. Immediately, she set it aside.

I burped in my mouth and waved my glass at Armel, asking for more.

Frowning, he poured me a stingy amount. I kept shaking the glass under his hand until he reluctantly poured another dollop.

"Armel," Galina began. "Let us set aside our petty jealousies and disagreements of the past."

"What?" he asked, blinking in surprise. He pointed at me. "Has this one been telling stories?"

"Nah," I said. "I didn't even know you were the tribune of this zoo."

At the term "zoo" Armel's eyes narrowed. It was a relatively new derogatory word the legions had decided to give Blood Worlder outfits. The military had always been full of special words—both the official and the unofficial.

Galina reached out a hand and touched my wrist. "McGill, you must make an effort to be more polite."

Armel noticed that touch, and I got the feeling he'd heard rumors about Galina and I. In fact, I braced myself for a whole new slap-fest of insults on our sexual relationship.

But that never came. Instead, Armel leaned back behind his desk, sipped his brandy, and nodded.

"All right," he said. "I agree with you, Turov. We have both been mistreated by our superiors. The only way to get back what we once possessed is through cooperation."

Galina nodded. "I'm glad you see reason in this instance. We must win this battle. We can't be outdone by the Wur."

"Agreed."

And that was that. They'd started off all catty and hissing, but after getting some of that out of their systems, they decided to put away their knives and treat each other right. I was surprised and happy about the development.

"So," Armel said. "We must assume that the Wur will attack Fort Beta just as they did your pile of sticks to the north."

"They'll come," Galina said. "I only hope we can kill them all this time."

"When can your troops arrive from *Legate*?"

"As soon as I give the order. Do you have room for them all?"

Armel shrugged and made a pouty face for a moment. "We will have to build more bunkers. In the meantime, I suggest your troops come down and sleep on the lifters. I'd rather have them close in case the Wur make a serious move."

About then, I stopped listening. They worked out how many troops could man the walls, how long the shifts would be, and a dozen other dull details.

The next thing I knew, a sharp jab in the shins woke me up.

"Stop snoring and drooling, McGill," Galina said. "It's time for you to gather your skinny blue friends and post them at the main gate."

I blinked the sleep from my eyes. After fighting most of the day, I found I was more than a little fatigued.

"The Scuppers? Why are they going to the walls?"

"Because the rain is picking up—they don't mind getting wet, do they?"

"No… I suppose not."

"Then, get out there."

Galina dismissed me with a wave. Armel poured another brandy, but he excluded me, even though I shook my glass at him.

"One for the road?" I asked.

He frowned at me and then glanced at Galina's glass, which was untouched. "Perhaps McGill would like to share your beverage, hmm, Tribune?" Armel asked.

"What? Oh… you want this, McGill? No wonder you're falling asleep on me. All right—take it."

I snatched it from her and downed it in a gulp before anyone could change their minds. Armel looked at me like he smelled crap. Galina turned away, disinterested.

I could tell Armel wanted Turov to get drunk. Maybe I'm paranoid, but that was my honest impression. Hell, I might have wanted the same if we'd been alone tonight…

That thought gave me a chill. What if Armel was about to put the moves on old Turov? Should I try to protect her—was I even justified in doing so?

After all, she was a grown woman, and our occasional hook-ups weren't anything serious. Still, I found myself lingering at the exit. My eyes roved over the two.

Armel had poured her another drink, and he looked pretty lit himself by this point. He swirled his glass around, sniffed it, and talked about the bouquet.

Galina finally took a sniff, and she was about to drink. I could tell.

Now, you have to understand that I knew Galina Turov pretty well. She didn't drink often, but when she did, she often lost control. Armel, on the other hand, was a crafty, high-functioning alcoholic.

I cleared my throat loudly.

They both turned a cold eye in my direction.

"Sorry sirs," I said. "Do you want me to ask Graves to begin landing the troops? I'm—"

"Yes, yes," Galina said, flapping a hand at me. "Get on with it. Dismissed."

Trying not to look sour, I nodded and left.

But as I was exiting, Armel caught my eye. He made a tiny kissing motion with his lips, just for my benefit. Galina didn't notice, as she was taking a burning swallow of his overpriced brandy.

*Dammit.*

I left, and the big doors swung shut behind me.

# -44-

Walking out, I was fuming mad.

Sure, the last time Armel and I had met up, we'd fought to the death. But that had been an honorable thing to my mind, a challenge made and executed to the finish. I'd won in the eyes of the worldwide audience, but we'd both been dead within the hour, making it close to a draw.

But this? This was different. He was seducing a girl he knew full well I was involved with. What's more, I thought he was doing it out of spite.

Sure, Galina was a lovely woman. She kept herself fresh as an orchid, dying and coming back again as young as young could be every few years. But still, I'd be willing to bet a stack of credits tall enough to buy one of his fancy bottles of brandy that Armel was only doing it to bug me. That made things personal.

Unfortunately, I couldn't think of an easy way to remedy the matter in my favor. Sure, I could go back in there under some pretext and then maybe assassinate him. That would be satisfying for a few minutes at least—but then his damned Blood Worlder apes would tear me apart. They were already eyeing me like they had special orders to keep me out of the office—who knew? Maybe they did.

Worse, Armel would just pop back out of the oven downstairs a few hours later and have me shot.

Nope… I just couldn't think of an easier path. This was going to take more work than my usual violent outburst.

Checking my tapper, I found a raft of messages. I paged through those, and soon realized there were *way* too many to bother with. Irritated, I contacted Natasha who was up in orbit, aboard *Legate*.

"James?" she answered immediately. "I see you didn't die, and you're at Fort Beta. How'd you pull that off?"

"I'm slippery," I said.

Natasha was a tech—possibly the best tech in the legion. She'd had a thing for me that stretched all the way back to our first campaign together, so I couldn't very well ask her for help rescuing Galina, but there was more than one way to skin a cat.

"Natasha," I said, "I need a crisis. Go through today's news for me—here, I'll give you access to my official email."

"Um… you *want* a crisis?" she asked. "I don't understand."

"I need a pretext to barge in on Tribune Armel, and I need it fast."

She sighed. "Again with the brass? Why don't you hang out with people on your own level, Centurion? There are plenty of—"

"Specialist Elkin," I said, "I'm needing some help, and I need it right now. Can you do the job, or do you want me to call Kivi?"

Natasha's voice stiffened a bit. She was jealous of Kivi—always had been.

"There's no need to mine your email," she said. "There are a half-dozen crises in progress right now. Any of them should suffice."

"All right, list them."

She muttered something, but I didn't quite catch it, and I had a feeling I didn't want to know what she'd said anyway.

"First off," she said, "there's the fact that thirty-eight percent of Legion Varus is still dead, sitting in the revival queue. Then there are the enemy troop movements to the north, where they're clearly gathering strength to hit Armel's fort next."

"How long do we have?"

"Maybe three days—Storm World days."

I computed that, and shook my head. Three Storm World days lasted about thirty-six hours. "That's way too long. What do you have right now?"

"Um… there are always rumors."

"About what?"

"Native troop movements, and that strange ship that's lurking among the outer planets."

My ears perked up. "A ship? What ship?"

"Unknown. It's thought to be a Nairb ship, coming to spy on us. But it could be a Wur ship. We just don't know. Either way, it's keeping its distance, hanging around the gas giants in the outer system."

My mind raced. "I think that will work," I said. "Thanks, Natasha."

"Uh… okay."

I did an about-face and marched back toward Armel's office.

"One more thing," I told her. "Contact Graves and tell him Turov wants him to land now. He's to bring down all the lifters, and he's to report in person to Armel's office."

"Uh… isn't he supposed to get a message like that from Turov herself?"

"Good idea… that's good. Tell him to call her to confirm the details. Maybe she'll have an agenda all printed out for him."

"You're sounding kind of strange, James," she said. "What's this all about?"

"Nothing," I lied. "I'm just trying to be a supportive officer. We were hurt pretty bad down here. Except for Turov herself, I'm the most senior surviving Varus officer on this entire planet."

"Ah," she said. "Turov is making you her gopher, and you want an excuse to get out of mundane work. Now, I get it."

I let her go with that one. It was as good a cover-up story as I could have created. Better even, since she'd come up with it herself. The most convincing lies are the ones people invent and tell themselves to explain the actions of others.

Marching back to Armel's office, I tried to enter—but the two Blood Worlder giants didn't open the door. I pushed, but it didn't budge.

Suddenly, the odd design of Armel's doors seemed more than cosmetic. By making these massively thick doors, he effectively kept people out.

Looking up at the giants, I glared at them.

"Do you two know who I am?" I asked loudly. "I'm James McGill. The Hero of Blood World!"

They stared at me with slack faces for a few seconds. Finally, the one on the left worked his rubbery lips.

"...McGill..." he said in an odd, rumbling voice. I got the feeling they weren't used to talking much.

"That's right. Open this door! I command you!"

They did it. I was as surprised as anyone, but I didn't let it go to my head. After all, there was still the inner door to contend with.

Six sweeping strides took me to the second set of doors. Two heavy troopers stood there, looking at me curiously.

"Official business," I said. "Open the doors."

They didn't answer, they didn't budge—they didn't do anything. They just stared at me.

To me, that indicated they had orders from Armel to leave the big doors shut.

Some secretary person was talking off to my right, but I was losing my cool by this time. The staffer wasn't armed, so I ignored him completely.

Instead, I marched to the doors, and I hammered my fist on them. Then I tried to pull them open. They didn't budge.

The heavy troopers didn't try to stop me. They just looked at me like I was a crazy person. Maybe, just maybe, they were right.

Why was I doing this? I had to ask that, although I usually didn't bother when I got into a bad mood.

Did I care about Galina? Or was I simply pissed that Armel was lifting his leg on what I considered to be my territory?

It was hard to say, but I *was* angry, and I'd lost it.

Drawing my pistol, I made ready to burn a hole in the door.

A massive hand came down from above and gripped mine. The Blood Worlder's paw was so big it looked like somebody's dad had grabbed hold of his child.

I looked up at those, piggish, stupid eyes. There was wisdom there. I could see it. Sure, he wasn't going to ace the SATs, but he knew I was headed down a dark path, a path he was going to have to interrupt.

"Yeah…" I said. "You're right. I'm sorry."

My gun went back into my holster, and the massive paw that had gripped me slipped away.

Heaving a deep sigh, I turned around. I was just going to have to walk out and save what I had left of my dignity today.

Then, the door opened.

Surprised, I turned around. I expected to see Armel giving me his widest, shittiest grin.

But instead it was Galina. She had her clothes on and everything.

Frowning, I watched as she walked out. Behind her I saw Armel trotting after.

"But Tribune," he said. "Can I count you as my guest for dinner tonight?"

"Of course," she said.

They both glanced up, noticing me.

"McGill?" Turov asked. "Do you have something to report?"

"Yes sir. There's a strange ship in the system. I… I think we should discuss it."

Her eyes widened a fraction then diminished again. They slid from side to side in a calculating way. Inside her head, I knew the demons of worry were whispering.

Galina knew I'd recently been involved in a foray to the Core Worlds. If this was a Nairb ship, it couldn't be good news. Possibly, she could be under investigation herself.

She was more right than she knew. I hadn't even told her about how I'd murdered old Xlur. There was much more going on than she suspected.

"I must go—right now," she told Armel. He had a few grasping fingers on her elbow, but she pulled away and went with me.

Turning back, I took a quick look at Armel. One glance told me the tale.

He seemed annoyed—and that was all I needed to know. He hadn't gotten anywhere with Galina.

I began to smile.

# -45-

"How can you be in such a good mood?" she demanded when we were a hundred steps away from Armel's overgrown set of doors.

"Um..." I said, unsure of how to answer. I couldn't admit I was happy she'd obviously refused Armel's attentions. A quick lie usually sprang to my lips at moments like this, but I was empty right now.

Her eyes searched mine for a moment, but she apparently didn't like the blank look I returned.

"Are you really an imbecile?" she demanded in a loud whisper. "This ship is probably a Nairb vessel. They haven't come out here to Province 921 for years."

"Well, technically," I said, "this isn't Province 921. We're out past the rim. This is frontier territory, what used to be Province 929."

She stared at me in surprise. I'd dumped a little info on her partly to throw her off—but mostly because I didn't like being called a dummy.

"How the hell did you know about that?" she hissed.

There… that was perfect. She was off the track and running the wrong way again. I allowed myself a tiny smile of victory. She had no idea I was here due to jealousy.

"I know lots of stuff," I said.

"No one knows about old 929. No one knows the Empire has had… difficulties in recent centuries."

"Difficulties? You mean like civil war, decay, and outright shrinking borders?"

Her eyes inspected the Blood Worlders and squids that wandered the halls. The squids were watchful, and when you saw them staring, you always had to wonder what evil thoughts were going on inside their alien minds.

Apparently, Galina felt the same way. "Not another word. Come with me."

She led me to her newly assigned courtesy quarters in Gold Bunker. A primus had been kicked out to give it to her, and he was just packing up as we arrived.

"Oh…" I said, recognizing the guy. "Primus Fike! Good to see you again, sir. We'll soon be in battle together, shoulder-to-shoulder."

He gave me a sour glance. He'd once been a proud leader in the Iron Eagles, and I'd made his acquaintance on Dark World. Unfortunately, he'd died the hard way back then, and he seemed to recall the event vividly.

"McGill…" he said. "I remember your unit. You stood by as my troops marched into a Vulbite ambush."

"Nonsense, sir!" I said enthusiastically. "Don't sell yourself short! You guys gave them hell, but there were just too many of the enemy. By the way, your fresh younger body looks good on you."

I grinned at him the whole time he glowered and hauled his stuff out of the tiny apartment. There was a desk, a bar, a bed and a bathroom. That was about everything a man needed to be comfortable in my book.

The minute he was gone, I stretched out on the bed and sighed heavily.

Galina stood over me with her fists on her hips. "What do you think you're doing, McGill?"

"Taking a break. My bones hurt after fighting all damned day and night."

"It is late…" she said, glancing at her tapper. "I should probably send you to one of the other bunkers. I don't want people talking."

"Aw now, come on! Squids don't care about where humans sleep."

"But Fike does. Why do you have to antagonize people like that? You should be polite to him."

"I thought I was. I never even mentioned his humiliating transfer to this zoo legion."

"Zoo legion? More insults? That's it, you're out of here."

"Hold on, hold on," I said, seeing she was seriously considering throwing me out. I had plans, and they didn't include hiking in more mud and sleeping on a rolled-out mat in some basement full of Blood Worlders. "We've got to talk. For reals."

She took my measure again, and she sighed. "All right. What are you hinting about?"

I told her then. She was the first person, besides myself, to learn what had really happened out on Mogwa Prime.

Galina wasn't happy. She pulled back a long ways, and then she came at me with a roundhouse, slapping me a good one across the cheek. I let her do it, not even trying to block her hand. A trickle of blood stained my teeth.

"Are you *shitting* me?" she demanded. "You killed Xlur *again*? On his home planet, no less?"

"Yeah…" I admitted. "I think it was right next to his own bedroom this time. I just didn't see another way out. I didn't have the book, he was figuring that out, and I—"

She slapped me again, from the other side. This time, it landed on my ear and kind of hurt. I hadn't expected that second one, so I looked up in annoyance.

Galina put her face down into mine, her teeth clenched and angry. "You should have killed yourself without harming Xlur. The Mogwa will never believe this was a legitimate suicide."

"Why not? He was kind of a sad failure."

"Because Mogwa don't kill themselves. They aren't fools—they're narcissists."

I thought that one over, and I had to admit, she had a point. The Mogwa weren't human. They were aliens, and they followed their own behavioral rules. Hell, for all I knew, they lacked the capacity to feel depression at all.

"But… all he did was complain about being sent out to dismal frontier provinces as an exile. A governorship out here is like a prison sentence to them."

"That's very interesting, McGill. But even if I accept your credentials as an unlicensed xenologist, the fact remains you risked Humanity because you were bored with the Core Worlds."

I scratched my neck, feeling a trifle self-conscious. "Well… you've got a point there."

That hand came up again, but she didn't slap me this time. Instead, she wrapped her arms over her breasts and started pacing around like she was comforting herself. My dreams of a sultry night were fading fast, I don't mind telling you.

"A massive fuck-up," she said. "You've turned a humiliating defeat into a full-fledged shit-show. How are you going to get us out of this?"

"Um…"

"That's what I thought. You have no idea at all."

She stopped pacing and propped her butt up against Fike's desk. She was thinking hard, I could tell.

"We have to try to establish communications with the Nairb ship," she said at last.

"But we don't even know if it *is* a Nairb ship."

"What the hell else would it be? You've seen them operate before. The first thing any cautious delegation of Nairbs does is scout the system in question from a safe vantage point in the outer system. Then, when they understand the situation and the players, they move in and make their demands known."

She was absolutely right, of course. I'd seen the Empire's most bureaucratic race behave like this more than once. I still had my doubts, but the odds were she was correct.

"Okay. What are your orders, sir?"

"What can we do…?"

"We could blow up their ship. We did that back at Rogue World."

Galina closed her pretty eyes for a moment as if in pain. "Why would you remind me of that disaster now?"

I shrugged. "Just a thought."

Her face screwed up with horrid indecision. Finally, she contacted Graves. Despite the fact it was about midnight local time, he answered immediately.

"What is it, Tribune?"

"Graves… contact that ship: the one lurking among the outer planets."

"We don't know who they are, sir. We don't have probes out that far, and they—"

"It's the Nairbs, Primus. It has to be."

He was quiet for a second. Galina had him on speaker through her tapper, and I could hear it all.

"Are you saying that because you have some inside knowledge on the topic?" he asked at last.

Galina glanced at me, and I gave her a tired thumbs-up. She rolled her eyes.

"It doesn't matter. Assume they are Nairbs. Greet them with enthusiasm and inform them Earth is responding to a distress call in the frontier region. Suggest they are welcome to watch, but should stay out of weapons range as we can't guarantee the safety of civilians."

"Do you want this going out in the clear?" Graves asked.

She hesitated, but only for a moment. "Yes."

"Got it. Will transmit. Due to the range, however, it will take about four light-hours to reach them, and four more to get a reply—should they choose to answer at all."

"I understand. Turov out."

Sighing, she collapsed on the bed beside me. "Between you, this ship, Armel and those shitty trees today, I can hardly breathe."

"Armel really worked you over, huh?" I asked.

She looked at me quizzically. Then, suddenly, a sly smile appeared on her face. She sat up and touched my cheek with one finger.

"You're jealous," she said. "Ah-ah—don't even bother to deny it. I saw something on your face before, but I didn't quite understand it then… now I do."

"That's crazy-talk."

"Sure it is. Don't worry, your secret is safe with me. But I have to admit, I'm feeling better—proud, even. After all, how many girls have wasted their hours worrying about you? This is an opportunity to even the score for them."

I didn't like the way she was talking, so I didn't answer.

She continued to run her finger over my cheek. It took me a moment to realize she was outlining the mark she'd left on my face with her previous slaps.

"Armel did give it a try," she told me, moving closer. "But you already knew that, didn't you? It takes one cad to know another.'"

My eyes studied the ceiling. I tried to look unconcerned, but I didn't think it was working.

"No interest, huh?" she said, getting up and standing at the foot of the bed. "Well… I'm not tired. I think I'll go for a walk. Don't wait up."

She didn't make it to the door. I was up, and my arm was blocking her before she took three steps toward it.

"I could have you up on report," she said in a silky tone.

"You can report me in the morning, sir."

I kissed her then, and she responded nicely. Somehow, I was more into it than usual.

Did that mean I had serious feelings for Galina Turov? Lord, help me...

When I lifted her up and carried her back to her bed, she whispered in my ear. "Armel didn't get anything."

"I know."

She laughed. "Yes, I suppose that you do. He tried, mind you, but I didn't even let him kiss my fingers. Why do men do that, anyway? I don't like it. Such an act makes them seem weak to me."

Tired of talk, I grabbed her, and she went with it.

A short time later I was busy demonstrating I was anything but a weak man. She liked that, and we fell asleep soon after.

# -46-

Morning came all too soon. Galina and I barely had time for breakfast before we were receiving emergency messages on our tappers. The lifters were on their way down from the transport and due to land outside shortly. Graves was in charge of the deployment, and he'd apparently been working the whole time we'd been sleeping together.

But that wasn't the big news. What concerned us more was the unidentified ship—it was on the move.

"What's going on?" Galina demanded when we reached the command center.

The squid ops officer eyed her for a moment then glanced at Armel for approval. After all, we were in his legion's headquarters, not our own.

Armel gave his officer the nod.

The sub-centurion squid shuffled his many thick appendages around to face us.

"The ship lurking in deep space has reacted to your query from last night," he said. "It is transmitting messages and flying closer."

"Let me see what they have to say," she said, stepping toward the main screens.

Again, the squid checked Armel's mood. After getting a second nod, he touched his console.

An old, grizzled Mogwa appeared in the holo-tank. His body was bloated and his limbs squirmed impatiently. Unlike the usual black sheen of a Mogwa body, this specimen was pale in patches that looked fleshy and wrinkled.

Could it be they shed their chitinous shells like hermit-crabs as they got older? I wasn't sure, but that's what it looked like. When I was out there, I hadn't seen too many old-looking Mogwas. No matter what the reason, he was sinfully ugly.

"Slaves," the Mogwa began, "I am Sateekas. I'm the new governor of Province 921. I'm here to witness Earth's capabilities firsthand. When the enemy arrives, you are instructed to engage in battle immediately. Behave as if I'm not here. When I pass judgment, rest assured that I intend to implement an honest verdict."

Galina, Armel and I reviewed this message together.

"Sateekas!" I boomed.

They both gave me blank looks.

"Don't you recognize him? That's good old Grand-Admiral Sateekas! He's been out here a few times... The last time he was in the province, in fact, he was commanding Battle Fleet 921."

"Ah..." Galina said. "That old bastard... How could I forget?"

"They do all look similar," Armel said, "but he's clearly an ancient specimen. What alarms me most at this point is your apparent familiarity with this Mogwa, McGill."

"Oh yeah," I said. "Sateekas and I go way back. *Way* back. I know him almost as well as I know Xlur."

"Speaking of whom," Armel said, "where has Xlur gone? He's apparently been replaced as our governor, but I don't recall hearing anything about the transition, or why it happened."

"Well Tribune," I said, "that's a funny thing—"

"Shut up, McGill," Turov said, cutting me off.

"Yes sir."

Turov stopped staring at the message, which she'd been replaying over and over while we talked.

"What matters most are the unspoken details of this message," she said. "Sateekas mentioned passing judgment. He mentioned coming to a verdict. Could that be related to our performance here on Storm World?"

"Maybe he wants to see if we can beat the Wur," I suggested. "We are the local enforcers."

"But…" Armel sputtered, becoming alarmed. "He can't possibly be weighing Earth's capacity to wage war *now.* It would be monumentally unfair. We are grossly outnumbered. We can't launch a serious offensive at this time. It will take days just to get the rest of your legion back into the field."

Galina shrugged. "You're right, of course. But the Mogwa rarely consider the fairness of their judgments. It's my assumption we must win this planet in short order. Otherwise, there's no telling what they might do."

"How are we going to do that?" Armel demanded. "Your legion is half-dead, and mine—"

"Is made up of half-trained apes, yes, I know," she interrupted. "We're going to have to request reinforcements from Earth."

"I'll go!" I boomed.

They both cast me sour glances. They knew about my occasional side-trips home during far-flung deployments.

"I don't think so," Armel said.

"I agree," Galina said. "It will not be McGill this time."

"Good," Armel jumped in. "I'm glad that's settled. You're easily the best of us, Turov. With you serving as our ambassador to Earth, we're sure to get the forces we require."

Galina looked annoyed and worried at the same time. "All right," she said, surprising everyone. "I'll go."

I'd expected her to put up a fuss. By the way Armel's eyebrows shot up, I knew he'd expected the same.

That left us both pondering while she replayed the message a few more times, tapping at her lips with a carefully painted fingernail.

We were surprised because whoever went back to Earth would be carrying bad news home to Central. Galina generally avoided being the messenger bearing bad tidings as much as she worked to take credit for every success.

But not today. She just kept replaying that message, frowning and studying it.

"Uh…" I said. "Why are you playing that over and over, Tribune? I think we've got the gist of it by now."

She aimed a fingernail at the screen. "Watch this part. Listen to what he says again."

"...When the enemy arrives, you are instructed to engage in battle immediately..."

I shrugged. Armel frowned. She looked at us with a worried expression.

"He's been watching for days," she said. "We know that. Why would he talk about the enemy arriving soon? The Wur are already here."

"Perhaps it's a translation failure," Armel suggested.

"Or maybe he's talking about the next attack," I said.

They both looked at me. I grinned back. "Don't tell me no one has figured out yet that the Wur are going to try to take this fort out soon? Just like they did the last one?"

"Of course we've considered that..." Turov said, "but I don't feel one hundred percent certain that's what Sateekas is talking about."

I shrugged. For the zillionth time, I was glad I wasn't running an entire legion.

"All right," she said at last. "McGill, you shall return to the walls. Help Graves arm and organize everyone he can. I'm leaving for Earth."

She marched quickly out of the control center, and we both watched her go.

The moment she was gone, Armel gave me the boot out of his command center.

I was happy to leave. I kind of wished I was playing messenger-boy by going back to Earth using the gateway posts, but that dream seemed out of reach now.

Gathering my gear and my troops, I went to find Graves. I had most of my unit cobbled together by now, plus a couple of hundred salamanders.

Graves eyed me critically when I reported for duty. The rains were watering the planet again, and the wind was blowing at a slant. Even with our visors down, we had to shout to be heard.

"McGill shows up at last," he said.

"Um... We got in last night, sir."

"Last night? Who's we?"

"A few survivors of my unit, Tribune Turov, and my friendly native heroes."

I indicated the throng at the base of the wall we both stood on. They were sheltering from the storm up against the puff-crete.

"Turov…?" he asked. "I thought she'd been evacced."

"That was me again, Primus. I showed her my underground system of tubes, and… well, we used it to come here. Currently, she's headed to Earth to sweet-talk somebody into sending us reinforcements."

Graves nodded after checking my story on his tapper. He was the kind of man who often professed to believe me—but then checked every word I'd said against the record just to be sure.

"I've been so busy marshalling the legion and redeploying," he said, "I hadn't heard that part of yesterday's events. I'm impressed. There *were* very few who didn't board the lifters to get out of Fort Alpha and yet still survived the night."

"That was us, sir. Where can we help now?"

"Right here. You're the new gate commander."

Sub-Centurion Churn sidled up to us as we spoke. At about this point of the conversation, it became clear he was listening in.

That wasn't any kind of violation, as we were using local chat on purpose. If we'd wanted to exchange words discreetly, we could have created a private channel.

"Yes, Sub-Centurion?" Graves demanded, looking up at the squid.

Churn was impressively large, just like all squids. He had to weigh close to five hundred kilograms, and that's a whole lot of raw calamari.

"Excuse me, Primus," he said. "But I do believe an error has been made."

"You're right," I said. "Your mama sewed too many arms on you."

Graves slapped my chest plate with the back of his gauntlet, and I shut up.

"What error, Churn?" Graves asked.

"There was some discussion of putting this person in command of the gateway. That is not possible, as I'm in charge of the gate."

"You're challenging my authority?" Graves demanded.

"Not at all, Primus. I'm merely challenging your grasp of certain realities. Tribune Turov has left the planet. Tribune Armel outranks you and therefore it is he who must be obeyed."

The squids could be kind of prissy when it came right down to it. You wouldn't think it to look at them, but it only made sense. After all, in their culture, there were only two possible roles: that of master, or slave. Middle men played both parts, of course.

In such a rigid society, no one messed around second-guessing as to who was in command. It had to be very clear at all times—otherwise, it was a squid free-for-all. They'd murder each other until someone proved himself to be top dog.

"You've got a point," Graves said reluctantly. "I've been operating the defensive effort based on the fact Turov is a tribune in command of a real legion. Since Armel and Turov are of the same rank, she had the authority."

"A real legion, that's right," I chimed in.

They didn't even look at me. Churn was aptly named, because his tentacles seemed to squirm around a lot when he was ticked off. I could tell he wasn't happy we'd even tried to depose him. Squids were even more territorial than humans under these circumstances. They were sure to take any removal of authority personally.

"Tribune Armel?" Graves asked, talking through his tapper again. Before he said anything else, he switched to a private link.

While he talked, I stepped up to Churn and pointed. "You see that man? He's older and more experienced than any squid that ever lived."

"I find that difficult to—"

"What's more," I said. "He's not just a primus. He's what we call a blood primus. His rank insignia—see that star? It's got a ruby in the center. That means he's the most senior ranked individual in Legion Varus, short of Turov herself."

"I fail to see—"

"I'm trying to tell you, squid. He's in charge of Varus, and any human legion supersedes yours."

"That's not my understanding of the command structure."

I crossed my arms. "Well, we'll see."

Graves faced us again a few moments later. His expression was stony.

"The gateway is to be bolstered with a larger force. We'll have a full cohort of heavy Blood Worlder troops up here, plus McGill's rag-tag army and some more elements from Varus."

"Uh…" I said. "But who's in charge, sir? Please don't tell me I've got to take orders from Inky, here."

At the label "Inky" Churn stiffened, and his tentacles whipped around like snakes.

"Armel has decided to deploy Primus Fike at the gatehouse as the overall size of the force has grown too large for a centurion to handle. Both of you will place yourselves under his command when he gets here."

After handing out these orders from on high, Graves marched away, his boots splashing.

Churn and I eyed one another in distaste. This wasn't going according to any plan of mine. I could tell Churn wasn't happy, either.

At least that was something.

# -47-

Primus Fike was a true asshole. It could be said—and had been said by many—that his entire home legion known as the Iron Eagles was made up of a parade of assholes just like him.

But even in such company, this man stood out. It wasn't his effectiveness, his professional qualifications or his fighting abilities I objected to. It was his insufferably superior attitude. He considered all troops from Legion Varus to be trash, and he let us know it at every opportunity.

Fike didn't like Blood Worlders much, either. As a result of these poor opinions of everyone he was commanding, he wasn't happy—and neither were we.

"All right, people," he said to a collection of centurions and a few other supporting officers. "Let's see if we can mount a proper defense without screwing up as badly as Varus did at Fort Alpha."

Harris tossed me a glare, and I knew he was wondering if I was going to mouth-off. He clearly wanted me to, as he lacked the balls and the rank to do it himself.

Stoically, I ignored Harris and stared at Fike with my arms crossed over my breastplate.

"McGill," Fike said, zeroing in on me, "I want you and your freaks stationed right here at the gatehouse itself. You'll provide overwatch and check every ground vehicle that comes in or out of the compound."

"Uh…" I said, lifting a finger into the air.

"Do you have a question, Centurion?" Fike demanded.

"Just a suggestion, sir. My unit has fought these Wur before—several times. I think we should be on the walls."

"Do you have any 88s?"

"No sir. They were all destroyed or abandoned back at Fort Alpha."

"Exactly. You can't stop a walking tree with a snap-rifle. You'll man the gatehouse."

"But sir… our heavies have force-blades. We killed a lot of the enemy with those. Besides, I was figuring we'd get new gear. Lots of transports are shipping stuff down from orbit every hour."

"You figured wrong," Fike said, looking down at his portable battle-table. It glowed, casting a blue-white glare up into his faceplate. "All equipment being distributed right now is going to successful units, not failures."

"Successful?" Harris spoke up, unable to stay quiet any longer. "What has this *zoo* legion every done?"

Fike looked at Harris balefully. His two sub-centurion squids did the same.

"We haven't lost our fort yet, for one thing. We're going to get our chance to shine soon. You Varus people had your shot—stop complaining. If things go badly enough, I'll throw you into the fight. Until then, you're strictly reserves."

Fike went on, detailing the placement of forces along the rain-soaked battlements. When he'd finished, I realized he'd skipped over my native troops. There was nowhere near enough room for them inside the gatehouse, there were too many.

"Sir?" I asked.

He sighed, flashing his eyes up at me. "What is it, McGill?"

"What about my Scupper troops, sir?"

"Your what?"

"My native levies. They can't all fit in here."

The gatehouse was about the size of a large multistory house. Leave it to Armel to build something complicated out of puff-crete and put it on top of his walls. I thought maybe he had some kind of a hard-on affair with medieval days, as his wall looked more like a castle structure than our usual simple designs.

"Your what? Oh right… those tree-frogs…"

"Salamanders, sir."

"What's that?"

"Their morphology more closely resembles—"

Fike made a sweeping gesture with his arm, and I shut up.

"Whatever," he said. "Just keep them out of my way. Put them inside the walls, near the road. If anything gets past our defenses, tell them to attack it."

Harris and I glanced at one another and shrugged. Really, it was hard to complain too much, as the deployment made things easy on us. All we had to do was back up Fike's gorillas.

Oh sure, I knew what he was doing. He wanted to make sure that we stayed out of this fight in order to give every drop of glory to his troops. The good Lord knew they needed it. These Blood Worlders looked tough, but they weren't experienced. They'd yet to prove themselves in battle to anyone.

The briefing droned on, but I'd tuned out. I messed with my tapper instead. That brought me to an interesting tidbit of information that Natasha had passed my way.

My hand shot up again, and I waved for attention like a teacher's pet.

Fike ignored this for several minutes, but at last he pointed at me.

"What is it now, Centurion? Do you have to go to the bathroom?"

There was a general wave of laughter at that. Even the squids bubbled a little.

"No sir," I said. "But I thought I'd mention that this planet is being invaded."

Fike rolled his eyes. "Yes, I know. We're the invaders."

The group laughed again.

"Um… very funny, sir. But I'm talking about the new ships that have just arrived. They've warped in close, and they're slipping into orbit. Check your tapper."

He did, and he frowned. "Uh… you all have assigned stations! Dismissed!"

I turned around, but I heard heavy boots behind me. Fike was marching in my direction with a scowl on his face.

"That information is need-to-know, McGill," he told me. "Didn't you read the entirety of the message? I can't believe Armel even put you on the distribution list."

"Um..." I said, realizing that Natasha had stolen the information and passed it on. Whenever I had a good inside channel to spy on the brass, it wasn't a good idea to give it up. Accordingly, I lied.

"Sorry sir," I said. "I was startled by the message. I guess I didn't realize it was classified."

Harris was watching this exchange like a man watching a naked Ping-Pong tournament. His eyes flashed from one of us to the other with every word.

Fike looked at him. "Take a hike, Adjunct," he ordered.

Reluctantly, Harris walked away.

Fike lowered his voice and got closer to my ear. "Armel specifically warned me about you. Now I can see why he bothered. You're a loose cannon."

"That's right, sir," I said. "But I can still shoot pretty straight."

He blinked at me for a moment, then the frown returned. "Listen, I don't want you here. I don't want any Varus trash under my command at all. You'll only bring me down somehow in the end."

"Aw now, that's not a fair characterization, Primus. You can't tell me you're still sore about dying back there on Dark World? That was over a year ago. Get over it man. A death is a death. It's no big deal to a real legionnaire."

Fike's face darkened further. Before, he'd been glaring like an angry old man with kids on his lawn. Now, he looked like I'd tipped over his outhouse and set it on fire.

"You'd best not antagonize me, Centurion."

"That's the furthest thing from my mind, sir."

"Good. Dismissed."

"Uh... there is one more detail."

"What now?"

"What about the invading ships, sir? Are we going to set up defensive measures to meet the new threat?"

He blinked again. "Surface-to-air missiles?"

"That'd be a good start. I haven't seen any deployed here except at Gold Bunker. Surely, you have more than a single battery."

Fike looked concerned for a moment, and I almost grinned.

He'd skipped over preparations for a serious strike from above. That's because, in my opinion, the Iron Eagles were glorified color guards. They'd been polishing gear and standing watch over alien princes for so long, they'd forgotten how to fight a real war.

Unfortunately, this was beginning to look like one.

"Look, sir," I said. "I'm seriously suggesting we build up our air defenses—and we scatter them all over the fort. We've got lots of alien ships in the system, and there's no way *Legate* could take them all out if they decide to strike at us."

"But..." he said and consulted his tapper again. At last, he nodded. "I'll talk to Armel about it. We'll request and deploy missile batteries. But you—you're to report to your new station immediately."

I grinned. "I'm already here, sir. I'm your gatehouse watchman, remember?"

He gave me a sour salute and rushed away, talking to his tapper.

The whole scene worried me a little. These troops all thought they were hot-shit, but they didn't seem to have things completely in hand yet.

The next two hours slid by in a boring fashion. As my men hadn't been given much to do, we lounged around indoors and made trouble with the Blood Worlders. We got them to arm-wrestle each other, and taught them various games of chance. Somehow, the near-humans always seemed to lose their money to the Varus troops.

As the third hour began, things changed. Darkness had fallen outside, and the rain had finally died down to a drizzle.

"McGill!" my tapper spoke to me. I opened a channel, recognizing the caller as Natasha. "Look at this—I can't believe it."

She passed me a vid feed. It was from space, and I recognized the cloud-smothered planet below our ship—the video was looking down on Storm World.

"Looks like rain," I said, laughing a little.

Natasha didn't share in the joke. She sounded a bit panicky. "They're about to fire on those alien ships!"

My mouth fell open, my eyes widened, and I stepped outside into the rain. Standing on the battlements, I tilted my head back and stared up into the dark skies.

Above me was a gray-black wall of ever-lasting cloud-cover. I knew *Legate* was on the other side of the storm, cruising above the atmosphere in a high orbit.

To my surprise, I saw her fire her broadsides. The orange flashes were so bright they came through the clouds like lightning and made the sky shine like daylight for a second or two.

Now, I have to tell you that when a dreadnought fires her primary armament, it's a big deal. Sixteen cannons, carefully constructed to fire sixteen fusion warheads all at once—that packs a powerful punch.

"What's that? Lightning?" Harris asked, joining me on the battlements.

Together, we gawked up at the clouds.

"What's up, McGill? You know something, don't you? You're holding out on me—you're holding out on everyone!"

"Shut up," I said. "Just watch the sky."

Sure enough, the clouds flashed again. There was another rippling series of flashes, as if someone had set off a dozen firecrackers in rapid succession, a split-second apart. As it was all happening up in space, the explosions were eerily silent.

At least ten more times, something big lit up the sky.

"They're firing again," I whispered, checking my tapper feed for confirmation.

Harris grabbed my arm to look at my screen, and I let him.

"The broadsides… they're firing the broadsides?" he asked, letting go of me.

I shook my head. "They already did that a few minutes back. They couldn't have reloaded them all so fast, and besides, the broadsides fire in unison."

"Well then what's going on?"

"Remember those new missile pods Turov showed us at the briefing?" I asked him.

His face went ashen in sudden comprehension. "They're firing everything they've got."

"Seem like it."

Harris peered up into the cloud cover fiercely, as if he could penetrate the gloom with the power of his will alone.

"What are they shooting at, McGill?" he asked me.

"They've spotted alien ships up there," I said.

"You mean the Nairbs?"

"Not just them. Someone else has arrived. They came out of warp real close to the planet."

Harris looked at me in shock and alarm. "We should get below ground. What if one of those shells strays down to here?"

I laughed quietly. "Well Adjunct, in that case we'll be transformed into a spreading cloud of atoms a split-second later. Armel hasn't deployed anti-air batteries or shields. There's no point in running now. We might as well enjoy the show."

Together, we continued to gawk up at the sky.

All over the fort, the word had spread. Troops and vehicles rushed this way and that, and sirens wailed.

But we stayed put, walking on the battlements atop our gatehouse. After all, we were already at our assigned battle station.

# -48-

Natasha kept streaming vids to me from space. Otherwise, I might not have known what was happening up there.

It was disturbing. Three ships had arrived—three *more* ships. It wasn't clear what kind of ships they were due to the range, but I didn't think they were friendly.

Allied ships didn't just pop into disputed star systems, coming out of warp close to a planetary gravity-well, if they had friendly intentions. First of all, appearing next to a planet was a dangerous stunt. Warp drives weren't super-accurate, as you had to navigate blind while you flew a ship in warp. It was like coming up for air from the bottom of the ocean. You weren't always exactly sure where you would surface.

In addition to the navigational hazards, it was just plain rude. Hostility would be assumed, and rightly so, by any local inhabitants.

But neither of these concerns had impinged on our new visitors. They'd appeared about a hundred thousand kilometers out, and were coming into orbit at speed.

"Are you getting this, McGill?" Natasha asked me.

"I sure am—thanks."

"Don't share it around. I could get into trouble. Not even every primus is seeing this."

"Are they worried about morale?" I asked.

"Maybe..." she said, "or maybe there's more to this than we know about yet. Maybe this is someone's dirty little secret."

"Hmm..." I said thoughtfully.

In Earth's past, some of our militaries had been outstanding and purely professional. Others, sadly, had been shams run by dictators and the like. Our modern armed forces were worldwide, and therefore they operated similar to what the old defunct United Nations may have fielded back in the day… In other words, our military was functional, but far from perfect.

For a long time, Hegemony hadn't been run in an entirely up-and-up fashion. Corruption, shenanigans, and even treason had frequently reared their ugly heads. Natasha was hinting that this might be a private deal. It could be Claver, for example, coming to do a deal under the table with Turov, or Armel. Neither one was springtime fresh as far as dirty dealing goes.

But if that was the case, why were they shooting at each other? At the very least, if this was some kind of smuggling operation, it had almost certainly gone off the tracks.

"Oh shit!" Natasha hissed less than a minute later. "I don't believe it!"

"What?" I asked, but right about then a nose appeared near my left arm.

It was Leeson's nose, and he had planted it way too close to my tapper.

"What you got there, Centurion?" he demanded.

Adjunct Leeson was a fairly short, stocky man, but he was tall enough to see my forearm clearly.

"Is that…" he said, grabbing my arm.

Before I could shake him off, he'd gotten an eye-full.

"Jumping Jesus! Is that a squadron of enemy ships bearing down on *Legate*?"

"We don't know that," I told him. "They might be making a special delivery."

"I don't think so, James," Natasha said, sounding freaked out. "Those salvoes weren't just warning shots. I think one of the enemy ships has been hit."

My heart sank. This wasn't a good sign at all.

Planting my hand on Leeson's face, I pushed him away—but he'd already seen too much.

"Those streaks," he said, his eyes bulging. "*Legate* is firing on them! One against three? We're doomed!"

"Shut up," I told him. "Get all the men under any kind of cover you can find."

"I thought there was no point," Harris boomed.

Turning the other way, I saw he'd come up surprisingly close. He was glaring at me the way a man might glare at his cheating wife.

I sighed. "Okay," I said, "if a fusion warhead lands here, we're dead. But if it's only wreckage, or a stray shell comes down a few kilometers away, shelter will save us."

"So I was right before?"

"Yes," I admitted.

"Damned straight I was right…" Harris said, stomping away.

Harris and Leeson were both marching around shouting orders. They were trying to pack up the gatehouse, demanding that pigs be sent to the walls to help dig an emergency bunker—all sorts of things.

I let them handle it. My eyes were glued to my tapper. Up in space, I could see the streaking fusion shells now. They were leaving trails that soon vanished—but they didn't have all that far to go. Any thoughts of digging a new bunker in time—that was a fantasy.

But I let them do it. Sometimes, keeping troops busy was the best policy. It stopped them from panicking on you.

Adjunct Barton showed up next. I guess I shouldn't have been surprised. All the junior officers depended on me to provide filtered-down information from on-high.

"Sir?" she asked. "What's the panic about? Are the Wur close?"

She was trying not to look worried, but I could see she was failing at it. She'd died during the last battle, after all. She was a Victrix officer, which meant she had good discipline and probably an excellent GPA from college. However, she wasn't used to fighting and dying hard in trenches. She'd gotten a taste of that in her short time with Varus, and her outlook had shifted accordingly.

My first instinct was to shine her on with a smile and a lie—but I couldn't do it. Leeson, Harris, Natasha—hell, half my unit already knew what was really going on. Probably, the only reason Barton didn't know was because she was new and hadn't gained the trust of those who networked privately. It didn't seem fair to me.

"It's worse than that," I told her. "Check out my tapper feed."

She glanced at my arm, then back up at me. She hesitated, but finally stepped close enough to see my screen.

The strange reaction made me wonder if the other women in the unit had warned her about my frequent relationships. I found that annoying, as I was no fiend. The women I pawed on a regular basis were always willing partners—always. They were just trying to warn off the new girl.

Adjunct Barton finally caught sight of the approaching ships and the icy vapor trails left in space by our barrage of fusion shells. She gasped and grabbed my arm with two sets of fingers that felt like claws. Damn, did everyone have to do that?

"We're under attack? Seriously? From space?"

"Looks like it."

"But… the Wur are already down here. Who else would…?"

I shrugged. "It's a mystery to me, too. I suspect Turov and Armel are both filling their pants over it right now."

"*Legate* can't take down three alien ships—can she?"

I shrugged again. "Maybe. I've seen Imperial transports blow down aliens, but I've also seen them get crushed. *Legate* is an Earth-built ship, but she's similar in design to countless other dreadnoughts that serve the Empire. It's a workhorse design. Nothing special—but always effective."

Right about then, Barton realized that she was holding onto my arm like a tree branch in a flood. She let go and took a step back.

"Sorry, sir."

Carlos happened to be wandering by, and he made an obscene gesture behind her back. I ignored him, as I didn't want to add to Barton's embarrassment.

"Adjunct," I told her, "I've got special orders for you. Have your light troops break out their tents. Tape up all the windows in the gatehouse—pronto."

She blinked at me, and she almost said: "Why?" But then, she got it. "Fallout? Okay… I'm on it, sir!"

Barton ran off, full of purpose. I had no idea if my instructions were worth the effort, but I figured it couldn't hurt to give her something to do.

While she ordered confused light troopers to dig into their packs, I faced Carlos. He'd come to stand by me and ogle her.

"That's not your usual type," he said. "She's too buff. Too much of a—"

My open hand slammed the back of his head. "Haven't you got something better to do than mock your officers, Ortiz?"

"Ow! You don't have to be a tool about it, McGill."

"Report to Harris and ask for a job to do."

"But I'm a bio—I don't get busy until *after* the battle."

"Well then, I've got—"

"Whoa! I spoke too soon. I just remembered I've got critical work on the lower floor. Thanks for reminding me, sir. That knock on the head must have jarred my memory back into place."

"Anytime…" I said, and I watched him run for the stairs.

Looking back at my tapper, I heard Natasha saying something. She'd been squawking in my ear while I dealt with Carlos, but I'm not good at listening to more than one person at a time. Some would say that listening to even one was a major problem for me.

"James! *James*!"

"What's wrong, girl? Oh… I see it."

One of three ships was gone, but there was a swarm of missiles flying toward *Legate*. The Rigellians had finally gotten into range, and they were fighting back.

"How many missiles is that?" I asked Natasha.

"At least sixty in each group. There are three groups—it looks like the ship we took down fired before she was destroyed."

"Nearly two hundred birds?" I asked in concern. "Our defensive guns can't stop that many at once."

"No, not by the specs I know. *Legate*'s defenses will be overwhelmed in about ten minutes."

We watched as the ship that had been shattered stopped burning. Fire never lasts long in space, as it must have oxygen to burn. Once the initial fireball had dissipated, we could see the dead ship had been transformed into an expanding field of tumbling debris.

"Who is commanding Legate now?" I asked.

"It's Turov herself," Natasha told me. "She used the gateway to return to Earth to ask for reinforcements, but she wasn't gone long. She came back today."

"Did she bring back help from Earth or not?" I asked.

"I don't know. All of this—it's kind of sudden."

"No shit… But anyway, Turov has to retreat," I said. "*Legate* can't take that many missiles. Connect me to her on Gold Deck."

"Are you crazy?"

"Yes… but do it anyway."

There were a few moments of delay before Turov came onto the line. "McGill, this had better be good."

"It's not good, sir—not at all. I don't think they'll fall for the same trick with the broadsides again."

One of the reasons our broadsides and missiles did so well is they appeared to be dumb weapons—but they really weren't. Each warhead had a cagey AI built-in, and the software helped them get hits reliably. They did this by either changing course, or blowing up early—or some other dirty trick. That sort of thing generally worked against new opponents better than it did against an experienced opponent. Once you'd laid your cards down, the surprises were over.

"Thank you for that sage advice, Centurion," Galina said. "I'm so glad you interrupted me at my command post to inform me about how I should be running this battle. Wait… hold on. How do you even know about the battle up here?"

"Let's just say you're streaming live."

"I suppose it doesn't matter. McGill… you called to check up on me, didn't you? You're actually concerned for my safety?"

I hesitated. Possibly, just possibly, she was right. But on the other hand, there were lots of good reasons for me to worry about the status of our only ticket back to Earth.

"Uh..." I said. "Of course I'm worried about you, sir... I'm also tired of Armel ordering us around down here."

"What?" she demanded angrily.

"He's superseded Graves, and he's giving us orders since you're not here."

"But I told him... dammit!"

"Don't worry about that now," I said. "Take *Legate* and pull out before those missiles hit."

"So you *do* care if I live or die? That's sweet. Rest assured, I will survive. Make sure you do the same after the enemy land."

"Uh... what?"

"Didn't you recognize these ships? They're Rigellian transports. They're coming to Storm World to push us off, just as they did at Dark World."

"Oh..." I said.

I opened my mouth to say more, but the channel was dead. Then the streaming video from the heavens died, too.

Pacing on the battlements of Armel's castle, I stared up at a fresh, churning storm. The clouds began to roil and they spit rain at my visor in gusts. I couldn't see any ships through the storm, neither theirs nor ours.

Without input, my mind was free to ponder grim possibilities. Why had the feed cut out so suddenly? Was *Legate* already a spinning wreck up there above the endless clouds? Was Galina dead?

If she was, we were all likely to join her soon.

While I stared upward, I saw an alarming sight. A white zone of luminescence appeared, lighting up the clouds.

Harris and Leeson rushed outside to crane their necks and watch. The white oval of light streaked off to the west then vanished. It was like the biggest spotlight in the universe had just swept over the hanging storm clouds—but it had been shining on the top side of the clouds, from up in space.

"Holy shit!" Harris said. "Was that lightning?"

"Nah," Leeson said. "That was a warp bubble seen from *way* too close. Turov probably fried our nads with radiation when she hit the gas."

Harris looked at him in alarm. "A warp bubble? *Legate* has ditched us on this mud pit?"

"Looks that way."

They moved off to attend to their respective platoons while I marshaled my troops and placed them as I saw fit.

The Wur were out there in the dripping forest, gathering strength, but they hadn't seen fit to attack us yet. That said, no one knew how much longer we had.

Then, about ten minutes after Turov had left with our ride home, Tribune Armel contacted me.

I was surprised to hear from him directly.

"What can I do for you, Tribune?"

"You can tell me the truth, for once," he said. "I've traced down all the recent communications with *Legate*—her last call with the planetary surface was to you. Imagine my astonishment upon learning of this..."

"Uh…" I said, trying to think fast. I couldn't come up with a good reason to dodge him, so I went with the urgency of the situation. "That's extremely interesting, sir, but if you could just send me a few replacement 88s—"

"If I relieve you of your command, you will not need them. Now that Turov has fled, or died, or whatever, I'm in total control of this ill-fated garrison."

My heart sank a little. Mostly, because he was right.

"Okay sir. But if I cooperate fully, can I have two 88s at the gatehouse?"

"Fine," he said in disgust. "Now, tell me the truth."

"What do you want to know?"

"Why did the tribune choose to call you, rather than Graves or myself?" he demanded.

"She didn't, sir. I called her."

"For what reason?"

"Uh…" I said, thinking hard. "Well see, when a man and a lady are intimate, Tribune, the nearness of death sometimes causes them to yearn for one last contact before—"

"That's absurd," he said flatly. "I'm not buying any nonsense about you two being madly in love. She's a manipulative harlot, and you have no more emotion than a rutting boar."

"I'll be sure to share these opinions with her the next time I see her."

"If you don't start being more forth-coming, you won't be seeing anyone soon."

"Well sir," I said, "I don't know what else to say. I've told you the God's-honest truth, whether you like it or not. Galina was in danger, so I called her to suggest she should run from the system. She took the call for the same reason I made it—we both care about each other."

He was silent for a moment. "Is this really the story you wish to employ? This amounts to a blatant refusal to answer a simple question from your commanding officer. That's a punishable offense, you know."

"Blatant refusal? That's a gross mischaracterization, Tribune," I said sternly. "I'm telling you the truth."

And I was, to some extent, telling him the truth. I felt somewhat annoyed with him for taking such a hostile position—but then, I knew he was pissed off that his efforts to get into Galina's pants had failed. There was plenty of bad blood between us besides that, but he was just going to have to suck it up and get over it.

"Very well," he said. "Remember your choices today, McGill. You may come to regret them."

Frowning, I began to speak further—but he was already gone.

Harris came near then, grinning.

"Natasha told me you were talking to Armel. You guys are soul mates now, right Centurion?"

"We're blood-brothers now, Harris. That's what I'd prefer to call it."

He kept grinning. He was getting pretty good at deciphering my bullshit at times like this.

"Well sir, the enemy is on the move."

"The Wur are coming?" I asked, checking my tapper. The motion sensors, drone-scouts and satellite feeds were all blank. "I don't see anything."

"Not them, sir. I'm talking about the Rigellians. While you and Armel were squabbling, Natasha tapped into the feed from our spy satellites in orbit."

He showed me his tapper.

"Pass me that feed," I ordered. "Now."

He did so with a few swipes and a tap. He grumbled a little. "I never get to see any of this cool hacker-shit. Does Armel know you've been watching and listening to encrypted channels?"

"Nope—and I want you to keep it that way. Dismissed, Harris."

He stalked off with a dissatisfied air, and I watched the feed.

It displayed the two transports the Rigellians still had gliding above Storm World's clouds. Instead of chasing after Turov, they were unloading troops—thousands of them.

As far as I could tell, they were coming down right on top of us.

I thought about talking to Armel again, but I passed on the idea. There was no way he wasn't watching this same feed by now, and there was no point in letting him know I had unsanctioned connections with the best of our tech specialists.

Instead, I watched the skies. It took a few minutes, but soon the telltale streaks of reentry were undeniable. The Rigellians were using drop-pods, invading Storm World just as we had done some weeks ago.

The first pods landed inside our walls four minutes later, and the battle was on.

# -49-

Fortunately, no matter how much Armel hated me, he did send two 88s down to bolster my position at the gatchouse. He was a real dick sometimes, but I was grateful for the support anyway.

"Leeson!" I roared. "Get those 88s turned around! Aim down into the compound!"

"On it, Centurion!" he shouted, and said something else, but the whipping winds of the storm made him unintelligible.

"I don't know if that's a good idea, sir," Harris said, standing by my side. "The Wur are marching, too. They'll hit us from the forests. We'll be squeezed in-between."

"I'm well-aware. But we have to take out the internal enemy first. If the fort is to stand, we can't have troops in our midst. Killing them is our first priority."

"Roger that—but sir, there's something else I have to tell you."

"Spit it out, Harris. I'm hoping for good news."

"Um… it's about your army of skinny snake-men—they've vanished."

I turned slowly and met his eyes. He didn't look like he was kidding. Then I examined the muddy ground at the base of our walls, where I'd last deployed them. The region was empty.

"All of them?" I asked, crestfallen.

"As far as I can tell. You think they're in on this? With Rigel, I mean?"

I shook my head. "It doesn't make sense…"

"You know what doesn't make sense? These stupid Rigellians dropping right into the center of our base. They've got to be the most arrogant, crazy sons-a-bitches I've ever laid eyes on—except I haven't really seen them yet."

"They're either crazy or highly confident. We'll see which it is in about a minute."

Harris left me, and he soon led a platoon into the open on the inside of our walls. Rippling snap-rifle fire was going off now, firing orange streaks through the pouring rain. I couldn't even see what they were shooting at, so I switched my faceplate to night vision mode and examined the scene.

Standing out in bluish-white and black, the night scene was almost as clear and clean as it would have been at high noon back home. Dozens of drop-pods were landing in groups, a full squad coming down together every few seconds. But these Rigel-made pods didn't operate quite the way that ours did.

Each pod landed with a gush of retros, thrusters flaming so as to slow down their descent. This was normal, but I noted that the jets had the side effect of kicking up a hellacious amount of smoke and steam. Each area where the pods landed was immediately shrouded in thick mist.

Our troops were firing into each LZ anyway, sending bright lines of accelerated steel into those billowing regions of mist.

I crouched on the wall, adjusting my own morph-rifle to fire long-range bolts. I waited until I saw a target before sending any bolts downrange.

There was a good chance, of course, that I would *never* see this enemy in the open. Rigel often deployed Vulbites to do the fighting. Vulbites were insectile creatures with pinchers, about a hundred legs and a bad attitude.

Vulbites were also masters of stealth, possessing gear like Cooper's ghost shroud.

That thought reminded me: I needed intel.

"Cooper!" I boomed.

To my surprise, he popped out of nowhere at my side. Suddenly, several things made sense. Could he have gotten orders from my own officers to spy on me? They'd been very noisy lately about my hacked vid streams.

Not for the first time, I felt myself commiserating with Graves. He'd run this unit of devious misfits before me, and he'd suffered a lot due to our naturally inquisitive natures.

"Get out there, Ghost," I told him. "I want intel. Penetrate those misty areas and report."

He looked like I'd sentenced him to death—which I probably had.

"Is this about the spying, sir?"

That confirmed it. He *had* been tailing me, probably reporting on who I was talking to back to Harris and Leeson. Sneaky adjuncts. You'd think a pack of experienced soldiers could fight and die at my whim without pulling shit like this—but then, I'd never played it that way.

"Of course it is," I lied. "Now, get out there and report!"

He vanished again. I saw a few splashy steps on the wall's walkway, but then I lost him.

"Leeson," I shouted again. "Have you got those 88s turned around?"

"I do, but the angle is bad. I don't recommend—"

"Don't give me that," I said. "You see those Blood Worlders closing in on the nearest patch of mist? Help them out. Light up that steam with a warm welcome for our guests."

"Roger that."

The 88s blazed into life a few moments later. The results were dramatic. Broad beams of intense heat and radiation struck a lot of raindrops, then a dense mass of mist. The beams were partially absorbed and deflected—but they were too powerful to shrug off entirely. The enemy LZ was lit up, and the mists expanded into hot steam.

It was like firing spotlights into a dense fog bank. To us, it looked like a wall of white had suddenly appeared.

"Sir," Leeson called out. "We're just making the mist thicker."

"Give it another sweep," I ordered. "Cross-wise, this time. Slice-and-dice."

Leeson sighed, but he gave the order. Soon, the zone hissed and roiled again. It was like the biggest damned kettle of dry ice the universe had ever seen.

Finally, fleeing figures appeared. They were coming out of the mist, rushing toward our walls. They seemed disorganized, almost panicked.

"Are those Vulbites?" Harris demanded on tactical chat.

"I don't think so," I said. "They're not stealthed, and the shape is wrong. They look like small men."

"You sure they're not our troops?" Leeson demanded. "Aw, dammit. Armel will have me up on charges if—"

"They're too small," I said, getting a close-up view with my HUD. One of them had run past a pig, and I'd gotten a quick comparison. The fleeing soldier was just over a meter tall, if I had to guess.

"Barton!" I shouted. "Take every light you've got and advance. Cut them off—don't let them get up onto the walls with us."

"On it!" she called back, and as if she'd been waiting for the order, I saw her group spring out of the base of the gatehouse and sprint forward.

"Look at that, Harris. That's how a Victrix girl leads troops."

"Yeah, yeah…" he said.

Harris had been in charge of my light platoon for years, but his troops had never looked so eager.

My morph-rifle was taking shots now, driving bolts into the approaching line. The first three shots missed—but then I nailed one.

He flipped and rolled, knocked right off his feet by the force of the bolt. I whooped—but the battle cry died in my throat.

"He got up!" I shouted, pointing in surprise. "Did you see that, Harris? That little bastard got right back up after taking a bolt in the chest."

"I've seen a lot of that. They're all getting back up. Plasma bolts don't seem to stop these little bastards."

For the first time, I felt a thrill of concern go through me. It wasn't fear—not exactly—but I was worried. Real worried.

Then I realized Barton and her eager-beavers were colliding with the enemy line. Light troopers weren't going to stand a chance against these invaders. I thought about calling for her to retreat—but it was already too late.

Putting my rifle to my shoulder, I fired bolt after bolt. Sometimes, I knocked one of them flat, but they almost always got back up.

Barton and her troops put up a good show. Snap-rifles blazed away on full-auto—but nothing seemed to stop the advancing line of mini-troops.

In response, the advancing devils were shooting powerful one-blast guns. Something like a shotgun, or a small belcher. Each shot that landed not only killed one of my troops, it blasted the body to smoldering fragments.

In the chaos of the one-sided battle, I came to several quick conclusions. For one thing, our opponents seemed to have very tough, light-weight armor. Compared to our breastplates, it was dramatically superior.

The second thought that occurred to me was this: why did they have single-shot super-powered shotguns as weapons?

After a moment the answer seemed obvious: they were geared to fight their own kind. Since they wore battle suits that were almost impenetrable to small-arms, they carried serious guns designed to penetrate tough armor like their own.

The final, sad thought that came to me as I witnessed Barton's platoon being blasted to pieces one man at a time on the battlefield, was that we were all well and royally screwed.

# -50-

We discovered several key things over the next few minutes.

One was that these troops were actual Rigellians. Now, that made purely good sense to me. In order for those vicious bear-like people to be ruling one hundred-odd star systems, they had to have something on the ball. You didn't just dominate and rule a race like the Vulbites, for instance, without being a pretty damned mean killer-species yourself.

We'd all seen the captured vids. Rigellians looked like under-age bears. They were just over a meter tall, but estimated to be about the same strength as a full-grown man—as were juvenile bears back home on Earth.

They might look cuddly, but such looks were grossly deceiving. They tormented the species' they enslaved, snipping off body-parts when displeased by a servant. They were tough, well-organized, and just plain mean.

All that said, we'd never met them in open battle before. This was our first direct encounter—and we were being humiliated.

The biggest problem was both sides were geared to fight troops that matched their own capabilities. We had guns that did pretty well against humans and other races similarly equipped—but the Rigellians had never seen a human fight before.

Mentally, I corrected myself—they *had* seen us fight.

Back on Blood World, Rigel had sponsored the Vulbites to fight for them. That must have meant they'd watched and analyzed our capacity for close combat. Then on Dark World, I'd met up with one of their kind and bamboozled him into letting me escape.

Even so, what had he been doing there, on the front lines inside a Vulbite mound? Why, gathering intel of course. He'd as much as told me so. He said he'd hoped we'd be easier to deal with, that he was disappointed… that extermination of Humanity looked like the only viable option.

Had that moment translated into this? A scene where their troops were mowing ours down with ease? It was hard to know. Possibly, this was how Rigel's troops always operated. It seemed pretty damned effective to me.

The key to their kit was that suit. I didn't know what it was made of, but if any man could shake off a direct hit from a plasma rifle, well, only our artillery hit harder than that.

"Primus Fike?" I called as the enemy finished off my light troops and began assaulting the entrances to the gatehouse. We'd buttoned up and locked them out—but I doubted that would last long.

"What is it, McGill?"

"We're under assault here, sir. The gatehouse might fall."

"Listen to me, Centurion. You will not fall. You will stand. You will fight, and you will die, but you will not lose your position. If you do, the Wur will roll right through us when they get here."

My heart sank another notch lower. It was down somewhere inside my ball sack by now, if I had to guess.

"Uh…" I said. "Soviet Order 227, sir?"

"That's right. Not one step back. Die well, McGill."

Fike disconnected, and I withdrew off the wall and into the gatehouse. Back in World War II, Stalin had given Soviet Order 227, commanding Russia's defensive forces to hold the Germans back at all costs. The order had become the slogan of the war for their side.

I could only dream I'd manage to execute it as well as the Russians had.

"All right," I said. "Churn, I want every Blood Worlder heavy we've got to the bottom floor of the gatehouse. You'll hold them there, fighting hand-to-hand if you have to. Here's how—"

"But sir," Churn objected, flapping his limbs around in an agitated fashion. "The enemy troops are shrugging off our weapons just as they do yours. I don't think our swords will fare any better against their impenetrable armor."

I got up into Churn's face, and a couple of his eye-groups glared at me.

"Listen, squid," I said, "I've got a new plan for your men."

Walking toward a Blood Worlder, I grabbed his rifle from his hands, reversed it, and aimed it into his guts.

They all watched with alarm. His eight brothers twitched and stared. They didn't like me threatening their relative, but they were too disciplined to attack me outright.

"See that?" I demanded. "That's what you're going to do. Don't shoot them. Don't hack at them. Grab their guns out of their hands, turn them around, and blast them in the belly. You got that?"

They shuffled and stared at me with piggy eyes—but a few of them nodded.

"Outstanding! Churn, lead these heroes downstairs. If you come back up before this is over, I'll make calamari out of you."

With poor grace, Churn led his troops downward, and I pulled all the humans back upstairs. From the walls, we did our best to make the Rigellian troops hate life. We dropped grenades, popped shots off at them to kick them around and generally behaved like apes in trees.

They fired back now and then, but they were well-disciplined. Their weapons were very short-ranged and probably required heavy ammunition. Those bears could only carry so much, and their transports were way up in the sky. They couldn't afford to waste it by missing their targets.

The door went down with a crash in less than a minute. That was impressive all by itself, as the door had been built out of puff-crete and crystalline steel. Some of the hardest substances Humanity had access to.

I wasn't down there as it was cramped, and I didn't want to get in the way. But due to the beauty of drones and tappers, I got to witness the action up-close and personal.

The bears blew the big door's hinges off with charges—but things didn't go the way they were supposed to after that.

First off, the door was damned heavy, and the squad of Blood Worlders behind it shoved hard in unison when it came free of the hinges. That sent the doors out and down, instead of inward.

Two of Rigel's finest were squished right then. I didn't know if they were still alive under those two-ton planks of metal and condensed mass, but it probably didn't matter. They weren't going anywhere even if they were still kicking.

Snarling, the invading team rushed inside to meet our defenders. As I'd ordered, the littermates stood off to the sides and snatched the little guys up like ogres grabbing children.

A vicious, strange fight broke out. Sometimes, a Blood Worlder would manage to pluck a gun from one of the smaller troops and blast him with it. But almost as often, the growling little monster would manage to tear up the bigger man.

"They've got force-blades!" Harris shouted. "Just like ours, but shorter. They use them like claws. Nasty!"

It was true. The Blood Worlders were massive and powerful, but they couldn't tear an arm off the smaller enemy. About the only thing that worked was taking the guns away and shooting them, point-blank.

Unfortunately, my guys were simple-minded. Once they'd lost a few of their number, they went berserk with rage and forgot about killing them with their own guns. They tried to use their traditional tactics—and got themselves killed by these vicious dynamos.

"That's it!" I shouted. "Heavy troops, on me! All of you sling your rifles and extend force-blades. Set them for about a meter in length. We're going down there!"

Roaring, we rushed to the defense of our near-human comrades. By the time we got down there, most were dead. Churn was standing to one side of the smoking room, firing over and over with a gun he'd wrestled from a Rigellian. He worked the weapon like a pro with his tentacles, despite the fact two of them had been blown half-off.

I was glad to see the enemy had taken serious losses too. At least fifteen of them were down.

My heavies tramped onto the floor, and we squared off with the bears. To my surprise, they fought like martial arts masters. Force-blades slashed and sizzled. Thrust, parry, and thrust again.

Every trooper on my side was well-trained with these weapons. We had one on each arm, and we used them to block as well as attack. It was like a good, old-fashioned sword fight.

We soon learned that we had a single advantage—and it wasn't skill. These guys clearly were well-trained with these weapons. They were quick, accurate, and instinctual killers. Several heavies fell with their guts steaming on the floor before they realized these bears weren't kids, no matter how short they were.

But then we discovered their blades didn't extend. They were a fixed length, about half a meter long.

All we had to do was engage a bear, trade a few cuts, then surprise him by extending a hot blade into his guts. My first bear was a whirlwind of blows, I caught them all, reeling back, but then turned a parry into a sliding disengage and—zap, I extended my blade and ran him through the skull with it.

That armor had held back every ballistic weapon we'd thrown at it. No grenade fragment, burst of radiation, or plain old accelerated sliver of metal had penetrated. Maybe it was reactive armor, triggered by high-speed kinetics to realign molecules into a solid—I don't know. But whatever the case, it was a sucker for a force-blade.

We killed them all, in the end. We'd lost six of my men, and fourteen out of eighteen of Churn's platoon—but we'd won.

After the fight, I spread the news as fast as I could. The Rigellian troops *could* be beaten. They were at least equal to a human in heavy gear, or a Blood Worlder littermate. There was a downside since a light soldier stood no chance at all, but I was quite pleased to share that our foes *could* be killed with the right tactics.

# -51-

All over the fort, there were reports of hard fighting. Others had come up with strategies that worked—but my gun-snatching idea was probably the most effective.

The key was in the arm strength of your average Blood Worlder. Their size, reach, and vitality allowed them to disarm the smaller troops. Even if they often received mortal wounds in the process, they were still able to complete the job of murdering their unarmed opponents before they sagged down, joining them in death.

Overall, there was a hell of a lot of dying going on. The fight was bloody, and corpses were everywhere. Part of that was due to the natural ferocity of the opposing sides, but it was also related to the simple fact the Rigellians had nowhere to retreat.

They'd dropped right into the middle of our walls. That took brass balls, as they must have known they weren't going to walk out alive unless they won.

Fortunately for us, they didn't win. They'd dropped an estimated three thousand troops, and they'd lost them all.

"The enemy troops aren't the only ones taking this hard," Harris told me.

Glancing at him, I saw he was leaning on his rifle, but I didn't admonish him for using it as a prop. That was about all it was good for today.

"The littermates?" I asked.

"Yeah. They're despondent. Virtually every square of nine lost half or more."

I shook my head. "We had to use them—yeah, even overuse them. They took the brunt of the losses in the end."

"Have you checked in with Graves and Armel?" he asked. "We need reinforcements. In fact, I'd like to send any squad that's lost more than two back to Blood World. Let them switch out for a fresh group."

I thought that over. "I'll ask."

When I talked to Armel, he laughed at me.

"Are you kidding? Build new squads. Every group of nine—since they seem so fascinated with that number—can form into an effective force again."

"But sir," I said, "the Blood Worlders don't want to fight without their real brothers. How many revival machines do we have that can handle big bodies?"

"This nonsense again? I don't have time for your hand-wringing, McGill."

"It's far from that, sir. I'm concerned about the readiness of my troops. The Wur are approaching, and I'm sure there are more than three thousand troops on those transports."

"All right, all right," Armel said irritably. "I'll put you in contact with Raash."

I blinked when I heard that name. Raash was a saurian who'd once killed me and Floramel back on Earth. He'd died at my hands too, and that didn't leave us on the best of speaking terms.

I'd heard that old Raash was working revival machines for Blood Worlders again. The legions used saurians because they were larger and stronger than humans, as well as more technologically competent than Blood Worlders. The bodies of the troops being birthed by these extra-large revival machines often weighed a metric ton or more. Hegemony had seen fit to employ Saurians like Raash to man these outsized machines for them.

"Uh…" I said, but by the time I considered objecting or maybe disconnecting, Armel had switched me over.

"Raash speaks," an oddly familiar, raspy voice said. It was his translator, but I still recognized it.

"Raash…?" I said. "So, you're really on Storm World?"

"This is the McGill? Ah yes, I see the identification on my com unit. You are correct, I'm on Storm World. However, you are not wanted in my vicinity, McGill."

I blinked twice, letting that flip over in my mind a few times. Raash always seemed to have an odd turn of phrase, and today was no exception. Figuring he was saying he wasn't glad to hear my voice, I decided to press ahead anyway. After all, orders were orders.

"I've been directed by Tribune Armel to talk to you about revival rates."

"Your complaints are uninteresting. I have work. This call ends."

He disconnected before I could say more. That left me a bit ticked off. Glancing at my tapper, I had him pinpointed inside the bunkers on my mapping app.

"Kivi!" I called out. "How long until those Wur hit the walls?"

"They're not in too much of a hurry. They're massing up in the forest. If they behave as they did up at Fort Alpha, we probably have an hour at least."

I glanced at the dreary sky and thanked my lucky stars it wasn't hurricane time. "An hour… They'll hit us just before the local version of dawn then, right?"

"That's what I expect."

Nodding, I set Leeson in charge, with Sub-Centurion Churn backing him up. Then, I marched out into the smoldering battlefield inside our walls.

As I trudged through the mud, I noted that I couldn't find a single undamaged structure. They'd tried to pry their way into every bunker, even Blue Bunker where I was headed now.

A solid ten minutes after I'd started walking, I found my way down into what served the bio-people as a basement. There, I found Raash and about thirty other lizards, working oversized revival machines.

As I watched, they birthed a giant. The process was both impressive—and disgusting.

Then I caught sight of the last person I'd expected to meet down here—Floramel. She was lingering in the brightly-lit hallway behind me.

"Floramel?" I boomed, throwing my arms wide. "Sorry I never got a chance to look you up. So you're serving with the Blood Worlder legion?"

"It's a near-human formation," she said. "Isn't that where I belong?"

"Um… sure. I guess. As long as you're happy…"

Floramel and I had had a strange, on-again, off-again relationship for years. Now, that could rightly describe my entanglement with any number of women, but with her, the pattern seemed even more pronounced.

She studied the floor with down-cast eyes. Every now and then, she glanced up to look at me squarely, before going back to studying the deck again.

"Sure is good to see you," I said, and I meant it. She didn't quite have the raw sexual intensity of a girl like Kivi, or the cute youthful looks of Galina—but she did have the regal, queenly look nailed.

Taking a chance, I stepped forward and extended my arms. For a long time, we'd had a private means of communication. I would touch her shoulders lightly, giving them a squeeze.

Since physical contact among Rogue-Worlders only happened when they were suggesting a willingness to mate, what might look like an innocent gesture of friendship to a human was really an open invitation to her.

"Stop!" boomed a voice behind me.

I looked over my shoulder in surprise.

Raash stood in the doorway of the revival chamber. His jaws were open, and his nasty-looking tongue was squirming inside his mouth.

Now, I'm no expert in saurian facial expressions, but seeing as he'd exposed just about every tooth inside his toothy head, I figured he was upset about something.

"Hey, Raash!" I said, lowering my outstretched hands.

I hadn't touched Floramel, but it'd been a close thing.

"I didn't come here to dispense sexual functions, James," Floramel said unhelpfully.

"Uh…"

"You've been rebuked, human," Raash told me. "It is time to withdraw while you still possess a tail."

Raash had always had a weird thing going for Floramel. He'd followed her around, spied on her, and eventually killed her back on Earth. All of that hadn't quite soured her on the crazy lizard.

I threw up my hands and laughed. "Look, I don't know what's going on, but I'm glad to see you both breathing again."

"That does not match my own thinking," Raash said. "I enjoyed every moment of your most recent interval of nonexistence."

"Still full of love and biscuits, aren't you, Raash?"

"Your statement concerns sex and food, but it is nonsensical. I will assume it is an insult."

So far, I wasn't losing my temper. Raash was just the kind of alien you had to acquire a taste for—but I'd never acquired it.

But then he did something I really didn't like. He pushed past me, knocking my shoulder with his, and put his big claws on Floramel.

My own teeth made an appearance. My hand went to my morph-rifle—but Floramel stopped me.

She put up her hand, palm out. "James… I see you don't understand."

"Understand what?"

Raash put his scaly hands higher, gripping Floramel. He reached up and gave her a squeeze at the shoulders. She winced a little, as if he'd hurt her, but she said nothing. She just stared at me.

Finally, that dormant organ inside my skull got the message. It was loud and clear. Raash and Floramel were… intimate.

"Aw now…" I began, feeling disgusted. "Don't tell me…! That's just *wrong*, girl!"

"Why?" Raash asked. "Over time, we've become physically compatible."

"Jeez," I said, not wanting to think about it. "A human woman and a lizard? That's not right. He's an *alien*, Floramel! You're not even from the same food-group!"

"I thought you of all people, James, might understand. After all, you and I mated many times, and I'm not completely human."

"That's not the same thing at all," I argued. "Besides, he's an abuser. I've never hurt you."

"Not physically perhaps," she said. "But all couples fight."

She shrugged, and Raash's claws rode her shoulders. He maintained a constant possessive hold on her.

"He's worse than an abuser," I continued. "He's a murderer! This lizard *killed* you back on Earth!"

"I killed you when we first met," she pointed out. "And you told me stories of your odd relationship with Della. And let's not forget you and Turov. Or—"

"Yeah, yeah, yeah… Okay. I get your point. Some of my relationships have been imperfect as well. But this…"

I gave a little shudder. I couldn't help it.

"Wait a minute..." I said, my eyes narrowing with a fresh suspicion. "Did you two have a thing going back on Earth? Back when I first met Raash?"

"Yes," she admitted.

"Well then… Why didn't you damn-well tell me, girl?"

She lifted her hands toward me, palms upturned. "Isn't that obvious? Look how you're reacting. You can't even deal with the news years later."

I sighed, shaking my head. "Whatever. I hope you two are happy together."

"You hear that?" Raash rasped. "I told you he would lie. He lies constantly. The truth will burn his throat, if he ever dares to utter it."

My finger came up, and I pointed it at him accusingly. "Raash, you told me you were an agent. You said you were trying to get back to Steel World, back into the favor of your prince. You expressed contempt for Floramel then—for all humans."

Raash's face twitched, as did his tail. Was that a sign of surprise? Perhaps he'd hoped I'd forgotten our conversation in

Floramel's apartment. There had been plenty to distract me, as we'd fought over her dead body.

"What's more," I continued, "Claver told me you worked for him. You were *his* agent. You were after the book, weren't you? Maybe you still are…"

Floramel frowned, and she looked up over her shoulder at Raash.

The saurian still gripped her in his powerful claws.

"You see?" he rasped in her ear. "He flails with pointless words. He is wicked. He seeks to hurt our minds, and he is forever untruthful."

Floramel lowered her head to look at the deck for a moment, but then she looked up again and met my eyes.

"You have to go, James. Whatever we had before—it's gone now."

"All right," I said. "I'm out of here!"

I threw up my hands. The gesture made them both flinch.

Marching away, I left Blue Bunker. The air outside wasn't exactly fresh, but at least it was laced with honest stinks.

Armel contacted me the second I left Blue Bunker.

"Ah, McGill!" he purred smugly. "I see by your location tag that you've exited the revival chambers. Here's hoping you've had an enlightening discussion with Raash, hmm?"

The delight in his voice was obvious. Right off, I knew the truth: I'd been set up. Armel had known about Floramel and Raash. He'd sent me down there, not for any information about revival rates, but to rub my face in the clear light of failure.

What a devious bastard he was. I could only wonder, as I returned to the gatehouse to await the arrival of the Wur army, how this new feud between us would end.

In the past, such things had never gone well for anyone.

# -52-

Returning to the gatehouse, I was feeling low. Far from the hero's welcome I'd hoped for, I'd been booted out of Floramel's presence. Sure, we'd won the battle, but Armel had gotten the best of me. Raash had also gotten to take a turn at kicking old McGill in the tailpipe.

Shaking it off, I took stock of the tactical situation. Now wasn't the time for introspection, heartache or any other form of self-indulgent mental masturbation. A legionnaire on the front lines couldn't allow his brain to get tied up with nonsense.

I ordered Kivi to project a tactical map on the puff-crete walls with her computer. The display showed the Wur, who were clearly using the same tactics they'd used before against Fort Alpha.

And why shouldn't they? That effort had been successful. Even a race of oversized plants were smart enough to stick with a winning formula.

Within an hour of my return, the Wur spiders scouted us. These spiders were the smartest form the Wur took—except for their Nexus plants, which looked like giant cacti.

The spiders came poking up out of the brush to peer at our walls warily—and we gave them a hot greeting.

Unlike past encounters with these creatures, we were ready for them. Snipers began peppering their ugly faces the moment they appeared.

Hissing and reeling back, they quickly faded into the ferns again.

The troops hooted and whooped, as if we'd won some kind of major victory. Those who'd fought and died on the walls back at Fort Alpha, however, presented a different mood: they were tense, quiet, and fatalistic.

"Another bug-hunt," Harris complained. "I can't wait for the full on piss-party to show up and educate Armel's fools."

Counting noses among my troops, I came up with a paltry number. We'd lost so many fighting the Rigellians, we'd been left somewhere below half-strength. Reinforcements were trickling in from the revival machines of course, but it seemed like too little, too late. The worst part was the Scuppers had abandoned us entirely. They hadn't been all that useful, but it was always demoralizing to have friends run out on you.

Tapping on Kivi's helmet, I got her to contact HQ for me.

"Get Graves on the line."

"He's dead. Didn't you hear?"

I blinked at her. "Nope… Did the Rigellians get him during that landing?"

"Yes. He tried to hold the entrance to Gold Bunker using your new tactics. I guess he pulled a gun out of a teddy-bear's grip—but he got shot in the process."

"Teddy-bears…" I laughed. "That's the opposite of what those snarling little bastards are like. Teddy-bears from Hell, maybe."

"Yeah."

My eyes narrowed. "If Graves is dead… who do I ask for reinforcements?"

"Primus Fike is your immediate commander, sir."

My face twisted up into a grimace. "Primus Fike won't give us shit."

She squirmed. "You're probably right. If you want to go over his head… it has to be Armel."

"Damn."

I'd been hoping someone else from Legion Varus would have taken on the role of quartermaster or executive officer—but there was no such luck. Eventually, after complaining to an army of snotty staffers, I got through to Armel.

"Again with the sniveling?" he asked. "What is it now? Do you wish I should wipe your tears for you?"

"Tribune, we've got problems. We're being scouted by spiders—that means an attack is imminent."

"So? Repel the invaders! You've got new weapons courtesy of Rigel. Grow a spine, man!"

I closed my eyes. Armel never made these things easy. I wanted to disconnect and curse up a streak, but I held my anger in check. It would only make him happy and leave my troops in the lurch.

"Sir," I said patiently, "the enemy broke the gates at Fort Alpha, and we were full strength then. Once they get past these walls—it's over."

Armel made a pffing sound. "I will send you a full unit of heavy troopers from my reserves."

"That's excellent, sir. But I need more. I need giants."

"Impossible!"

The wrangling went on for a time, but I eventually shared a few choice vids from the battle at Fort Alpha, and a few more from Death World. I showed him what a full-on pod-walker charge looked like from the ground. He was grudgingly impressed.

"These walking trees are unnatural," he complained. "Do you think our walls can hold them?"

"I suggest we seal the exterior gate with fresh puff-crete. Anything that makes it over the wall after that, your giants can deal with."

"I only have a force of sixty here… I will give you half. But do not fail me, James McGill!"

"I won't, sir."

Harris eyed me after I'd finished the negotiation. He looked impressed.

"You played that straight, McGill. No lies, no shit, no nothing."

I shrugged. "Sometimes the plain truth can be useful."

He grunted, and we went back to waiting. We didn't have to wait long.

Right on schedule, the forest floor began to shake again. The pod-walkers were coming.

The rain had slowed to a drizzle, allowing our troops to see a decent distance into the forest. Our snipers began to plink away. I could have told them it was pointless, but they wouldn't have listened.

"Hey!" Leeson called out excitedly, slapping my armored shoulder. "I see *giants*! On our side, I mean."

The biggest near-humans of all came marching toward the gatehouse from the middle of the compound. There were thirty of them, just as Armel had promised. They marched two abreast from the center of the fort, and I quickly realized, without any surprise, that they were coming directly from Gold Bunker. Perhaps Armel had been keeping them down there as his personal Praetorian Guard.

These giants weren't the small kind like the littermates. They were much taller and heavier. True monsters, they stood six meters tall or more. A glittering shield of force created a glassy nimbus over their bodies, and they each carried a massive energy projector that was bigger than a belcher.

My heart swelled to see them despite their disturbing faces. They wore idiot grins on heads that were slightly too small for their swollen bodies.

Somehow, despite all that, these stinking primitives always lifted the spirits of the men who fought with them—and caused those who opposed them to feel real fear.

My troops began to cheer as the giants took up positions behind the walls and around the gates. They were too big to enter the gatehouse itself, but their job was to destroy anything that broke inside, so it didn't matter. They were my back-up, my reserve, my ace-in-the-hole.

Turning my attention back to the forest, I saw a charging line of Wur outside the walls. There were a lot of them. We were going to need every asset we had.

Steadfast, we braced ourselves for the initial shock. The Wur soon broke out into the open, and the battle began in earnest.

This time, I played it smarter. I ordered our light troops to get off the battlements. Armed with snap-rifles, they were only good for shooting spiders and acid-monsters. I redeployed the light troops well back inside the compound. I wanted them to act in support of the giants, killing anything that made it inside.

The pod-walkers strode into the open, leaving the trees behind. But this time they didn't pick up acid-monsters and throw them over our walls. Instead, they just rushed right at us.

The 88s sang, and a dozen pod-walkers warbled in agony as their trunks caught fire—but they still charged toward us.

Blind, but determined, they reached the base of our walls. The tallest of them couldn't reach the top of the walls, not by five to ten meters. Construction crews had measured it out that way months ago.

"What are they doing?" Harris laughed. "Permission to use our heaviest guns to shoot them in the face, sir?"

Harris wanted to deploy the shotguns we'd captured from the Rigellian troops. I thought that over for about a second, but I shook my head. "We have to keep every round we have that can penetrate Rigel-made armor. Morph-rifles only, set for assault mode."

Disappointed, he ordered his troops to advance, and I joined them. Together, we poured fire down the wall into the confused, scrabbling enemy walkers.

But then, a second line of pod-walkers appeared at the tree line. They too, charged our walls.

Howling and beating their great fists on the puff-crete, the first group met their dooms one at a time. Concentrated fire chipped and tore leaking holes in their bodies. Like real trees, the flesh inside the rough exterior was white. Inside their hollow trunks and limbs, I knew, were strings of nano-fiber that resembled corn silk. These strings reacted to stimuli as did our muscle fibers, contracting to cause movement.

Two went down, then four—but the party didn't last long. The second wave of Wur soon reached the first.

These monsters were already scarred by our 88s, but they kept coming. They seemed more purposeful than they had been during the previous attack. Could it be they were learning? Could the spiders have taken careful notes and worked out a new strategy?

I wasn't sure, but their inexplicable behavior was beginning to worry me.

"Are these walls going to hold?" Leeson asked. "There's no way they can beat down puff-crete, right?"

"No way in Hell," I told him with absolute confidence. I forced a grin. "This is a turkey shoot! Burn them all down before they run back into the woods!"

Leeson smiled back weakly. He wanted to believe my overconfident boasting—but he couldn't quite do it.

Still, we kept firing, killing them one at a time. What else could we do?

That's when the third wave of pod-walkers thundered out of the forest. This group was made up of the largest of their kind.

"Burn the new ones!" I shouted. "Take down those big bastards in the rear!"

"Can't do it, sir!" Leeson shouted back.

The 88s were too busy buzzing and scorching what they could of the enemy at the base of the walls. They'd all tilted over, nearly ninety-degrees, doing their best to nail the enemy that was so tantalizingly close.

The fresh wave of monstrous Wur made it to our walls with only a few dark stripes on their hides. Most of them still had orange fronds out, whipping like snakes. Their sensory organs had stayed intact, and that meant these new giants weren't blind like the others.

Coming upon the frothing mass of their smaller brethren—who were maddened by pain and beating themselves to a pulp on our walls—they touched them.

The survivors of the first waves reacted strangely to this touch, which was almost a caress. They froze their bodies into place.

Looking down from the wall-top, the frenzied invaders all seemed to pause at once. They soon resembled a forest of trees swaying in a winter breeze. Those who had taken the worst of our defensive fire had taken root.

A curious transformation took place. Ladders were formed—or at least what looked like crude scaffolding. The survivors interlocked arms and transformed themselves into a series of living, smoking ladders.

Then the third wave of pod-walkers, the greatest of them all, began to climb their brothers' backs.

"Burn their fronds!" I shouted. "Blind the big ones!"

My men hastened to obey, but I already knew it was too little, too late. The taller walkers soon managed to reach the top of our walls—which were, after all, carefully measured to be out of reach for the biggest known walker we'd ever seen.

Unfortunately, the Wur had learned to climb.

# -53-

The skies overhead seemed to know we were fighting hard. They darkened, the winds gusted up, and rain began to pour down with sudden fury.

Feeling a sense of desperation, my wall-defenders gave their all. We blasted, cut and stabbed. Leeson pulled back his 88s, waiting until a climbing pod-walker was inside point-blank range before unleashing a deadly spray of radiation. This last effort had a serious effect. Out of the initial wall-climbers, only half made it over the top.

When they got there, a fierce thirst for vengeance overtook them. No longer were they struggling painfully, stung by a thousand tiny burns and pinpricks. Instead, they slapped us from the walls with greedy abandon.

Men flew from the rain-slick walls, wailing and broken. The lightning that now played overhead lit the frantic scene periodically. Every flash of brilliance brought a new horror to my eyes.

I saw a littermate snatched up. His guts were squeezed by thick brown fingers until his eyes popped from their sockets. Even so, his sword arm kept hacking with rhythmic determination.

Then I saw two blinded walkers grab hold of a single slaver at the same time, pulling the lanky near-human apart in their frenzy. They must have each thought the tugs of their comrade were desperate efforts by their prey to escape—but since his head was missing, I knew they were mistaken.

“Retreat!” I roared, sounding a bugle call on tactical chat. “Withdraw to the base of the wall!”

The survivors scrambled to obey. Six of the walkers now stood on the walls themselves, reaching with their long, long—*impossibly* long arms to pluck weaponeers from those hated 88s. The artillery pieces were cast down in their great fists to crash into the soggy earth far below.

Rappelling down the inside of the wall and casting off the emergency lines, I retreated with the rest. Some men didn’t get their lines cut fast enough, and they were snatched back up to the howling monsters on the battlements above them.

That’s when our giants got into the game. I didn’t order them to do so—perhaps one of the squid sub-centurions had picked up on the opportunity and given the fateful command.

Reaching up with fists the size of a man’s torso, they grabbed hold of the lines that we’d used to escape. Far above, the pod-walkers were still in a frenzy, and they yanked on these monofilament ropes with greedy intent.

The giants yanked back.

Breathing hard, bleeding, I stared with my mouth open. Watching the giants in action was always a fearsome vision. They were humanity taken to a logical extreme, a breeding experiment in genetics and hydraulics. They were as big as a human could be, requiring massive hearts and comparatively tiny brains.

Veins popped out in purple ropes on those fists. The muscles were unnaturally strong, even accounting for their vast weight. They had to be. With our natural muscular density, no normal human could have grown so large and lived.

The Wur, so far above us, were caught by surprise. Tangled on lines they’d been hauling upon like fishermen pulling in nets, they found themselves overpowered by groups of giants. One at a time, they came crashing down to the mushy dirt. Brown waves of mud surged like ocean waves, flattening and choking regular troops who were too close to the impact point.

Heedless of the smaller figures fleeing between their legs and rolling to dodge their monstrous feet, the giants advanced. Drool ran from their mouths, and their eyes stared without blinking. They were hungry for battle, and they made grunting noises of obscene excitement.

The Wur were far from finished, however. Some had suffered snapped limbs, but they struggled to stand anyway.

Our giants closed in, and a horrible melee began. The giants thumped the Wur with massive fists, burned away their organs with chest-mounted projectors and tore their branch-like limbs from their flailing bodies.

The pod-walkers killed a few giants, usually by finding a wattled neck and throttling it—but it was too little, too late.

"Hold your fire!" I ordered, and those of my men who'd been spraying rounds into the mess halted. The chance of hitting our own giants was simply too great.

Harris and Leeson high-fived one another. I grinned at them both. Even Carlos was impressed.

"That's got to be the best mud-wrestling free-for-all I've ever seen, McGill," he said. "You must feel right at home."

"Get in there!" I shouted in his ear. Placing my hand on his shoulder, I shoved him and sent him staggering toward the fight

He glanced back in shock.

One look at my laughing face, and he relaxed.

"Evil sir," he said. "Positively evil—and well-played!"

We all enjoyed the show, but it didn't last. More Wur had climbed up onto the battlements, and they weren't content to watch us dismember their comrades.

Acid-monsters had joined their ranks. First a dozen of them—then two dozen.

"Fall back!" I ordered, and my men began to pull out.

The giants, however, didn't withdraw.

"Sub-centurion Churn!" I called out. "Get control of your men. Pull the giants out—the Wur at the base of the wall are all dead."

"I'm sorry, sir," Churn responded. "But that's not possible. Your cousins are in a blood-rage, and they won't withdraw until the enemy has been torn apart."

I did recall then, at some boring briefing or another, that giants had trouble breaking out of combat once they were in an up-close melee. They seemed to lose their minds and beat dead horses until there was nothing left other than flat road-kill.

Knowing Armel wouldn't want me to abandon his idiot giants, I reversed my command.

"Take up firing positions! Target the acid-monsters—put them down one at a time!"

Uncertain, but still game for the fight, my troops obeyed. They formed a ragged line, knelt and released withering fire on the enemy up on the walls.

The Wur were already tossing acid-monsters into the middle of our giants. Some of these splatted down, crushed into a smoking mess by a bad landing. Others struck giants and slathered them in corrosives. Usually, the giants could rely on their personal shields to protect them, but not always. Puddles of mud and acid, when stepped into, proved highly dangerous.

The giants, feet burning, lost what little they had left of their minds. They fought with these new invaders, corpses, and even one another at times with equal ferocity.

Now and then, one of them thought to use his projector and beam the Wur above him, but that was the exception rather than the rule. I realized that Churn wasn't so much a commander of disciplined troops as a herder of a stampede. For the most part, the giants did as they wished once they were engaged.

They began to fall after thirty seconds of fighting. First one, then three more—by the end of the first minute, the count of dead giants stood at six.

I felt sick. I knew what I had to do, but I didn't want to do it—I contacted Armel.

He didn't answer my channel request, and I cursed him and the devils who'd spawned him.

Then… I heard the loud peal of a horn. My troops blinked and craned their necks. Our plinking fire slowed…

"They're coming from Gold Bunker!" someone shouted.

It was true. A column of giants, led by a man riding a pig, were advancing rapidly.

It was Armel's reserves—the other thirty giants—and he was riding the drone at the head of the formation.

Tribune Maurice Armel was nothing if not a showman. I'll never know what had possessed him to ride a buzzing, Clydesdale-sized drone into combat—but I was glad he'd decided to join the party.

"Good to see you on the front, sir!" I called out on tactical chat.

"I'm less pleased with your performance, McGill," he said sternly. "You've failed to hold the gates, and worse, you've lost a third of the precious giants I released into your care!"

He sounded pissed, and although I didn't think he had any right to be, I decided to let it go. At least he was here and willing to fight. Say what you will for the pompous bastard—he was no coward.

"Glad to have you, sir, all the same." That's all I said, then I went back to firing into the mess at the bottom of the walls.

Soon, Armel and his men rushed right through our lines. Kivi was trampled to death, and I thought that was rather rude. Maybe Armel figured he was getting even for losing his precious giants—but it wasn't professional.

Still, I didn't complain. Armel himself rode right into that mess with his giants swarming all around him.

The enemy had started making headway with more pod-walkers coming down off the walls and throwing more acid-monsters—but the thirty additional giants proved decisive.

Armel seemed to have much better control of his minions than Churn had exhibited. He didn't simply let them go wild, howling and forgetting to use their beam projectors. Instead, his troops had a reasonable level of discipline, and they used it mercilessly.

They beamed the Wur to death and rescued their injured comrades. When it was all over, I joined Armel on the bubbling field of battle.

"Well-fought, Tribune," I said, and I meant it.

He turned toward me. His kit was muddy, and his drone was staggering on three legs. For a moment, he stared at me—but then he relaxed. He must have seen that my praise was honest and real.

"Yes," he said. "It was well-fought. The enemy pressed here at the gates with the greatest ferocity. I have to admit, when I saw your men fall back from the battlements, I thought they would keep running—but they did not. You turned back, you stood, and you supported my engaged giants."

"Damn-straight," I said. "Those giants can't be revived on this planet. Can we even get more of them sent out from Blood World?"

He opened his visor and gave his head a shake. He seemed to instantly regret this, as fetid air assailed him. Even the storm wasn't able to keep the stink down completely.

"No," he said. "They're too large for a simple set of gateway posts. We can get littermates, maybe a few Cephalopods and slavers, should we want them—but not more giants."

I nodded, understanding how Armel felt. He didn't want to lose an elite force he couldn't replace.

"But you came out and risked the rest of your force anyway?" I asked.

"Of course," he said. "The lack of choice in this matter was so obvious I'm surprised even you did not see it."

There he was, falling back on insults again. Armel could fight, he was a good commander—but he was a hard man to like.

"I had to release the rest of my reserves," he continued. "If you'd been wiped out here, I wouldn't have bothered. I would have stayed in my bunker and hoped for the best. But, since you were in an even struggle, I released the reserves to break the back of their offensive."

"Well… I'm glad you did."

So saying, I offered him a dirty gauntlet. He looked at it as if it were a serpent, ready to strike. I kept the hand out there, ready to shake.

"Look, sir," I said in a lowered voice. "We've got to pull together out here as best we can. We've got little bear dudes in unbreakable armor, and about a zillion trees trying to kill us. They all hate us—both of us."

I still held out my hand, and Armel still hesitated. Finally, however, he noticed several other officers were watching. Among them was Primus Fike, Sub-Centurion Churn and

Centurion Leeza, who'd apparently been reassigned to this legion along with Armel.

Always political, Armel slid from the saddle of his crippled drone and slammed his gauntlet into mine. His grip was solid, if less than impressive.

I grinned, and I shook that hand as if I'd met a long-lost cousin. Armel gave me a pained smile in return.

"This is for show, McGill," he said in a low voice. "The troops need to keep up their morale."

"Don't I know it, sir."

He nodded then, and we let go of each other's hands.

The situation was clear. We didn't like one another—not at all. But we had to depend on one another in order to survive this campaign.

# -54-

In the aftermath of battle, Graves was revived. He demanded a briefing, and he reviewed every aspect of the conflict.

Some hours later, he got around to talking to me.

"McGill? What happened to those skinny blue natives you had following you around earlier? Were they all wiped out?"

"Um… that's a funny thing, Primus. They disappeared on me, just before the big attack landed."

"Hmm… I don't like the sound of that. According to our deepest drone reports, the troops from Rigel have landed in force in the mountains to the east of the fort."

That was the first I'd heard of any enemy landings. I turned to the east and examined the peaks that stood there. They were hazy in the drizzle, but I could see a row of dark mountains squatting beyond the trees.

"That sounds bad, sir," I said. "They might find good artillery placements up there—provided they have artillery."

"Agreed. McGill, you've dealt with Rigel infantry face-to-face, and you've talked to a representative of Rigel in person. Why do you think they chose to invade our camp so blatantly? They could have landed more safely from the start and begun a campaign of eradication with a much more traditional approach."

"Honestly, sir, I think they're pretty full of themselves. And to give them credit, they almost took us out with their arrogant attack."

"That's true... They don't think much of our fighting capabilities. Well, what we need now is human intel—eyes on the ground. You up for some in-country action?"

"Uh..."

"Really?" he complained at my lack of enthusiasm. "I would have thought you'd be bored by now patrolling inside these walls."

"It's been anything but dull, sir. But if you want intel, I suppose I could gather my unit and go for a walk."

"That's not exactly what I had in mind. By all reports, we're in for a lull. The Wur have taken a beating, and the boys from Rigel are setting up a new camp. I want you to use these hours wisely by finding your native friends and seeing if they can help you penetrate the Rigellian camp."

"Oh... sounds great, sir. I'm not sure where the locals went, however—"

"Seriously, McGill? Do you think I was born yesterday? They've got a network of subway tunnels or whatever you want to call them directly under our feet. They obviously went slinking down there when things looked dangerous. Reestablish contact and report back. Graves out."

Sighing, I saw the green com light die in my helmet. I really had been looking forward to a shower and a few hours of relative peace—but that never had been the fate of any star-faring legionnaire.

After making sure my unit was recovering and placing Leeson in command in my absence, I contacted the one man who might know more than I did about our lanky blue friends.

"Cooper?" I asked. "You awake?"

He yawned in my ear.

"Just what I thought. If I catch you sleeping somewhere in that stealth suit, I'm pulling your name as a ghost candidate."

"That's harsh, Centurion, so harsh. I'm ready for action."

"Meet me at the gates."

After filling a ruck with basic supplies, I found two footprints that didn't fill with mud near the gatehouse. I elbowed Cooper, and he grunted.

"Oh no, sorry man!" I exclaimed, slapping him on the back until he coughed.

"It was the footprints, wasn't it?" he complained. "That's the worst thing about this form of stealth. It doesn't do much for you when there's an absence of volume. In fact, when the rain is really coming down in sheets, you can see me better by the empty, rain-free space than you could if I was just standing there without this damned poncho."

"You want to give it up, then?" I asked, calling his bluff.

"Hell no."

"That's what I thought. Lead the way."

"Um… to where, sir?"

"You going to pretend you haven't been shadowing me? That you have no idea what Graves wants us to do? Really?"

He pulled his suit over his head and blinked in the rain. He didn't have a helmet on, and rain ran down over his squinting eyes.

"You've been tracking me?" he asked.

I nodded. "Now and then, when the mood strikes."

"Sir, Graves said you were supposed to go out into the brush and find those blue deserters. I don't see why—"

Nonchalantly, I put a big hand on his shoulder. He shut up immediately, but he didn't flinch away.

"Listen," I said. "You're coming with. Be happy—what good is a scout if he's not off doing some kind of recon?"

Cooper grumbled, but he soon led the way into the muck outside the walls. The land was a mess consisting of endless mud, Wur sap, bubbling craters of acid and countless other nasty things.

Following him as he led the way to the edge of the forest, I felt a twinge of concern. I'd figured he was shadowing me, goofing off, and probably following attractive females around in that ghost-suit of his—but I hadn't really figured he would have overheard my conversation with Graves. I made a mental note to investigate that detail later on—maybe one of our techs was feeding him info.

He took me to a secret spot where space warped. There, a "fall-in" zone could be used to gain entrance to the underground labyrinth of the Scupper. We both hesitated before jumping into it.

"You sure this is the spot?" I asked.

"Stalling, huh?" Cooper asked. "I don't blame you. In fact, I'm more than willing to call the whole thing off and tell Graves we tried and failed. I'll back you up one hundred percent, sir."

"We're not giving up before we even try. That's not going to happen."

Cooper sighed. "We're going to get permed down there, you know. We almost did the last time."

"Maybe," I agreed. "You first, scout."

He continued to linger. "Can I ask you one thing first, Centurion?"

"Nope. Get into that frigging hole!"

My boot swept toward his tail-section, but he'd already dodged forward and slipped away into nothingness. It was the damnedest thing to watch. One second, he was falling into a patch of muck, and the next he was gone.

Following him, I slid down into the ground, and what passed for the gray daylight of Storm World was lost above.

I landed inside a tube as before. Lit with a glimmer, I applied my suit lights and soon realized I was alone. I saw two smaller muddy footprints on the deck—but no Cooper. Judging by the look of the prints, I figured he wasn't still standing there—he would have been right under my balls if he had been.

So… where had he gone? There was only one obvious answer. He'd jumped up and flown away, using the unique properties of these transportation tubes immediately upon entering.

But why?

"Cooper?" I called out quietly. "You still around?"

There was nothing. The deathly silence of the grave met my ears, and pounded on them. Compared to the endless splattering sound of the rains above, the sudden silence roared in my head.

"Cooper?" I called again, a little louder this time.

There was no mistaking it. I was alone.

Cursing, I gave a little hop and began flying away downstream—in the direction the builders of this place had intended.

According to my tapper, I was going east. That was positive, at least. I was supposed to scout in an eastern direction at some point. Why not start now?

The tunnel was a fairly short one. A kilometer or two farther down, I began to drift then landed. I'd learned over time to do it gracefully, and I marched down the tube toward the endpoint where one of those doors stood open.

Seeing muddy footprints that weren't my own, I felt a deep frown overtake my features.

"Cooper?" I demanded loudly.

"Shhh!" he hissed back.

Slowing, I looked carefully at the end of the tube. The door was there, hanging open. In general, doors down here always closed themselves. That meant someone I couldn't see had to be holding it open.

I walked up quietly behind the stealthed Cooper and crouched behind him. Fortunately, there was enough muddy debris on the ground to let me track him. Vaguely, I wondered how they kept the tubes so clean when their planet was nothing but one giant pit of filth.

Peering into the void beyond Cooper, I saw it was a shaft, one that went both up and down. I wanted to ask him what the hell he was doing, but he was my scout, and I'd found him, so I figured I'd let him explain himself in good time.

"Dammit," he said, in a whisper. "I can't hear him anymore."

"Hear who?"

"One of those blue cowards was waiting for us down here. When I came down, I almost landed on him. I think he was posted here to see if we followed that 'Second-man' dude. Well, when I showed up, he bounced into the air and flashed away. I followed, but I couldn't quite catch up. He went through that door into the shaft beyond."

"Yeah… so? Just run out there and see which way the wind blows."

"Not so simple. Remember those shafts that go both up and down? This is one of those. I'm not sure where he went."

Leaning forward, I pushed Cooper aside and poked my head into the shaft. Cooper was right—there was no telling which way the salamander had gone.

"We could split up," I said.

"And double our chances of a perming?" he complained. "No thanks."

I was frowning again. Somehow, that happened almost constantly when dealing with Cooper. He'd never quite grasped the twin concepts of authority and duty. He was a dishonorable cur at heart, always forgetting who he was talking to.

In a way, he was like me when I'd been younger—but much more snotty.

"All right, you pussy," I said, and I pushed past him into the shaft. "I'll take my shot."

"Up, or down?" he whispered.

I considered. "Above us should be the mountains where those troops from Rigel are setting up camp. If I were on the run, why would I go there?"

"Maybe. If you were really allied with them, not the Earthers."

"Huh…" I said, having not considered the idea.

Shrugging, I jumped out into open space, and I shoved off, sending myself into a fall. I'd made my choice, right or wrong. If we just sat around, there was no way we'd ever catch up. This way, at least it was fifty-fifty I'd guessed right.

I fell like a stone. The air came up and whistled into my face, and I couldn't help but feel the growing creep of panic.

Was I falling faster, due to the additional tug of real gravity? It felt that way. Would this shaft's safe-landing sensors be switched off by the blue bastard we were chasing, since he was a native and no doubt had more control over this system than we did? There was no way to know until I slammed down dead at the bottom.

There was nothing for it now other than to enjoy the fall. I tried to do so, but my body wouldn't let me. I knew better than to relax and create a bloody splat on some distant landing pad below. I wanted to reach out and touch the sides of the shaft as they flashed by.

I didn't dare, of course. I'd go into a tumble, unable to stop. When travelling in the lateral shafts, at least you could roll out of it and end up on lying on the bottom of the tube.

Not so in this shaft. I'd bang my body against one wall then carom over to the next—I doubted I could survive.

The fall went on for what felt like a long time. At points, I thought I saw other passages and doors at the sides of the tunnel—but I didn't stop falling deeper into the planet's crust.

That worried me a little, I don't mind saying. What if our treacherous friend had turned off the automated features of this tube? Wouldn't it look like this? Flashing by one stopping place after another in rapid succession, like a runaway train sailing through stations full of startled passengers at breakneck speed?

Soon, I became convinced that I'd been tricked. How easy it had been to best old McGill. Some salamander had left a door open as a baited trap, and I'd willingly jumped to my death like the true-blue fool that I really was inside.

# -55-

Landing at last, I was relieved to find myself standing on my feet. The tubes had decelerated my mass at the last minute, leaving me in a comfortable stance.

That was about the only good news of the day, however, because the place I landed in was unlike anything else I'd encountered on Storm World.

It was a city. An underground city inside a vast cavern.

The feeling was similar to being outside. There wasn't even much of an echo, so I knew the place was big. Really *big*.

What's more, there was a wind whistling along—an actual underground wind. To me, that seemed weird.

Off to my left, I saw a river of sorts. Surprised I could see that at all without night vision toggled on, I realized there was light down here. It came from dim yellow globes of unknown girth that gripped the ceiling. Electrical? Chemical? I didn't know, but they did give off a definite wan glow. Just enough to see by, like something a half-moon would do to light up your backyard on Earth.

Nearer at hand, encircling the landing pad area I'd ended up on, were a whole lot of Scuppers. Hundreds of them stood in loose ranks with their spears pointing in random directions.

At my sudden appearance, dropping down out of the ceiling with a war-whoop, the demeanor of the army changed. They came alive, no longer leaning on their spears but rather aiming them at me. The nearest fifty or so stalked forward, heads down, tails sticking out stiffly behind them for balance.

Automatically, I put on my best Georgia smile.

"Hey there," I said, "well met, boys! I'm James McGill, and I'm a First-man."

I'd turned on my translator, which gurgled and plopped in what I fervently hoped was an appropriate manner.

The front rank of advancing salamanders paused, glancing at one another and croaking in confusion.

"That's right," I said. "I'm here to find my Second-man. He's disappeared, and I'm hoping there's a damned good explanation. I wouldn't like to think any Scupper was a cowardly deserter."

One of them nosed through to the front. He was a big green specimen, both taller and broader than my own Second-man. This Scupper had some meat on his bones.

"You speak insults? You dare come here and call us cowards?"

"Not all of you," I said. "Just the man who swore allegiance to me, then bolted when battle came. He's the one I want to talk to."

"You mouth impossibilities. No Scupper would serve a human. No Scupper officer would abandon his station without being destroyed by his own men."

"Is that so? Well, take a look at this video on my tapper."

I held up my arm, and they shuffled closer, blinking in suspicion. Soon, they caught on as I played a vid of my Second-man fighting at my side on the walls of Fort Alpha.

"You see that? He was a good sort, until the boys from Rigel landed. Then, he bolted."

"Ah," said Big Green, lowering his spear and placing the butt of it in the dark, wet, sandy soil. "Now I understand. He would of course retreat from battle with Rigel. Honor would demand no less."

It was my turn to stand and stare in confusion. "Uh... why's that?"

"Because Rigel troops are our guests here. Just as you are."

"Guests? They're invaders."

"Maybe to you, but not to the natives of this world. I see you don't understand. Perhaps you are as simple as the other humans we've met."

"Let me see if I've got this straight, my amphibious friend," I said, as thoughts clicked into place inside my thick skull. "You asked us for help against the Wur, correct?"

"Yes. Earth is strong. We needed troops, so we called for your aid."

"And we answered with two legions. But… if I don't miss my guess, you guys also made the same plea to Rigel. Right?"

The salamander shook his sucker-cupped fingers at me. "Of course. We would have been fools to do anything else. You are strong. They are strong. We needed help, so we requested it from everyone who might be able to help us."

"Didn't you see how that might cause trouble? Between Rigel and Earth, that is?"

Again, the big green bastard shook his cups at me. I was beginning to think the gesture was equivalent to a human shrug of the shoulders.

"That was of no concern. The Wur have eaten up half our landmass. There was no time or enthusiasm at the prospect of picking sides. We had no way of knowing if either Rigel or Earth would even show up to help."

Slowly, I began nodding. I was able to see the Scupper's reasoning. They were like a small country under attack from a larger one. Desperate, they sent envoys to all the local powers for help. They got both of us to show up—but from their point of view that was way better than choosing one and being ignored.

"All right," I said. "I can accept all that for now. But how does that absolve my Second-man? He still ran out on me, no matter why he did it."

"That was a matter of honor, as I said. Your auditory organs seem to fail you often, despite their great size and ugly nature."

He reached out a glistening finger and poked at my ears. I pulled back in irritation.

"I heard you," I said, "but I don't get how honor can force a man to desert his post."

"It's simple enough. We invited both of you. If you choose to fight one another, we can't interfere."

I narrowed my eyes at him. I wasn't born yesterday, and even if I had been, this story would have stunk up the gigantic cave I was standing in.

"One of you frogs must have been bright enough to know that we'd fight if we met up together. This whole thing was a setup from the beginning."

The green guy waved his fingers again. Another shrug of disinterest.

Now, I've never been known to have a short fuse—but I've definitely got a long one, and I'd reached the end of it at last.

Reaching out and grabbing hold of his waggling hand, I gave it a yank, pulling him toward me, off his feet.

He stumbled forward, croaking in surprise. A dozen or so of his soldiers became alert, gripping their weapons and encircling us.

"Maybe I should fight you," I said. "You're a First-man, aren't you? Maybe I'll make you my second. Or maybe I'll make your second serve me instead."

"Have a care, human brute. You are not a welcome guest here now, as we are already entertaining another. We cannot have both. Do not make us force you from this place."

I let go of his hand, and he snatched it back, working it as if it was sore. It probably was.

"You already have a guest?" I demanded. "Who?"

"That is of no concern—"

Suddenly, the light went on inside my fridge. I smiled and grabbed hold of the slimy green bastard again.

"You've got a Rigel-man here, don't you? Where is he?"

He pulled away from me. "I informed you, we cannot have two guests in conflict—not here."

"No problem! I won't be here long. When my legion arrives, we'll make short work of this dump of a place and leave what's left behind for Rigel."

He listened to the translation and looked at me warily. "You are alone. You will not return to your fortress if you make threats."

"Want to kill me, huh? It won't matter. You know we men from the stars live a thousand lives, don't you?"

"I've heard such fantasies, but I disregard them."

"Well, how about this: did your spy tell you I was alone when I entered the tunnels?"

He paused. "We have no spies."

I laughed. My translator gurgled at him.

"Aw, come on, green-finger. I saw him when we first came down here. He bolted to tell you we'd entered the tunnels. We chased him, and he ran straight here."

"You are mistakenly speaking in the plural form. You are alone, Earth man, and—"

Here, another form slunk up to join us. It was a brown salamander, built with a long neck and short limbs that left him low to the ground as he approached.

"First-man," he said, "I beg to speak."

"You dare much, but I will allow it."

The brown slime-ball eyed me repeatedly as he gave his report. "The brute speaks correctly, First-man. There were two of them when they first came down—maybe more. I can't know, as I returned to make my report as ordered."

The green bastard backhanded him, sending him rolling ass-over-tea-kettle onto the dark sand. "You dishonor us all with your words!"

The spy scuttled off, and the green officer turned back to look at me.

"Where is your companion?" he demanded.

Lifting my fingers, I did my best to imitate his waggling gesture of disinterest.

"Who knows?" I asked. "He's not here, but he knows how to get here. As I said, when my army comes—"

Big Green changed his attitude in a flash. He was pissed.

"You've come here to our sacred city to deliver idle threats?" he demanded. "You are no ally of ours! You are rude. You are duplicitous. You are unpleasant in both manner and appearance."

"That might all be true," I said, waggling fingers at him again to show him how little I cared. "But we humans are better killers than your people are, and we've been deceived. Do you really want to find out what my troops can do against your pathetic army of spearmen?"

His eyes shifted, gazing around himself at the watching, listening troops.

"What is it you propose?" he asked at last.

That's when my grin came back—right then, and not a moment sooner. We'd just had ourselves a good, old-fashioned country stare-down, and Big Green had blinked first.

"Do you frogs really lay eggs?" I asked Big Green. "We're low on fresh meat back at the fort, and real predators like us humans only enjoy fresh meat."

He had twin eyes the size of cue balls on top of his head, and they popped out a little.

I laughed.

"Nah…" I said. "Just kidding! We don't eat babies. Adults-only."

"You are an unpleasant being."

"So people keep telling me... Now, listen up big guy. This is how things are going to go down."

The First-man listened, but as he did so, his eyes began to puff up again. By the time I was done, I was wondering if his eyeballs were going to fall out and roll away on the sandy floor of the cavern.

# -56-

Big Green obeyed me with a decidedly poor attitude. He led me deeper into the cavern along a sandy road. The road wove between lagoons of lapping black pools, fields of mushrooms and racks of blind, pale-skinned cavefish. It wasn't paved, but it was well-used enough and clearly marked.

As time passed, my eyes adjusted so I could see farther into the cavern. It was a gloomy place, several kilometers wide and deep. The roof was only a few hundred meters above our heads, and it was covered with moss and vast hanging stalactites that resembled fangs festooning the roof. Now and then, we passed a fallen pile of shattered rock, and I realized that anyone unlucky enough to be under one of these stone daggers would surely be killed when it fell.

That would be a certain perming if it happened to me now. That's what I was thinking about, and it made me feel kind of itchy.

After all, I had no idea where Cooper was at the moment. He *might* be stealthing along in my wake—or he might have gone back to the surface. It was hard to tell, and he hadn't bothered to give me any clue as to his whereabouts or his intentions.

But Big Green didn't know that. It was funny how often a small missing bit of knowledge could expand to be worth a man's life.

All around me, big Scupper-feet slapped and crunched on the sand. I whistled as we marched along to pass the time.

After a few minutes, Big Green turned to me and croaked in irritation.

"Could you stop making that noise?" he asked. "It sounds like the squall of a dying mollusk."

"Really?" I asked. "I don't think I've ever heard a mollusk make a sound that I could hear."

I kept right on whistling, of course. If a man can't face mortal danger in his own way, well, there's no justice in the universe.

Besides, my careless willingness to irritate my hosts could only serve to prove to them that I was feeling confident. A man's boasting could be easily unraveled by hesitation and overthinking. When you're living a lie, you've got to go all the way.

In time, a bigger structure loomed ahead of us. It wasn't a nice-looking place. It was more like an underground termite-mound made out of dark gray basalt stone.

"Huh…" I said as we passed inside the mouth of the main entrance. "Is this some kind of cathedral?"

Big Green puzzled over that for a moment. "It does have mystical significance," he agreed. "But the word you've chosen is improper. We call it the Citadel."

"Fair enough. Lead on."

He eyed me in annoyance before again complying with my commands.

His irritation made me feel good. Sort of… prideful. I swear, a man like me could get pretty far with an arrogant attitude and a believable bluff. Today was proof-positive.

As per my instructions, Big Green didn't announce my arrival. He just marched me into the heart of the place, leaving his army outside the gates. We got plenty of looks from the locals, but no one stopped us outright. I gathered from that simple fact that my escort was respected and highly ranked.

I didn't care either way, of course. I had bigger fish to fry.

When we arrived at last and stepped into a cold chamber full of black, ashy stone, I halted. There, squatting on a dark throne, was another Scupper. She was similar in appearance, but vastly over-sized.

The throne itself was at least a ton of polished black stone. Ebony? Dark quartz? I couldn't tell, and I barely cared.

What caught my attention were two key details. One was the massive queen herself. An outsized Scupper big enough to fit her massive throne, she was at least *shaped* like her smaller subjects. She was as big in comparison to Big Green as one of our Blood Worlder giants would be if they stood side-by-side. If I had to guess, I didn't think I'd come up to the top of her folded, warty kneecap.

But the second thing that caught my eye was even less pleasant. The queen—because that's what I'd deduced she was—was in the midst of entertaining another visitor.

The nature of this visitor was known to me. Short, stocky, and generally bear-like in appearance, the creature appeared to be in a conversation with the hulking monarch on the throne.

*A Rigellian.*

There was no getting around it. They'd made it down here before us—and now I was face-to-face with one of them.

The alien turned to look at me. He didn't jump up or draw a weapon. He didn't nod or wave. He just stared at me.

That let me know that Big Green had kept his word. He'd led me here unannounced. The little bastard was surprised to see me.

Two steps forward, and I placed my fists on my hips.

"I'm Centurion James McGill," I said loudly. "Emissary from Earth. I'm here to demand an audience with the Scupper queen."

The queen, for all her bulk, spoke quietly in deep tones. "This is… unexpected."

"It's rude," the Rigellian said in a strange voice. It spoke with a warbling, underwater sound, as if it had already drowned in one of the inky black pools that dotted the cavern. "It is foul, and it is known to me."

That made me blink. My mouth, already open wide, sagged and I stopped talking. Leaning forward and peering in the poor light, I finally released a bray of laughter.

"I know you!" I boomed. "You're that pathetic dummy I met back on Dark World. How's tricks, dumb-ass?"

My translator clicked and chirped. The necklace of metallic snake-bones that hung around his neck did the same. At last, the small figure turned away from the queen's towering shins and walked toward me confidently.

"At last we meet again. Perhaps all your words were not lies—as you have come again into my presence. This cannot be fate or chance."

I wasn't too sure about that, but I thought I'd let it ride.

"That's for certain," I said. "I'm here to square things up between you and me. Last time out, you managed to drive humanity off Dark World. That can't stand. This planet is going to ally with Earth."

The bear-dude tilted his head. "You spout grandiose concepts," he said. "None of your fantasies shall come to pass. I've concluded a bargain with the queen. Earth has been defeated by the Wur, and you by Rigel. You've been publicly shamed, and you shall be whipped from here as is only right."

I laughed loudly. "What? The Wur didn't beat us! We sent them packing just yesterday."

"One battle does not a war make. You've lost one of your legions and one of two fortifications. Your ship has fled from ours. That makes a string of humiliating defeats."

"Not so fast," I said. "We beat your asses inside our walls. That's right, you dropped right on top of us, and you were wiped out down to the last bear cub."

The Rigellian made an irritable gesture. "All of this is moot. It has been decided."

He turned back toward the queen, who all this time had squatted, gurgling softly on her throne.

"My Queen," he said. "Tell this creature of our arrangement. Tell him who your allies are now."

"It's true," she said in that vast voice. "Storm World serves Rigel. This being is now my leader. I am sworn to him."

This was a conundrum, I don't mind telling you. For about three long seconds, my jaw sagged low. I gaped at the two of them.

*Dammit!* I'd gotten here too late. Maybe by an hour, maybe by a minute, but it didn't matter. This smooth-talking bear had convinced her holiness that he was the one to sign on with.

But then, slowly, my overstimulated brain began to cook up an idea.

It wasn't going to be an easy play, but as best as I could figure, it was the only move I had.

I laughed. I laughed long and loud, grabbing my belly like a boozy Santa who deserved to be fired on the spot.

"That's great!" I boomed. "That makes my job all the easier!"

"Madness," the bear said. "These Earthers truly suffer from it. The last time we met, this creature insisted a box of glucose was an explosive. After careful analysis by a dozen of our demolitions experts, however—"

"Never mind about that!" I said. "Don't you understand, fuzz-ball? Don't you grasp the mistake you've made here?"

"No error has been committed. Notwithstanding the possible misstep of allowing you to speak your nonsense for so long—"

"No, no, no," I interrupted. "I mean culturally. Hey, Queenie! Tell me if I'm wrong: is this bear-fellow your boss now? Do you serve him, the way a Second-man might serve a First-man?"

"Your analogy is insulting—but essentially correct. We are the junior force in this alliance."

"Excellent," I said to her. "Now, what happens if I challenge pipsqueak here to a duel. What if I beat him six ways from Sunday, fair and square?"

Her big, bulbous eyes blinked once in slow-motion. "Then, his forces would become yours."

"Nonsense and idiocy," the Rigellian sputtered. He turned to the guards who stood around the chamber. "I order you to arrest this ape. Restrain it, so that I might dissect it alive. I wish to both learn of its nature and to enjoy its anguish simultaneously."

My hand crept to the butt of my gun, but I needn't have bothered. The guards made no move to advance.

Agitated, the bear turned to face the queen. "I demand you relay my commands. This creature must be restrained."

The queen ruminated. She seemed slow of mind, but intelligent. Maybe once you got to be five meters tall and several centuries old, your brain worked on a different schedule.

"No," she said simply. "The challenge has been offered, but as yet it has not been accepted. This annoying creature is the leader of a great people, and therefore has the standing to make this challenge. Until the matter is resolved, I cannot follow your orders. That is our way."

I wanted to laugh. I wanted to guffaw and to cheer so loud a dozen spikey rocks would come flying down and bury this arrogant little teddy-bear.

But I thought of something better to do instead.

I clocked him one, from behind. One gloved fist, one fuzzy skull. The two cracked together—and the fight was on.

# -57-

The bear didn't go down with my first strike. That, all by itself, impressed me. Most men would have been knocked senseless by the blow I'd given him—but not this frigging little bear. He was one tough bastard.

Ever seen a baby gorilla out-wrestle a grown man? It's not a pretty sight, but it's not uncommon. Wild animals frequently have greater muscle density than humans. In my experience, that went for plenty of varieties of alien beings, too.

It wasn't just a matter of size, or of ferocity. Being male, or from a higher-gravity world, sure, that kind of thing helped.

But it was more than that. Each critter was simply built differently than the rest. Humans, for beings of reasonable size, were on the low end of the strength-to-muscle-mass ratio in my experience. Most predatory species were more powerful than we were kilo for kilo.

This frigger from Rigel was no exception. He'd probably had an easy time of it earlier today, beating down whatever champion had been unlucky enough to fight for the Scupper queen. Hell, these salamanders weren't very tough—but I wasn't a salamander, and neither was he.

He absorbed the thumping I'd given his skull, pitching and rolling away from me. A moment later, he came back up with a growl.

His disengage maneuver had been performed with a practiced air, which told me two things: one, I hadn't hurt him much, and two, he was a well-trained fighter.

As there was no backing out at this point, I waded into the fight. Attempting to use whatever initiative I'd gained by striking first, I reached for his furry throat and grabbed hold of him. Lifting and squeezing hard, I tried to throttle the life out of him.

It was a mistake. Despite my long arms, I wasn't far enough away from him to prevent him from retaliating. He squirmed in my hands, but didn't break free. He didn't even try. Instead, he slashed up at my face with those hind legs of his.

Now, I'm a long-armed galoot of a man. Just ask anybody. But even I didn't have a reach that exceeded the one meter distance over which this bear-thing could deliver a hard kick.

My faceplate starred and cracked. That surprised me. Sure, it wasn't invulnerable, but bear claws shouldn't have been able to break the ballistic glass. Did he have something on those claws? A diamond-tipped enhancement, maybe?

I didn't really have time to contemplate the answer. The bear was kicking my ass, and strangling him didn't seem to be slowing him down much. I had to come up with another tactic immediately.

I threw him across the room. It was instinct and probably a mistake. It allowed him to scramble back to his feet and advance.

Equally instinctual was my grab for the pistol on my belt. A rumbling word from the queen stopped me.

"Introduction of weaponry will nullify the results of this contest. It must be even in its beginning and at its ending."

My hand slipped away from my pistol, and the bear gave me a feral show of teeth. He advanced confidently, determinedly.

How do you wrestle with something so small and so powerful? I wasn't accustomed to this kind of fight, so I tried to keep my distance. Using my superior reach, I tried to land blows and keep the bear at bay.

My size-thirteen boot flew out first, striking for the snout that was coming in at about my gonad-level. The bear twitched and dodged, then reached up and gripped my ankle. He tried to flip me, he really did, but I was ready for that, and I pulled away.

We circled, my hands thrown wide like a wrestler. He did the same.

"You have made a gross error, human," he said. "The stupidity of your species continues to astound us at every turn."

"At least I didn't live in terror of a juice-box for better than an hour, you dumbass bear."

I laughed loudly at my own joke, and that seemed to piss him off. His eyes were those of a snake, resembling two drops of glistening black oil. For the first time, he came at me with true rage in those beady eyes.

His rush was easily sidestepped. As he went by, I got an idea.

Long ago, when I'd been dating girls under more earthly circumstances, I'd discovered they liked cats—but that the cats rarely liked me.

Countless were the times when some fuzz-ball would sidle up and sniff, nip, claw or otherwise interrupt my relentless pursuit of their mistress. It was as if they figured I was a rival, an interloper in their territory.

Naturally, as a gentleman caller, I couldn't very well drop-kick the housecat. Instead, I would wait until the girl was distracted, then clamp a hand down on the offending animal's neck, pinning it down.

This did nothing to harm the kitty—but they sure as hell didn't like it. After counting to five or so, I would snatch my hand away. Invariably, the pet would slink away and hide, staring at me with dark hatred from under the furniture.

My problem had therefore been neatly solved with the girl in question none the wiser.

Taking a page from an old book, I clamped down on the back of the bear's neck and shoved his snout into the stony floor of the queen's chambers.

Unfortunately, this alien was much stronger than any housecat ever born, so he bucked up again—and I landed on his back with the full force of both knees, driving them into his fur-covered spine.

Down he went again. I heard a small, angry grunt. There was quite a bit of scrabbling, but I was on him now. Not just sitting, but kneeling on his back.

He didn't give up easily. I'll say that for the little dick. He bucked and squirmed and snapped desperately. I rode him like a cowboy breaking a fresh mustang stallion.

Whooping and laughing, I bounced and jounced, somehow always finding a way to drive a knee, fist, or even an elbow into the small body under me.

At last, he paused, sides heaving. He was exhausted.

"Kill me," he said.

"What? Why? This is too much fun."

"You intend to humiliate, not just to abuse?"

"Yeah, I sure do. Aren't you having fun, little guy?"

He bucked a few more times, and he managed to claw my knee. I frowned and bashed his skull several times—hard.

"Now, now, that's no way to treat your new master, Mr. Bear. You'd best learn some manners."

"You must slay me. This is dishonorable."

I glanced over my shoulder at the queen, who still squatted on her stone throne, contemplating the situation.

"What do you say, Your Majesty? Should I kill him?"

She waved her finger-cups at me. A shrug.

"It is your right. Your prerogative."

"Do you accept that I won this contest fair and square?" I asked her.

"I do. I have witnessed the struggle, and it is clear you are the victor. My armies are now in your hands—you may command them."

I licked my lips and looked down at the bear. I was running out of ideas. Should I kill him? Or should I let him go?

It was a question with no clear answer.

## -58-

"Let's negotiate, bear-buddy. Your people are slavers, right?"

"I know where you are going with this, human. The answer is 'no'. I will never serve you."

"Not even for a day or two?" I asked in honest disappointment. "I had plans… you could wear a funny hat or something. Maybe I could teach you to dance with a chain around your neck. My buddies would like that."

"Your suggestions are as impossible as they are cruel."

"That's a damned shame… Well, if we can't work anything out…"

I dug a combat knife out of my gear. The blade had a silver edge that glimmered in the dim-lit chamber.

"At last," he said, "this humiliation shall end."

Getting an idea, I put my knife away again and pulled back my sleeve to expose my tapper. I had to do this with my teeth, as my other hand was pinning him down.

"What are you doing now, slow-witted human?" he demanded.

"Just a second. Don't get your fur all in a bunch. I'm making a vid and transmitting it."

The body under me heaved a little.

"What? Why can't you end this?"

"Don't worry, don't fret. I'll kill you soon enough. I just wanted old Sateekas to see the situation firsthand before I send you to bear-Nirvana."

His ears twitched. "Stop!"

My tapper glowed, and I began recording. I spoke into it as I filmed the pinned bear, the hulking queen, and the cavern around me.

"Now, if I can only get this damned thing to transmit…" I said, fooling with it.

The bear snorted and relaxed a little. "You will fail. Your technology is pathetic. Cast-offs from your superiors the Galactics, every piece of equipment you possess is—"

"Hold still and shut up for a minute, will you? And hey, Cooper, could you get this relayed up to the surface?"

"Sure thing, Centurion," Cooper said.

The bear's eyes rolled around in his skull. "Where—who is that speaking?"

"One of my many companions. You didn't think I'd come down here without a full combat team, did you?"

I laughed at him then, like he was the biggest idiot at the party. Maybe he was, at that.

"I've got a signal, sir," Cooper said. "I've been working on that since we came down here."

"I'm not surprised," I said, and I meant it. Always thinking of number one, Cooper had been working hard to prevent our likely perming if we died down here.

I had him pinpointed by now. He was over to the left of the entrance, standing near a guard. Although he still had his stealth suit on, his footprints were distinctive in the soft sand of the cavern floor.

"This invalidates the contest!" the bear said under me. He squirmed and tried to aim his snout toward the queen. "Monarch! Stop this farce!"

"On what grounds?" the Queen asked reasonably.

"Interference! Two combatants have conspired to foul the third, an innocent who acted in good faith. That nullifies these proceedings!"

"Getting a little desperate, shorty?" I asked. "Cooper didn't do anything. He was ordered not to. All he's done is discover a way to communicate beyond this underground lair."

The real reason Cooper had done so was obvious to me: to avoid being permed. Legionnaires from every outfit feared being off-grid. Without a body, a soldier couldn't be revived. If we could at least report our status, we were much closer to being revived if this whole adventure went tits-up by the end.

"Okay," I said, "I've queued up the feed. Can you relay it—and our latest engrams?"

"I'm on it, sir."

I didn't ask how he'd gotten access to the outside world. That was because there was very little chance that his methods were legitimate. I strongly suspected Cooper had been hacking into the Scupper networks. What else did he have to do while watching me fool around with a bear and a giant salamander queen? He sure as hell hadn't felt like revealing himself and helping me out. The only reason he'd done so now, I'd wager, was that he figured I'd clearly won.

Despite the squirming, the insults, and the desperate growling sounds of my opponent, I managed to connect my tapper with Sateekas' ship.

"Ah…" he said as he examined the live vid I was feeding him. "The McGill-creature reports in directly. Why am I not surprised?"

"I have great faith in you as well, Governor," I said.

He shuffled his bulk around and stared. "Is that the representative of Rigel? Have you slain him?"

"No, sir! This bear is as fresh as a daisy. The representative is—uh—he's just resting."

Using my off-hand, I clamped the bear's snout closed. He didn't like that anymore than your average animal did. He struggled, and blew snot on my gloves, but I kept him quiet.

"What is the purpose of this communication, McGill?"

"Just to show you who's in charge down here," I told him. "As a representative of Earth, I've defeated the champion of Rigel. We Earth folks are clearly superior in every way."

Sateekas released a farting laugh. "Your efforts are amusing, but insufficiently conclusive. The contest will end when one of your species is kicked off this planet, or has at least eradicated the Wur entirely."

"A tall order, sir," I said. "But we'll do it—somehow."

Sateekas signed off. Disappointed, I released the bear and stood up.

Getting to his feet, the Rigellian seemed a bit on the sore side. That was probably due to the kneecap I'd kept planted in his back for a good ten minutes now.

"You might have a few bruises in the morning," I told him. "But it was all in good fun."

He glowered. I'm not always good at reading expressions, but I was pretty sure he was hating on me with every fiber of his shrimpy being.

"This humiliation will not go unanswered, ape," he said. "Know that no species has ever bested Rigel! Our people are indomitable!"

I made a rude blatting noise with my lips.

"Come on, bear-dude," I said. "You've got to be kidding. You're out here to win favor with the real power in this galaxy—the Empire. Just the same as we are. In fact, you're trying to take our job. You're *begging* to serve the Galactics."

If he'd been pissed before, I'd gone and made it worse. His claws shook a little as he lifted them and pointed at me with his entire, bloody paw.

"McGill..." he said as if my name was a swear-word. "I shall remember that name."

"Yeah, okay," I said. "By the way, what's your name?"

"I am called High Lord Squanto."

I blinked, and for a second, my mind froze over.

Now, I'm not a complete idiot. I could tell when enough was enough—but I couldn't help myself.

I doubled over in laughter. "Squanto!" I shouted. "Really? You're not shitting me? Your name is *Squanto*? That's great."

"You mock even my name...?" he asked seriously. "This has become personal between us. It will never be forgotten—"

"Yeah, yeah," I said. "Listen, are you going to serve me and swear your army to me, or what?"

His glass-bead eyes blinked once. "Certainly not. The absurdity of such a suggestion proves—"

"It proves you're a dishonorable cur," I said, and I turned toward the queen. "Did you hear that? He's a First-man, bested by another fair and square. Yet he refuses to relinquish his power and serve the new First-man. What should we do about that, Queenie?"

The queen stirred at last. Her limbs creaked, and she stood up. She was so tall she had to hunch so she didn't scrape the vaulted ceiling.

In her hand, her spear seemed to sense her intent. It crackled into life.

"This creature is dishonorable!" she boomed, suddenly loud beyond belief. The walls shook with her croaking words. "We shall expel him from our sacred cavern!"

Squanto took a step back, then two. Behind him the guards came to life as well and gripped their spears. They meant business.

He ran for it then. I couldn't blame him. Sure, he'd begged me for death, but I was recording all this on my tapper, and I was grinning big.

He knew I'd spread the vid file far and wide. It was one thing to be beaten down in an honorable fight and killed—it was quite another to be jolted in the ass by a crowd of angry salamanders.

The chase was on in an instant. I had to give Squanto credit—for all his haughty nature, he was a scrapper. He dodged, he weaved, he darted between gangly legs and knocked guards down like bowling pins.

We chased him all the way out of the cavern. I waved my own army of amphibians back, and they reluctantly let him pass.

The queen though, with her long-legged retinue, they just wouldn't give up the chase. They railroaded his furry butt all the way to the entrance.

There, however, we ran into a bit of trouble. A full squad of Rigellian troops was on the scene, squaring off with an army of Scupper regulars.

Apparently, Sateekas hadn't been the only interested party who'd viewed my vid as I uploaded it.

# -59-

A terrific fight broke out. My new salamander buddies must have thought they had it in the bag at first—but they'd thought wrong.

The Rigel troops were unstoppable. They were stronger than they looked—easily stronger than the Scuppers. Worse, they had on that flexible armor that couldn't be penetrated easily.

The Scuppers swarmed forward, jabbing with their shock-sticks, and I was surprised to see them scoring some hits. They couldn't penetrate and kill the Rigellians with their weapons, but they could give them a jolt. Apparently, the suits were designed to stop kinetic damage, not electrical charges.

Still, despite being stunned and goaded, the Rigellians began to win. They deployed their boom-stick shotguns and blew down two or three salamanders with every blast.

"Hold on, hold on!" I shouted. "As your First-man, I order you to pull back!"

Startled, the Scupper officers looked at their queen. She was at the back of the pack, standing and leaning on her massive spear. She looked winded. I got the feeling she didn't march off to battle all that often.

"Obey the First-man!" she said.

The Scuppers fell back, and the Rigel boys circled up. They helped their stunned troops back onto their feet.

"Squanto!" I called out. "I've decided this isn't the right place for battle. We came here in peace, and we should part ways in the same fashion."

Squanto eyed the crowd. More and more salamanders were marching up every minute. It was obvious that he might kill a thousand—but he couldn't kill them all. Eventually, they'd run out of ammo, or be stunned over and over until their hearts stopped beating. However this was going to end, it wasn't going to be pretty.

"I will withdraw," he said.

"Good. Let's let bygones be bygones. I can forgive and forget about this day, if you can."

Squanto stared. I got the impression my offer surprised him.

"No, McGill," he said. "The events and words spoken today can't be so easily forgiven. This is not finished between us."

"That's a crying shame…" I said, watching the Rigellian troops turn and limp away toward the tubes.

A familiar figure approached me then. He was tall, blue, and skinny. He'd been my Second-man before running out on me days ago.

"Second-man?" I demanded. "Where have you been?"

"Let me apologize for my absence, First-man," he said. "Your unexpected arrival here has cleared my mind. I now live only to serve you."

"Yeah, yeah… right."

"I have a suggestion," he said, sidling closer. "We can manipulate the fields inside the tubes. My people did construct them, after all."

"Uh… what are you suggesting?"

"A simple matter," he said, waving his cups delicately in the air. "We'll turn them off at an opportune time, such as when a journey is near its ending. Without any braking action… well, the soldiers of Rigel will experience a difficult landing…"

He painted a grim picture. I looked after the Rigel troops. Could it really be so easy? Would it be worthwhile?

I could order them all murdered. Rigel would know, of course. They'd know I'd fought with Squanto, publicly humiliated him and his men, then arranged to have them killed as they withdrew under the terms of our truce. We transmitted these details on open channels to impress Sateekas.

"No," I said at last. "Don't do anything to the tubes. Let them find their way to the surface again."

Second-man waggled his fingers slowly, clearly disappointed. "It will be as you command. All agreements shall be honored."

He slunk away, and I looked after him. I wasn't sure if I liked the guy anymore. In fact, I was beginning to think I didn't like him at all.

After the troops from Rigel had all left, I stared after them. How would things turn out in the end with old Squanto? I'd bested him twice, but he seemed determined. It would be hard to trick him a third time.

Try as I might, it was hard for me to visualize us becoming friends someday.

Being First-man of the Scupper forces wasn't quite like being the Pharaoh of Old Egypt. Instead of wielding absolute power, I found I had to do a bit of convincing and cajoling to get their cooperation.

My first idea was simple: gather all the salamanders I could and take them up the tubes with me to Fort Beta. That idea was met with laughter.

"Impossible," Second-man said.

Somehow, despite the fact I didn't really know or like him, I was saddled with him. The queen had decided that he would act as my Second-man to their entire Scupper force. This seemed to make perfect sense to them, while the logic of it completely escaped me.

"Why is it impossible?" I growled at him.

"It simply cannot be done. There are too many commitments. Everyone can't go on a mad adventure."

"This is your planet," I said. "We're here to help you out. Why do we have to fight and die when you refuse to?"

"You don't," he said.

"And if we threaten to withdraw? If we return to our ships and exit this world?"

"Faced with such a cowardly act," he said, "we'd be forced to swear allegiance to Rigel."

"Right… that's what I thought. Your word means nothing."

"It means much—but we can't allow our species to be exterminated on your whim. Most of these soldiers are only militia—meaning they are only bound to fight when defending the city. They can't be forced to march to the surface and fight off-world armies."

I scratched at my face. The world down here was kind of… stanky.

"All right. How many troops can I take topside?"

"A thousand, or maybe twice that if your manner is convincing. They must all be volunteers."

"Wonderful. What about other cities, other queens?"

He blinked in surprise. "There are other dwellings, but most of them exist under the sea. We shelter there from the endless storms that disturb surface waters."

"Will they join me?"

Second-man considered carefully. "They might, if you can defeat their leaders. Soon, however, they will hear of such an effort and move to stop you."

I threw up my hands. "I'm trying to help you people! I'm not here for my health, you know. I'd rather go back to Earth and let Rigel enslave the lot you."

"It is fortunate, in that case, that your superior officers have given you orders that conflict with these base impulses."

Second-man really had my number. These guys seemed primitive, but they weren't, not really. They had decent tech and they were cunning when it came to diplomatic matters. They knew I couldn't just pull up stakes and take off. Central would never go for it.

"All right," I said. "What if we send out messengers to the other cities asking for adventurers to join us?"

Second-man brightened. "Will there be looting?"

"Uh… looting? What do you want to loot?"

"The bodies of fallen Rigellians, of course. They have excellent weapons and even better armor suits. We would like to study them."

Knowing full well I was on shaky ground, I grinned and nodded. "Sure thing. If you can get me a few thousand more soldiers, you can loot what you want after we beat Rigel. I guarantee it."

"This is excellent news. I will spread the word, and I'll take on the task of requesting aid from other cities personally. If you'll wait here for a few weeks, I'm sure—"

"Forget it. Send an electronic message."

He looked crestfallen. "But… First-man. The cities are distant. They aren't culturally aligned with us directly. The personal approach, sucker-tip to sucker-tip, is bound to be more successful in winning support."

"Is that so? All right… follow me."

He did so, but he moved apprehensively. I found Big Green and ordered him to accompany me to the queen's chambers.

We found her snoring on her rocky throne. After clearing my throat a few times, I got her attention at last.

"What is it, Champion?" she asked. "I thought you'd gone to relieve my world of all invaders. Please, make haste."

"I surely will, your majesty—but I'll need a bigger army."

I quickly explained my plans. Both Big Green and the queen seemed alarmed at my ideas.

At last, however, I managed to get the queen to order Big Green out to the depths of the ocean. He was to journey from city-to-city, using the tubes that ran along the seafloor.

With luck, he'd send up a steady flow of recruits. Even if that failed, well, at least there would be one less hater behind me prattling to the queen.

Big Green left after an hour of objections and weaseling. As good as he was at coming up with excuses, the queen was better at swatting them aside. Watching her get her way and rule her subjects, I began to appreciate her capabilities as a ruler.

She knew how these salamander troops thought, and she'd heard it all before. She didn't take any crap from anyone, wet-skin or dry.

Before the day died in the cavern, Big Green was on his way, and I went in the opposite direction. He travelled out to the sea, downward at a slant into the deep. I led three thousand odd troops back to Fort Beta.

Would they be able to stop Rigel, or the Wur? I had my doubts, but they were better than nothing.

# -60-

By the time I got back up to Fort Beta, Graves was annoyed.

"What took you so long, McGill?" he demanded in my headset.

I considered telling him the truth—but quickly passed on the idea. He didn't like it when I dealt with foreign dignitaries on my own. Hell, no one did.

"I apologize, Primus," I said. "But I've got a little surprise for you."

"What's that? Did you give one of these salamanders the clap?"

"Uh… I'm not sure that's even possible, sir. But no, I've brought back some of them. Several thousand of them, actually."

Soon, they were popping out of the ground, exiting the underground subway system at speed. As they were well-practiced with the procedure, they came out fast, at least one a second.

Graves took in the camera feed I relayed to him, and his manner changed.

"Well, I'll be damned… You did it. It's raining lizards down there. I'll report this to Armel. Good work, McGill."

The channel closed. Carlos swaggered up to stand at my side. He clucked his tongue as he watched my fountain of amphibians.

"Most of them are blue," he said thoughtfully, "but there are about thirty percent green ones, and maybe fifteen percent brownish, or mixed."

I glanced at him. "You're keeping score, huh?"

"Yeah. There's this bio chick who's trying to work her way into the xenobiology corp. I promised I'd get her some firsthand data on the locals."

"Hmm," I said, considering. "Well, I've got some more info for you, in that case. You want to see something… unusual?"

Carlos sidled closer. "You *know* I do. What did you do? Pierce it?"

It took me a second to interpret his comment and his odd grin. When I did, I almost clocked him one, but I settled down instead.

"Check this out," I said, and I played him a snippet of the vicious fight I'd had with Squanto.

"That's *awesome*!" he exclaimed. "You've got to pass me that vid, McGill. I'm sure to get in tight with this girl in Blue Bunker with that."

"No way," I said. "You can't show anyone. That's a private vid, like I said."

"You cock-blocker," he said, throwing up his hands. "Everyone is out to shut down old Carlos."

"I just can't—"

"Fine. Whatever. If that's the way you want to play it, forget I asked."

Carlos stalked off, looking pissed. I shook my head. I shouldn't have shown him the clip, I realized that now. He was the last person a man could trust with a secret. I just couldn't afford to have the brass find out how I'd gotten my native army.

I'd been under the impression Graves would be so impressed with my efforts he'd overlook what I had to do to get these results. Unfortunately, he didn't seem all that appreciative. I'd gone to insane lengths to get him his army, and he was off to report the news to Armel. He hadn't told me to report to Armel in person, oh nooo. He was going to do it.

Maybe he'd even forget to mention my part in the effort. That wouldn't be like him… but sometimes people changed.

Could Graves be hoping for advancement to tribune? Did he want to run Varus himself? I supposed it might be natural for him to want more recognition after having spent ninety-odd years in the service of the legion.

"This whole thing seems unfair," Cooper said in a conversational tone. "I mean, you're not getting much of the credit here, and it's like I'm invisible or something."

I jerked my head, looking around. Of course, no one was there. Making an educated guess, I reached out a glove and caught a hem of fabric.

"Hey!" he called out, but I didn't let go.

"You're going to rip it!" he complained.

"Then take it off."

He did so reluctantly.

"How long have you been standing around spying, Cooper?"

He sniffed. "I don't know… maybe a few minutes."

I tossed the stealth suit at him, and he caught it.

"Leave it off," I told him. "Come with me."

We began walking toward the bunkers. Cooper joined me in the chow line, as it was just after dinner time. The KP bots tried to tell me it was too late to eat, but I pulled rank on them, and they backed off. We got our food and ate it in silence.

"Ah…" a voice said. "McGill and Cooper… Our heroes of the hour."

Tribune Armel swaggered up to our table. "May I join you gentlemen?"

"Of course, sir," I said with my mouth full.

I was pretty happy to see Armel. Obviously, Graves *had* told him where the reinforcements had come from. I shouldn't have mistrusted him.

Armel pulled up a chair and sat down. "You have done something…" he said. "Something I didn't expect. What was it?"

I froze, mid-bite on a pork chop.

There were, as a matter of fact, several very large possibilities he could be referring to. I'd gathered an army, sent out representatives to muster more, fought Squanto nearly to the finish—and contacted Governor Sateekas directly without authorization. I didn't want to forget about that one.

Armel looked at me expectantly.

After a big swallow, I smiled back at him blankly.

"Uh…" I began, stalling for time. My mind is fertile, if not the quickest. Dredging for ideas, I brought up the best I could come up with on the spur of the moment. "We brought an army of salamanders back home to defend our walls, sir. Is that what you're thinking of?"

"That you did," he admitted. "But there's more to the story than that… isn't there?"

"Um…" I said.

Cooper cleared his throat. "Maybe, sir, you're talking about—" he began.

But Armel raised a finger and put it into his face. He didn't even look at Cooper. He kept staring at me. "Silence, little insect. You're like a mosquito—almost invisible, and that's good, but also no one wants to hear your tiny whine in their ears."

Cooper looked pissed, but he shut up. He was new when it came to talking to arrogant brass like Armel.

Despite being shut down, Cooper had given me time to think. "Are you talking about the queen, sir? The giant alien I met down there?"

Armel's lips formed a tight line. I could tell right off I'd guessed wrong.

*Dammit.*

"That does sound frightfully interesting," he said slowly. "But I was thinking of a conversation you had with an even more critical personage."

I got it then. He wasn't happy about me contacting Sateekas directly. I could understand that, as the Governor of Province 921 had the power to summarily erase our species from existence.

"Oh…" I said, chewing slowly. "You must mean Sateekas."

I just stared at him after that, chewing. He stared back, growing increasingly annoyed.

Twitching his head toward Cooper, Armel curled his upper lip. "Begone."

Cooper slid away like the ghost he was studying to become. I watched him go—but he didn't make it all the way to the door. He shrugged on his stealth suit and vanished instead.

That sneaky bastard…

"You dare to smirk?" Armel asked dangerously.

He was watching me. To him, Cooper was unimportant.

"Uh… no sir. I'm just enjoying my dinner."

I chewed some more, face slack, utterly without guile or comprehension.

Sometimes, this tactic worked on folks, especially those who didn't know me very well. They assumed I was an ignoramus, and they left with a snort or an insult.

But Armel knew me better than that by now, unfortunately.

He slammed his fist on the table. "We had an agreement, McGill. One based on mutual respect. You have violated that agreement."

"I don't see how, sir," I said, as unconcerned and unflappable as he was pissed.

"You don't? You're playing political games again. Not only do you threaten Earth with regularity, you also threaten my advancement."

"Ah…" I said, catching on at last.

Armel had ruled Legion Germanica for a long time. Being reassigned to running one of the near-human legions wasn't pleasant to him. Near-human, or "zoo legions" as rude people called them, didn't even have names, only numbers.

"You've been hoping to gain something from this venture, is that it, sir?" I asked. "Maybe… an improvement in status?"

I gave him a little smile then. It was a mistake to do so, and I knew it. But I didn't care. He was starting to piss me off.

"Your conversation with Sateekas was intercepted, McGill. The hubris demonstrated was incredible, even for you.

"Why… thank you kindly, sir!"

He glowered and hunched his shoulders. "You can't go around transmitting things to Galactics, McGill! I don't want to ever see this happen again!"

"Sir, I apologize profusely. I was an idiot and a fool of the first order. I want you to know, I hereby swear to *never* do anything so stupid and downright evil again. I do so swear it, and I hope to die."

Sucking a breath through his tight nostrils, Armel stood up and pounded the table one last time, making the silverware jump and jangle.

"Very well, McGill," he snapped. "I too, hope that you die."

He stalked off, and I ate my food in peace for a goodly ten seconds. It was a rare moment. But then, even as I reached for my third tangerine, I saw it vanish.

"What'd you think, Cooper?" I asked conversationally.

"That was quite a performance, sir. I continue to learn from you."

"Really? Like what for instance?"

"Well sir, I wouldn't have thought you'd be a man who could apologize so nicely. So utterly. It was a bit of a shock to hear it."

"Oh… that. That's no big deal. Unless I'm really angry and losing control, I always apologize immediately and without reservation to anyone who asks."

"But it just seems out of character, Centurion. I mean, you're usually such a stubborn hard-ass type."

"Mmm?" I questioned, chewing. Then I swallowed, and I laughed.

"No, no, no," I said. "You don't understand, Cooper. You see, I *always* apologize. Especially to women, and men like Armel who value such things. But, you have to understand: I never mean it."

Cooper laughed quietly, and we both ate our fill. After all, it'd been a long, tough day.

# -61-

"You've got to be shitting me," Carlos said the next day as we headed outside for some PT before manning our posts. I was a firm believer in maintaining physical fitness, even when we were in a combat zone.

"It's true," I said.

"Squanto? His name is frigging *Squanto*? That's just too good. That's rich. He wins the prize for worst-named alien of all time. Even that squid-clown called Bubbles—"

"Shhh," I shushed him. I was smiling, but I didn't want our near-human friends to know I mocked their non-coms.

"What?" Carlos asked. "Did Bubbles die, or something? Did you have him executed and chopped into calamari like Sub-Centurion Silt?"

My face grew annoyed. I should have known not to talk to Carlos about this, but I was trying to make him happy after upsetting him yesterday. He loved a good joke, and he was good at coming up with them, but he always took it too damned far.

"Shut up about that, too," I told him.

"Okay, whatever. But… Squanto? That's so great!"

He wandered off chuckling to himself to join the other bio-people near the gates. I went in the opposite direction, into the open fields. There, a mass of slimy-looking blue and green shapes had gathered. This was my new army of recruits, salamanders one and all.

"Look at this asshole-parade," Cooper said next to me as I halted to inspect the troops. "You think they'll fight this time, or will they run again?"

Glancing around in irritation, I noted he was nowhere to be seen. He was abusing his stealth-suit, as usual.

"I should never have given you that suit," I told him. "And I'd better not hear anymore rumors about you haunting the rooms of young ladies at night."

It was a stab in the dark—literally. I hadn't heard any such rumors. But, given Cooper's personality and his love of stealth, it stood to reason it might be true.

"That's a highly insulting suggestion, Centurion," Cooper said. "The thought has never even occurred to me."

Right then, I knew he was lying. Sure, Cooper was a slippery man, but it's hard to lie to a master of deceit such as myself. He shouldn't have even tried it.

"One more report, Cooper," I said sternly. "Just one more mystery-man leaving footprints in the wrong places, and you can kiss your specialist rank as a ghost goodbye."

Cooper sighed. "Thanks for the warning, sir," he said.

"Now, get your tail out onto the far side of that wall and start scouting."

He left, and I grinned a little. Cooper's opinion of me must have shot up in several ways, and I hadn't even done anything.

I spent the next three hours drilling the Scupper troops. They weren't accustomed to organized exercise—or even to lining up for that matter, but they quickly got the hang of it. Talking to Armel, I got him to release ten squids from his Gold Bunker into my custody.

These were all non-coms who'd lost their squadrons of near-human troops. They'd been given desk jobs in the HQ. I figured it was about time they earned their reputation for handling recruits of different species.

They both exceeded my expectations and disappointed me at the same time. They were harsh. Squids were cruel task-masters who meted out physical harm thoughtlessly. By early afternoon, at least a dozen Scuppers had been laid out, knocked cold by the long slithering tentacle of an angry squid.

At that point, Second-man sidled up to me.

"Excuse me, First-man," he said. "May I discuss a delicate matter with you?"

"Of course. What's the problem?"

"Centurion, we appreciate your intensive training, but many of the men are unhappy."

"It's not my job to make them happy, Second-man."

He blinked his big bulbous eyes at me twice. "But… how will you get them to fight for you if they hate you and your sub-officers?"

I frowned. "They aren't thinking of deserting, are they?"

"Six already have, by my count."

"Six! How do you figure that? These squids keep a tight roster of their charges. If that many had slipped away…"

Second-man shook his head. He'd learned the gesture from humans, I guessed. "The six have all awakened after being stunned by unjustified attacks from these unpleasant and giant aquatics. Maybe they have been deemed unworthy of counting, or perhaps they haven't yet been missed."

Aquatics was a term the Scuppers used to reference the squids. It was apt enough, I supposed.

"I see… Did they escape into the underground subway system?"

"They did—at least, that's my assumption. In any case, they've vanished."

"Desertion in the face of the enemy. That's an offense worthy of execution, Second-man. Do they understand that?"

"Indeed they do. The threat lingers in every man's mind in this entire army. Most of them are beginning to rethink the wisdom of their volunteer efforts, and they're scheming to escape in spite of the risk."

"Hmm…" I said, thinking it over. "Maybe I need to change things…"

"That would be an excellent idea."

"You will help me," I told him. "Tell our troops that we've come to an understanding. No more of them will desert."

He seemed to brighten, standing taller and holding his shock-spear like a weapon instead of a walking stick. "I will do so immediately!"

After he left, I got Kivi to help me contact the Scupper queen. I discussed the matter with her, and I offered my solutions. She agreed eventually, and the job was done.

Swaggering out in front of the entire throng, I had the salamanders brought together as a group. They lined up neatly enough—the training had taught them that much, at least.

I nodded to Sub-Centurion Churn. "Good job, Churn. They're already getting it."

"It's been difficult," he admitted. "They're wild-things by nature. Barbarians. Part devil, and part child—but… I thank you for the words of praise, Centurion."

Once the throng had quieted, I took up a bullhorn and roared into it so they all heard me. We'd issued translators to the lot of them by now. You couldn't very well command troops who had no idea what you were saying.

"Scupper Militia. We men of Earth have come a long way to intervene on your behalf. We hope to save your planet from the uninvited and hostile forces of the Wur."

I didn't get a cheer, not exactly, but I did get some upraised fists, hissing throats and shaken spears. I guessed that for this army, that was an exceptional response.

"Sadly," I went on, "a small handful of your number have tried to abandon this fortress. They've all been captured and executed, as is our custom."

Croaks of dismay swept the crowd as they heard my translated words.

"You'll be happy to know," I continued booming, "that I've taken steps to remedy this lack of courage among a few cowardly members of your species. I understand you aren't professional soldiers, and at times, your fears might override your will to serve and save your planet."

One of the blue men in the back bolted then. I saw it, as did Sub-Centurion Churn. He gestured to me with an excited tentacle, but I directed a flat palm toward him, and he restrained his urge to go after the deserter on the spot.

"That's right," I said, continuing my speech to the assembled native troops. "Your queen and I have decided to end your torment. We've shut down the tubes. From now on, no one can enter or exit the access points in this vicinity."

Another murmuring rumble swept the crowd like a forest fire. They only quieted down when I continued speaking.

"No need to thank me!" I shouted, my voice rolling like thunder over the assembly. "Your leaders back in the Sacred City are the ones who manipulated the tunnels. It was a simple thing, and it's been done. No longer will you be tempted by thoughts of returning home. You will fight here, and some of you will die here, but those who live will be better men for the experience!"

I had the squid noncoms call at-ease, and the Scuppers fell to talking among themselves. Most of them milled around looking stunned.

Several skulked away and attempted to enter the various access-points—but all were rebuffed. They looked even more dejected.

The Scuppers were under my command, and since there was no way to run home now, they began training harder. Soon, they marched and formed squares like they meant it.

Discipline had already been ratcheted up at least two notches.

# -62-

As the afternoon wore on, I began to get disturbing messages. Several came from HQ, requesting reports as to our readiness. I declared myself, my unit, and my entire army of reluctant natives to be fit and anxious to fight.

That was a bald-faced lie, of course, and I figured they knew it. But they appreciated the gesture and gave me accolades anyway.

After that, the level of chatter on command-chat elevated. The brass was seeing something. I contacted Natasha to find out what it was.

"You know I can't do that, James," she said. "They're watching my traffic. I'm not getting any feeds from space—not a thing."

"So hack into a proxy or something. Spoof the bastards. These poor buggers down here in the trenches are going to be permed if we get surprised. They aren't like Earth regulars, you know. They've only got one life to live."

Natasha sighed. I knew how to push her buttons. She was a sucker for life-and-death situations. Many legionnaires yawned at such things, but not good old Natasha. She was a softie, and she always had been.

"All right, I'll see what I can do."

I waited for about nine impatient minutes. My finger had just lifted up, poised to buzz her again, when she called me back.

"James," she said, her voice a whisper. "Something's wrong. At first, I thought I was seeing a battle, but now… I'm not sure what it is."

Frowning, I tried to make heads or tails of a battle map projection she'd forwarded to my tapper. But the screen was too small and the data too abstract. It just looked like a sea of red contacts, like a mound full of fire ants.

"Uh…" I said. "I've got to see this on something bigger."

"Come to Gold Bunker. They've got big displays everywhere."

I did as she suggested, putting Sub-Centurion Churn in charge of my Scuppers and Leeson in charge of my human unit.

A few minutes later, I talked my way past the entrance security and stumbled into Natasha.

"Jeez, these apes are touchy," I said, glancing back over my shoulder at the twin near-human giants who were watchdogging the entrance. "You'd think I resembled a teddy bear the way they grunted and frowned at me."

"Armel's personal guard," Natasha said, "yes, I know. They don't smell too good, either."

She led the way into the interior of the bunker, and I followed.

Watching the way she walked, I felt a familiar pang. Natasha and I had been close long ago, and I don't think she'd ever quite gotten over it. Maybe I hadn't, either.

She led me into an empty meeting chamber and flicked the table and walls on with her fingers. They lit up, and the gloomy room swam in imagery.

I whistled a long one. "By damn… Armel doesn't spare the budget down here, does he?"

"No, he doesn't. He's more like Turov than you probably knew."

I glanced at her sidelong, but she was bent over the table, tapping at it. Was that remark some kind of a dig at Galina? Natasha knew Galina and I were an item, and she was never happy about any of the women I dated—except when I dated her.

"Uh…" I said, "show me what you've got."

She did so. With expert touches, she brought up a system-wide forces display. This laid out the planet with realistic textures then overlaid it with crawling symbols. The symbols represented troop formations, ships, fortifications—the works.

Quickly sorting through it all, I found the oddity that Natasha had been trying to describe to me.

"Is this right? Are the Rigel boys in the thick of it with the Wur?"

"It would seem so," she said. "Their forces are right on top of each other."

I released a war-whoop. "That's great! Let *them* fight it out for a change. Legion Varus is sick of playing punching bag on this rain-soaked rock!"

Natasha wasn't smiling, however. Her arms were crossed, her frown was firmly in place, and she stared down at the maps with a decidedly worried expression.

"What's wrong now?" I asked, figuring that some people were never happy.

"James," she said, "the Wur and the Rigel forces have been occupying the same geographical areas for hours. They're not destroying one another. They aren't even moving around much."

I gaped at the table. "Is that so?"

After watching for a time, I caught on to what she was saying. "You would think there would be some explosions or something…"

"There's nothing. No heavy radio traffic. No emissions indicating missile launches. No… anything."

"Uh… why not? Have the Wur surrendered?"

"I thought about that," she admitted. "But it seems unlikely, doesn't it? I mean, the Wur are plants. They never give up. The Rigellians don't impress me as quitters, either."

I thought about Squanto and the fight he'd given me down in the Scupper city. "I've got to admit, you've got a point there. This is weird."

As we puzzled over the feed, a large red box popped up on the screen. It was a warning of some kind.

*Sniffer detected*, the message read.

"What's that?" I demanded. "Are they attacking us?"

Natasha didn't answer. She quickly swiped at the screens shutting them down. Some of them lingered. Cursing, she opened up her ruck of tricks and powered down her computer.

Now, that was a big deal for a tech. They never shut down their portable rigs.

A pounding began at the door of the conference room about two seconds later. When I say a pounding, I mean it was loud. It sounded like the hammer of the Almighty himself was beating on that door.

"Shit!" Natasha hissed.

I stepped to the door as it opened. I don't know what I expected to see on the far side, but the reality of it surprised me.

There, standing in the broad hallway, was a massive giant.

Six meters tall if he was an inch, he reached in and grabbed me around the waist. I was hauled out of the room and out into the open like a doll.

With his other hand, he grabbed Natasha. She squeaked in pain.

Those fingers were as thick as my calf and they were impossibly strong. Fortunately, I hadn't been caught entirely off-guard. I had one hand free, and I was wearing combat armor.

My force-blade extended to a half-meter's length from my right gauntlet. It blazed with hot kinetic force. Plasma ran like flame down the length of the blade.

One down-stroke. That's all it took.

The giant, who'd just begun striding along the passageway with his two captives in his hands, stopped and looked down stupidly.

His right thumb was off. It had tumbled, splattering blood, all the way down to the deck under his massive feet.

His small head and stupid eyes stared at that, dumbfounded.

In that instant, I could have killed him. I was in the mood, that was for certain—but I held off. After all, I knew these ogres were Armel's personal pets, and they were just following orders.

The moment of bewilderment passed, and the giant seemed to become aware again. I was halfway down his body, having escaped his hand, which was now just a ball of flexing fingers and blood.

A transformation overcame him. He reached for me again—and I slashed him open.

A howl came out of that massive throat. It was the kind of noise that hasn't been heard on Earth since the last Ice Age.

Rearing up, the giant took the only thing he had handy, and he threw it at me.

At the last second, Natasha screamed.

"James!" she screeched as she went flying by.

The giant had thrown her at me with all his terrible strength. What could I do? I stood my ground and switched off my force-blade so I wouldn't cut her.

The impact knocked me right off my feet. Worse, I wasn't able to hold onto Natasha. She banged into the wall, the deck, then the wall again.

Each of these surfaces was raw, unforgiving puff-crete. By the time she stopped tumbling and flopping, she was stone dead.

After that, I lost consciousness myself. I think the giant might have bashed me one on the head, but it was hard for me to be sure.

# -63-

I passed out for a time. I wasn't sure how long. But when I woke up, I was sure I hadn't died and come out in the revival chamber again.

Partly, my certainty was born of the simple fact I was lying on my back in the passageway of Gold Bunker. In addition to that, a familiar, unpleasant face was blocking my vision of the place.

"Resisting arrest again, eh, McGill?" Armel asked.

He straightened up and made small sucking sounds with his mouth. "That's simply unacceptable. If you were one of my officers, I'd demote you."

"How's Natasha?" I croaked out.

"Hmmm…? Ah, the tech girl. She's been… mangled. It seems she did an excellent job of cushioning your fall."

"It was the other way around," I said, struggling to stand.

"A pity in any case. Now, back to why you're under arrest."

"I'll bite," I said, getting to my feet and rubbing my neck. "Why did you send a giant down here to pester me?"

"Correction: the giant was sent to *arrest* you."

"Why's that?"

"Because you hacked into our battle streams. This is not Legion Varus, McGill. I demand adherence to the chain of command. We have strict protocols here, and we don't appreciate data breaches."

"Uh…" I said, looking around.

There were three giants nearby now, not just the one. Of the three, one of them had his hand wrapped up. I gave him a little smirk and a rapid up-down motion with my eyebrows. Unfortunately, he just stared at me in resentment, cradling his hand. I figured my taunts were wasted on him.

"Are you considering attacking me and my troops again?" Armel asked.

"No," I lied. "I'm just confused, that's all. Natasha said she had something to show me, and I came here to see it. There was no indication that it was secret data. Who would I tell out here on this rock, anyway?"

Armel wagged a skinny finger in my face. "Some things are classified, McGill. What goes into that category is for me to decide—not my underlings."

"Of course, Tribune. Can I go now? I've got a headache."

He looked at me oddly, suspiciously.

"What did you see in those streams?" he asked.

Right then, alarm bells went off inside my head. I'm a slow man on the uptake, just ask any teacher who's had the misfortune to try to teach me anything. But I could tell Armel was hiding something. Something so big, so heinous, he was willing to kill over it.

I looked him right in the eye, and I let the left half of my mouth curve up into a smile. "I saw the Wur cooperating with a lot of Rigellian troops. It looked like they were having a big pow-wow out there. Maybe, even, they were preparing to—"

That finger of his came back into my face, and I might have cut it off—but my gauntlet seemed to be missing.

"Shut up," he said suddenly, making a flicking motion.

I complied, and he frowned.

"Something you said has intrigued me, despite my irritation," he said at last. "You will follow me."

I did as he asked, and the three giants thumped along in the rear. I could hear their ragged breathing, punctuated by loud swallows and incomprehensible grumbling.

Armel led me to his personal office. We pressed through the first door into the waiting area. There he left the giants behind, ordering the wounded man to take his thumb to Blue Bunker so the bio people could reattach it.

Leading me into his inner sanctum, I wasn't surprised to see he had a similar battle map displayed on the central conference table.

Graves was there as well, which also didn't surprise me. After all, in Turov's absence, he was the top ranking man among the Varus officers.

"Hello sir!" I boomed, grinning.

Unfortunately, Graves seemed less excited to see me.

"What are you doing here, McGill? I don't recall relieving you of your post on the wall."

"Uh… no sir. Tribune Armel here asked me to accompany him."

It was more of a twist of the truth than an outright lie, so I looked at Armel, hoping for confirmation.

"McGill has made a suggestion. A disturbing one."

"Let's hear it then," Graves said, crossing his arms.

I wracked my brain, but I had no idea what Armel was talking about.

"Uh…" I said.

Armel rolled his eyes briefly. "It was something about having a meeting…"

"Oh yeah," I said, brightening. "That's what it looks like to me, sirs. The Wur and the Rigel-boys. They're having a good old-fashioned sit-down. A conference, maybe."

Suddenly, Graves stiffened. He looked at the map in alarm.

"Could that be true?" he asked. His head snapped up, and he glowered at me again. "You know something about this, don't you?"

"I know all kinds of stuff, Primus. Just ask me."

"I'm not talking about how to count, McGill. I'm talking about the fact you've been interacting with the leadership of Rigel, the Scuppers—and the Wur? Have you been talking to the Wur, McGill?"

That question put me in a tough spot. If I lied now, and I told him I had been talking to the Wur, he'd most likely believe me. That meant there was a golden opportunity for untruth staring me right in the face.

But the question was whether I wanted to take him up on that offer. Sometimes, just because a cover story is being dangled under your nose, that didn't always mean you wanted to take it.

Twists and turns. They'd gotten me into all kinds of trouble all of my life. I guess it's just part of my nature.

At last, I sighed and looked down. "I suppose, sirs… I suppose that maybe I have been."

There it was. You could have heard a pin drop. I'd released a dangerous lie, one with no real purpose behind it—and I couldn't take it back now. My only hope was it would turn out to be useful at some point in the future.

Glancing up, I snuck a peek to see how it was going over. One glance, and I cast my eyes back down again. I studied the floor like a man convicted of a heinous crime.

They were buying it. Both of them. Hook, line and sinker. Normally, people scoff when you tell them a whopper they don't believe. These two looked deadly serious.

In a way, I supposed, I was a convicted man now. I'd convicted myself.

The only thing left to do now was to decide what my crime had been, and why I'd done it.

## -64-

Fortunately, at times like these my fertile mind goes into overdrive. A dozen scenarios sprang up, all shiny and new, in rapid succession.

I thought of telling them I'd met up with the Wur in the forest—which was true enough—but this time I'd embellish the tale, adding a Wur Nexus.

The Wur could only be described as an odd race. They were plants, but it was more than that which set us apart from them. They were downright *weird.*

Most of them had only rudimentary brains. Not much more than an insect might possess. But a few, a select, secretive cabal on every world they inhabited, were called Nexus plants.

These plants were the brains of the outfit. They were giant, green-blooded cacti, in fact. Full of juice, spines and evil, they squatted in dank holes here and there on every Wur world, plotting and chemically transmitting orders to their countless underlings.

All I had to do was tell Armel I'd run into one of these immobile monstrosities, and that could be a pretext for every other indiscretion I'd indulged in recently.

Opening my mouth, I almost brought up the Nexus plants—but Armel beat me to the punch.

"It's Claver, isn't it?" he asked, leaning on the table.

His fists formed two shimmering zones on the smart-table as he leaned on it. The table was trying to interpret this odd gesture from its master.

"Claver…?" I asked, truly baffled. I blinked in confusion.

Armel stalked forward. "Yes, I can see it now in your eyes. Guilt. How infuriating you are. Do you know I sometimes dream of your murder, McGill?"

"Uh…"

"Tribune," Graves interjected. "Let him speak. I want him to tell us more without us offering up our own suspicions."

My eyes slid to glance at Graves. There he sat, acting all smart and everything. His advice was dead solid, of course. The quieter Armel stayed, the easier it would be to catch me as I spun my tale. If he told me up front what he thought I was going to say, well, that just gave me something to work with as I formed my fabrications.

Graves was a hard man to fool, and he already suspected I was full of shit. Accordingly, it was time to regain the initiative with a play of my own.

I selected a barb, and went with it.

"The primus has it right, sir," I told Armel as I crossed my arms. "You haven't even let me talk yet. I bet you have no idea why Claver is interested in me."

Armel showed me a line of teeth—and he took the bait.

"I *do* know. It's that damnable book!"

That got my attention for reals. I didn't think Armel knew about the book.

Surprised, I gave him a real look of shock. That was a mistake on my part, of course. Perhaps he'd been fishing for just such a response.

Quickly, I down-shifted the expression to one of slack bafflement—but it was too late. The damage had been done.

"Ah-ha!" he said, pointing a gloved finger at my face. "There it is! I see the truth in your eyes. You had no idea I knew of this dangerous item until now, did you? Have a care, McGill, I know more of your nefarious dealings than you might be aware of."

"Uh…" I said, playing dumb out of sheer desperation.

"What book?" Graves demanded.

Armel and I didn't even look at him. We locked eyes instead.

"Now," Armel said in the voice of a hunting snake, "time to tell me the rest of it."

"Sure thing," I said. "There's this book, see, and Claver has been chasing me halfway around the galaxy to get it. So far, he's failed."

"Yes, yes," Armel said, leaning over his desk in an eager manner. "But where is it now? Does it still exist in some form? Anywhere?"

I thought about his words for a second—they revealed even more about what the man knew. Graves was frowning hard, and I was beginning to agree with his sentiment. Armel was way too excited about this subject for his interest to be purely academic.

"Um…" I said, mentally stalling for time. After a few seconds, during which Armel made nearly frantic hand-gestures for me to hurry up, I spoke again with confidence. "There's always another copy. Not easy to get, mind you, but it exists."

Armel sucked in a breath and let it out slowly. A long, drawn-out sigh. "Excellent. In this case, you will provide me with a copy—immediately."

"Sure thing, sir. Just as soon as I get home to Earth—"

Armel's face hardened again. "That's too late! This is a golden opportunity, for me, and for Earth herself."

My face twisted up. That was a puzzler. "Uh…"

Graves didn't like it either. He pointed a finger at Armel.

"Tribune," he said. "We're getting badly off track. We've got two enemy forces gathering strength nearby. If they're combining their armies, forming an alliance against us, we must move quickly to halt that process."

Armel's eyes slid toward Graves. He smirked.

"It's too late for that. We've lost this campaign."

"I don't like to hear this kind of defeatism," Graves said. "Especially from someone of your rank."

"Get over it, old man. Rigel and the Wur have allied. It's obvious. It's time to grab what we can and run."

"Run? How? They chased off the *Legate*."

Armel made a pffing sound. "We've got the gateway. Once the battle begins, we'll march our officers through and tell our tale of woe."

"But what about the troops you'll be leaving behind?" I demanded.

Armel shrugged. "There are always casualties in war. We'll print out those who deserve to live again, and we'll honor the rest with a pointless ceremony."

Graves stood up suddenly. I could tell he'd had enough.

"In that case, sir, I'm out. Please dismiss me from this conference. I want no part of it."

Armel shrugged again and pursed his lips in a disgusted fashion. "As you will. You're dismissed, Primus."

Graves walked out. He got to the door, lifting a gloved hand... But he didn't reach for the touchplate. Instead, he groped at his back. At that moment, I noted the dark circle in his lower spinal region.

Sagging first to his knees, Graves groped for his pistol.

Armel fired his gun again. It was a slim laser with a wickedly thin beam. I hadn't even heard him fire it the first time, but I could smell the tell-tale acrid scent some lasers left in the air. It reminded me of the special stink burnt hair made.

Before he could shoot Graves a third time, I slammed the gun out of Armel's hand. It went flying and clattered on the floor.

Graves never died easily. Still on his knees, he struggled with his lower body, but he couldn't rise. I figured his spinal cord had been badly damaged.

"Armel," he rasped. "I want you to know all of this has been recorded and transmitted. You won't get away with any of it."

So saying, he pitched forward and began convulsing on the deck. He was having a seizure.

"Such bravado," Armel complained. "As if I would allow an errant transmission to escape my own office while in the field. Absurdity. Graves, if you can hear me, your transmission has gone nowhere."

"What kind of bullshit is this?" I demanded.

Armel glanced at me. He pointed to Graves, who still quivered and jerked now and then. "You're partially to blame for this mess. You should have let me finish him, McGill, for pity's sake."

I stood over Armel now, close to twice his size, and there was stark murder in my eyes. No one have could have missed it, least of all Maurice Armel. He'd felt my wrath before.

"Don't be a fool," he said. "Attempt to predict your immediate future, for both of our sakes. If you kill me now, who will be the sole individual to come out of my legion's revival machines? You, Graves… or me?"

I controlled my baser instincts with difficulty. My arms shook a little. My blood was up, I don't mind telling you.

We locked gazes. I wanted to kill him sooo badly—just for spite, if nothing else.

"All right," I said. "Talk to me. What the hell are you up to? What makes the book worth so much at this point?"

"You haven't guessed yet? Really? With a skull so large, I'd calculated there must be a brain of considerable capacity within. That was my mistake, and I'm disappointed."

My hand shot out and grabbed him by the tunic. I gave him a good shaking, and he pulled a vibro-knife on me, but I batted that away.

"Since you insist," he said, "I will explain. We have a buyer. Right here, in this star system."

"A buyer…? Who?"

"I can't reveal that—but again, I'm astounded at your lack of intuition in this matter. I was told you possess a certain animal cunning that belies your brutish nature and your obvious lack of intellect. Perhaps the individual who so informed me was wrong."

"Who told you that? Who set this all up?"

I gave him a shake as I demanded these facts, but even as I did so, I knew the answer in my heart. To a certain degree, Armel was right. I should have known.

"Claver…?" I asked aloud.

"Damn straight, you moron," said a familiar voice behind me.

Setting Armel back on his feet and turning around slowly, I saw Claver-Prime. He was flanked on either side by two third-rate Clavers. These two said nothing, but they did brandish rifles in my direction.

I let go of Armel, and the trio of Clavers approached. They hadn't entered through the main office door, but rather some kind of side passage. Leave it to Armel to pour a puff-crete bunker and add secret doors to it.

The Class-Threes were wary, but the Prime was all grins.

"Oh, no!" he said sarcastically, slapping his own cheeks. "Is that Graves? Did he trip or something?"

"He chose to stand on principle," Armel said, "rather than firm ground."

Claver put his fists on his hips, shook his head, and tsked. "It's a shame, really—but predictable. Graves always was a boy scout. I'm not even sure how he's managed to last so long without a solid perming. He's even older than I am, you know."

"You used to serve with Graves," I said. "Back in the day. Graves told me about it once. Don't you care about those memories, when you were young and real? Can you even remember those times, Claver? Or have you had too many revives by now?"

Claver looked troubled for a few seconds. That was a big deal. No one got to Claver.

But there were theories. I'd heard them, and I believed them.

Mankind wasn't meant to die and live again over and over. We aren't designed to live forever in a thousand disjointed chunks.

People often experienced serious changes to their personalities when they were reproduced so many times. Some said it was because our brains weren't built to hold the memories of so many lifetimes. That we simply couldn't connect to our past—not forever. We weren't designed to hold a thousand years of time in our heads, only a hundred or so.

Others said that subtle errors were inevitable after so many repeated copies were created. That biology wasn't quite like a mound of printer paper. You couldn't get precisely the same cell when you copied it—you could get close, but not an identical copy. Over time, the body and the mind warped slightly, the way a copy of a copy of a photo became increasingly blurred.

Still others said it wasn't that complex. Back in the old days, when we'd first gained control of the revival machines—mistakes were made. Our tech had been primitive, and the machines were experimental. Some of those who were copied early-on had come out wrong, that's all. The oldest legionnaires, like Claver and Graves, were bound to be at least mildly insane. They were, in effect, mildly bad grows that had never been properly recycled, and the original copies had been lost over time.

These thoughts played out on Claver's face as he gazed down at Graves, a man he'd served with long before I was born. He had to know all the theories—perhaps he'd heard others that were even darker.

Snapping out of it, Claver drew in a sharp breath through his nostrils. He looked at me. "Everyone says you're a card-carrying retard, McGill. But there's more to you than the ape that meets the eye."

"That's what you keep saying," Armel said, crossing his arms and looking bored. "But I still don't see it."

"Well… never mind. The question is what do we do now?"

Armel shrugged. "Torture him? Gather his women from around the camp and abuse them until he cooperates?"

Claver seemed to consider these ideas.

"Nah…" he said at last. "Such things have been tried before. It's never worked out. How about this? I'll take him off your hands. I'll get the book, and I'll make the trade."

"You're cutting me out?"

"Of the small details, yes. Let an old pro handle the dirty work."

Armel seemed to consider. "Our original deal stands?"

"Of course. Indirectly, you gave me the book. I'll get it to the client, and you'll get the credit."

"Hmm…" Armel said, seeming to consider. At last, he smiled. "How can I say no? As of now, McGill is your problem. Get him out of my office."

That was it. Claver and his muscle-bound copies marched me out of the office. Armel announced I'd been placed under arrest for killing Primus Graves, and no one was to interfere.

It was a situation I'd been in before, so I wasn't worried. Not worried *much*, anyway.

"Chain him up, boys," Claver said in a cold voice.

"What's this?" I demanded. "I'm a legion officer. You can't just—"

A rifle butt cracked into my jaw. That hurt pretty good.

I struggled, but there were two armed men, and I was stunned. They managed to get manacles on me. It wasn't a pleasant feeling, let me tell you.

"If you want me to cooperate, Claver," I told him in a rough voice, "you're going about it in the wrong way."

The Claver-Prime grinned at me. "You're out of the picture now, McGill. I don't need you to get a copy of the book. I know all about Floramel and her memory. I'll get my own damned copy."

I frowned. "Well then… why'd you go to all this trouble? Why'd you make deals with Armel about me?"

Claver released a dirty laugh. "Such a moron! You still don't get it, do you? This is about a *second* deal, McGill. This time, *you're* the merchandise."

I let that thought bounce around inside my skull for a time. After a while, I decided I didn't like the sound of it.

The Clavers marched me down the main passage, and I called out to a few legionnaires for help.

No one moved a muscle to come to my aid. They'd all gotten the word from their tribune that I'd been legitimately arrested for killing Graves. Sometimes, having a reputation as a troublemaker wasn't a good thing.

One face among many others, however, did give me a second glance. It was the odd, tree-frog like face of Second-man. He watched in alarm as I was hustled on by.

"Hey!" I shouted at him. "I'm under false arrest!"

A big hand came up and clubbed my mouth. One of the dumbass Clavers had done it without even looking.

The Claver-Prime at the front of the pack laughed. "Don't bother, McGill. Everyone knows you deserve whatever's coming to you. Not even your own officers will lift a finger to help."

Looking back, straining my neck, I saw that Claver was partially right. Harris, Barton and Leeson were circled up, staring, muttering and shaking their heads. None of them looked too keen on getting permed on my behalf.

The squid sub-officers, on the other hand, were delighted. They were slapping tentacles and swiveling their eye-groups excitedly. Ding-dong, the big bad witch was finally dead.

Only Second-man truly looked upset. He trotted after me like a lost dog for a time, but then slowed and stopped. He went slinking back toward the mass of Scupper troops.

Did that mean he was pining away for his master? Or was he plotting his own move up to fill the First-man's shoes? It was hard to tell.

I noticed the number of Scuppers was significantly greater than it had been. Craning my neck, I thought I saw Big Green, the guy I'd sent off deep under the ocean to look for more native recruits.

Second-man and Big Green were both here at Fort Beta, willing to fight. It would be a crying shame if they'd come all this way for nothing.

Soon, we passed by the salamander camp and kept going. Seeing as I was being dragged along in chains, I kind of expected to end up aboard a ship. Maybe I'd be hauled aboard a small vessel, of the type Claver used to travel the galaxy.

Instead, he took me to Blue Bunker. That was kind of surprising. Claver generally had few friends among the bio-people and xeno-nerds who dwelled there.

Marching by several challenges, he was allowed down into the bowels of the bunker. Down here in the basement, that's where the revival machines were kept.

Was I going to be recycled? I wasn't sure, but I began to drag my feet. Lifting me up with bulging biceps, the Class-Threes barely slowed down.

The humid stink of the machines was nearby. This was the region where near-humans could be revived. Somehow, the bigger machines produced a bigger stench—I supposed it was only natural.

Claver tried the last door on the left, but it was sealed shut. He ordered his Clavers forward to kick it in—but that was almost hopeless.

At last, the men grabbed me and rammed me against the door, making certain my face was against the steamy porthole-like window.

The window was triangular and fogged-up, but I could still see inside. I didn't know why they were pushing me up there—but after I got a look inside, I knew what the score was.

A big, flaccid-bellied revival machine was in there. Working beside it was Raash and two other saurians.

None of that was terribly interesting. This was, after all, a near-human legion's revival chamber. Working such machines was Raash's job.

But there was someone else there—a woman who wasn't a bio tech or even a saurian.

It was Floramel, and she was looking at me with a puzzled expression.

# -65-

I shook my head. I swear I did. I did everything I could to warn her.

And I shouted, too. “Floramel! Don’t open the door!”

But I should have known she couldn’t hear me. These revival chambers had solid doors, meant to survive assaults.

The Clavers took turns bashing my skull, trying to quiet me. All that did was splash some blood on the triangular window. I didn’t shut up.

“Floramel! Stop!”

They pulled me away, and Claver-Prime got into my face.

“Now, don’t you mess this up. She’s mine. All I want is what’s in her head. I’ll let her go afterward.”

“Is that a bargain?” I asked him.

He hesitated. “Yes,” he said finally. “That’s a deal between us, McGill. You know I keep my deals.”

Before we could say more, the door swished open.

We all turned, expecting to see Floramel’s pretty face. But instead, we were greeted by the snarling features of Raash.

“You are not to be here. This man,” he pointed at me, “he speaks nothing but lies. If you have listened to him, you have been misled.”

Claver-Prime released a dirty, wheezing chuckle. “He knows you, McGill! Even this shit-for-brains lizard is wise to you!”

I said nothing. My muscles were tense, waiting for a solid opportunity to act.

"He plots!" Raash said. "You don't know him as I do. He's a devil in pink skin."

"That he is indeed," Claver said. "We're here, in fact, to gather witnesses for McGill's trial. Would you like to testify, Mr. Lizard?"

"My name is Raash."

"Of course it is. McGill here is up on charges. We've arrested him, see? We just need a few more witnesses, and he'll be permed this time."

"Permed? This concept pleases me."

"What's going on?" Floramel asked, stepping up behind Raash.

My body tightened up, and my lips drew into a line. I wanted to shout for them to run for it.

But Claver was eyeing me, shaking his head. He had a beamer in his hand, while Raash and Floramel were unarmed.

It was hard, but I kept my mouth shut.

"A lovely young lady," Claver said, addressing Floramel. "Let me guess: you too are familiar with the accused, one James McGill. Isn't that so?"

Floramel's eyes slid from me to Claver and back again.

"Yes…" she said hesitantly.

"Good, good. It's just one big happy family down here on Storm World, isn't it?"

Suddenly, Floramel's expression changed. "I know your face. I know these words… you are the Claver! A thief in the night who steals our technology! Raash, throw them out of here!"

Raash moved to close the door, but a huge arm from one of the Class-Threes barred his path.

The saurian roared and attacked. The Three fought with genetically-enhanced strength, but the contest was uneven. Raash was bigger and stronger than most humans, even pumped-up clones. More importantly, he had teeth.

He got hold of the man's thick neck, tore it open, and blood sprayed.

I struggled with the remaining Three, but he had my hands tied, and he was hauling on my arms to hold me back. Even so, I bashed him into a few walls.

Suddenly, a beamer sang.

Dazzled by the flash, I fully expected to feel my own hot guts slipping away over my belt buckle—but it wasn't me that Claver-Prime had shot. He'd gunned down Raash.

Floramel ran to the crumpled form and wept.

"Seriously?" Claver laughed. "Are you some kind of a pervert who likes lizards, girl?"

Floramel didn't answer. She stood, and she might have attacked Claver, but he had his beamer on her.

Leaving behind Raash and the Class-Three who'd battled to the death on the deck, we marched out of Blue Bunker. My own personal guard still had my arms behind me, and the Prime had Floramel with a beamer's muzzle in the small of her back.

The various guards among the Blue Bunker staffers glowered at all of us as we passed by, but they clearly had orders from Armel not to interfere.

We were half-marched, half-dragged to the blast-pans. Here, lifters had once ferried back and forth troops and supplies from *Legate*. But that was the past. *Legate* had gone back to Earth, and she'd taken the lifters with her.

Now, only one vessel sat in the midst of the central blast-pan. It was a small ship, something about the size of an Imperial patrol boat.

But the markings were all wrong—in fact, they were absent. It was a quiet, unassuming ship with no flags, emblems, or visible guns.

I knew it had to be Claver's.

We were forced aboard, but then a howling rush of wet blue flesh came out of the rainy gray light and attacked.

Second-man and Big Green led the charge. Behind them was a pack consisting of hundreds of Scuppers. I was impressed. Big Green really had managed to drum up some support from other native cities.

This ambush took Claver by surprise. He didn't even seem to know enough to blame me for the attack. He had no idea, apparently, that I'd been snake-charming these odd people for weeks.

"What in the holy hell—?"

His shock was brief, however, and he came up with a simple expedient. He kicked his last Claver-Three in the ass, pushing him out into the howling mob that rushed from all sides of the ship.

"Kill them!" he ordered. "Kill them all!"

The big, dumb Claver whirled to see the ship's door closed. He knew he was screwed—he was at least that smart.

The salamanders were on him in an instant, and he fought as best he could. The native warriors were smaller, weaker, and less well-trained—but it didn't matter. There were lots of them, and they took him down in a matter of moments.

Inside the small ship, I got to my feet and looked around for a weapon. I looked for something to free my hands, but I was knocked onto my face.

The ship had surged upward, lurching into flight. Claver had hit the jets, and we were soaring.

Under the belly of the small ship, dozens of faithful Scuppers were flash-fried.

*Dammit.*

I hoped Second-man had managed to get clear.

Flipping on the autopilot, Claver had his gun turned on us before I could take him out. Still, I stood over him, and the look in my eye told the tale. I was going to try to take him out, hands or no.

Claver's wrist flicked, directing the gun toward Floramel.

"Sit down, McGill," he said. "Or all of our deals are canceled. *All* of them."

It was clear he meant to kill or at least mistreat Floramel.

Growling, I sat down on a bench seat and decided I'd bide my time.

Claver sniffed, and he turned to face Floramel—appraising her.

"Impressive," he said. "You must be something special, little lady. I don't think I've ever met a woman who could get two muscle-bound retards to kill themselves for her on a single day."

"You misunderstand the situation," Floramel said.

"How's that?"

"McGill is not allowed to mate with me."

"Oh no? But he did at least once, right?"

She didn't answer, and Claver started up with his dirty laugh again.

"Claver, where are we going?" I demanded.

"Isn't that obvious? No?" He sighed and rolled his eyes. "Let's do a little math, shall we McGill? How many starships are in this system right now?"

"Uh…" I said. "Three last I knew."

"Right, right. Two transports from Rigel, and one light cruiser from the Core Worlds."

I blinked at him. None of these destinations were very appetizing to me.

"Now," Claver continued as if talking to a slow child, "I'm planning to sell both of you. Who do you think might be the highest bidder, respectively?"

I blinked some more.

"*Sell* us?" Floramel asked in alarm.

"That's right. I'm a trader. Trading is what I do. It's nothing personal, doll. Now, I happen to have here two valuable specimens, if I can only find an interested buyer. Can you figure this out, Rogue-Worlder? People keep telling me how smart you are and everything—but I haven't seen any evidence yet."

Floramel glowered. I knew she was proud of her intellect, the same way a man like me might be proud of a pair of thick arms, a kill-count, or even how much he could eat at one sitting.

"You know of my memory," she said. "You know I've memorized the book."

"Yes! That's right. Who would want that tidbit the most?"

She shrugged. "It seems like half the galaxy wants it."

"Right again! Maybe I was wrong to think you were some kind of organic robot. Maybe you really *are* as smart as they say. Both of the potential buyers in this system are interested in what you have to offer—but really, I can't sell you off to the Empire. They might misguidedly blame me somehow, or even think—wrongheadedly, of course—that they can suppress the information by killing all of us."

"Therefore… I must go to Rigel?" she said in a small voice. She sounded horrified, and I didn't blame her. We'd all seen how those miserable bears treated their captives.

"Stands to reason!" Claver said. Then he looked at me, and he waved his gun in my direction. "Now girl, let's see if you can apply the same logic to the case of this overgrown idiot."

Floramel looked at me thoughtfully. "It's hard to say. Both parties probably hate him. He's probably wronged them all."

Claver cackled then. He outright *cackled* like a happy witch.

"Exactly right!" he laughed. "That's been my dilemma, until I gave the matter a careful five minutes of deep thought. You know what I came up with?"

Neither of us answered. We just stared at him.

"Nothing, huh? I'm disappointed… but never mind. What I realized was that if I flew to meet with Rigel, the Galactics would notice. And vice-versa. What I needed, therefore, was a cover-story. A reason I could give to the second ship as to why I'd visited the first. McGill's here partly for that purpose."

My eyes and my mind were wandering. I was thinking of all kinds of nasty ways to kill Claver. I'd done it before, after all, plenty of times. I kind of thought that this time around might be special. I was really going to enjoy this murder, when I got the chance.

"…very good, Floramel!" Claver called out, smiling at her.

Floramel looked troubled.

"Uh…" I said. "What'd I miss?"

"Thinking of pork chops again, McGill?" Claver asked.

"Now that you mention it, I could use a snack."

"No doubt you could. You eat like a cow eats grass. It's a wonder you don't shit yourself with every step you take."

"James," Floramel said quietly. "He means to give you to the Galactics. He's going to pretend he picked you up from the Rigellian ship—therefore providing an excuse for not going directly to the Mogwa ship."

I almost blurted out that didn't make much sense—but I managed to shut myself up.

"I get it," I said. "A double-deal, just like you said. There's just one thing… why would Sateekas want me? He kind of likes me, if the truth were told."

Claver gave me a predatory smile.

"Maybe he does right now," he admitted. "But what do you think he'll say after I inform him of certain recent… indiscretions on your part?"

"Huh?" I said, playing dumb.

My heart was pounding already. I didn't like where this might be going. I didn't like it at all.

"James, James," Claver said, clucking his tongue. "How could you forget so quickly? You'd think even an interstellar murdering sociopath like yourself would recall the most heinous act of perming a Mogwa!"

I snorted and laughed. "You're crazy, Claver. Is that really what you're going to try to pin on me? No one would believe it."

Floramel was leaning way forward. Her long, lovely neck fully extended. Her mouth was unaccustomedly gawking at me, too.

"James?" she asked in a near whisper. "Did you *really* perm a Galactic?"

"Not just *any* Galactic," Claver said with glee. "Our beloved ex-tyrant, from right here at home. He permed Xlur, none other than the duly appointed governor of Province 921."

Floramel searched my face, but I didn't meet her eye. Instead, I stared at Claver.

"That's not just a lie, sir," I barked at him. "That's a *damned* lie!"

Floramel gave a sigh that sounded like something my mother would have released after an angry teacher called home.

"James…" she said. "How could you?"

Claver howled with laughter and slapped at his knees. He was almost crying, he was so fucking happy.

"She really *does* know you, McGill!" he said. "You know what? If you two weren't both about to be traded off into servitude, I'd recommend you give marital bliss a shot. It's a shame that will never happen. A damned shame."

"James," Floramel said. "Is that what happened to Governor Xlur? Everyone at Central—the entire Hegemony Government—they're all in the dark. They've had countless meetings about it. This means… Now, what will happen next is…"

I shrugged, and I met her eye at last.

"Sorry," I said. "I had my reasons."

She flopped back in her chair, defeated. "I'm sure you did…"

# -66-

When we docked with the ship from Rigel, I wondered if Squanto was around. I didn't think Claver knew how much he hated me—but maybe that was just as well.

There wasn't much to the transfer. The hatch opened, and Claver gushed pleasantries. Then he scraped and bowed like some kind of medieval servant.

The bears took custody of Floramel, and I began to object. I had things I could tell them, if they would only listen.

I was ready, in fact, to use the name of Squanto and demand an audience with him. Hell, if I was going down, I figured I might as well throw a wrench in Claver's carefully laid plans.

Claver seemed to catch my mood.

"Ah, one thing!" he said. "I'll be back in three days to collect this lady intact. That's agreed, yes?"

The bears looked at each other doubtfully as their metallic snake-bone necklace things clicked. They finally agreed.

"It seems pointless that we should be inconvenienced by your mating habits," said one of them.

"Um…" Claver said. "Oh… right. We'll go with that. I ask that you indulge me on this point. I'll be back with even better deals soon."

"We very much doubt it. But this formula is useful to us. We'll submit to your demands on this occasion."

"Excellent! Thank you, gentlemen! Thank—"

But they'd already clanged the hatch shut behind them.

We were soon flying away, leaving orbit. Storm World fell behind us, but it didn't vanish.

"Hey Claver," I said, coming up with an idea. "You remember when you told me about your sister?"

He glanced at me sharply. An instant frown overcame his face. That was noteworthy, as he'd been as happy as a pig in shit up until now.

"I have no sisters, McGill."

"Aw, sure you do. I'm talking about your clone-sisters. The female Clavers. You told me all about them once—but then, maybe that's a memory you don't have anymore..."

Claver led a strange life. He'd come up with the idea of transmitting his body-scans and mental engrams from one place to another instead of his physical being. Essentially, he used death and revival as a means of mobility. After all, it was easier to send a signal across countless lightyears than it was to send a flesh and blood person.

All he had to do in order to cross great gulfs of interstellar territory quickly was off himself, then make a copy wherever it was he wanted to go. Once he awoke in a new place, he could make deals then transmit his updated memories back home after that copy died.

The process left plenty of chances for gaps in his knowledge, however. If one copy had experiences after the transmission point, for example, those were lost forever when the clone died.

"You're lying," he said. "None of us would talk about—"

"She wasn't bad-looking, the one I met up with on Dark World. We thought she was a ghost, you know. She was transmitting sobs and tears across the station. We tried to find her, but by the time we did—it was too late."

During this short speech, Claver turned around and fixed me with a serious glare. I could tell I was on a taboo subject.

"McGill," he said. "I'm warning you, this isn't a topic you should poke at. There's no way—"

"That I could know about your clones? Don't you remember? I've been out to your little hideaway planet twice. The little fart-bag flying things outside the windows. The building, set up like a mini-version of Central. It was kind of cute in a way—"

"You've only been there once!" he said loudly.

I looked startled. He was, of course, correct. But I was messing with his mind. He had a weakness in this area. Anyone who lived and died over and over, with various clones running around doing random stuff—how could a man be *sure* his memories were complete? I myself had often run into people who remembered events I had no recollection of. It must be chaos for Claver.

It wasn't a pleasant feeling. In fact, it was downright disturbing.

He must have felt the fear such discrepancies created: a gnawing worry that your own mind wasn't complete. How could anyone feel hale and wholesome if they didn't know what had happened to some of their own existences?

That special little mind-fuck—that's the one I was working on now. It was the only card I had left.

Shrugging, I leaned back and made myself comfortable.

"Don't worry about it," I advised. "None of that stuff really matters. You're just one Claver-Prime among many. From your point of view, you're probably right. I've only been to Claver-land once, and I never met up with any lady-Clavers. Just forget I brought it up."

Claver stared at the deck for a moment. He was thinking hard.

"What did I say?" he asked quietly.

"Huh?"

"About the female, you moron. What did I say about her?"

"Oh… oh yeah," I laughed, and he frowned. "Kinda funny, me having to tell you what you said yourself."

"What did I say?!" he demanded.

I shrugged again as if I barely cared. This gave me a moment to dream-up something good.

Taking the timeout seriously, I dug into my brain. Claver was upset about this talk of different memories, and any talk of a female version of himself. Why would that be?

My fertile mind conjured up some awful thoughts. Could a renegade Claver have created a female just to abuse her?

Maybe a bad grow—or maybe the girl herself was a bad grow. Sometimes, copied genetic material got twisted up a little. Could it result in a change of gender?

Either that, or one of them had done it on purpose. Maybe… just maybe, not all Clavers were completely trustworthy. Maybe some of them hadn't wanted to die for the greater good of the others. That could cause all sorts of trouble.

Given the paranoid way he was acting, I figured it had to be something like that. Something bad had happened in Claver-land.

A smile began to flicker into life on my face. I tamped that down immediately, though. Never let your mark see you grin. Not even when you've got him by the gonads—never.

Forming up a serious expression, I screwed up my face and put on my best thinking-hard expression.

"Hmm…" I said. "I met up with the female Claver on Dark World—on the factory satellite to be clear. I thought I saw one again back on Claver planet—your home world."

"That's impossible," he snapped, "a dirty lie. Females are forbidden."

"Ah-ha!" I said. "That explains it."

"Explains what?"

"Why all of you Clavers freak out when I bring her up. It's a taboo among your tribe, huh? I understand."

"You're a simpleton. You understand nothing."

I stared at the bulkhead as if seeing across the years and the countless lives and deaths I'd experienced.

"As to the last time I talked about the girl, well, that happened when you revived me a month or so back."

"What are you talking about? It was a year ago when—"

I shook my head. "Like I said, maybe you're a little befuddled. You revived me, asked me a few questions about the girl—the one I'd met on Dark World—and then put me down again. It was rude, actually."

Claver blinked, staring at me. "You're claiming that another Claver-Prime has been shielding his memories from the rest of us? That he's been storing them somehow, and searching for Abigail in his spare time? That's a lot to swallow, McGill."

Blinking, I almost blew it. I quickly contorted my surprise with a dumb-ass expression.

"Uh…" I said. "I didn't say anything about one of you Clavers being a renegade, or anything about Abigail. Didn't even know that was the lady-Claver's name. I just thought any confusion between our recollections must be due to some natural trimming of our minds. You know, how you wake up feeling your old self must have died… but that you can't quite remember the details? Don't you ever wonder if that last guy really did bite it… or if maybe he somehow survived and went into hiding?"

Claver was studying the deck again. "A deal is a deal," he said firmly. "Without that single principle, we've got no basis for interaction!"

I watched him. He seemed to be talking to himself as much as he was talking to me.

Could this mean there was less than a state of total bliss in Claver-land? If there was a rogue copy—or one that showed up from time to time—that might explain the uneven nature of his recent behavior.

More importantly, it gave me another idea.

"When do we get to Sateekas' ship?" I asked brightly.

Claver studied me for a moment before answering. "You seem suddenly interested to meet the Mogwa. That seems odd."

"Oh, I've met him before. *Many* times. Sateekas and I, we go way back. *Waaay* back."

Claver was eyeing me with vast distrust now.

"What was the nature of these… meetings?"

"Well, it all started when Battle Fleet 921 came to Dark World. You were out of the picture by that time—I think the Rogue-Worlder's caught you in a stasis trap."

"Don't remind me of that nightmare."

"Okay, we'll skip all that. Anyway, I'd already seen the girl by that time—or rather her body—and I'd told one of you Clavers about it."

"Go on," he said, gritting his teeth.

"Well, later on, I was revived at Claver-land. Again, one of you Primes asked me about… uh… Abigail, was it?"

He nodded sourly.

"Right. I was questioned about that, and when I didn't give up much information, I was put down again, quite rudely."

Claver looked out the front viewscreen at the swimming stars. The Galactic ship was a white dot now, growing rapidly.

"Hey!" I said suddenly, "maybe that's why you seemed surprised the last time I killed you."

"What do you mean, boy?"

"Well, you were surprised I was all pissed off at you—but maybe you didn't know you'd mistreated me recently, from my point of view. Just a thought. If it wasn't you—I mean, if it was some kind of evil, rogue Claver… well… I guess I sort of owe you an apology for killing you off last time around."

Claver looked pissed, but he also looked a little heartsick.

Now, you have to understand, I was absolutely joyful inside. I'd managed to get him to doubt himself—whether or not there was any reason to. That made me very happy.

It's one of my personal theories that all of us live in two worlds at once, the mental and the physical. Sometimes one is happy, while the other is miserable.

Right now, I was likely to be physically abused—but I'd abused Claver mentally. Who was the winner in such a case? It was hard to say, but I felt pretty good about the exchange this time around.

# -67-

We docked up with an Imperial heavy cruiser. It was an impressive vessel, about two kilometers long and maybe one eighth as wide. Old Sateekas was traveling in style.

Walking behind Claver with my hands chained up, I whistled and hummed.

Claver, by comparison, had his neck all scrunched down like a turtle.

"Could you stop making that noise?" he growled at me.

"Sure thing…"

I stared at him for a second. He really didn't seem happy. "Do you like the Mogwa, Claver?"

He turned to look at me as if I was insane. "Like? That's not a word I would use."

"Fair enough. I bet they don't like you much, either."

He gave me an odd look, and I returned it with an idiot's grin.

Finally, he turned away and led me deeper into the ship, shaking his head and muttering.

The floor lit up as we walked, showing green arrows where we were supposed to go. The chambers and passages lit only while we walked in them, then immediately fell dark again in our wake. It was kind of a spooky effect.

"It's like a ghost ship in here," I said. "They're always like this, these Empire ships. You know why that is?"

"No—but I've noticed the same thing. I've noticed it for years. It's a mystery."

"I bet I know why they're empty. It's Mogwa psychology. You see, they don't like leaving Mogwa Prime. These ships are almost unmanned because coming out here so far, to the fringe of the frontier, that's a form of banishment for them."

Claver stopped and peered at me. "That might be the most astute thing I've ever heard you say, McGill."

"Uh… thanks."

After the arrows finished up at a big sealed door, we waited until it opened. There, several Nairbs humped around inside a large chamber. In their midst squatted an old, nasty-looking Mogwa.

It was Sateekas, as I live and breathe. I smiled to see him. Of all the Mogwa I knew, he was one of the few reasonable types.

He wasn't a nice guy, don't get me wrong. He was an old spacer at heart. He was a realist and a creature who understood something of honor. These rare traits had made him a good naval leader but a poor politician. As a result, it looked like they'd given him the governorship, which I'd learned from Xlur was equivalent to banishment from the point of view of the Mogwa.

"Hey, Grand Admiral!" I shouted. "It's me, McGill!"

Startled, Sateekas shuffled his pile of floppy limbs around and studied me, peering with eye-groups that probably didn't see as well as they used to.

"The McGill-creature?" he asked. "How is it you've been brought to me?"

Claver slapped at me and stepped forward. "Silence, prisoner," he said importantly.

Right about then, I figured that I'd possibly done Claver's little act some damage when I'd managed to get rid of his two bodyguards. He couldn't really manhandle me into cooperation now. All he could do was threaten me with his pistol—but that only went so far.

When a man's facing possible torture and near-certain execution, there just isn't much reason for him to cooperate. As I was in that position now, I was feeling kinda ornery.

"That's right," I boomed at Sateekas. "I'm the McGill-creature, and I've brought you a prisoner. He's a traitor and a vicious—"

Right about then, Claver tried to cow me. He went for a pistol-whipping, if you can credit it as such. It was almost laughable, but I didn't laugh. This was part of my plan.

I took a gun-butt to the cheekbone, and it surely did hurt, but at that same moment I swept my big foot under his. He went down and did a facer.

In retrospect, I figured all our talk about lady-Clavers and my complete lack of physical threat had put him somewhat at ease. He just wasn't expecting me to pull a move on him. Also, as I was chained up, he probably figured he could handle me.

But I wasn't the same fresh recruit I'd been thirty-odd years ago when we'd first met up. I was a very well-trained fighter. Being hand-cuffed was an inconvenience, but it by no means meant I couldn't take action.

Claver struggled to rise, but I kicked away his gun and planted a boot between his shoulders. I pushed him back down again and kept pushing, ramming the air out of his lungs. He coughed.

"We had a deal!" he managed to wheeze out. "Ask your Nairbs!"

"Now, now," I said. "I'm sorry about all this, Sateekas, sir. I should have brought him in here unconscious."

So saying, I stomped methodically on his skull until he quieted down. I might have killed him, but I was pretty sure he was just in a coma or something. I didn't really care.

Once he'd stopped struggling, I squatted over him and touched his tapper to my manacles. They instantly fell away.

A few Nairbs advanced and circled around the scene suspiciously. They tried to get Sateekas' attention, but he brushed them back. He'd never had much love for bureaucrats, not even his own.

Sateekas shuffled a few paces closer.

"Tell me, McGill," he said. "If you are the captor rather than the captive, why were you the one who was wearing restraints on your limbs when you arrived?"

"What, these?" I asked, rattling my crys-steel chains. "They're just for show. We use them to train ourselves to fight under any circumstances. Also, I know Mogwa consider Earthlings to be useful slaves."

"This is correct."

"Right. So, I figured it would only be proper to come into your presence dressed for the part."

Again, I shook my chains. The Mogwa and the Nairbs conversed among themselves for a moment. I watched with a confident air that I didn't really feel inside.

After a few minutes, I saw a troop of guards show up. They were Mogwa regulars, young males, armed and armored with exoskeletal suits.

"Uh…" I said, looking around myself. "Is there something wrong, your Grace?"

"Indeed there is. My sycophantic underlings have annoyed me with some unpleasant facts. We were scheduled to meet with the Claver creature who lies at your feet."

I glanced down at Claver, and I wasn't really sure if he was breathing or not. That could be bad, I realized now.

"Oh, oh, oh! Right, of course!" I said, laughing. "You guys must have gotten caught up in my ruse."

"Ruse?" Sateekas asked. "I'm not fond of trickery of any kind, McGill."

I was very pleased that Sateekas seemed to be buying it at least a little, but his chief advisor was clearly agitated. A fat Nairb shook his puke-green face in a negative jiggle, and sloshed from flipper to flipper.

"This is absurd," the Nairb said, speaking up at last. I had the feeling they'd been under orders to keep quiet. "I don't understand why you would continue to entertain the fantasies of this over-sized ape-creature, Governor. It defies all logic." He gnashed his short yellow tusks in frustration.

I clucked my tongue loudly and shook my head. "Wow! Do you always talk to your master like that? Back on Earth, you'd have been stomped flat and hung out to dry long ago, Mr. Nairb."

The Nairb looked at me with a prissy mix of disgust and outrage. "Governor Sateekas, I insist that you—"

"Jeez!" I burst out. "That's a low-blow, reminding him of his demotion to Governor. You just have to rub it in, don't you?"

The Nairb blinked at me. "Your nonsensical statements aren't helpful. Governor Sateekas has been awarded a title and duties. There's no insult implied by using his correct title."

But I knew different. I took a glance at old Sateekas to see how he was taking this exchange. The truth was, he looked kind of pissed off. To his way of thinking, as a Navy man, being turned into a governor of a benighted province like 921 was an insult indeed.

Sateekas suddenly back-handed the Nairb. Normally, if any other being had taken such a blow, it wouldn't have meant much. Hell, my daddy had bashed me like that any number of times when I was a kid—for excellent reasons, I might add.

But Nairb physiology wasn't quite like that of a human or even Mogwa. Nairbs were like bags full of green snot. You could see their rubbery bones and organs inside there, excreting and absorbing… It was kind of sick when you thought about it.

So, a powerful blow to the back of the noggin did more damage than one might expect. The Nairb slumped forward, leaking fluids and shivering on the deck.

"Irritating creature," Sateekas complained. "Take that mess away. It smells."

The Mogwa troops dragged the carcass off. I wasn't sure if he was dead—but he probably was by the time they were done tossing him around.

"Sorry about your servant there, Sateekas. I hope you're not inconvenienced."

"Don't worry about it. He'll be recycled and come out to annoy me again shortly. Now, however, we still haven't sorted out your status… McGill-creature, let's postulate for the moment that I believe you. A creature named Claver contacted us, promising us a prisoner of great value. Instead, you arrive, a Hero of Earth by all accounts. How has this come to pass? Who should I believe in this instance?"

"That takes a bit of explaining…" I admitted. "But it's simple enough. I couldn't tell you about the real reason I'm here. The *real* trade I have to make was a secret up until now.

This Claver-creature—he's one of the worst of the worst. He's human in name only, totally untrustworthy."

Giving Claver a kick, I caused his body to roll over onto his back.

Old Sateekas was confused. Various eye-groups blinked at me in sequence. That state of bafflement wouldn't last long, of course. The Mogwa didn't like to be confused. They soon became wrathful and dangerous when confronted with something they didn't understand. The Nairb agent that was even now being scraped off the deck was a testament to that.

"Here's the deal," I said, lowering my voice a notch. I took in a deep breath then paused.

I slid my eyes to regard the other Nairbs who were skulking around the chamber. They were listening quietly, intently.

They hated me, one and all. They always had, just like every government stooge I'd encountered in my long and storied life back on Earth. I was anything but the compliant type such creatures preferred.

"Uh..." I said, "maybe we should remove the rest of these agent-critters."

"What?"

"The Nairbs. They might be plotting revenge for their fallen comrade."

Sateekas laughed until he shook and farted. "No need, McGill. You imbue them with far too much bravery. They'd never dare take action to avenge a temporary death. They don't have that kind of warrior spirit. But I understand, as a warrior yourself, how you might expect them to react like creatures with a spine."

I nodded slowly, but inwardly I was cursing. I'd hoped to get rid of all the Nairbs before I told my tale. They were far too likely to find holes in my story—because, after all, there were *lots* of holes...

Tons of them.

# -68-

With one curious Mogwa and a half-dozen angry Nairbs listening to me, I began my tale.

"You see, it went like this..."

I told them then of Claver going to the Core Worlds—Mogwa Prime to be exact—to do a deal in person.

The mere idea of it stunned the Nairbs in particular. "That's a violation of at least seven statutes," complained one of them.

"That's right!" I said loudly. "That's what I told the man! But he wouldn't listen—he and his accomplice."

"Accomplice?" Sateekas asked.

"Yes, sure. Didn't I mention him?"

"Who is this accomplice, McGill?"

Giving a sniff and putting on my most trustworthy, honest-John face, I spoke with firm certainty. "His accomplice was none other than Governor Xlur himself."

This elicited a round of barking and squawking from the Nairbs.

"Absurd!"

"A treasonous lie!"

"An eighth count against Earth for uttering baseless falsehoods!"

Shrugging, I looked at Sateekas. He looked guardedly interested.

"Your tale intrigues me," he said. "Continue."

Angry Nairbs slithered in circles around us like cats.

"Well sir, as I understand it, you can't get to Mogwa Prime as a human being—not even using a revival transmission approach. You can't, that is, unless you've been invited by a Mogwa."

Sateekas hesitated. "What you say is essentially true."

"Damn straight it is!" I said, glaring around at the Nairbs. "Do any of you want to explain why Sateekas here is wrong?"

A few hissed, but none of them dared to speak.

"Animal," Sateekas said sternly. "You'll do well to ignore them and continue with your story."

I looked at him, and I figured he was deadly serious. My life hung in the balance.

Still I felt a certain confidence that some might have called unwarranted. As wild as my tale seemed, I knew that it was backed up by certain facts. After all, a human *had* recently been revived on Mogwa Prime. Of course it had been me, not Claver—but that begged the point. Galactics tended to confuse puny races like humans. One of us looked like the rest. They didn't bother to track our genetics or anything, any more than humans would track individual sardines in the sea.

We were like a bucket full of slugs to them: distasteful and almost identical.

Even more importantly, the event *had* happened at Xlur's insistence. He'd been in on it, and he'd died suddenly afterward. Governor Sateekas had to know about that.

"Well sir," I continued, "I don't know that much more about the story. I know Claver went out there—illegally, but with the blessing of Governor Xlur. Soon thereafter, Xlur vanished and you became our governor."

"...aggravated violation..." muttered a Nairb in the back.

"Yes!" I called out, pointing in his direction. "Yes, it was a sickening violation. One committed by Xlur—and by Claver. That's why I came here today. I thought it was too important to leave to chance. So, I brought you one of the culprits personally, your honorship."

"Why would you bring me this beast?" Sateekas asked.

"I thought that was clear," I said, pretending to be startled. I pointed a long finger at the end of an even longer arm in the direction of the swarming Nairbs. "They would blame Earth—

all of humanity for the mistake of one being. I couldn't let us be falsely accused."

"But Claver *is* a human!" pointed out the Nairb in the back. "The crime is so great it can't be washed away with the blood of an individual!"

"Precisely so!" I shouted back. "Xlur must be brought to justice! And I've got Claver right here to share the guilt."

"...unbelievable hubris..."

"...outrage..."

"All humanity is on trial here, human!"

Again, I leaned and shrugged as if disinterested. "I don't see it that way. Xlur invited Claver to Mogwa Prime. He had to do that, or Claver couldn't have gotten there. Then, after performing some kind of deal, Claver came back to our local space to plague us."

The Mogwa watched me closely. I definitely got the vibe he was trying to digest it all. He had to know that certain elements were true.

"You're saying," Sateekas began, "that the fact Xlur invited Claver absolves the human of his crimes."

"Nooooo," I said, drawing the word out. "Not at all, sir. I'm just saying that the fact Xlur invited Claver decouples the responsibility of humanity at large. He's still guilty as Hell for succumbing to temptation!"

"Hmmm..." Sateekas said, ruminating. "Are you aware that Xlur is dead?"

I gasped and almost swooned. Staggering a little, I grabbed onto a bulkhead for support.

"Are you certain?"

"Absolutely."

"Well then, that is grim news indeed, sir!" I said.

Then, as if a thought had struck me out of the blue, I leaned forward and lowered my voice.

"You don't think..." I said, toeing Claver's unconscious form. "You don't think *he* had anything to do with it, do you?"

"The investigation has thus far been inconclusive."

One of the Nairbs dared to slither closer.

"The suspicion of human involvement is a definite maybe," he said as if he was announcing my doom. "That's one of the reasons we're here—to evaluate Earth's loyalty and possibly take punitive action."

Sateekas wheeled on him, slapping at him with his limbs. The Nairb scuttled away.

"The witness is giving us vital testimony, fool!" Sateekas told him. "Do not interrupt!"

"Uh…" I said.

Suddenly, I was wondering who was being manipulated. Oftentimes court actions involving Empire officials didn't go the way a man intended. In the long run, Sateekas might yet order us all to self-execute.

Sateekas turned back to face me again. "So, loyal slave, now has come the time to tell me what Claver was peddling. What item could be so valuable that he would give his life multiple times? What might interest Xlur to an equal level?"

There it was, out in the open. They wanted to know about the book, about the formula—about the death spores that only affected Mogwa.

"Uh…" I said. "I'm not sure. But I know who does know the truth."

"Who?!" demanded the Nairbs. They leaned in, hungrily listening.

Again, I nudged Claver with the toe of my boot.

"Why, I'm talking about this here traitor. Surely he must know the answers to your questions. You have only to rouse him and ask."

Sateekas slid a long limb forward to lay it upon Claver's back. After a moment, he spoke. "It breathes still. It can be repaired. Slaves, come forward and heal this criminal."

The Nairbs humped near and took Claver away. I grinned and nodded to each of them when they got close and peered up into my eyes.

When they noticed my scrutiny, they shuddered and scuttled away quickly.

At last, only Sateekas and I were left in the room with a few stern Mogwa marines.

"McGill-creature," Sateekas said. "I know that you're lying."

My blood ran cold. "Uh… I'd never do that, sir."

He made a dismissive gesture. "Don't worry about my marines. They aren't equipped with translators. There's no point in forcing them to listen to the bleating and cursing of those they slay."

This thought struck him as funny, and he gave one of those farting laughs.

"I see, sir…" I began, not sure what to do.

"I've noticed that you've never dared refer to me as governor," Sateekas said, "despite the fact it is now my proper title."

"Um…"

"You are wise not to do so. The mere thought of it—a masterful naval commander banished to a governorship… One would think I was as reviled as Xlur himself."

My lips were clamped tight, even though my mind churned with questions and retorts. I'd always suspected Xlur was considered to be an asshole, even by his peers.

"To explain," the Mogwa said, "you are essentially correct. A human *did* come to Mogwa Prime. And that human, it has now been determined, did murder Xlur. It was a perma-death too—professionally done."

My lips parted to show my teeth. I was worried now. My eyes slid to the marines. They were watchful, but seemed unaware of the intensity of the conversation Sateekas and I were having. Could I possibly rush one of them, take his weapon, then manage to kill the rest?

I wasn't sure, but I was about to try it.

## -69-

Governor Sateekas and I contemplated one another for a few seconds. I was waiting for his attention to shift. I needed a moment during which the guards were distracted somehow. Perhaps a Nairb would wander back to report, drawing everyone's eye for a few critical seconds…

"And so you see," Sateekas said, "I know it was you who killed Xlur, not Claver. For that, I owe you a great debt."

"Huh…?" I asked, blinking in confusion. I quickly recovered and straightened up my spine. "That's great, sir. I'm glad you see it my way."

"Yes. You've removed Xlur—your reasons are your own, but I can understand why. He wasn't well-liked by anyone. And this job I have now—the governorship, it's not what anyone would want, but it's better than being retired permanently."

I didn't entirely know what he was talking about, but his mood was positive, so mine was as well. I found myself nodding in agreement with everything he said. Inside, I felt a wave of relief.

"Anything to serve, sir," I said.

"An amazingly loyal beast you are. That you should have given up your existence this way for my comfort—yes, it's an honor to thank you personally."

"Uh…" I said, unhappy again. "What was that part about my existence, sir?"

"Yes, truly magnanimous. By slaying Xlur, you placed me on his throne by default. This is automatic, as I was the only other official assigned to this province by the Empire."

"I see."

"Clearly, you did. What's more, you saved my own life. As reluctant as I am to accept the mantle of a governor, it's better than what happened to my replacement who led Battle Fleet 921 on its final mission."

Sateekas seemed to think I knew what he was talking about—perhaps because he knew I'd been on Mogwa Prime recently—but of course, I was completely in the dark.

"Right sir. I know the outlines of that terrible disaster—but maybe you could fill me in on the specifics?"

"Of course. A loyal slave such as you deserves to know why his fate has befallen him. Battle Fleet 921 was deployed against a neighboring rival near Mogwa Prime. Unfortunately, the ships in that formation were both out of date and used on the front lines of the conflict. All but a few vessels—such as this cruiser we're aboard now— were destroyed."

I was stunned. The Battle Fleet was *gone*? That was grim news indeed.

Battle Fleet 921 was like our local police force. Sure, sometimes they bothered us, or they might seem overbearing, but to most folks, the concept of living without any protection at all from the wilds of the frontier… well, that was downright scary.

"What was the fighting all about this time, sir?" I asked.

"The same thing that usually ignites such fires. The Empire has always been plagued by revolts and civil wars. Recently, however, we reached a crisis state. The Senate hasn't met for years. The representative Galactics each vie for supremacy. You see, we have a critical problem."

"What's that, sir?" I asked, sincerely fascinated. I'd already started recording his explanation with my tapper, but I adjusted the microphone pick-up just to be sure. Central would want this someday—if I was ever lucky enough to get home.

"We are an empire without an Emperor. Isn't that obvious?"

"Uh… yes, I guess it is."

Thinking about it, I found it hard to believe I'd never really thought about who the Emperor was before. Ever since my birth and education, we'd been told about the distant, infinitely superior Galactics. We'd been told we were part of an Empire, a grand community made up of billions of stars and peoples—but no one had ever shown us who was at the top.

To think that maybe nobody was—the thought was disturbing.

"An Empire *needs* an Emperor, McGill!" Sateekas boomed at me. "They call me old-fashioned for having such thoughts. They urge me to update my body scans and go through a recycle to be young again—but I suspect them. You see, far too many officers I've known have done just that and returned with gaps in their memories. I'm not willing to go through with that process—not until there's no other choice."

Suddenly, old Sateekas had my sympathies. Maybe he had problems just as big as mine—or bigger—to keep him awake at night.

"What's the civil war about then, sir?"

"Succession, of course," he said. "Every major species is at the throats of the rest. Sometimes, one faction or another gets an upper hand, but then they're ganged up upon and cast back down. Often, periods of peace reign when a truce is signed—but always, eventually, the peace is broken again. We *need* an Emperor!"

He seemed almost to be talking to himself at this point.

"Um… sir? You mentioned something about my existence, earlier?"

"Yes, of course. A deal has been struck with these irritating creatures from Rigel. They clearly have more star systems than Earth has, and they're about to destroy your outpost on this planet with their superior forces. There's no easy way to put it: Earth is about to lose her status as my local enforcement species in the province."

I rolled that one over and over in my mind for a moment.

"What, uh, happens to an enforcer species that's been replaced, sir?"

"They're expunged, of course."

"Of course… but sir, what if we win? What if we destroy these crap-eating bears?"

Sateekas let his limbs rise and then flop down again. Was that a shrug? Something like it, I suspected.

"Then you may continue in your present capacity. I must warn you, however, the odds are very long indeed. The Nairbs have confided in me that you've got less than a one percent chance of weathering the combined assault that they're planning right now."

"One percent?" I asked excitedly. "So… you're saying there's a chance, right?"

"A very, very slim one."

"Hot damn! Well, I really do love chatting up here with you, Grand Admiral, but—"

"Governor," he corrected.

"Right," I said, but I carefully avoided using the term anyway. "But I really do need to get back down to the planet. I wouldn't want to miss all the fighting."

"Impressive…" he said. "The bloodthirsty nature of your race never ceases to amaze. By all means, you must depart to slaughter your opponents!"

Without another word, I rushed to the tiny patrol ship, boarded her, and flew back toward Storm World.

The cloud-cover obscured ninety-plus percent of the surface. Unlike Earth, Storm World had a turbulent atmosphere most of the time. I plunged into those misty shrouds and broke out into a lower level of grayness. Soon, the mists transformed into silver sheets of lashing rain.

At high speeds, rain doesn't bead up on your windscreen. Instead, it forms a continuous sheet, a thin film that spreads and slips away quickly.

The ship banked on auto-pilot and homed in on Fort Beta's signal. Within minutes, I was landing on the ground and surrounded by troops.

When I walked out onto the gangplank, I waved like I was surrounded by adoring fans. Those legionnaires in the crowd who knew me lowered their rifles and shook their heads in disgust.

"Take me to Armel!" I shouted with my hands on my hips. "I've got some important news for him!"

Instead, they arrested me and threw me into the brig. That was some kind of shitty welcome for a returning hero.

# -70-

When I woke up the next morning, there were base alert sirens going off. A few troops rushed by my cell in the brig. They were arming up, shrugging into their gear.

"Hmm…" I said, rubbing the sleep from my eyes. "Hey Santos… what's up?"

One of the specialists stopped. His name was Bob Santos, and he knew me, but not well.

"McGill?" he asked, belting on an extra power-pack for his snap-rifle. "What are you doing in there, Centurion?"

"Just catching up on some beauty sleep. What's happening Bob? My tapper is blocked."

It was standard procedure to disconnect tappers from the local net when you were incarcerated. Otherwise, prison wouldn't mean much to most folks.

"The Wur are on the march, sir—but that's not the bad news."

"Don't keep me in suspense!"

He looked around, as if he was passing on a rumor he'd been told to keep to himself. "They say the Rigel troops—those little bear guys—are marching with them."

I nodded, not too surprised. "Damn… I'd kind of hoped they'd take a few more days to get their alliance operating."

Santos stared at me. "You knew this was coming?"

Shrugging, I looked past him at the view screens. The guards had cameras operating inside and outside the bunker.

Outside, I could see formations of troops gathering and organizing.

Shaking his head, the specialist ran off.

About an hour passed. Bored, I kept expecting the battle to kick into gear, but despite all the prep-work it hadn't broken loose yet.

The sky did stop raining for once. A rare shaft of sunlight touched down in the camp. Shining brilliantly through a thousand shimmering drops of water, it looked like a miracle.

"McGill!" someone whispered.

I looked around, but there was no one there. The lone guard was focused on the view screens. Lots of people were checking out the sunlight. They looked like kids playing in the first snows.

"Where've you been, Cooper?" I asked quietly.

"Here and there. I'm a ghost, remember?"

"What do you want? A laugh?"

"No sir, I'm breaking you out."

As he said these words, the door clicked open and slid away.

"What the hell?" the guard demanded, standing and hitching up his belt. "What are you up to, McGill?"

I backed away from the bars, throwing my hands up. "Nothing! Maybe it's a power problem."

Suspicious, the guard took out his pistol and approached me cautiously. He reached the door and—

*Wham!* He went down.

"You hit him kind of hard, Cooper," I commented.

"He's a big boy."

Accepting the invitation, I stepped out of the cell and looked around.

"Now what?" I asked. "You realize they're going to blame me for this, right?"

"I'm kind of counting on that, sir."

"Great…"

"Centurion, if you'd prefer to step back in there and close the door—well, it's up to you."

I thought about that. I seriously did.

The reason I wasn't escaping was because it seemed pointless. Without an answer to one simple question, I wasn't going to leave my cell.

"What am I going to be able to do alone that could change the doomed battle that's coming?" I asked.

"It's up to you, sir. I'm taking off to man the walls.

"Sure you are…" I said, and I frowned at the open cell door. Finally, I figured I had an answer to the question I'd asked myself.

"I'm going to talk to Armel," I said. "I know what's coming. I know what the stakes are. He needs that information."

There was no response.

"You still here, Cooper?"

There was nothing but sirens and pounding feet outside. Soon, there would be the crack of gunfire, along with the snap and whine of the star-falls launching plasma into the forest toward the approaching enemy.

Grunting unhappily, I left my cell and headed to the stairs. The big storm doors at the top of the stairway swung open the moment I put my foot on the bottom step.

Bright sunlight glowed down into the brig. It made me squint, as my eyes weren't used to it.

"McGill?" asked a familiar voice.

Armel sighed. He had two heavy troopers with him.

"Hello Tribune, sir," I said brightly "This is quite a coincidence. I was just coming to talk to you in person."

Armel came down the steps haltingly. He looked at every shadow with a stern, wary frown. "Have you murdered another of my guards?"

"Uh… I don't think he's dead. He had an accident. It was the damnedest thing, sir."

"Of course he did... What did you want to tell me?"

I went ahead and spilled my guts then. I told him almost everything. All about meeting with Sateekas, and the deals Claver had made with Rigel.

"Why didn't you tell Sateekas about the formula?" he asked. "Don't you think he'd have been enraged by Claver's actions and sympathetic with yours?"

"That's a good point, sir—but you're absolutely wrong. The Mogwa don't think like that. They still tend to think of humans as a single group. If I'd told him Claver had threatened billions of Mogwa citizens, well… he'd blame every human that ever drew breath for the crime."

"Hmm… so the individual crime of slaying Xlur—that was more palatable?"

"Normally, it wouldn't have been. But Sateekas told me it helped him survive by getting him out of the navy right when he needed an out. He doesn't like being a governor, but it's better than being a dead admiral commanding a dead fleet."

Armel gazed at me with squinched-tight eyes. People did that when they wanted to shut out an image they were viewing. In this case, the offensive image was my face.

"I'm not sure what to believe…" he said at last.

"Well sir, I can help you on that front. I'm the most honest, trustworthy, and downright unassuming—"

I'd been about to give him the full Boy Scout list, but another figure arrived at the top of the steps.

We all squinted up into the unexpected glare of sunlight. There, at the top of the stairs, was Claver.

He descended one step at a time, joining us at the bottom.

"Is this the man you left on Governor Sateekas' ship, awaiting torment and execution?" Armel asked me.

"Uh…" I said, honestly dumbfounded.

"Aw now," Claver said, "don't torture this farm-boy. He's not used to brain-twisters like this."

Armel laughed. "Yes… I admit that I'm puzzled as well. Exactly how did you escape the Mogwa?"

Claver shrugged. "A man has to have a few secrets. You won't deny me that, will you, Tribune?"

He gave him a significant glance, and Armel cleared his throat. "Very well. You asked to come here and speak with McGill. By all means, speak!"

"It might be better if he were back in his cage."

Armel considered it, but he shook his head. "No. I will need him on the wall tops in ten minutes. All my troops will fight today—no matter their criminal status. I have to go now and marshal our defenses."

He left, but he didn't leave Claver and I alone. He assigned the two heavy troopers as bodyguards to Claver, but they didn't look happy about it.

"How'd you get out, Claver?" I asked.

"I didn't, you fool. I'm a different Claver."

"Ah…" I said, catching on. "So they offed you that quick, huh? I'm surprised. I would have expected old Sateekas to take his time killing a fiend like you."

Claver glared at me. "What'd you tell him exactly? What crime did you hang on my neck?"

"Don't you remember? Well, maybe you were out by then. I told him you killed Xlur."

Claver looked truly surprised.

"And he bought that?"

"Nope," I said, shaking my head. "But he liked the story, so he decided to go with it."

Claver took a few halting steps down into the brig. He stared past me, his eyes darting as if thinking fast.

"Uh…" I said. "What kind of evil is going on inside that big brain of yours?"

"This is going to be a difficult play—mostly due to your ham-handed con job."

That made me blink in surprise. "Ham-handed? I thought it was rather neatly done. After all, it worked, didn't it?"

"Listen McGill, do you understand the stakes here?"

"Um, yeah… Sateekas said something about us losing our status as local enforcers."

"That's right. The Mogwa have gone sweet on Rigel. These bears are dynamite fighters, and Sateekas knows we're half-assed at best."

"Well, if that's all you wanted to say…" I began. "I think I need to be getting to the walls. This fort could fall."

As I stepped past him, he did a dangerous thing. He reached out and gripped my arm.

I frowned down at him. "I'vc killed for less."

"I know it—but hold on. Hear me out. I'm not Claver—not the one you know. That other Claver Prime, he's in the Mogwa ship getting eviscerated."

"Uh... you duplicated yourself? That's a Galactic crime right there."

He rolled his eyes. "I'm well-aware. But the situation is... complex. I'm not in complete agreement with all my brothers, see."

All of a sudden, I *did* see. This Claver was the renegade. The man who the others I'd met had long hinted about.

"Seriously?" I asked. "You're a different breed of Claver? Have I met you before?"

"Yes. Most recently, I came to tell you about the deal with your daughter."

"That was you, huh? I killed you."

He shrugged. "It happens. I have some resources—but I'm not as invincible as the primary Claver line. In fact, I'm hunted by them."

"Why are you telling me all this now?"

"Because you outted me. I listen to the traffic between Clavers—they have their own private com system—and they're talking about a rebel in their midst. A mole."

"This is really something," I said, scratching my head. "When did it all start? This deviation in your line of clones, I mean?"

"Remember the man who you exiled among the Wur back on Death World?"

"That guy? Wow, that's waaay back."

"Sure is. That was me. It was sometime after that, when I wandered in the forest of the Wur, that I deviated from my brothers. We had just established our enclave—our own colony. But I had a difference of opinion from the rest. Maybe it was those long lonely months I spent in those empty Wur forests. Or maybe it was the mind-bending toxins the Wur Nexus plants inject into your brain when they talk to you. I don't know..."

He looked haunted, and that alone intrigued me. Claver had never seemed like an introspective man to me.

"What's your problem with the rest of them—or their problem with you?"

Claver hesitated. "I've got a flaw. I need companionship. Women, specifically. I wanted to bring women to our colony world. The rest of the Clavers disagreed, of course. You see, the firm rule of the colony is that every citizen must be genetically related to the original Claver. That way, we reasoned, we could stay in agreement. It gave us all unity."

I thought that one over, and it was weird, but I could see it.

"So... they didn't want you to import women. Didn't want children, either? Is that it?"

"Exactly. If we introduced non-clones, they could only vary from our thinking, from our goals, from our commitment to self-sacrifice. I mean, any given Claver knows he can go on a mission, die, and come back whole again. But what if we had kids? Would the kids follow those rules? It seemed doubtful."

"Yeah... That's really weird..." A thought occurred to me then. "Hey!" I shouted, and I slapped his chest with the back of my hand.

This made the two heavy troopers step from foot-to-foot anxiously. They glowered at both of us, trying to decide if Claver had been attacked or not.

Ignoring them, I grinned. "You're the dirty little bastard who cloned up a lady-Claver, aren't you?"

He pursed his lips and looked troubled.

I laughed hard. "You old goat, you!"

"Creating a female was within the rules we'd laid out," he said stubbornly. "A female Claver was just a variation of all Clavers."

"Sure, sure, sure," I said. "You discovered a whole new form of masturbation! You should feel proud! In fact, you've given a whole new deep meaning to the phrase: Go F yourself!"

"Yeah, yeah, thanks, McGill." He looked dejected. "Ridicule, rejection. I'm used to it. They didn't accept Abigail. They banished her. After that, they discovered my engrams had deviated too far from the rest—and they took steps to erase me as well."

"Seems like that didn't take."

"No, but I can't go back to them. I'm an outcast now. So, don't kill me without good cause, McGill. I'm not like my brothers. I can't pop up in a thousand places, like one more rabbit escaping the warren."

I considered that. This Claver *did* seem different to me.

"You're a bad grow, aren't you?" I said. "Or rather… a good grow? A Claver with a conscience?"

"Something like that."

"Good enough. Let's say I'm willing to believe all this—and I am, as I found that lady-Claver myself, and I've seen for years how the others don't like to talk about her. Given all that, why are you here now? What are you trying to pull?"

"I need Earth to stay in this game," he said. "This is the final chapter—or it could be. I'm here to win this war, to help Earth keep her status as enforcers."

"Why does Earth…? Oh, so you can find, um, *companions*. Is that it?"

He shrugged.

Outside, the sirens wailed again. The Wur and their allies from Rigel were about to attack. I could hear star-fall artillery firing from the center of the fort. Each plasma ball carried death with it out into the endless forest. When a warhead struck down, it took out a giant tree or an entire formation of smaller enemy troops.

The battle was on.

"We need to win this battle first," I said.

"We can't. No one can. Too many will come. Thousands upon thousands… But, there's another way…"

# -71-

When I heard Claver's plan, I knew it was a winner—it was also ironic.

"Let me get this straight," I said. "You want me to locate and kill the last Wur Nexus? The brains of the enemy?"

"It's the only way. Rigel tore up the rest, which brought the Wur to the negotiating table. However, if that last one fell, the Wur would have no brains left on Storm World."

"But back on Death World, you were totally set against that same tactic."

He shrugged. "Of course I was. Back then, I wanted to make a deal with the plants. Today, I want to stop them."

A voice spoke off to my left then. It was Cooper, who'd apparently been hanging out quietly all this time.

"This guy is a snake, Centurion," he said. "He's full of shit. I can kill him for you, if you don't want to do it."

Claver looked startled. "A ghost, huh? I'd heard about you guys recruiting slime like that. No wonder you're hard to keep in a cage, McGill. You're a cheater."

"What about it?" Cooper asked. "Should I off him? I've got a blade at his throat, and he doesn't even know."

Claver tried to look brave, but he took a half-step back and gulped anyway.

Mystified by the situation, the two heavy troopers looked around with rolling eyes. They reminded me of horses that were about to start kicking things.

"Nah…" I said. Giving my head a shake, I looked at Claver thoughtfully. "You really *are* a different kind of Claver. Either that, or you're extra-tricky today. What should I call you? I mean, you're not exactly a Claver-Prime."

"That's true… Call me Claver-X. I like the sound of that."

Cooper snorted.

"All right, X," I said. "How do we do this thing with the last Nexus?"

He worked his tapper. "First off, I'm sending a message to Armel right now informing him that you've agreed to this suicide mission."

"Uh…"

"See?" Cooper asked. "What did I tell you?"

"What's the problem?" Claver demanded, lowering his arm. "Did you think Armel walked me over here to spring you out of prison as an act of sheer love? Grow up. We made a deal, and I just sealed it."

"Uh…" I said, thinking hard. "This is going to suck then, I take it?"

"No, no, no," Claver said sarcastically. "It's going to be a springtime walk in the woods. Assemble your unit and a few hundred of your crappy natives. We'll break out over the mountains while the main attack advances on the walls."

Grumbling and hustling, I gathered my gear and trotted to where my unit was stationed. I considered going AWOL, of course, but how would that turn out? I was on a craptastic mud-ball of a planet. If all the humans were killed, I couldn't imagine I'd have a fun life outrunning the victorious Wur.

At least this way I wasn't going to have to sit out the battle in a prison cell. I could die in style.

"McGill?" Harris called out to me the minute I showed up. "What have you been doing? Screwing some kind of salamander princess?"

"That's pretty close to the mark, Harris. Gather up the unit, we're moving out."

Shaking his head, he turned and began to bellow at the unit. They were embedded in nice muddy foxholes and huddling on the wall tops, but if you thought they'd jump at the chance to get outside the walls and get some fresh air, you'd be wrong.

"Where are we going, Ace?" Leeson asked me.

I pointed vaguely into the mountains.

"Um... you do realize, Centurion, that we're dealing out effective punishment just hugging the mud and laying on heavy artillery fire don't you? Those Rigel nut-sacks have put up screens, but star-falls can punch right through that stuff. They'll be here soon, and they're coming in vast numbers according to every report. We need to whittle them down all we can."

Glancing at him, I gave him a disinterested shrug. "We're leaving the fort, but we're not walking straight into the enemy lines. We're going up there, into the mountains."

"Ah..." Leeson said, craning his neck around. "I like that better. Barton and her lights are on point, right?"

"No, I'm sending about a hundred of the Scuppers in first. Then Barton."

He slammed his gauntlets together and grinned. "Sounds good to me! Once we get up there on top of those cliffs, I can set up my 88s and—"

"No," I said. "Forget the 88s. We can't drag them into the mountains. Leave them here for the boys who are manning these walls."

Leeson looked crestfallen, but he didn't argue. He just turned away and began to get his platoon moving.

Soon, all of my people were organized into a column. We began trekking toward the cliffs to the rear of the compound.

Behind us, the battle was heating up. Snap-rifles popped and whined. The star-falls kept up their thrum followed by a pounding sound that released a slow-moving plasma ball. Punching through shielding that domed both sides now, it fell in what looked like slow motion among the huge, shadowy trees, many of which were now burning.

By the time we exited the rear gate of the fort and began marching up a winding trail into the mountains, we could see the Wur hitting the walls. 88s flared into life, a thousand guns fired, and a pall of smoke rose up to obscure the battle.

Veteran Moller began slapping heads, screaming for members of my platoon to turn their heads back to the trail. She shocked me into motion again as well. We all marched together up the rocky path until we couldn't see the battle any longer, obscured as it was by the black, wet cliffs.

"Contact!" Barton called out on the tactical chat channel.

"What have you got, Adjunct?" I demanded, but she didn't answer right away.

"I… I'm not totally sure, sir. The Scuppers are fighting up ahead."

Claver-X tapped me on the back. "You'd better get up there, McGill. These lizards are no match for Rigel regulars."

I knew he was right, and I began to press my way forward, passing troops on the trail. I had to shove my way past my own platoon and up to Barton's lights.

They looked scared and wet, but ready for anything.

In my headset, I could hear the yammering voices of Scuppers. They were shouting excitedly in their own language.

I kept moving up the line. Breaking past the lights, I came up on Barton. She was aiming her weapon forward, trying to get a shot.

Ahead of her, the scene had changed dramatically. The landscape had gone from a gully between two cliffs to a narrow path cut into the wall of the cliff on our right—and a sheer drop on our left.

Due to the rain and mist, I couldn't even see the bottom of that fall. It was black, volcanic-looking rock and scrubby green growths all the way down.

"Shit…" I said, leaning against the cliff wall on my right.

"Something is killing my Scuppers, Centurion," Barton told me. "But I can't get a shot in. They're just around a few bends up this winding path."

Putting my visor down, I used my HUD. Automatically, Kivi's drones were engaged. Some of them were programmed to fly and investigate anything the commander looked at. Normally, that tech feature didn't matter much. But with this low visibility and rough terrain, it proved useful.

I soon got a visual flow. There were small figures up there, a long, long line of the friggers. Right off, I knew what we were facing. The enemy was distinctive due to their size and tenacity.

"Rigellian regulars!" I shouted, relaying the feed to the rest of my officers. "They must be coming this way to scout the rear of the fort."

"I bet they planned to infiltrate and slip into Armel's backdoor," Harris said, laughing. "We're a rude surprise for them!"

"It's rude for our native troops, too," Leeson added. "They're killing our Scuppers ten to one."

It was true. Using their shotguns and superior strength, they forced the salamanders back. The Scuppers tried to fight, and they made a good show of it. They applied their spears with vigor, jabbing and shocking the oncoming soldiers.

But it was an uneven contest every time they met in battle. Single file the Scuppers edged up closer and closer to the advancing Rigel line coming the other way on the narrow path. Each time a Scupper met up with a Rigellian regular, a fight to the death began. Behind each man was the pressing mass of their own troops, which didn't allow them much room to maneuver on the narrow, slippery path.

The worst part for our side was the uneven weaponry. Spears have reach, but shotguns have more. The usual process had a Rigellian soldier methodically blowing the guts out of one native after another, until he had to reload.

At that point, the next desperate Scupper would charge in and thrust.

Even then, it was far from a certain kill. These boys from Rigel were strong and mean. They'd often grab hold of the taller soldier's spear and hurl him over the side. Even if they took the shocking blow, they didn't stay stunned for long. They got in close, and fought until one of them was dead.

Now and then, a Scupper got lucky and jolted one of the enemies in the leg or foot, and he'd go down and slide away into the abyss to the left. Once, I saw two of them go over the edge in a deadly clinch.

The Scuppers were too weak to hold up against this enemy, of course, but they had weight and leverage. After the first took one bear with him, I saw more decide to go for it. Grappling with a bear and then clutching it firmly, he would go over the edge taking his hated foe with him.

"Goddammit!" I roared. "They're dying hard up there. I'm moving up!"

Barton gave me a startled glance. "If you let the Scuppers wear them down, sir—"

"Forget it. I'm not watching a hundred of my troops die ten-to-one against those fucking bears. They've already lost half their number. I'm going up."

It was easier said than done. The pathway was only half a meter wide in spots. I had to literally lift terrified Scuppers bodily at times, placing them behind me on the path and moving forward a single slot.

Up ahead, the battle was fierce and desperate. Even the bears looked tired and worried. They'd lost plenty of men, too.

After scooting up a dozen spots in line, and seeing another dozen Scuppers die against one single Rigellian casualty, I was finally able to get a shot.

The cliff curved a little, and the enemy troops were on the opposing wall. There was a spur of rock between us, and I hid behind it.

For openers, I tossed a grav-plasma grenade.

Apparently, none of these fellows had ever seen one. That made sense, as our two species had only done battle on a couple of occasions. We were both due for some surprises.

A few of the enemy eyed the glowing device for about a second, and one moved to pick it up and toss it off the cliff.

Before he could let go, it went off in his hand. Plasma grenades were strange weapons. They picked up elements of their environment and hurled them outward with terrific velocity. In this case, there was plenty of shrapnel to be had. Rocks, pebbles—even raindrops were transformed by a blue-white flash into a brilliant spray of death.

Their tough suits kept them from being killed outright, but they weren't happy. Two toppled off the cliff, knocked senseless. A third was in combat with our line of Scuppers, and he took a spear in the guts. That was the end of him. Stunned and limp, he toppled from the path.

"Pass up more grenades!" I called. "Pass them *all* up, one at a time!"

Behind me, the Scuppers and the light troopers did as I'd ordered. The native troops only had their spears, but each light in Barton's platoon had been issued a single grenade. They were soon flowing up at a steady rate.

The first thing I did was shorten the timer down by two seconds. That was dangerous, but I didn't want them to have a chance to toss one back or for the grenade to roll harmlessly off the cliff.

Again and again, I tossed them at the enemy. They were blown off the cliff as each new group came marching up to replace the last.

"How many of these fuckers are coming up this mountain?" Harris demanded in my earpiece.

"Let's hope it's all of them," Barton said. "McGill is screwing them over badly."

After about a hundred kills, my luck ran out. Someone noticed me through the swirling mist, tossing grenades into their ranks.

I'm no expert on alien expressions, but—they looked pissed.

# -72-

What had covered for me up until that moment—besides the rain and the mist—was the fact the enemy were rounding a corner. They kept marching along the pathway around a fold in the mountain that prevented them from clearly seeing the source of the grenades. They'd probably figured the Scuppers were throwing them—until somebody saw me.

Pointing and snarling soon gave way to blasting at me with their shotguns. Fortunately, I was far enough away that their first blasts spread wide.

Still, I was hit and almost slid down into the abyss at my feet. Scuppers grabbed my arms and strained. One of them was shot down—but another took his place. They dragged me back around the spur of rock and down the trail until I was sheltered from enemy fire.

My left leg was a mess. I took some stims and allowed my suit to patch up the bloody holes. Shotgun pellets, driven with terrific force, had penetrated my armor and made a few marble-sized holes in my thigh.

Carlos and my suit worked together. He patched me up, and the suit tightened so I could walk with a limp. Afterward, I was breathing and talking between clenched teeth.

"They finally got you, huh?" Carlos laughed. "That was unbelievable, McGill. We were all watching on the drone-feed. Such a bunch of morons—you must have killed fifty of them."

"More like a hundred."

"Yeah, sure. Whatever you say, Centurion. You want some drugs?"

I considered the offer. I would be less sharp, but the pain had a way of dulling a man's mind anyway.

"Just some local stuff. We're not off this mountain yet."

We were sitting in an alcove, a deeper spot along the trail that was a good two meters from the cliff edge. I soon closed my eyes. I needed a second to rest.

Next thing I knew, Barton's light troopers were stepping right over my sprawling form. Had I passed out again?

"What's going on?" I demanded. "Barton? I didn't order an advance. If you press the Scuppers too hard they'll go down faster."

"Sorry sir," her voice buzzed in my helmet. "I've been reporting directly to Leeson since you passed out."

"I didn't pass out," I grumbled. "Carlos, did I pass out?"

"Uh... do you really want to invite me to some kind of piss-party over this detail, Centurion?"

I considered. "No. I don't care. Why are you advancing, Leeson?" I called out on tactical chat.

"Because the enemy is pulling back. They're in retreat, sir."

Slowly, a grin dawned on my face. The Rigel boys had had enough.

"Are they running, or out of troops?" I asked.

"I'd wager it's a little of both. They're backing down the mountain, setting up ambushes—but they aren't willing to take more losses. Each time we rush one of their set-ups, they've already withdrawn farther."

Claver-X appeared. Maybe he'd been waiting for this moment. He squatted and looked me over.

"You feeling like a quitter today, McGill?" he asked me.

Shaking my head, I began to struggle to my feet. Carlos arrived and tried to push me back down.

"You've lost a lot of blood, Centurion," he said.

"Then pump some fresh stuff into my veins," I told him, giving him a shove.

He teetered on the edge of the cliff, cursing, but Moller came along and pulled him back onto the ledge again.

"That was uncalled for, even for you," Carlos complained.

"Just keep me walking. I can't stop now, or the wounds will stiffen up."

I looked around for Claver, but he'd moved on. I was still not a hundred percent sure I trusted him—by that I mean I didn't trust him at all. Maybe he'd flipped over a new leaf, or maybe he'd come up with a cock-and-bull story to get me to escort him into these mountains. Either was possible.

Having been shot any number of times in the past, I knew all too well the feeling of one's muscles contracting painfully. I had to get up and keep moving. My body didn't like getting shot much. I could hardly blame myself for that, but this war wasn't going to win itself.

Using a cocktail of drugs from Carlos' magic bag and my suit's emergency injury management system, I was able to keep on my feet.

Soon, the sporadic gunfire up ahead slowed, petered out, and died completely.

"Report from the front line!" I demanded. "What do we have up there?"

"We've lost contact with the enemy, sir," Barton responded. "They've withdrawn down the mountain. My platoon can press forward to pursue, but we've got a lot of wounded, and your Scuppers are spooked by their heavy losses."

"Right…" I said unhappily.

I didn't like the idea of losing my native troops. We were heading into their territory now, and we weren't doing it in a stealthy fashion. We were certain to meet up with further resistance as we moved deeper into the mountains.

The march turned into a slog after that. We suspected an ambush after every bend. We sent drones flying ahead, but the enemy deployed countermeasures to take them out. Soon, our techs were down to a handful of camera units, and I ordered them to preserve the rest.

The effect was chilling. It was one thing to march down into territory you could see on your tapper, but quite another to advance when you're essentially blind.

Feeling dread with each step, my troops soon stopped joking about the last battle. The Rigellians might be seeking revenge. We all had the feeling they'd never let a humiliating defeat like that stand for long.

As we walked steadily downward into a gorge, we saw few signs of the enemy. The rushing sounds of a turbulent river roared, coming closer and closer. Instead of being encouraged, we were filled with unease.

At last, we reached a muddy strip of land near the river. The water was so violent, it threatened to sweep away the whole unit.

"Where did they go?" I asked, looking around. "There's nothing down here!"

Sure enough, as the group gathered, we found ourselves alone at the bottom of the gorge. We looked for a path out of the region, but the only one we saw was the one we'd followed down here.

Claver came down to have a look.

"Hmm…" he said. "This is a poser. You didn't kill them all, did you?"

"Negative," Leeson said. "No way."

Claver smiled. "But you might have. This gorge… you see the walls? Do they look like they've felt a rush of water lately?"

"This whole planet is nothing but a frigging sponge!" Leeson argued.

"Whoa! Wait a second," Harris said, walking around and looking up.

The black cliffs were about a hundred meters apart, and they seemed to rise up to space itself on both sides. The sky was a ragged, gray-white line far above.

"What if a big wave came down this gorge?" Harris asked.

We all looked around in alarm.

"Kivi," I said, "link me up with the satellite feed. Do we still have some eyes in the sky?"

"Negative," she said. "The Rigellian ships took them all down."

"Dammit…"

Looking around, I caught sight of a few Scuppers. I got them to find Second-man for me.

Second-man didn't look happy to be on the muddy shelf of shore with us.

"This is a dangerous place," he said.

"Yes, I think so. We followed the Rigel troops down here. Do you think they've been swept away?"

He walked around on his padding feet and inspected the environment. "There has been a surge—but it has not gone higher than this level for days. You can tell, by looking at the way the striations—"

"Okay, okay," I said. "I believe you. But if the enemy wasn't carried away in a flood down this gorge, where did they go?"

He blinked at me. Two slow blinks.

"They are below. Can't you see the tracks?"

I examined a region he pointed at. It did indeed seem like there were footprints—small ones—but then the trail ended at the far end of the spit of land we were standing on.

"You mean they walked down into the river itself?"

"No, no," he said. "The river has shifted, that's all. Wait. It will shift again."

That was about all I got out of him. My officers circled around, grumbling.

"We ought to go back," Leeson said.

"Not going to happen. The fort might have fallen by now—we're not getting any kind of signals."

"Signals down here?" Leeson laughed. "We're not getting bird shit down here, Centurion. Not without a satellite."

I looked up, and I figured he was right. On a wild planet with a turbulent atmosphere, you needed satellites to communicate over long distances. We were at the bottom of a wet gorge with nothing in that narrow strip of sky to relay our signal.

"All right," I said. "We're going to wait. Everyone but our scouts should head back up on the trail, in case a wave comes by and takes out this shoreline."

They grumbled about not being on flat ground, but I knew if I took them all down here, they would have grumbled about all being drowned any second, too.

About thirty long minutes passed. Kivi tried to send a few swimming drones into the flooding waters, but there was no point. They were swept into the rocks and smashed almost as soon as she deployed them.

At last, something unexpected happened.

A rushing wave of water flashed into sight from the north. It swept along, scooping up a dozen or so Scuppers I'd left down there.

Panicked, my troops tried to retreat—but there was no running now. We were too bunched up on the trail, and the water moved too fast.

It roared, sounding like a subway train flying along at out of control speeds.

This planet had vicious tides. We'd never managed yet to get a good working computer model of the behavior, as there were too many moons, and thus too many variables. On top of that, the harsh wet weather caused flooding all by itself.

The surge went by in the span of a minute. A few light troops were swept away, along with the Scuppers. There was no hope for them, given the violent power of the water and the rocky walls that smashed their bones and clawed at their thin skins.

But, after the wave went by, the waters receded rapidly. The water fell farther, in fact, than I would have thought possible.

"Is this a low tide?" I asked Second-man.

"This is a cross-tide," he said. "One moon crosses another's path in the sky, and it can cause the water to dance in a peculiar rhythm."

"That's just great. Let's try the path."

Trotting over the soggy shore, I found the path now continued on the other side. The water level of the river was falling…

It went down a hundred meters, then two hundred. We rushed down the slick path as fast as we dared.

"This is insane," Harris complained. "You might be perming the whole unit. Have you thought of that, McGill?"

"Listen, don't lose your nerve. The whole legion might be permed—or at least wiped—if we fail."

Shaking his head, he fell back and rejoined his heavies. He admonished them to greater speed, kicking the iron ass of any soldier who lagged behind.

# -73-

At the two hundred meter mark, I sent Harris and his heavy troops back up. They were slowing us down, and it wasn't their job to scout and die—that was job of Barton's platoon.

Taking a fast-moving force of light troopers and Scuppers only, I jogged with Barton down the newly revealed pathway. Every step hurt, as my thigh was still torn up.

Modern medicine, with flesh-printers and nano-surgical gear, had given us much better wound recovery times than troops had had in the past. Since no bone or organ had been struck by the pellets I'd taken earlier today, I was able to move with speed.

But I was gritting my teeth and grunting every step of the way, let me tell you.

It felt eerie to be winding down deeper into a gorge that had so recently been underwater. Any second the water could come back. Without satellite coverage, we had no real way of knowing.

After we'd made it another three hundred meters down, I realized that even if we did get a small warning now—we couldn't survive. The tidal waves moved with such sudden force that we could never outrun them. We'd be overwhelmed and crushed.

"Pick up the pace! Double-time!" I ordered.

"Centurion," Barton said from behind me. "We're going to lose people. They'll fall off this ledge, and we'll never get them out of that water."

"That's what revival machines are for," I shouted over my shoulder. "Keep moving."

She shut up and jogged after me. Claver was right behind her, running and panting with the rest.

He'd given Barton plenty of thoughtful glances. Could that really be his motivation? Was this particular Claver just a horn-dog?

He'd tried to make a woman of his own, and failed. Was he helping us in hopes of finding someone like Adjunct Barton to be his companion?

Giving my head a shake, I got my mind back into the game at hand. Each stomping boot might slip, and if it did, I'd go right over the edge.

Up ahead, the column slowed. Barton slammed into me—maybe she was distracted. I put a hand back and pushed her toward the wall.

She was so light, especially since I was wearing a breastplate, that she didn't do much more than cause me to rock forward. But for some reason, she'd clearly been knocked forward and almost over the side.

"Sorry! Sorry, dammit!" Claver said.

Glancing back, I saw Claver's hands were all over Barton, helping her back to her feet.

She gave him a jab with her elbow and a shove.

"Watch what you're doing, civvie!" she snapped.

"I was distracted," he admitted.

Turning forward again, I saw the line snake downhill.

"Point-Man!" I called out to the Scuppers I had leading the advance. "Report!"

"The trail has ended, First-man."

Frowning, I began to pass people again, grabbing them, lifting them up, and placing them behind me. Each human and Scupper I did this to squawked in alarm—but I didn't care.

Coming to the front, I saw that the trail again ended in swirling water.

"Shit…" I said, looking around at the echoing black walls. They were shiny with slick mud and running droplets.

How long did we have before the tide reversed again? I had no way of knowing.

"Give me your spear," I demanded of the point-man.

He handed it over without an argument.

Using the spear, I tapped ahead of me, probing the flood near the cliff. There was solid ground down there—solid enough. My boots were soon submerged as I waded in—then my kneecaps.

Looking back, I saw the point-man wasn't following.

"The path is here, it's just submerged. You can come after me."

He looked worried. "First-man, I'm not wearing a tunic of metal. I'll be swept away."

Realizing he was right, I nodded. "You hold on here. Let me scout."

"That's wrong," he said. "I should die in your place."

"Don't worry, you'll get your chance soon enough."

Tapping and taking cautious steps, I felt the water push at my legs. Fortunately, I'm a very tall man. Standing at exactly two meters, I could wade into deep water and keep my feet longer than anyone I knew. On top of that, I was carrying armor and a lot of other gear. That weight, borne high on my body, helped keep me from lifting up and floating away with the current.

Rounding a bend in the cliff face—I saw the end. The path turned and went up again to a plateau. Planted up there was a Nexus, which amounted to a Wur brain.

It reminded me of those barrel-like cacti they had in deserts back home. This one stood maybe five meters across and more than twice that in height. Every half-meter or so, the gray-green hulk sprouted long yellow spines.

"Claver!" I shouted over tactical chat. "I can see it! This has to be a Nexus plant. I can't believe the thing is so far down here. It must be underwater most of the time."

"Get in there and kill it!" he urged me. "We can't follow, the water is getting deeper!"

Looking back the way I'd come, I realized in alarm that he was right. The water was rising—fast. Soon it would reach the gnarled roots of the Nexus.

I splashed toward the big plant, circling it, seeking higher ground.

"I'm cut off from you guys," I called out. "Barton, withdraw and pull back the entire unit. If I fail to take out the plant, you'll have to send more people forward later—and bring demolitions! It's a big bastard!"

Advancing until my thighs came out of the flood, then my knees, I soon stood panting on the plateau.

There, I discovered the Rigel troops—or some of them. I counted eight dead bodies. They were all around the Nexus, and it appeared they'd been guarding it.

They'd all drowned.

On the far side of the plant, the trail continued. It too, soon went back down into the flood.

Looking over the scene, I caught on. The Nexus was located at a high point between two lower sections. Once here, you were pretty much cut off by the tides. These eight enemy troops might have been posted here to protect the plant while the rest of their company retreated farther.

The ploy hadn't worked. They'd all been overwhelmed and drowned before we could even get down here to shoot them.

Striding to the base of the Nexus, I gave it a tap with my spear. A spark leapt and it could have been my imagination, but it seemed like those meter-long needles had shook—just a little.

Tilting my head back, I grinned up at the plant. "You can feel something, huh? You're going to love this."

I reached for a grav-plasma grenade—but of course, I didn't have one.

"Shit…"

I'd thrown them all at the Rigellians a long time ago.

Hearing some splashing, I looked around and saw the water was closing in. Some of the dead bears were floating.

"How am I going to kill you, you big green bastard?" I asked the Nexus.

The plant remained silent. It stood still, ominous, as if watching. I had no idea if it had sensory organs or cameras of some kind nearby, but I got the feeling it was aware of my presence.

Grabbing up one of those Rigel-made shotguns, I boomed three times at point-blank range. A hole was punched through the plant's outer skin and green slime gushed out—but it wasn't enough to kill something so large.

The water was at my knees this time. The current didn't seem strong here—but I was soon going to be underwater.

Producing my force-blades, I sliced a triangle out of the giant cactus. It shivered again, and some of those long yellow needles rattled. I'd hurt it, but I had to be sure it died.

I was as good as dead myself, of course. I knew that. After a man dies around a hundred times or so, he gets a feel for his own imminent doom.

The water surged closer greedily while I was carving a second triangle. It touched my force-blade and shorted it out.

*Damn*, that stung!

Soon, I realized I'd be underwater completely. That was a bad thing, as the current might get pretty rough down at the base.

Climbing… I had to climb.

Shucking off my armor after punching the emergency releases, I put my combat knife in my teeth and I climbed those nasty-looking needles. They were spaced about a meter apart, and they held my weight.

A part of me was trying to survive, of course. It's hard to break that habit. If I managed to get to the top of the plant, maybe, just maybe, the flood wouldn't reach that high. I might wait this out until another team came down this way—or even exit this trap on my own two feet during a low tide.

The hope was a slim one, but when you're as good as dead, you'll try anything.

Up the plant's side I went. My thigh injury ached and tore. Fresh blood dribbled, then ran. I ignored it all. This was it, I didn't have another play.

Far below, the dead Rigel boys sloshed around and were impaled over and over on the needles. They couldn't feel this abuse, but it made me wince anyway.

Reaching the crown at last, I sprawled out and gasped for air. Coughing and bleeding, I wondered if I had the strength left to kill this thing with only a knife.

A tickle. A tiny thread of… electricity? No… more like a chemical trace in my blood, in my mind. A thought that had leaked from somewhere else.

Worried that I was dying due to lost blood, I surged up and gasped.

That's when I saw and felt the pain in my hand. It was flush down on a rosette of spikes. The spines—small ones, hair-thin, were clustered at the apex of this monstrous plant.

My blood had mixed with those spines. They'd tapped into me, and they were trying to communicate.

Curious, and a little bit high from the intoxicating effects of the Nexus venom, I accessed an old app on my tapper. It was one that Claver had given me a long, long time ago.

The app translated the chemical tickling, turning drugs into words. It was a strange way to communicate, but that's how the Wur did it.

"*...creature...*"

"What?" I asked aloud, bleary-minded.

How long had I been lying on that cactus, dreaming due to its powerful intoxicating effects? I wasn't sure, but the water around me certainly looked deeper. I didn't know how much higher it would go, but I knew I couldn't survive if it rose to the top.

"*...how is it that utter-cruelty can speak to me now? I've tried and tried to contact utter-cruelty, with no success...*"

After a blurry second or two, I realized I must be 'utter-cruelty'. I guessed that the plant was pissed at the wounds I'd inflicted at the base of its vast girth.

"I'm James McGill, a human legionnaire—and I hate plants," I told it. "I've just gotten started digging into you."

"*...you are a dead-thing, utter-cruelty. You've ingested too much of my blood. I've tasted yours, I've analyzed it, and I've determined you will not survive the hour...*"

"That's okay," I said, coughing. "You're not going to enjoy the next hour much, either."

After that, I began stabbing and hacking.

Before I'd dug my way through the crown, a drone came down and landed next to me. I picked it up, my bleary eyes refusing to focus properly.

"Who sent you?" I asked the drone. "Let me guess—Kivi."

I touched it to my tapper, and it absorbed my information. Then I tried to coax it into flying off—but it just sat there, grounded. Maybe it was programmed to watch me die.

Shrugging, I went back to my crude knife-work.

It took a long time to dig my way from the crown down into the meat of the plant. Once I'd cut a hole into the top, I let myself fall into the slippery, lumpy guts inside. There, I kept on hacking and slashing.

Stringy ganglia slapped and splashed. The plant wailed and complained in my thoughts—but I never stopped cutting at it. Not until long after it had fallen quiet.

Even then, I wanted to keep chopping it up just to be sure, but my arms wouldn't obey me anymore.

So I laid on my back and relaxed.

I was going numb, becoming paralyzed. It felt like my body had swollen up and become feathery light.

Staring up at the jagged hole I'd cut in the roof, I saw the gray skies of Storm World beyond. I thought to myself that the inside of the brain-plant looked kind of like the innards of a pumpkin—but the walls were green, instead of orange.

I heard as much as saw the little drone that had sat with me, waiting patiently for me to die. It rose up, buzzing and whining like an insect. Spiraling higher and higher, I saw it leave the hole in the roof.

Mumbling, I wished it well.

After that hazy thought, I died.

# -74-

Coming back to life is always something of a trial. Today was no exception—in fact, I thought it might have been a worse experience than the norm.

"Get him up. Get this lout off the table!"

*Armel…* That was Armel's voice. I'd know that Frenchie accent anywhere.

"He's not ready yet. You pushed the revive, and now his nervous system isn't a hundred percent."

A female—a bio, I supposed. I didn't like what she was saying. They'd "pushed" the revive? What the hell did that mean?

My first action was to try to move my arms. That's my usual opening move—but they didn't move. Not even a smidgen.

"You, orderly," Armel said. "Stand him up. I've waited long enough."

Hands gripped me under the armpits. I felt my head loll back. I was all floppy and loose—my muscles were like rubber.

"He looks like a ragdoll," Armel complained. "I thought you said he was fully grown."

"He has full height, full weight, all his parts are formed," the bio explained patiently. "But his nervous system hasn't quite knitted up yet. He has paresthesia—like when you sleep on your arm and it goes to sleep. Except in this case, his entire body is in that state."

"Then he's useless!" Armel complained. "Why even accelerate the process if you end up with a cripple?"

"He's not a cripple. He will—well, he *should* recover."

"How long?"

"Come back in five minutes. We'll test him again then."

Armel made a snorting sound of disgust. "We might as well put him into that lawnmower thing over there and start again."

"That's your choice, sir."

I heard footsteps pacing around me. Boots. Armel always wore boots with sharp heels. I figured they gave him a few extra centimeters in height.

"Fine!" he said at last. "Five minutes. I will return. If he's not moving, we're going to recycle him."

Now, I'm not a squeamish man, but no one would be happy hearing a superior officer openly discussing your violent demise. What made the situation worse was my relative helplessness.

Right about then, however, I began experiencing a new discomfort. My fingers were burning, tingling like someone jabbing about fifty pins into my hand at random spots.

Experimentally, I flexed my fingers. That made them burn even more. But I kept it up.

My lips curled then, and my head bobbed. I couldn't open my eyes yet, I didn't even want to, but that could wait. I worked my hands, enduring the pins-and-needles pain of revitalization.

"That's it…" the bio said, lingering near me.

I felt her light touch on my forehead. It was a kindness, but it hurt. She might as well have been petting me with a hot frying pan.

The five minutes passed, but Armel might have become distracted. He hadn't yet returned. By now, I was able to roll onto my side. Weakly, I propped myself up. Putting my head against a pillow, I breathed steadily, and I tried to speak.

"What's your name?" I asked the bio.

"Sarah," she said softly.

That made my thoughts wrinkle up, just a little. Most people would have given me a last name, not a first name.

But then, I had it.

This was *my* Sarah. She'd been a regular in my unit for years, but she'd recently moved up to specialist and become a bio.

"I thought that was you," I slurred out the lie. "I'd know your sweet voice even with these defective ears."

"You can't hear properly?" she asked in concern.

Again, that soft hand touched me. My bare shoulders this time. At least it didn't burn anymore to be touched.

"It's coming back," I said. "It's all coming back. Don't worry. You did a fine job."

"I didn't want to push the revive," she whispered. "I'm sorry McGill. Armel ordered me to do it."

"How'd the battle go?" I asked.

"What?"

"The battle, girl! When I died, we were fighting Wur on the walls."

"Oh… well, we mostly lost."

Groaning with the effort, I turned around and sat up. I forced an eye open.

There was Sarah. She looked a little blurry, as if she were underwater or something, but I knew her face well enough.

She had narrow shoulders and wide hips. Her blonde hair was cut so it encircled her sweet, small-featured face. She'd always looked like an elf to me, and I'd always liked her.

Forcing a smile, I felt half my lips draw up on the right side. The other side was still kind of numb.

About then I heard some high-heeled boots snapping on the deck.

"Ah!" Armel called out. "So, you are awake at last! I hope you are feeling fit, McGill!"

"Never better, sir."

"Excellent. We can begin the process immediately then."

"Uh…" I said, tearing my eyes away from Sarah and looking at Armel at last.

He seemed bitter but happy. That had to be a bad combo.

"The Mogwa Governor has passed judgment," he said. "He has summoned one human and one representative from Rigel to his ship."

"Um… maybe you should go, sir," I suggested. "I'm not sure that—"

"Generous to the last!" Armel announced, slapping me hard on the back. This resulted in a new blaze of fire from my overstimulated nerves. "But alas, Sateekas has specifically requested *you.*"

"Oh… Okay then. Just let me get dressed…"

Armel waited impatiently while I sprayed off some goop in the shower and forced a uniform over my wet skin. The cloth felt like sandpaper, but I tried not to show it.

"Come on, come on. We're hoping that if he perms you he'll spare Earth. It's a slim hope, but there you have it."

"Always keeping others in mind, aren't you sir?"

He twisted up his lips in disgust.

I stretched and approached Sarah. With a sudden move, I dipped my face down and kissed her.

"What's this?" Armel demanded. "Have you been romancing your physician in such a short time? One would think you're part goat, McGill."

"Goats are very intelligent animals. Did you know that, Tribune?"

"No… I didn't."

Sarah smiled at me, and I knew my play had been a good one.

"If you come back," she said, "I'll want an explanation."

"You've got it. Sandwiches, wine, and a detailed accounting."

She smiled again, looking a little shy.

Armel rolled his eyes and marched out, heels clacking. He motioned for me to follow with a crooked finger. I did so, and we were soon walking up muddy steps into daylight.

"Uh…" I said, looking around in shock. "I thought we were in Blue Bunker."

"This charming mess *is* Blue Bunker—what's left of it. The fort has been leveled."

Coming out into the gray daylight, I saw it was true. The puff-crete walls were shattered all around us. Only a few towers stood. Even the bunkers were flattened and torn apart.

Bodies were everywhere, lying in the muck. Giants, various Wur, humans, slavers… Now and then, I spotted a dead Rigellian. They'd all fought to the last.

"Hmm…" I said. "Seems like we were overrun. But did we win, sir?"

"No," he said. "The Wur went mad at the end, after they breached the walls. They turned on their new allies. The pod-walkers in particular raged all over the camp. They killed us and the aliens from Rigel indiscriminately."

"Oh…" I said, thinking of when I'd dug into the brain of the last Nexus plant.

The pod-walkers, the spiders, the acid-creatures—all the various forms were attached to that single Nexus. By carving it up, I'd essentially driven the entire Wur army insane. I'd seen that effect before back on Death World—but I'd kind of forgotten about it.

"I wonder… what could have pissed them off so badly?" I asked, shaking my head as if I was bewildered. "It's a sheer mystery. We'll probably never solve it."

Armel eyed me coldly. "Get aboard the ship."

The same patrol boat I'd flown in days ago was sitting on a mound of wet debris. It must have withdrawn into space when the battle had started, or it surely would have been destroyed with the rest of the place.

Roaring up into orbit, I wondered why Sateekas had asked to see me in particular. Being a naturally upbeat person, I dared to hope he'd come to value me as a friend and planned to toast my victory.

But a meaner, more negative version of James McGill, one that was buried deep inside my mind—that pessimist told me I was wrong.

Deciding I'd find out the truth soon enough, I sat back and let the autopilot do its work. Humming an old tune from Georgia Sector's ancient past, I gazed out the window and watched the Mogwa cruiser grow steadily in size.

Don't get me wrong. I did hope I'd come back from this little jaunt alive. After all, a good date was almost certainly riding on the results of this journey.

# -75-

After following arrows around onboard the Imperial cruiser, I found Sateekas again. He was spanking Nairbs and seemed to be in his normal, irritable mood.

"Your lordship!" I called out. "I got your message and raced right up here. I've even got a bottle of champagne to celebrate!"

I'd found a bottle of creamer in the patrol boat galley and dumped out the contents, replacing it with water and some coffee grounds. I was pretty sure, after all, that Sateekas wouldn't care about drinking champagne with me—but just in case he did, I had a prop to wave around enthusiastically.

"You are an odd beast," Sateekas said. "Can you truly be so generous in nature that you would celebrate an enemy's victory?"

"Uh… well… no sir. Not exactly. I kind of figured that we'd celebrate Earth's victory. I mean… we did win down there. We killed the Wur."

Sateekas flapped some of his disgusting limbs at me. "Ah, that. I see the source of the confusion. It's almost endearing. You possess a true warrior-spirit."

"Um… what's endearing, your overlordship?"

"The fact you would believe the goal of the contest was the sole criteria upon which you were being judged. Yes, McGill-creature, I did say the goal was to eradicate the Wur. However, the contest took on a life of its own."

“Uh…” I said, letting my fake champagne sag down to my side. “How’s that, exactly, sir?”

“Earth and Rigel engaged directly in battle. Your two technologically advanced species came into direct conflict. The Wur played a role, but it wasn’t pivotal. Once the battle began, I was fully engaged. It was quite entertaining.”

As he spoke, he spun up a recorded vid. I could see rampaging pod-walkers, marching squads of Rigellian troops, and desperate Earth forces battling them all.

“You see here,” Sateekas said, “where these bulky humans are being torn apart?”

A group of near-human blood-worlders had indeed been encircled. The pod-walkers were snatching them from the ground and ripping off limbs like children plucking petals from a daisy.

“Uh… I see it, sir.”

“This is a seminal moment. The Rigellian troops, at this point, had clearly won. They were superior in every way, abusing your last soldiers with impunity.”

“Yeah, but keep watching! We’re about to kill their brain-plant and set them all free. The Wur turn on Rigel’s army, and—”

“Yes, yes, yes… but that’s not the point. They were on the offensive, which is the harder position to take in any conflict. You managed to pull a stunt on them, but you’d already lost.”

“But… we won in the end!”

“No,” he said. “You did *not* win the real prize, which is of course my favor. I’ve rated both sides carefully, measuring prowess in battle—not just trickery and luck. As a professional, you must be able to see my point. When you battled face-to-face, those enemy troops outperformed your legion.”

“I witnessed no such thing, sir!” I lied. “Victory is victory. You can’t take that away just because one side operated with more style.”

Sateekas narrowed his eye-groups and waved an appendage at me. “I certainly can take it away, and I’ve done so. Don’t presume to lecture me, human. I’m fond of you, as any Mogwa might favor a pet that does amusing tricks—but I’m the governor of this province. I'm free to choose any species I want to be my local enforcers."

Just about then, I noted some Nairbs shuffling around in the back of the chamber. A small figure walked in their midst.

"Hey now," I said. "You should watch your back, sir. That runty alien is a fiend! A bloodthirsty mass-murderer!"

My long arm extended, and a long finger pointed from the end of it.

The object of my accusations strolled closer without concern. It was none other than my old wrestling-buddy, Squanto.

"I am here, beings," Squanto announced. "Make your entreaties as I am short on both time and patience."

Sateekas stomped a few of his hand-feet in irritation. "An impudent attitude," he said. "You should not speak to your new master in this insolent fashion."

Squanto looked up at him in surprise. His chain of snake-bones clattered and writhed as he spoke.

"No alien is my master. Nor will they ever be."

"You're incorrect," Sateekas said. "Know that the Empire has smiled upon Rigel. This is the most fortunate hour of your benighted existence. You have been selected to replace Earth as our local enforcers."

The bear rotated his head to one side. I interpreted this as a quizzical gesture.

"We came to this star system to gain its submission to Rigel. We are not interested in submitting to the toothless, geriatric Empire."

Sateekas reacted as if stung. "What! You impudent monster! Can it be you're as much an ingrate as McGill has claimed? I can hardly credit it.

As this discussion grew heated, I began to grin. I can't help it, when two rattlesnakes square-off, I always like to watch.

In a precautionary manner, I circled the room quietly with the Nairbs. When I was directly behind Squanto, I approached until I stood only two paces away from him—just in case.

"I can understand your disappointment," Squanto said. "The Earthlings are substandard either as opponents or allies.

Rigel would serve better—but, unfortunately, we're simply not interested."

"Why not?" demanded Sateekas.

"Because the Empire is a fossil. Once all-powerful, you have split up into factions that engage in fruitless civil wars. You offer us the task of patrolling this remote border—but we'd rather remain independent and carve out our own path."

It was a noble statement in my opinion. In a way, I admired the pluck of a species like these Rigellians. They were tough, and they had gonads to spare. Earth, by comparison, usually played it safe.

While I was impressed, Sateekas definitely wasn't feeling the same way. He puffed himself up like a cobra and loomed over Squanto.

"In that case, vermin, the offer is rescinded. McGill-creature! Execute this beast!"

"Uh…" I said. "Is Earth still your local enforcer?"

"Absolutely! Obey me!"

Squanto, to his credit, didn't just wait for it. He launched himself at Sateekas and managed to bite one of those floppy limbs before I could catch hold of him.

Having foreseen this possible outcome, I'd procured a heavy wrench from a storage cabinet earlier. The ship's AI had made sure I was unarmed—but you didn't always need a gun to be effective.

I brained the ferocious little alien a couple of times. That quieted him down.

When he was on his back, panting and mewing in pain, I bent over him.

"Listen up, Squanto," I whispered. "We had a deal about Floramel. You promise to give her back, and I'll get you out of this alive."

Squanto opened one eye that was crusty with blood. "Why would I trust you, prince of lies?"

"Because it beats being smashed to death with this wrench, and having your transport ships blasted out of space by this cruiser."

I hefted the tool menacingly.

Squanto thought that over for a few seconds. "I agree," he said finally.

Straightening up, I faced Sateekas.

"Grand Admiral," I said, "I know this alien has pissed you off—and rightfully so, sir. But… you *did* promise him safe passage to and from his ship. We had this meeting under a flag of truce."

"Are you refusing to obey me, McGill?" Sateekas demanded.

"Never sir! Not in sixty lifetimes would I dream of it! But… you did make a deal. As your local enforcers, you'll be making our jobs a lot harder if we can't parlay with Rigel in the future."

Sateekas breathed hard for a few long seconds.

"Distrust and dishonor…" he said at last. "I can't let them overtake me." He ruffled himself and straightened. "Very well. I lost my temper. In time, we will defeat these filthy beings and enslave them—but we won't go back on our word now. Escort the prisoner back to his vessel."

Not wanting to give Sateekas time to reconsider, I hauled Squanto's ass back to his ship. There, a group of his guards were waiting.

They stared at me with black, hostile eyes that glittered in the lights of the docking bay.

"Here's Squanto," I told them, tossing the limp form toward them. "He took a bathroom break and tripped."

Squanto rolled and flopped on the deck. His crew rushed to him and lifted him up.

"You have abused him!" one Rigellian thug exclaimed.

"Nah," I said. "Seriously, he did a facer on the toilet, like I said."

They produced weapons and approached. I shrugged.

"This is what I get for doing a man a favor? I should have known Rigel breaks their deals."

Squanto coughed then, and he weakly lifted a single claw. "Let the hairless ape go. Killing him will gain us nothing—not even his removal from existence."

The crew backed off.

Giving them all a happy send-off, complete with waves and hooting, I watched them pack-up and go. It was a moment to remember.

# -76-

Floramel was returned to us after I got back to Storm World—but not in the manner we'd expected.

"McGill," Armel said in my earpiece the following day. "Get over here to Gold Bunker. Stop loafing on those broken walls with your slimy friends."

The friends he was talking about were the Scuppers. They'd been very happy when the Wur went mad and began to wither away, and they weren't upset to see the Rigellians pack up and leave their world, either.

After wishing Second-man and all his confusable relatives good-bye, I headed for Gold Bunker—or what was left of it.

Cooper caught up with me soon thereafter. He was still wearing his stealth suit, but it had a few shorts in it after all the fighting. I could see flashes of his uniform revealed in midair now and then.

"Hey Ghost," I greeted him.

"You're going to do it then? You're going to recommend me for the new specialist rank?"

"That's right. Barring a solid perming in my near future, I'm putting your name forward for advancement."

"That's great, McGill. Thanks for coming through—sorry I wasn't able to help you with that brain-plant in the end."

"I was wondering where you'd gotten off to back then."

"Well... I'm not that good of a swimmer."

I let him off the hook with that. He'd played the bodyguard—to a point.

After a while, I noticed he was still pacing me. "Why aren't you headed off to rummage for supplies?" I asked him.

"Well… I'm kind of nervous. Now that I've got my promo, I want to keep it. I mean, if Armel is pissed about something…"

"You think he might still perm me? Even with seventy percent of our troops face down in the muck, you think he might find room in the graveyard for one more?"

"Maybe… You do tend to piss people off pretty bad. You know that, right?"

Nodding, I found I couldn't argue the point. After all, the evidence was overwhelming.

When I got to Gold Bunker at last, I found my way down into the bowels of it. They were using pigs and our last few unhappy giants to excavate. By this time, most of the basement level was useable again.

I found Armel in a grimy hole at the end of the complex. He was as far from daylight as it was possible to get.

He signaled for me to come to his side the moment he saw me.

"McGill, over here."

Grinning like he was my rich uncle, I marched to his side. "What's up, Tribune?"

He eyed me. "We have a strange transmission. A download, really. It's coming in now."

"From where?"

A single black-gloved finger pointed to the drippy ceiling. "From your friends, those obnoxious bears."

"Yeah? Squanto is sending us some kind of love-note? Let me see it."

I took a look at the slowly growing data file and frowned. "This is pretty long. Is it video?"

"If it is, they must like seventy-hour long presentations."

After examining the header of the file, I got a sneaking suspicion.

"Uh…" I said. "Hey, can I call someone? I think I might know what this is."

Armel eyed me suspiciously, but he nodded.

Working my tapper, I contacted Sarah. She wasn't part of my unit anymore now that she was a bio. I knew she'd be busy with revives, and I hoped I wasn't messing up my chances on our imminent date.

"McGill?" she answered immediately. "I can't talk. We only have two machines going right now, and the revival queue—"

"I'm with Tribune Armel," I told her. "Come on over to Gold Bunker. It's important. Let a flunky run the damned machine."

She stopped arguing and began slogging through the mud and bodies. Damnation, it was going to stink outside in a few days' time.

When Sarah joined me, I showed her the files. She recognized them immediately. "This is an engram. Do you have the body scan yet?"

"Nope."

"Who's sending it to us?" she asked.

"Squanto."

Sarah looked alarmed. I didn't blame her.

"James, it might be anything! We can't load up an unknown file. It might be a virus, it might—"

I put my hand gently over hers. "I don't think so. I think I know who it is. I need you to take this file and match it up to a certain body scan we should have stored in the data core."

"You know who…?"

Armel joined us then. "Ah, a sweet face returns—and already, I see the McGill is pawing at you again. Have some manners, you brute!"

My hand left Sarah's. Armel smiled at her like a hungry shark. "What is this file Rigel has seen fit to transmit to us as they leave our newly captured star system?" he asked her.

"It's an engram—the storage of a mental state."

"Who's?"

"There's one good way to find out," I said, joining the talk. "We can look for a matching body-scan in the data core and revive the person."

Armel frowned at us. "Are we talking about that furry scoundrel, Squanto?"

"Good lord no!" I said. "It's a human engram, right Sarah?"

She looked at me quizzically, and I nodded.

"Uh… I think so. Nothing else would match our data core files."

"There! You see? Just order the revive, and we'll know the full story."

Armel looked back and forth between Sarah and me. He seemed mistrustful.

"All right. I will allow it. You have piqued my curiosity once again. Do not disappoint."

"Wouldn't dream of it, Tribune," I said, watching him walk away to a screen which he brought to life with a gesture.

Sarah stored the file, which was finally finishing up.

"Ah-ha!" Armel shouted, pointing at his tactical battle map. "The Rigel ship has fled the system. The moment they finished that strange transmission, they left…"

He was eyeing us again, so I beat a hasty retreat, tugging on Sarah's arm every step of the way.

"James!" she admonished when we were out in the passages again. "I can't just revive this! We don't know—"

"Maybe you don't but I do—at least I think I do. It's Floramel."

I quickly fabricated a sad tale of Floramel being captured and dragged away by the Rigellians.

"That's awful. But James, she's been permed if that's the case. We can't revive her without knowing she's been killed. We might be making a copy."

Shaking my head, I disagreed. "I made a deal with Squanto to get her back. Apparently, he didn't feel like sending a shuttle down here to the surface."

"He executed her and sent the file? That's awful!"

"That's the Rigel way."

"But… we still can't just revive her. If she—"

"Listen," I said. "Armel just gave you an order to revive the person in this data file. That's a clear mandate. If you don't do it, you'll be disobeying orders and perming Floramel at the same time."

Sarah was flustered, but she went along with me in the end. That's why I'd contacted her. Unlike most bio-people, she still had a heart.

# -77-

Floramel came out of Blue Bunker in a dazed state. I was waiting around, as I was feeling concerned about her.

"James?" she said, her voice weak and introspective. "Where do we go when we die?"

I blinked at that. "Uh…" I said.

Now, you'd think that if anyone was qualified to answer such a query, it would have been me. But, unfortunately, I was as clueless as the next guy.

"I don't know," I said, "but you're alive again now. That's what counts."

Floramel, to the best of my knowledge, had only died three times. She was basically still a civvie by Legion Varus standards. Many recruits died three times before they had their first battle—our training regimen was legendary.

That lack of experience on her part was why she was in this odd mental state, I knew.

Taking her by the arm, I walked her toward the exit. It was raining outside, but at least it wasn't a vicious storm.

"McGill!" a voice called out behind us.

We turned and I saw Sarah, standing with her fists on her hips. She was still wearing her blue coveralls, which were streaked with stains.

One look at her annoyed face told me the story: she was feeling a little jealous. After all, Floramel looked like an exotic model, and she was leaning on me.

"Don't worry!" I shouted back down the hallway. "Floramel is in love with a lizard."

Sarah shook her head. "Just don't take advantage."

"I'd never!"

Sarah vanished after that, and I found Floramel studying me. "Is she jealous, or just looking after my welfare?"

"A little of both, I imagine."

"Does she have a reason to feel this way?"

I thought about all the times I'd stood one girl up for another—well, that's not true. There were too many such events in my long and storied lifetime to ponder them all at once.

"Maybe," I admitted, "but I'm mostly worried about you. I felt somewhat responsible for leaving you on Squanto's ship. How was that, by the way?"

"They were not considerate," she said. "They're apex predators. Quite different than humans. They lack compassion."

"Did you give them the book?"

She shrugged. "What choice did I have? Did you expect me to make up another story, perhaps?"

That made me think of the cock-and-bull story I'd fed to Xlur back on Mogwa Prime. I knew Floramel couldn't generate such a thing. It wasn't how her mind worked.

"So, they now have the formula? The bio-terminator is spreading? I thought maybe you'd alter it just a little, making it look good, but…"

Floramel shook her head. "They had a Mogwa captive. They keep many captives, and they meant to keep me. I had to give them the real formula, so it would kill the captive Mogwa. If it hadn't worked, they would have become very unpleasant."

"I understand. You had no choice."

"Not true, I could have made them false documents and suffered torments—but I chose not to."

"Uh… I understand. You did the right thing. No Mogwa would take a pinprick to save the entire population of Earth."

We walked out of the bunker and pressed through the rains to some muddy tents. The camp was shutting down soon, as we'd won the battle and gained the respect of the Scuppers.

Soon, we'd use the gateway posts buried deep under Gold Bunker to escape this world and withdraw to Earth.

"James…" Floramel said. "I think… I think I'm still up there, on Squanto's ship."

"What?"

"I mean, I suspect I'm a copy. Certain things they said… They promised I'd never leave Rigel."

My mind received that jolt without pleasure. I realized right off she was probably right. Squanto didn't care about Imperial rules. They'd happily keep an illegal double.

"That's crazy-talk, girl," I scoffed. "You're right here with me!"

"But why else would they have sent scan files instead of simply shipping me back down here?"

I stopped her, and we looked at one another in the mild storm. Her face was wet under her hood, and I wasn't sure if she was streaked with tears or rain—maybe it was both.

"Listen!" I said. "Squanto made a deal with me—twice. I reestablished that deal when I got him out of Governor Sateekas' ship alive. He's not a nice guy, but he understands the importance of keeping his word in a deal like that. He probably killed you and sent you down—it's easier that way. Hell, they do it all the time around here!"

I ticked off all the times I'd been killed lately as a means of long-distance transportation. By the time I was done, she was looking impressed, sympathetic, and hopeful.

"How do you stay with this grim life?" she asked. "I could never do it. I couldn't be a legionnaire. I'm not tough-minded enough."

"It's not for everyone, I have to admit. But… I've gotten kind of used to it."

Taking her below, I found Armel waiting for me. His arms were crossed, and he appeared to be angry.

"What's up, Maurice?" I asked.

He glared at me. He didn't like it when I used his first name, but we were both officers, and the battle was over—and I didn't give much of a damn.

"You dare to mock me?" he asked. "This is something you knew about, is it not? I find such pettiness disgusting, McGill. Drusus has kept you as a pet for too long."

"Um…" I said. "Could you give me more of a hint, Tribune? What's wrong?"

"As you no doubt know perfectly well, I'm going to be marooned here. My Blood-Worlder legion is not going to be missed on Earth, apparently. We're to be garrisoned on this rock to rebuild these broken fortresses."

"What about the gateway posts in your basement, sir? You'll be able to go back and forth at will."

"Not so! There is no escape that way, not even temporary relief. The gateway has been realigned to bring fresh troops from Blood World. We're to rebuild these shitty fortresses, gain the trust of the natives… The situation is depressing. To think of my talents being wasted in this fashion..."

His complaints kept rolling on, but I wasn't really hearing him anymore. He reminded me of Xlur at that moment, lamenting his fate at being assigned to run a distant sub-optimal outpost for a growing empire.

Musing while I pretended to listen, I thought about the situation as a growing trend. It only made sense that as we conquered more planets we needed more garrisons. It was turning into a common fate for legions everywhere. Legion Teutoburg, led by Tribune Deech, was still stuck on Machine World. Now Armel, with his Blood-Worlders, would be marooned here on Storm World.

I was glad I was in a mobile legion. We weren't well-treated, but at least we weren't stuck playing cards for decades on some rock a hundred lightyears from home.

"Sir?" I asked finally, breaking into his eloquent litany of complaints. "What about Legion Varus? How are we going to get home?"

"Why do you always ask for information that is common knowledge?" he scoffed. "Really, McGill, you should read the notices on your tapper more often. If you were one of my officers—but, never mind. *Legate* has returned to pick up the remnants of your pathetic legion."

Throwing up his hands in irritation, he left Floramel and me standing there in the mud.

My eyes swiveled immediately towards the only serviceable ship in the damaged base. It was, in fact, the same patrol boat I'd used to visit other ships in this system twice before.

"Should we?" I asked Floramel.

"You know that I'm only interested in Raash now, James."

"What? Oh—oh, right. Uh… he's dead though. You know that, don't you?"

"Yes, of course. I have a plan to get him back. I will go to Armel and offer to stay here on Storm World with him, if he revives Raash. He wants to mate with me. I'll suggest it's possible if he does this favor for me."

I laughed. "This is a sad, sad day. You're becoming more like a true human all the time."

"I must do what works. You've taught me that, James."

She gave me a little kiss then, and she left me smiling as she followed Armel into his torn-up Gold Bunker.

My eyes again slewed around, falling on the tiny ship sitting in its blast-pan. I almost went for it—but then I thought of Sarah. I'd as much as promised her a date. It seemed rude to not give an interested woman a shot at old McGill.

Going back to Blue Bunker, I lamented my weaknesses, but when I found Sarah that all faded.

"Where's Floramel?" she asked.

I told her, and she laughed. "You've corrupted her."

"Yeah…"

"This has been a rough deployment. I'm kind of regretting taking the role of a bio. I mean, it's scary fighting out on the line—but it might beat reviving a hundred people a day."

"You need a break," I told her. "Come on."

She followed me, and I led her toward the patrol ship, but I walked right past it. I'd come up with a better idea.

Instead, I took her down into the catacombs. The jump-tube network crisscrossed every kilometer of this strange world.

She liked the place immediately. It was quiet, alien and most of all, bone-dry.

After I taught her how to jump and fall sideways, traveling at wild speeds, she was laughing.

Catching her up in my arms when the moment was right, we kissed.

"I can't believe it," she said.

"What?"

"You've found a quiet place. How many women have you brought down here?"

"You're the first. I've been fighting a war, remember?"

Sarah had been resisting me, stiff and suspicious—but now she finally melted. We kissed some more, then we jumped and flew while we embraced.

"I've got an idea," she told me after our next jump. "Let's do it while we're flying."

My eyes widened. "That sounds kind of dangerous."

She nodded, and I couldn't deny her. She'd always been a bit on the wild side.

We ended up trying to make love while in mid-air but failed at it. The tubes didn't keep us in the air long enough.

But when we landed at last, we finished up—and it was glorious.

# -78-

About two months later, I was back home on Earth. My parents were happy I'd returned, but they were still dragging their tails concerning Etta. I came to realize they'd hoped I'd bring her back with me.

The legion had demobilized, and that was a pure relief to me. I could use a break. The last time around, I hadn't gotten much of a chance to rest at all.

Sarah and I exchanged some vid-calls on our tappers, but we didn't keep up the romance. We'd already tried that in the past. I don't think she really wanted me around when she was on shore leave. She liked to forget about her life in the legions and pretend it had all been a fevered dream. We decided it was best to remember our fine shared memories and leave it at that.

Winter had come, and the swamp had a chill on certain nights. The storms were mild compared to Storm World, and I often found myself walking outside while thunder and lightning played overhead, barely noticing Earth's best attempt to scare me.

The cold didn't last long, and the land soon transitioned into springtime. I'd fallen into my old routines, and things seemed right with the universe once again.

*Almost* right. There was still Etta. She sent me notes now and then on my tapper—but she stayed put out on Dust World.

Then came a strange night in April. It was perfect weather. Not too cold, not too hot—just right. I had my windows open and my door ajar with the screens up. Bugs buzzed and peeped all over, but they couldn't get in easily.

"Dad?"

Stunned, I got up from my couch and dropped my beer. I'd been watching the ballgame on my far wall. I froze the game with a gesture and walked to the screen door.

There she was, outlined by the porch light that shined overhead. She looked older, taller and more like a woman than ever.

"Etta? Is that really you, girl?"

"Can I come in?"

"You don't have to ask that! You *never* have to ask that! Get on in here!"

She walked inside, and I hugged her. As I did so, I felt her relief—but I also felt a certain tension in her. She kept looking outside, through the screen door.

Suddenly, I thought I got it.

How had she gotten here? Who had brought her home? Passage from Dust World to Earth—that wasn't cheap.

Peering outside, I scanned the yard for some slinking boyfriend. I didn't see anyone.

Turning back to Etta, I saw her face was haunted. A little freaked out.

"Who brought you?" I asked quietly. "Is he out there?"

She nodded, still peering outside.

"Who is he?"

Etta shook her head. "I... I'm not totally sure. He's changed..."

Defensive instincts kicked in. I reached for a gun and snagged it off the coffee table. I slipped it into my back pocket.

"Daddy..."

"It's all right," I said, shushing her. "I'm just going to have a little talk with him."

"He brought me home," she said. "Remember that."

I frowned at her, and she didn't meet my eye.

Walking outside warily, I searched the yard—and I thought I saw a shadow at the tree line.

"She's a fine young woman, McGill," a familiar voice called out. "I brought her home to you, safe and sound."

Stalking toward a tree with a shadow near its base, I kept my hand on the pistol in my pocket, and I let a false smile play on my face.

"Claver…?" I said. "You brought her home? Why?"

"I… I need a friend. Everyone needs a friend when times are hard. Just remember, I did you a favor."

My eyes were all squinched-up by now. I didn't know what was going on, and I *hated* not knowing what was going on. Especially when my family was involved.

"I better not find out you've been messing with my family again," I told him.

"I haven't. Ask her—I just brought her home. She wanted to come back, but she didn't have enough cash. She used most of her money helping out Dust Worlders. A lot of them are poor."

I was pretty sure that was true, but Claver didn't sound like Claver to me tonight. Right about then, I caught on.

"Claver-X?" I asked.

He laughed. "You're not as dumb as they say. I've got to go now. Just remember."

He turned away and walked off into the bog. I thought about going after him, but Etta called me back.

"Dad?"

Grumbling, I walked back to my tiny shack and looked my daughter over.

"That old creep didn't paw at you, did he?" I asked.

She blinked in surprise. "Oh no. Nothing like that. I would have hurt him if he did. He was a gentleman."

"I know for a fact that old man has a thing for the ladies," I told her. "He's not like the other Clavers. He's a horn-dog."

We talked about it, and I got the story out of her. Claver had approached her on Dust World, offering her a ride. She was homesick, so she took it.

I gave her a stern speech about not trusting men like that. She promised she never would again.

Neither one of us believed her.

That same night, after I'd handed Etta over to my parents to be fussed over and thoroughly debriefed, I slept in a chair in a wary state. My gun was in my lap when a hammering began on my door.

Throwing it open, I was surprised to see two Clavers. But these guys weren't Claver-Primes. They were Class-Three dumb asses.

"Uh… can I help you boys?"

"Where is the Prime?" one of them asked. I couldn't even tell which one had spoken.

"He's not—" I began, but then I halted. "You guys aren't looking for Claver-X, are you? The nice Claver? The one who made the lady-Claver?"

In unison, they surged one step closer. It was freaky how they moved in such a synchronized fashion.

"Where is the Prime?"

Right then, a light bulb went on inside my big skull. These guys were looking for Claver-X. Maybe they'd been doing that all along, hunting not for just *any* Claver, but a certain fugitive Claver. Maybe, when they'd bugged me until I killed them back on Dust World, they'd been searching for the fugitive Claver-X.

"He *was* here," I admitted, "but he's gone now."

"Where?"

"Into the swamp. I think he had a teleport suit. He's probably on another planet by now."

They turned and gazed out into the darkened bog. I thought about clocking them while their backs were turned—but I passed on the idea. They didn't seem to be after me, and they might not be alone.

"I know the swamp really well," I told them. "Maybe I can help. Maybe I can track him for you."

They turned back to look at me. "Help? We must find the Prime."

"That's right," I said. "Let's go on a midnight hunt!"

Leading the way, I marched them out deep into the swamp. After a time, I led them to the old, dilapidated barn. There, where I'd once killed a Claver who was much smarter than these two—I murdered them in the dark.

It wasn't a nice thing to do. But I was getting kind of tired of all these uninvited guests.

Lady-friends? Sure, I could deal with that. Even Claver-X was okay, as he'd brought my Etta home to me.

The motivations of Claver-X all made a lot more sense to me now. He'd come to my place as a hunted man. He truly *had* needed a friend. These two goons seemed unsympathetic and dogged, and I'd gotten rid of them for him.

As far as I was concerned, Claver-X and I were now even-Steven.

Going back home, I was surprised to see my light was on.

Now, that could have been Etta, or my folks—but I doubted it. My parents went to bed early these days, being well into their first decade of extended-life, and Etta probably wouldn't be running the lights at all if she was alone in there.

Eyes narrowed, I snuck up and peeked inside a window.

There, sitting on my dirty couch, was Galina Turov.

She was looking down at her tapper, but not for long. She looked up, exactly where I was peeking, and crooked her finger.

"Get in here, McGill!" she shouted. "Stop playing games!"

I walked in, throwing the door wide.

She started talking, but I ignored her and checked the bathroom, the kitchen and the closet.

"What's the matter with you?" she asked.

"There have been some strangers here tonight," I told her. "Lots of them. Something weird is going on."

"So paranoid…" she said. "Listen to me, I know all about your visitors. Pairs of Claver-Threes—the dumb, brutish types—they're combing Earth tonight."

She finally had my attention. I stopped looking behind curtains and stood over her.

"What's going on?" I demanded.

"It's important that we find a fugitive. One of Claver's clones has gone AWOL."

"I know about that. He made some lady-Clavers."

"What?"

"Never mind. Why are you involved?"

"Because this fugitive has sold the formula. We think Rigel might have it now—possibly others."

"Uh…" I said, thinking that one over. "I guess that's possible."

Internally, I was wondering which Claver I'd been dealing with at various times. Claver-X seemed to be the nice one—but that could have been an act.

"In any case, this renegade—"

"I call him Claver-X."

"All right, Claver-X. He's a menace. He must be stopped."

"Hmmm…" I said, walking into my kitchen. "You want a beer or something?"

"No. Not yet, anyway. I want you to tell me what's happened here tonight."

I gave her an edited version of the facts. In my tale I didn't kill anyone, for instance.

"It's very strange," she said. "Central is temporarily cooperating with Claver due to this special circumstance. He's helping us track down the bad clone, the one who is selling the bio-terminator formula to anyone who will buy it."

"That doesn't sound healthy for the Mogwa," I admitted. "You want a beer now?"

She looked at me thoughtfully. "All right," she said at last.

I gave her a beer and sucked one down myself before she'd taken her second swig.

"So…" I said, "why'd you come here?"

"We're helping Claver. We're hitting all the spots he's known to visit. It's so difficult to catch a man who has teleport suits. Nearly impossible."

"You're not here, then, just because you'd like to see me?"

Again, she gave me that speculative look. "I thought that things had ended between us, James."

"Yeah? Why?"

Galina blew out a puff of air, making her bangs fly. "Because you were chasing other women on Storm World and… never mind."

"Never mind what?" I asked, cracking open a second beer for both of us.

"You've been back on Earth for two months. You never even called me."

"Oh…"

She was right, of course. I'd been back for a long while, and we'd parted in a less than friendly mood when she'd bugged out and flown home. I guess I hadn't felt super-friendly after she'd stranded my legion on Storm World.

"Nothing to say for yourself?" she asked.

I shrugged. "War has a funny way of shoving people together then apart again. I suggest we start over. No recriminations. No regrets."

She drank her beer for a while, and she thought that over.

"No recriminations and no regrets... I like the sound of those rules… All right, I agree."

Smiling, I sat on the couch beside her. I didn't slip my arm around her—not yet. A man has to know how to pace these things.

She didn't object to my nearness, so we talked, drank, and eventually we laughed. Sometime before dawn, we were making love again. It was nice to have her back.

When we were at war, it was harder to be a couple. We never saw eye-to-eye on command issues. Now that we were on shore leave again, our mutual attraction had reasserted itself.

Just before Galina fell asleep, she mumbled something about the Core Worlds.

"What's that?" I asked her, trying not to tense up.

"An investigation," she said. "A problem—something bad happened while you were out there on Mogwa Prime."

"Uh… did you tell them I was the one that went out there?"

"No. They don't know who it was—but Sateekas does, doesn't he?"

My heart skipped a beat, then it started up again.

"He might," I admitted.

After that, Galina fell asleep.

I had trouble dozing off with her, despite the long, long night I'd just experienced. If the Mogwa were investigating Xlur's death, and they were coming here to complete that investigation…

Well, things could get sticky.

The main problem would be the Nairbs. The Mogwa themselves weren't meticulous. They couldn't be bothered to isolate an individual among our billions.

But the Nairbs… They might just find me.

Lying awake, I wondered about many things. The stars. How I really felt about Galina. What Claver-X was up to…

And the Nairbs. Were they coming to Earth, intent on opening a full-fledged investigation?

After fretting about these things, I decided to have one more beer. I finally managed to fall asleep just before dawn.

Books by B. V. Larson:

UNDYING MERCENARIES

*Steel World*
*Dust World*
*Tech World*
*Machine World*
*Death World*
*Home World*
*Rogue World*
*Blood World*
*Dark World*
*Storm World*

STAR FORCE SERIES

*Swarm*
*Extinction*
*Rebellion*
*Conquest*
*Battle Station*
*Empire*
*Annihilation*
*Storm Assault*
*The Dead Sun*
*Outcast*
*Exile*
*Gauntlet*
*Demon Star*

Visit BVLarson.com for more information.

Printed in Great Britain
by Amazon